Scars of Anatomy

Scars of Anatomy

NICOLE ALFRINE

by wattpad books

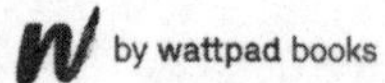

An imprint of Wattpad WEBTOON Book Group

Content warning: child abuse, drug abuse, underage drinking, child abandonment, childhood trauma

Published in Canada by Wattpad WEBTOON Book Group, a division of Wattpad WEBTOON Studios, Inc.

36 Wellington Street E., Suite 200, Toronto, ON M5E 1C7
Canada

www.wattpad.com

First W by Wattpad Books edition: June 2025

ISBN 978-1-99834-142-9 (Trade Paper original)
ISBN 978-1-99834-143-6 (eBook edition)

Library and Archives Canada Cataloguing in Publication information is available upon request.

Printed and bound in Canada

1 3 5 7 9 10 8 6 4 2

Cover illustration by Claudia Guariglia
Typesetting by Delaney Anderson

To the finches of the world: may you soar and find your flock.

ONE

Unknown

The sharp sound of Coach's whistle rings through the air, signaling the end of practice. It takes me only two seconds to claw off the sweat-drenched T-shirt clinging to my body, because of course Coach would put me on shirts the hottest day of the year.

Running off to the sidelines of the football field, I instantly find my water bottle and take a few swigs, dumping the rest of the water over my head and letting it run down my body in an attempt to cool down.

"Good job today, Bronx," Coach says as he walks by, clapping a hand on the top of my back, right over my tattoo.

Splayed across my back in black ink, shoulder blade to shoulder blade, is the word *UNKNOWN* in big, bold letters. While *Miller* is the name stitched on the back of my jersey, I feel like it's not my real last name. That it doesn't fit.

My mother got pregnant when she was a teen, and doesn't know who my father is. She was either too high or too drunk to recall who she hooked up with at some random party. Therefore, I had to settle for her last name and questions about this unknown variable in my life. Given my mother's track record, I don't expect my biological father to be a stand-up guy, but it would have been nice to know.

"Damn, man. Adrianna really did a number on you." I hear my best friend and roommate, Chase, laugh. He runs up next to me, bends down to grab his water bottle, and then, guzzles it down. Out of breath, he grabs a towel to wipe the sweat running down his face and body. Lucky bastard got to be on skins today. "Did she break off all her nails?" he asks, amusement dancing in his eyes as he rubs the towel over his sweaty light-blond hair.

I furrow my brows, momentarily confused, until I realize he's talking about my back. That would explain why it stings so bad—all the sweat seeping into the cuts from her nails digging into my back last night.

I can't help the smug smile that tugs at my lips. "Maybe," I quip back.

He lets out a booming laugh, wrapping the towel around the back of his neck. "It's not even the first day of classes and you two are already going at each other like that?" He shakes his head, an incredulous grin on his face as he gestures to my marked-up back. "It's going to be a long semester for you, man. Maybe she'll actually lock you down before graduation," he teases.

"She wishes."

If there's one thing everyone on this campus knows, it's that Bronx Miller doesn't date. Ever. I won't even take girls back to my own room. I go to their place or wherever is convenient, we have some fun, and then I leave. When the deed is done, it's just that. Done.

Some girls are repeats, especially Adrianna. But that doesn't mean anything other than that they're a fun time. Adrianna doesn't seem to understand that, though.

She's been after me since freshman year when we met at an opening weekend party. A raven-haired, emerald green–eyed beauty with a body that could rock any man's world—and as captain of the dance team, it's no wonder why she's so popular at Garner University. It's also no wonder why she's my most frequent repeat either. Adrianna is the hottest girl on campus, and she knows it.

If people didn't know any better about my reputation, they would think Adrianna and I were a couple because of how much time we spend together. Again, she's just my most frequent repeat. Nothing more.

Adrianna has always wanted more from me, though. She's always wanted to put an exclusive label on us and feed into the clichéd fantasy of the quarterback dating the captain of the dance team. From the beginning, I told her no strings attached. I'm not looking for anything serious. These are my golden years, and I plan on having all the fun I can before the NFL calls my name.

Football has been a passion of mine since I was a kid. It started out as a hobby my mom forced me into so she could get me out of the house so she could get high or do god knows what else. Then I started taking it seriously, hoping the skills could help me ward off some of the drug-addicted and abusive boyfriends she had.

In a way, football saved my life. Literally. Aside from making me physically stronger, football gave me a future I wouldn't have had otherwise. Because of it, I was able to go to college, something I didn't think I'd get to do.

Growing up, I never thought I'd amount to anything. I always thought I'd end up like my mother, a lowlife living in abandoned houses without more than forty dollars to my name at a time—or dead in a ditch somewhere before I got out of my teens.

Thankfully, I found sanctuary in football instead of drugs. By my senior year of high school I had college recruiters coming to my games, offering me full scholarships because of how well I could play. Lord knows I would never have made it into college based on my grades. That's how I ended up at Garner.

I'm in my senior year now, and I haven't slowed down one bit. I'm training harder than ever, and NFL recruiters are keeping a sharp eye on me. My goal is to get drafted after graduation.

"You going to the party tonight?" Chase asks as we head to the locker room, referring to the annual bash thrown by one of the biggest frats the weekend before classes start.

"What do I look like, a saint? Hell, yeah, I'm going."

>> <<

Chase cuts the engine of his truck and we jump out. The streets are lined with cars, forcing us to park a few blocks away. Even from here we can hear the thumping of the music indicating that the party is in full swing.

Eventually, we make it to the large house and walk up the steps, which are littered with people trying to get in. Even with all the people occupying the front and back yards, the house is jam-packed with people standing shoulder to shoulder. After fighting our way through the front door, Chase and I are intercepted by a handful of people wanting to chat before we can finally make our way to the kitchen, where we grab two red Solo cups of beer from the counter.

"Yo, Bronx!" I hear someone yell, and I turn my head to see Brennen, the team's wide receiver, waving me over. He's wearing his favorite olive-green button-up shirt, which complements his dark skin and bright hazel eyes. He claims that shirt gets him laid more often than not.

Pushing through the crowd, I make my way to the dining room, where the beer pong tables are lined up.

"Be my partner?" Brennen asks with a hopeful smile, tilting his head at the tables.

"Sure thing." I down the beer in my cup, ready to play. "Who are we up against?"

He jerks his chin at two guys standing in the corner. I recognize one from the baseball team and the other is a total preppy frat boy I don't recall ever seeing before.

"At least give me a challenge," I scoff, causing Brennen to laugh.

"That's my boy! Let's do this, Miller."

Not even ten minutes later I send the ball flying, sinking it into the last cup and solidifying our win. Cheers ring out and Brennen claps me on the back before pumping his fists victoriously in the air.

"They don't call you the beer pong champ for nothin'!" Brennen yells, excitedly shaking my shoulders.

He picks up two of the other teams' remaining cups on our end of the table and hands me one. He taps his cup against mine in cheers, then tosses the alcohol back.

Just as the cup hits my lips, a small, delicate hand wraps around the plastic, fingers brushing mine, pulling it from my grasp.

I look down to see Adrianna with my cup in her hand, smirking devilishly over the rim before tossing back the liquid herself. Wolf whistles fill the air along with some hollers, and Adrianna looks pleased with herself.

She's in a skintight, strapless black dress that leaves little to the imagination. Her heels are tall and strappy while her makeup is bold and edgy, her eyeshadow smoky and lips painted a dark red.

I grab her waist, pulling her flush against my body. "I believe that was my drink," I say, peering into her piercing green eyes.

"Oops." She tries to feign innocence, biting her lower lip and batting her dark lashes. Standing on her tiptoes, she whispers huskily into my ear, "I can make it up to you later."

I growl, my fingers flexing into her skin possessively. "Or you can make it up to me now," I challenge.

She grins. "Slow your roll, hot stuff. I just got here. At least get me another drink and dance with me first," she says, already squirming out of my hold before grabbing my hand and leading me to the dance floor.

>> <<

Adrianna giggles against my lips, her fist wrapped around the front of my shirt as she pulls me blindly down the dorm hallway. I'm not entirely sure how we ended up here, all the way across campus from the party, but I do know what her intentions are.

Since day one Adrianna has made it her mission to be the first and only girl in my bed. She was actually the first to find out about my rule—not letting girls into my room—since she was the first to be rejected. She's been rejected more times than I can count, but she's persistent. And tonight won't be any different.

As we rounded the corner to my room, her lips sealed to mine, her hand dips into the back pocket of my jeans. She sneakily grabs my key, assuming I don't notice.

I let her walk me to my door, thinking she's about to get away with finally accomplishing her goal.

Backing me up against the door, I let her fumble blindly with the key. I thread my fingers through the dark hair at the base of her head, fisting the silky smooth strands with just enough grip to pull a moan from the back of her throat, teasing her. When I hear her successfully slide the key into the slot, I place my hand over hers, stopping her.

She whimpers in protest when I take the key from her grasp and separate our lips.

"Not so fast, baby," I say.

She lets out a groan, pulling back with a look of annoyance on her pretty face. "Bronx! Come on, we're right here," she whines, gesturing at my door.

I shove the key back into my pocket before leaning against the door and hooking my thumbs through the loops of my jeans. "You know the rules," I remind her casually.

She rolls her eyes, crossing her arms over her chest in a way that accentuates her breasts and jutting out a hip to show off her curves. "Really, Bronx? Can't we just forget about your stupid rules?"

"I wouldn't roll your eyes at me if I were you," I purr, pushing off the door and advancing toward her. She retreats until her back is pressed against the opposite wall, my body trapping her there. "We can still have fun elsewhere. If you behave."

She pouts, looking up at me with those mesmerizing green eyes. "But I want you now." She seductively runs her finger along my jaw and down the vein of my neck, ending the trail of her wandering fingers with her palm flat on my lower abdomen.

I lean down, letting my lips rub against her cheek before fanning my breath over her ear. "Who says we have to go far?"

Taking her by surprise, I hook my hands around the back of her thighs and hitch her up to wrap her legs around my torso. She gasps as I press her body harder into the wall, my hips grinding against hers.

"Are you going to be good?" I grunt into her ear.

She bites her lip hard, nodding.

"That's what I thought," I say before claiming her mouth with my own.

She threads her fingers through my hair as I swallow her moans. My tongue slips past her parted lips to explore, licking deep into her mouth as she writhes with pleasure.

Making sure I have her secured against me, I pull away from the wall and walk backward down the hall.

"Where are we going?" she murmurs against my lips.

"You'll see."

Rounding the end of the hall, I grab the door handle of the men's communal shower room and pull it open. We tumble inside the empty space—no one is in here at three in the morning—and I lead us into a stall.

I push her up against the cool tile of the wall and she lets out a small hiss as her burning-hot skin meets the hard surface, not appreciating the drastic temperature change. Reaching for the knob, I turn it to full blast and warm water pours down on us.

"Bronx!" she scolds, whining about how her dress and makeup are going to be ruined.

I mold my lips to hers, silencing her cries of displeasure, which quickly turn to moans.

Skimming my hands up her thighs and over the curve of her ass, I push her short dress up to her waist, exposing her black lace panties. I place her on her feet and sink to my knees, pulling the thin scrap of fabric down her long tan legs to pool around her heel-clad feet.

Before standing, I look up at her. Her chest is rising and falling rapidly as she looks down at me, soaking wet, dress bunched up to her waist with nothing but desire in her eyes. As I stand, I pull my soaking-wet T-shirt over my head, struggling as the fabric clings to my body. I let it drop to the floor with a *plop* before reaching into my back pocket for my wallet. I fish out a condom and unbutton my jeans, pushing the fabric down my legs along with my boxers.

I tear open the foil packet with my teeth, then roll the latex on, gripping her thigh and hooking it around my hip before pushing into her. Sweet little moans pass her lips and mix with the pattering of the water before my name echoes off the tiled walls with a scream.

Scan the QR code to discover what Olivia is feeling right now.

TWO

Olivia

Groggily, I roll over to check my alarm clock and see that it's just past ten in the morning. With a groan, I throw back the blankets and force myself to get up. It's Wednesday during the first week of classes, and I've already skipped Monday and Tuesday.

Football practice has been kicking my ass, so I've been sleeping in. The first day of classes are all syllabus days anyway, so what does it matter? Kids are floating around with schedule changes, too, so it's not like teachers will assign any real homework. But today I have my anatomy class lab, and I don't want to get stuck with some random as my partner. I at least want some control over who I'll be paired with for the whole semester.

After a quick shower I get dressed in a simple black T-shirt and dark jeans. I manage to slip a pen into my back pocket, deciding to skip carrying my backpack around, before heading out the door to the science building.

I find room 109, the anatomy lab, and walk in. The stench of formaldehyde immediately wafts up my nose, and I look around to see that most of the tables are already full.

I'm glancing around, weighing my limited options, when long

raven hair and piercing green eyes catch mine. Adrianna looks up and I see a hint of a smirk tug at her plump lips. Her table of four is already full, but she waves me over.

I just give her a simple nod in greeting, refusing to comply. I know she wants me to be her partner, but I'm not willing to go down that road. I don't want to blur any more lines with her and give her any false hope.

I scan the room again, finding a table of three guys who all look like loners. They glare at me.

All right, clearly I'm not welcome.

There's a table of two girls sitting next to each other, looking at me intently, hunger in their eyes.

Pass.

The only table left has a boy and girl sitting together, both of them total nerds, but they'll have to do. Maybe I'll have a chance of passing this class if they'll carry the load.

I walk over and take a seat across from them. The boy has short dark hair, and he's pale as fuck. His rodent-like face is buried in his phone, and he doesn't even acknowledge me as I sit down. The girl next to him looks to be of Indian descent with dark curly hair and light-brown skin. Her narrow face and high cheekbones are nearly covered by large, thick-rimmed glasses. She looks up at me from the thick textbook she's reading, and her dark-brown eyes widen when she recognizes me.

She gapes at me for a few moments, and I pull my phone out of my pocket, staring at it to try to make things less awkward. I'm starting to rethink my decision about sitting here.

I look over my shoulder at Adrianna's table to see her and the other three girls in a heated discussion, keeping their voices low as they argue over who's going to be exiled to make room for me.

Maybe it wouldn't be so bad to have her as a partner . . .

"Olivia!" the girl across from me excitedly shouts, nearly giving me, and almost everyone else in the class, a heart attack.

I turn back to look at the girl sitting across from me, and she's looking at the door, smiling widely. Rodent Boy looks up from his phone, surprise written all over his face as he sits up straighter.

I look at the doorway and spot a tall, slender brunet standing there, a deep blush spreading across her cheeks. She gives a quick sheepish smile to the class while stepping over the threshold, keeping her head down as she briskly strides to our table, her long caramel-colored hair flowing behind her.

My breath hitches in my throat. She's beautiful.

She's not the conventional type—not drop dead gorgeous, sexy as sin, or hot as hell. No. She's the subtle kind of beauty; the kind that can easily be overlooked if you're not careful enough. She's not the kind to turn heads on the street—she seems far too shy and reserved to purposefully attract attention—but nonetheless, she takes my breath away.

Our eyes meet briefly as she gets closer, and she gives me a small, kind smile. It's like a breath of fresh air. I'm used to girls smiling at me, but they usually have some sort of motive behind it. Her smile isn't suggestive or seductive, and there's no hunger in her eyes or awe signaling that she knows who I am. Her smile is genuine and friendly, and damn does it make me feel good.

She's dressed simply in a white T-shirt and jeans, not a usual first-week outfit. Most girls go out of their way to dress up the first week of classes, wanting to impress everyone. Not this girl. Even in this simple outfit she manages to capture my attention, whether she intended to or not.

She stands next to our table and her warm honey–colored eyes meet mine once again. "Hi, is this seat taken?" her soft, melodic voice asks politely, gesturing to the empty chair next to me.

Caught off guard, I shake my head, my lips parted like a damn idiot as no words come out.

She gives me that smile again before shrugging off her powder-blue backpack, setting it on the floor, and taking a seat next to me. The faint smell of vanilla wafts over, giving me some much needed relief from the formaldehyde.

"Hey, Liv!" the girl across from us greets her.

Olivia.

"Hey, guys," she greets the two across from us.

"What are you doing in this lab?" Pale Rat Boy asks abruptly, some accusation in his tone.

"Oh." She startles, nervously tucking a strand of hair behind her ear. "Yeah, I had to rearrange my schedule a bit at the last minute. Professor Cooper's other lab TA had a scheduling conflict. She asked if we could switch times, and I didn't have to move my schedule around much to accommodate the change, so I agreed to help her out and run the morning lab instead," she says quickly, seemingly trying to brush off the subject.

"I swear, that woman's in love with you. Ever since freshman year she's found a way to keep you around somehow because you're her favorite. TA, grading assistant, tutor for her class . . . I swear Professor Cooper would let you move in with her if you asked. Yet she acts like she hates everyone else and barely let me pass her class with an A," the girl across from me scoffs bitterly.

Olivia rolls her eyes. "She's not in love with me, Dee. She's actually really nice. A tough professor at times, yes, but nice. And, hey, at least you got an A."

"Says the girl who passed the hardest freshman class with a ninety-seven percent," Dee grumbles.

Pale Boy sits forward in his seat. "You should have told me you were switching to this lab section. I would have saved you a seat so we could be partners."

"Gee, thanks. What am I, chopped liver?" Dee asks, offended. "Too bad you already promised to be my partner once you knew Liv wasn't going to be in this lab."

"Sorry," Olivia offers up. "So, did you guys do anything fun this summer?" she asks, quickly trying to skirt around the topic again, leaning over in her chair to pull a binder from her backpack.

Dee launches into her summer adventures, talking about all the trips she took and the fun things she did. I don't pay attention. My eyes are focused on Olivia's profile as she listens to her friend, amusement written on her face as the other girl goes on and on enthusiastically.

Dee's story gets cut short when the teaching assistant walks in, juggling stacks of papers in her arms as she shuts the door behind her. She drops the pages on the front table with a *thud* and walks over to the desk to wake up the computer and turn on the projector.

"Hello, everyone!" Her greeting silences the low murmur of the classroom. "My name is Tracy, and I'm going to be your TA for the semester."

She pulls up a PowerPoint that outlines the syllabus and passes out copies to all of us. When everyone receives a copy, she goes over it in great detail, explaining the class policies and procedures for nearly twenty minutes. Usually I'd just get up and leave, but I stare at Olivia as she reads over the packet intently, highlighting and circling.

Next, Tracy passes out a tentative class schedule that goes over weekly topics, including page numbers to study from our lab manual. She lets us know there will be a quiz covering the previous week's material every week and tests will be every four weeks, along with a final exam. Since we're not going over any material this week, there will be no quiz next week.

After wasting nearly thirty minutes of my life, Tracy takes it further, pulling up another PowerPoint presentation about herself, declaring we need to get to know each other since we'll be spending the semester together. I mentally groan as she goes on and on about herself.

"All right, everyone, that's me. Now let's hear about you!" She prances over to the whiteboard and picks up a dry-erase marker, scribbling a prompt for us to follow. "Whoever you are sitting next to will be your partner for the semester, someone you're going to have to spend time with, so I want you to get to know each other, as well as the whole class."

She continues writing on the board, making a list of questions. "I want you first to get to know your partner, find out their name, where they're from, their major, and what they want to do in the future. When you're all finished, I'll have you stand up and introduce your partner to the class."

Multiple groans fill the air, everyone hating the idea of having to introduce themselves to a class—let alone another person. But I don't find myself minding it as much as I usually would.

I twist a bit in my seat to face Olivia, and she turns her body toward mine as well, our knees almost knocking together.

She gives me a small, almost shy smile. "Hi, I'm Olivia McCausland."

I mentally jot that down.

"Bronx Miller." I extend my hand to her, and she places her small hand in my much larger one, shaking it.

"Nice to meet you. I don't think we've had a class together before."

Definitely not. I would have remembered. Regardless, I try to play it cool. "No, I don't think so. What year are you?"

"I'm a senior, graduating in the spring. You?"

"I'm a senior too," I admit, feeling disappointed to have only just met her. "What are you majoring in?" I ask, hoping maybe our majors are far off, and that's why we've never ran into each other.

"I'm pre-med with a minor in chemistry."

I frown slightly. "I'm health management: exercise science. How have we never run into each other?"

She gives me a tiny, one-shoulder shrug. "I've seen you around a handful of times, but I guess we've never had a reason to run into each other."

I nod once, disappointed that she's noticed me but I've never spotted her before. "Damn. I should pay more attention."

A small giggle passes her lips, and I'm pretty sure a blush is blossoming across her cheeks. "Are you originally from Georgia?"

I shake my head. "Nah, I just came here for college. I'm originally from Florida, I guess."

"You guess?" She grins, raising a curious eyebrow.

"Yeah, I moved around a lot as a kid, but I was born in Florida and spent most of my time there. Are you originally from here?" I ask, quickly moving away from any possible conversation about my past.

"Yeah, my parents have lived here their whole lives."

"That's pretty uncommon, kids from around here staying for college. You didn't want to move away? Experience someplace new?"

She shrugs. "I guess I like it here too much."

"So pre-med, that's pretty ambitious," I comment, twisting my body more toward her, getting comfortable in my chair.

She smiles. "Yeah. The plan is actually to become a cardiac surgeon."

My brows nearly shoot up to my hairline. "Whoa, a cardiac surgeon? Like, you literally want to have people's hearts in your hands and work on them?"

"That's what a cardiac surgeon does," I hear Rat Boy mutter, and it takes everything in me not to give him the finger and tell him to mind his own business.

Olivia nods, not hearing him. "I've always been intrigued by the heart and all it can handle. Then I did some shadowing in the OR and fell in love with it."

"Wow, that's more than ambitious, that's badass," I admit, making her smile.

"What about you? What are your plans after college?" she asks, and

I suddenly feel a little embarrassed; my aspirations are miles away from hers.

"Oh, uh." I awkwardly cup a hand around the back of my neck, massaging. "I actually plan on playing football. I want to get drafted by the NFL after college."

Her eyes widen. "Oh wow, that's really awesome," she says genuinely—not in the condescending or fake tone I was expecting based on her academics.

"Do you like football?"

She cringes in embarrassment. "I mean, I've watched a few games with my dad, but honestly, half the time I have no clue what's going on."

"Don't worry, I can teach you," I reply smoothly, proud of myself.

"All right, class!" Tracy yells over all the chatter, trying to take control of the room. "Are we ready?"

One by one, each pair of partners stands up and introduces each other to the class. When it's our table's turn, Dee quickly shoots up from her seat first, Rat Boy following suit unenthusiastically. I find out Dee's real name is Delilah Harper. She's a senior majoring in pre-med, wanting to become a neurosurgeon. Rat Boy's name is Quinton Barnsley—still debating whether I'm going to call him by his real name or not. He's also a senior majoring in pre-med, wanting to become an MD.

Once they're finished, I stand up with Olivia, actually looking forward to this. "Hello, everyone," I greet the class and gesture to Olivia. "This is Olivia McCausland. She's a senior from Georgia, majoring in pre-med. After college, she plans on going to med school and becoming a cardiac surgeon."

I look over at Olivia, who gives me a small, surprised smile and an approving nod for going off script, not needing notes in front of me like most students.

"And this is Bronx Miller." Olivia gestures to me. "He's a senior, originally from Florida, and majoring in exercise science. After college he plans on playing football for the NFL." Now it's her turn to look at me and I give her a grin, raising my fist to her for a fist bump.

Once we take our seats, the next table continues on with introductions, the class finally ending after the last pair goes.

THREE

Introductions Part II

After lab, I head to one of the dining halls on campus to meet up with Chase and some of our teammates. After filling up my tray and paying, it doesn't take me long to find them since they're sitting smack-dab in the middle of the dining area, causing a ruckus.

"Aye! Look who finally decided to roll his ass out of bed," Chase greets me with a grin on his face, prompting other members of the team to holler and give me a hard time as I sit down.

"Shut up," I say, picking a fry off my plate and throwing it at Chase, hitting him in the chest.

"Seriously, if I didn't see you at football practice I would've thought you were dead the past few days. You sleep like a rock, dude," he comments before picking up the fry I threw and eating it.

"Well, yeah, it's tiring carrying all of your asses out on the field," I comment, earning a bunch of "Ohhh"s and "Burn"s.

Chase shakes his head. "Whatever."

A well-manicured hand with black nail polish lands right next to my tray, causing the table to go silent. I look up to see Adrianna, her other manicured hand resting on her hip as she looks down at me.

"Bronx." She says my name in a tone that has me dreading this conversation.

"Adrianna."

Her eyes narrow and her lips tug up into a closed-lipped smile. "You didn't want to be my partner?" she asks in a sickeningly sweet voice that tells me she's actually pissed.

I shrug, taking a bite of my sandwich. "Your table was already full."

She lifts her hand from the table, crossing her arms and shifting her weight onto one hip. "Nessa was going to move, so you could have had her spot."

"Didn't look like it," I comment, continuing to eat my lunch. If I remember correctly, none of the girls at her table looked willing to move. "Don't worry about it, Ads. I like the partner I got."

She scowls. "You're at a table full of nerds."

"More chance of passing the class, I guess."

Fed up with me and my curt answers, Adrianna lets out a sound between a groan and a growl before stomping off. She's just mad that she couldn't snag me as her partner, trapping me for an entire semester. That and the fact that I left her low and wet after our little late-night rendezvous in the showers over the weekend and haven't talked to her since.

"You didn't want to be her partner?" Chase asks, slight amusement in his voice. He already knows the answer to his question, knowing my dynamic with Adrianna.

"Nope," I say simply, opening my water bottle and taking a drink.

"Ouch, harsh," Brennen comments, not sounding too sincere. "Who's your partner, then? Some random nerd?"

"Nah. Her name is Olivia McCausland," I say.

"Olivia?" I hear JC's voice pipe up, and look down the table a few seats to see him leaning in, looking at me. "Did you say Olivia McCausland?"

"Yeah," I say slowly.

A wide, fond grin spreads across his face. "Dude, Olivia's awesome! I had her as my physics lab partner last year, and she's so fucking smart. Get this, the TA for that lab was a total dick. He made the lab way harder than necessary, but Olivia breezed right through it. She didn't let me slack off either. Just when I thought she'd be the type to do all the work and ask me to stay the hell out of her way, she actually sat there and explained the material to me by having me help her. She probably taught me more than the TA and teacher combined.

"And back to the TA being a dick. Even after she would sit there and walk me through it, explaining everything, we'd still end up getting the lab done way before everyone else, but the TA wouldn't let us leave until another group finished. Even after he checked our work *and* interrogated me about the material—which I actually understood thanks to her—he wouldn't let us leave early. So to pass the time, Olivia calculated how much force it would take for both me and her to bust through the window and jump out." He laughs, shaking his head. "She's the best. You're lucky, bro."

I feel a smile tug at my lips. I already knew she was brains and beauty, but this just makes me even more excited for lab.

After lunch, I walk across campus to the language arts building for my English class. On my walk over, just ahead of me, I spot a powder-blue backpack and long caramel-colored hair pulled over a white T-shirt clad shoulder.

"Olivia!" I call, jogging to close the distance between us.

She looks over her shoulder, some wisps of hair flying in front of her face in the hot summer breeze. She tucks the strands behind her ear, smiling when she spots me and slowing her stride to let me catch up.

"Hey," she greets me when I finally reach her.

"Hey, where are you headed?" I ask, falling into step with her.

She pulls the textbook she's holding away from her chest, flashing me the cover. "English."

"Me too," I say, feeling hopeful as we reach the old cobblestone building. I hold the door open for her. "What teacher do you have?"

"Professor Hobb."

That name sounds familiar. I pull my phone out of my pocket, double-checking my class schedule to see that I'm in fact also heading to Professor Hobb's class. "Room 112, right?"

She grins, rounding the corner that leads to room 112. "Right."

"Looks like we have another class together," I gloat, following her into a small room that seats about twenty-five people.

She walks to the far side of the class and slips into a desk three rows back. I take the desk right next to her.

"I guess this means we'll be seeing each other every day," she notes, bending over to reach into her backpack, which is propped against the back leg of the desk chair. She pulls out a white notebook and a pencil, setting them on top of the textbook in front of her.

I think about it for a moment before realizing she's right. Our English class is Monday, Wednesday, and Friday, while our anatomy class is Tuesday and Thursday, with the lab on Wednesday. "I guess so." I smile, feeling excited that I get to see her more than once a week.

Suddenly, I feel a presence to my right. I look over to see a girl standing next to my desk, staring at me while tightly clutching her books.

"Um, hi," I acknowledge her, not recognizing her whatsoever.

Her eyes narrow and she quickly turns on her heel, scurrying to sit in a desk at the back of the room with a huff.

I stare at her for a moment before slowly turning back to Olivia, baffled. "Okay, I have no clue what all that was about."

Olivia bites her bottom lip, trying to suppress a giggle. "I think you stole her seat," she whispers.

"I stole her seat?" I look down at the top of the desk, as if it'll have the girl's name carved into it. "Were we assigned seats?"

She shakes her head. "No."

"Okay, then, at least now I don't feel like a complete dick." I chuckle. "From her reaction you would've thought I committed first-degree murder. Do you know her?"

That earns me a small laugh. "I believe her name is Lacy. She was the president of the chemistry club for a semester, and she can be a little intense at times," Olivia admits with a slight cringe.

"I believe it," I mutter, just as the teacher walks in.

Professor Hobb's heeled clogs click against the tiled floor, and her black flowy pants with a wildflower print swish around her ankles as she gets ready at the front of the classroom. She's in a long-sleeve V-neck shirt and her gray hair is tied up into a bun.

"All right, class," Professor Hobb mutters, loud enough for us to hear. She pulls out some papers from her tote, making stacks and laying them across the front of her desk. "If you missed the first day of class please come up and grab the syllabus, along with some other papers."

Olivia glances at me expectantly, knowing I missed the first day. I hop up from my seat to grab the papers—something I typically wouldn't do if she wasn't staring at me, because there's a 90 percent chance I'll lose them within the next couple of days anyway.

I make a slight show of grabbing the papers and taking them back to my desk, pretending to thoroughly glance over them to appease Olivia.

"Okay," Professor Hobb addresses us as soon as everyone is in their seat and class is officially scheduled to start. "It looks like we have a full class today, so why don't we do introductions since we skipped those last time?"

A low groan erupts from the class. I look over at Olivia to see her shoulders sagged and her lips slightly turned down into a scowl, also not thrilled.

I lean over and whisper to her, "I'll introduce you if you introduce me?"

That causes a spark to twinkle in her eye, and one side of her mouth tugs up in a smile. "Deal."

>> <<

"I didn't know you were double-jointed," I exclaim to Olivia, referring to the fun fact she'd mentioned when we had to list one about ourselves during our introductions. She even demonstrated her skill by bending her thumb all the way back to her wrist.

"Well, we just met, so we don't really know anything about each other," she states as we walk out of the building, our class over.

True, and I want to know more.

"Still, that's sick, Liv," I tease, feigning disgust and cringing at the thought of her twisting her fingers around in an unhumanlike way, imagining the pain it would cause if I even tried.

She shrugs, unaffected, a satisfied smirk on her face.

As we walk across campus, she opens up our English textbook, skimming through the pages.

"We have to read all of that?" I gawk, watching as Olivia rests the book on her forearm and uses her free hand to flip through the pages she bookmarked. Professor Hobb assigned us some poems to read and be prepared to discuss on Friday.

"It's only five poems." Olivia giggles, examining them.

"Yeah, but that one's two pages long," I retort, a slight whine in my voice, pointing to the text. "Aren't poems only supposed to be a few lines?"

She chuckles, closing the textbook and hugging it to her chest. "They can be longer. It's not that bad. It shouldn't take more than twenty minutes total to read them all."

"Still." I huff, exasperated. "Who assigns homework during the first week of class?"

Olivia presses her lips together, trying to suppress a smile while giving me a sympathetic look, but I can detect the laughter dancing behind her eyes.

"Yo, Bronx!" I hear someone yell, and look to my right to spot Brennen walking our way.

"Hey, man," I greet him with a bro handshake, and he falls into step with us. "What's up?"

"You going to Kohan's party tomorrow night?" he asks.

I let out a low curse. "I almost forgot about it. Yeah, I'll be there. You wanna come?" I ask, turning to Olivia.

Her eyes widen in surprise. "Oh, no. Thank you, though. Parties aren't really my thing," she admits nervously.

"You sure? It's going to be fun," Brennen tries to persuade her, leaning around me to talk to her directly.

"Oh, Olivia, this is Brennen. Brennen, Olivia," I introduce them.

"Hi," Olivia says, giving him a small smile and wave. "And, yeah, I'm sure."

"Positive?" I press, slight hope that she might change her mind in my voice.

"Positive," she confirms, and I feel myself deflate.

"Where you heading next, Miller?" Brennen asks, looking at his watch. "There's still over an hour before we have to get ready for practice."

"I have to run to the bookstore to pick up my books. Teacher's already assigning homework."

"Already?" Brennen asks, appalled, and I nod. "Damn, bro, that sucks."

"Tell me about it," I mutter.

From my peripheral vision I see someone approach Olivia, and I turn my head to catch Delilah looping her arm with Olivia's, and now walking with us. "Hey, girlie," Delilah greets her friend. "Since when do you hang out with football stars?"

"We're just walking together, Dee," Olivia states with a slight eye roll.

Delilah shrugs. "Ready to start MCAT prep?"

"Yep. We're meeting Quinton in the computer lab, right?" Olivia confirms.

"Correctomundo, but his class doesn't get out for another thirty minutes, so guess who gets to stand in that long-ass line with me at the coffee shop," Delilah sings cheerfully.

Olivia lets out an exaggerated groan. "Really, Dee? It's way past noon."

Delilah grins. "Really."

"You're going to get an arrhythmia from the amount of coffee you drink," Olivia mutters. "See you, guys," she announces to me and Brennen before she veers to the left with Dee, toward one of the campus's coffee shops.

"See ya, partner," I call after her with a wave.

"Ready to hit the bookstore?" Brennen asks.

"No," I admit honestly, but we head there anyway, Brennen deciding to pick up his books for the semester too.

FOUR

Bold

I jog up the steps of the science building two at a time, my heavy backpack beating against me with every jump. Damn, my back and quads hurt from practice yesterday—Coach has been really drilling our asses since the first game of the season is this weekend.

On the second floor of the science building, I head toward one of the large lecture halls for my anatomy class. Finding the correct room, I walk in, and my eyes automatically scan the area for one person in particular.

Toward the center of the fifth row, I spot Olivia sitting with Delilah. I take the stairs to the fifth tier, sliding into the row and claiming the seat next to Olivia.

"Ladies," I greet them, hooking my backpack onto the back of the chair before taking a seat.

"Hey," Olivia greets me with a surprised smile.

I take a quick glance around the large lecture hall that's already halfway full. "I swear, if we have to do introductions in this class . . ."

Olivia laughs, shaking her head. "I hope not."

"If we do, I still got your back if you got mine." I grin.

"Deal," she agrees. "Bronx Miller, exercise science, NFL."

"Very good," I praise her, pleased she remembered everything I told her about myself from lab. "And Olivia McCausland, pre-med, cardiac surgeon, weirdo who can twist her fingers in an inhuman way."

She grins. "Nailed it."

"You told him you're a freak?" Delilah chimes in teasingly.

"Actually, she told our whole English class," I say.

"Liv, you have got to stop using that as your fun fact." Delilah groans.

"What else am I supposed to say?" Olivia asks.

"I don't know, anything but that! And you definitely don't have to show everyone either."

During their banter, someone from the back of the room yells my name.

I turn my head and look over my shoulder at the rows behind me. It takes only a few seconds to spot Adrianna with her hand raised above her head, waving to get my attention. Once our eyes lock, she gestures for me to come sit with her and her friends a number of rows back.

Internally groaning, I flash her a meek smile and give a small wave before turning back around in my chair, clearly rejecting her offer.

"—tell everyone you have a third nipple." I just catch the end of Delilah's sentence.

"You what?" I nearly choke.

"Delilah!" Olivia scolds her friend, turning a deep shade of red. Her head quickly snaps in my direction. "I do not have a third nipple, by the way," she states.

"But, see, it really grabs someone's attention," Delilah teases.

"Just—ugh!" Olivia covers her face, slumping back in her chair, causing both Delilah and me to chuckle.

Before I can comfort Olivia, I feel someone looming behind me, and twist in my seat to see Rat Boy—Quinton—scowling at me.

"You're in my seat," he says coldly.

I make a show of scanning the desktop, and even the back of the chair. "I don't see your name on it."

His jaw ticks and his beady little eyes stare a hole right through me. Sizing me up, he realizes I'd knock him on his ass in point two seconds, and so his eyes shift to Olivia, waiting for her to say something.

She shrugs before pointing out, "There's an open seat next to Delilah."

Displeased Olivia isn't coming to his defense, he stomps past us to take the empty chair next to Delilah.

"Jeez, what's up with me and sitting in people's unassigned seats? This is college, not elementary school. Professors don't give a rat's ass about where you sit," I mutter so only Olivia can hear me, trying to make a joke to clear the air.

I watch as her lips press together, suppressing a smile.

Our professor walks in and sets up the projector. We spend the next hour jotting down notes from the PowerPoint presentation.

"Man, I didn't miss taking notes," I complain, flexing my fingers as we finish the class, students gathering their belongings and filing out of the room to flee to their next class.

"It only gets worse from here," Delilah says, shoving her binder into her backpack. "Oh, hey, Liv, I may be a few minutes late meeting you at the car. I have to meet Josie after class to grab a few things from her, and you know how she likes to yap."

"No problem, I have some reading to do for English class. It's hot out there so I'll just wait for you in the library. Text me when you're finished and I'll meet you," Olivia says.

"Shit, I forgot about that," I mumble, referring to the assigned reading for our English class.

I stand from my chair and grab my backpack, slinging it over my shoulder and waiting for Olivia to finish packing up her things. While waiting I feel someone sneak up behind me, a hand landing on my shoulder as a body presses up against my side.

"You're going to the party tonight, right, Bronx?" Adrianna purrs in my ear, her hand on my shoulder sliding down my back and slipping into the back pocket of my jeans.

I squirm, awkwardly clearing my throat. I feel uncomfortable with Adrianna being this assertive, and I can sense the rising tension radiating off Olivia.

"Uh, yeah, I might swing by for a bit," I reply, recoiling.

Adrianna grins triumphantly. "Perfect, I'll see you there," she says before standing on her tiptoes and planting a kiss on the corner of my mouth, taking me by surprise.

Anger and embarrassment bubble inside my chest as I watch her walk away, clearly pleased with herself, like an animal that's just marked its territory.

"Awkward," Delilah sings in a hushed tone as she, Olivia, and Rat Boy stand and shrug on their backpacks.

Olivia flashes her friend a warning look before we all file out of the room. We walk down the hall of the science building, and my mind goes haywire trying to think of something to say to clear the obvious tension still lingering.

Do I apologize?

But what do I apologize for? I did nothing wrong.

Do I not say anything at all?

"See you guys later," Delilah says as we descend the stairs to the first floor, Rat Boy following her down the hallway toward more classrooms as Olivia and I head for the exit. I make sure to grab the door for her.

"Thank you," she says, and we walk in silence, some awkward tension still lingering.

"You sure you don't want to come tonight?" I ask, stuffing my hands in the front pockets of my jeans.

She shakes her head. "No, thanks."

"Okay, well, I'll see you tomorrow in class?" I confirm, and detect the uncharacteristic sound of insecurity in my voice.

She gives me a soft smile, any lingering tension dissipating. "I'll see you tomorrow. Don't forget to read those poems."

"Yes, ma'am."

>> <<

The wall vibrates against my back as I post up against it, the bass rattling the entire house. I press a red Solo cup to my lips, taking a swig of the cheap, lukewarm beer inside. I'm surrounded by some of my teammates, talk of our first game this weekend fading in and out over the music.

Ciara sashays up to our group, her shoulder-length blond hair tousled from being out on the dance floor all night. She wedges herself between Taylor and me, taking a seat on the arm of the couch. Taylor wraps his arm around her waist as he chats with Brennen, who's sitting to his left. It's been rumored for the past week that Taylor and Ciara have been hooking up. Nothing serious, though.

"Where's your girlfriend?" I ask Ciara, bending at the waist to chat with her more privately.

She shrugs. "She's not my girlfriend anymore. We broke up just before the end of last semester."

"Oh shit. I'm sorry," I apologize, not realizing they'd broken things off.

She waves her hand dismissively, unaffected. "Don't be. I think you and I both know she wasn't quite up to my speed." She smirks.

Ciara is another one of my frequent repeats, after Adrianna. We started casually hooking up freshman year and slowed down last year when she started having a couple of exclusive relationships. She had a boyfriend for a handful of weeks and then she was with her girlfriend for about three months. During that time I kept my distance, respecting her relationships, but when Ciara approached me at a party last semester with her girlfriend, asking me if I wanted to have some fun with the both of them, I couldn't say no.

We ended up going back to Ciara's place and I could tell Molly, her girlfriend at the time, wasn't too into it. I kept asking her if she wanted to continue and she would always say yes, wanting to please Ciara. But I could sense she was uncomfortable, that this wasn't something she was used to, sharing Ciara and being intimate with a male. So I kept my distance and my hands to myself unless asked, letting her come to me and give verbal consent frequently during that night we all shared.

I guess Ciara became too much for Molly to handle. Or Ciara felt Molly couldn't keep up with her. Ciara is wild as hell, and I feel a little guilty for their split, but I know it's going to take someone really special to keep Ciara's interest.

Ciara peers up at me with hooded eyes, and I can tell that thoughts of that night are dancing around in her mind. She bites her lip, her eyes leaving mine to do a quick sweep of the house. When her eyes come back to me there's a naughty glint behind them, especially when that wickedly talented tongue of hers slowly pokes out to moisten her plump pink bottom lip.

Without a word, Ciara stands from the couch, Taylor's arm falling from her waist as she does, but he doesn't seem to mind, focused on his conversation with Brennen. Her body slightly brushes against mine, and she leans in to brush her lips against my ear. "Meet me in the upstairs bathroom," she whispers before disappearing into the crowd for a moment until I spot her form reemerge, walking up the staircase.

Not wanting to draw any attention, I wait a few minutes before downing the rest of my beer, dropping the cup on the floor, and casually walking over to the stairs. I make my way to the second floor and head for the bathroom at the end of the hall. After I knock twice, it doesn't take Ciara long to open the door and eagerly pull me inside by the collar of my shirt, the two of us going at each other.

Ciara stands as I zip up my jeans, wiping her mouth with the back of her hand. She walks over to the mirror, combing her hair with her fingers before reapplying some lip gloss.

"Always a pleasure seeing you, Bronx," she says flirtatiously, flashing me a smile over her shoulder. "Hope to see more of you this semester."

"Likewise." I chuckle, bidding her goodbye as she slips out of the bathroom.

I walk up to the mirror myself, straightening out my clothes and splashing some water on my flushed face. Once I look put together enough and some time has passed since Ciara exited, I slip out of the bathroom.

As soon as I do, I spot Adrianna leaning against the opposite wall, looking absolutely livid. Her green eyes are hard and dark as she scowls, her arms tightly crossed over her chest.

"Fuck," I mutter lowly, already knowing I'm going to receive a mouthful.

"Ciara, Bronx, really?" she says, voice dripping in disgust.

"Yep," I simply reply, breezing past her to head for the stairs.

Her hand grips my bicep. "Are you serious? You really just fucked Ciara in the bathroom?"

"I didn't see you judging or complaining when it was you the other night," I state, and her jaw nearly drops to the floor.

"You're a fucking asshole," she seethes.

"Why? We're not together!" I remind her, growing angry myself. "You don't own me, Adrianna. I've made that clear *multiple* times."

Her lips purse together and rage swirls in those wickedly green eyes. "You're right," she says, voice eerily calm despite her demeanor. "You're allowed to fuck whoever you want, and I'm allowed to fuck whoever I want."

Just as the words leave her lips, Colton from the soccer team walks past us, and Adrianna grabs him by the back of his shirt. He spins around and Adrianna pounces, shoving her tongue down his throat.

Surprised at first, Colton takes a second to respond, but nonetheless grabs Adrianna by the hips, willingly making out with her in the middle of the hallway. Adrianna makes a show of running her hands over his body, tugging at his hair. She makes sure to open her eyes to look at me, to gauge my reaction as she mauls Colton right in front of me.

I know she's expecting a rise out of me, or hell, even some sort of response or emotion to cross my face, but I can't find it in myself to feel anything. To care at all.

Realizing she's not going to get anything from me, she angrily shoves Colton away from her and storms down the stairs, leaving Colton confused as hell.

FIVE

Finch

Beep! Beep! Beep!

I fling my arm backward, blindly and aggressively smacking around for my phone on top of the nightstand to turn off the damn alarm. After much effort, the shrieking sound finally stops and I shove my face back into my pillow, ready to fall back asleep due to my raging hangover from the party last night.

Not even a minute later the door opens, and I hear Chase whistle a tune as he walks into our dorm room. "Bro, get your ass up," he says.

I groan in response, and shortly after something damp and hefty lands on my face, causing me to shoot up out of bed. "What the fuck?"

Chase laughs from the other side of the room, and I rapidly blink the sleep out of my eyes to see the bath towel that he must have thrown at me on my bed near my pillow.

"Come on, dickhead, we have biology in less than thirty minutes. You already missed Monday and Wednesday," he reminds me.

"Fuck off," I grumble, grabbing his towel and throwing it at him. It hits him in the side of his damp blond head as he bends down to pull on his jeans.

"Whatever, just don't expect to copy my notes when you miss class," he taunts.

"You don't even take notes," I call him out on his bluff.

"True, but at least I listen, which gives me a leg up compared to you. Do you really want to fail a class senior year?"

I wait a moment, letting out a heavy sigh after. "Fuck you," I mumble, grabbing my own towel and shower caddy, then walking like a zombie to the showers.

>> <<

"Dude, wake up," Chase whispers, elbowing me in the side of the ribs.

I jerk awake, ready to sock him in his pretty, boyish face when I realize we're in the middle of our biology lecture. It takes me a second to get my bearings. I must have dozed off while the professor droned on and on about different species of birds.

"And the next species we're going to discuss," our professor says, switching to the next slide of the PowerPoint, "is the finch."

The professor launches into a lecture about how Darwin proposed his theory of evolution by observing finches on the Galápagos Islands, going into great detail about how they differ in beaks, body size, and behavior.

"Finches are very quiet little birds," the professor continues. "But even though their chirps are soft and sweet—making them a great house pet—they are actually very social in their own little groups. Now, this poses a problem. Like I said, they make good house pets, but you really have to have more than one in your home in order for them to be mentally and emotionally stable. Finches need companions in order to thrive. They're not like a dog or a cat, forming special bonds with their owners, they prefer the company of other finches over human companionship. Out in the wild, they live in fairly large groups and rarely migrate."

My mind drifts to Olivia, her soft voice and tiny frame, and how she's never strayed from home. I feel a smile touch my lips, thinking about her sweet smile and melodic laugh.

"Dude," Chase whispers, nudging me and giving me a *what the fuck* look. I probably look like a loon sitting in the middle of biology grinning as the teacher spews out random facts about birds.

I shake my head, sitting up a little straighter in my seat to try to get through the rest of this lecture without falling asleep again.

>> <<

"You're going to need that," Chase snickers as I grab a coffee from the dining hall, setting it and a bottle of water on my tray before we head to the checkout line.

"Shut up," I grumble, taking a large swig of the coffee after paying, and we find a table where some of our teammates are already sitting.

"Whoa, look who showed up," Brennen comments. "I thought you'd be in bed, getting your beauty sleep after the party last night and before the game this weekend." I flip him my middle finger while taking another long drink from my coffee cup. "Damn, coffee? Someone means business today."

"I'm surprised you're even attending class after this. I would've thought the two you had this morning would have been your limit," Chase adds. "What class are you even prepping for anyway?"

"English," I say, downing the rest of my coffee and feeling a little more alive. I also perk up at the thought of a particular brunet I get to see shortly.

"Oh, yeah, for the teacher who's already assigning homework," Brennen says, remembering me bitching about it the other day while we went to go pick up our books.

My face blanches and I quickly twist in my seat to reach for my backpack on the floor, rifling through it to find my English textbook. I let out a curse, pushing my lunch tray to the side while I try to remember the page numbers we were supposed to read, flipping frantically through the book. How did I forget?

Finding the pages, I quickly skim over the poems while my teammates snicker at my odd urgency to actually do something that was assigned. I read the five poems, one about spring, one about grief, another about a boat lost at sea, and then there's that famous one about taking the road less traveled by, or whatever. But the one that really catches my attention is about a lonely man who stands at his window every day, watching for a bird he recently befriended. Captured by its beauty and melodic chirps, every morning he gets up to watch for this bird that sits on the edge of a low-hanging tree branch just outside his window, the little, colorful bird's appearance now a highlight of his day.

Quickly finishing up my lunch, I bid the guys goodbye and stroll to the language arts building.

Once I'm inside, I immediately spot Olivia through the door of our classroom. She's sitting at the same desk she was on Wednesday, her long hair curtaining the side of her face as she looks down at a piece of paper on top of her desk. The eraser at the end of her pencil is pressed to her bottom lip in concentration as her eyes scan the paper before she brings her pencil down to write.

I walk through the doorway of the classroom, claiming the empty seat next to her yet again. "'Sup, Finch?" I ask, shrugging off my backpack.

Her eyes lift to meet mine, her brows slightly pinching together and her head adorably tilting to the side in confusion. She looks over her left shoulder and then her right, trying to decide if I'm talking to her or somebody else. "Are you talking to me?" she asks, pointing to herself.

"Yeah, you," I say, trying my best to smother the smile threatening to split my face.

The pinch between her brows smooths out and she sets her pencil down and sits up straighter in her seat, giving me her full attention. "Finch?" she asks, an intrigued smile tugging at her lips.

"Yeah," I simply reply with a grin, stretching out my legs and leaning back in my seat, making myself more comfortable.

She props her elbow on her desk, resting her chin in the palm of her hand, looking at me expectantly. "Care to elaborate?"

My grin only grows. "Well," I drawl, sitting up a bit, leaning toward her. "I learned a lot about birds today in my biology class—specifically finches. I learned they're quiet, melodic, chirping little birds. They're colorful, social, and they rarely migrate from home. I don't know . . ." I trail off. "I guess they just made me think of you."

Her eyes grow soft and one corner of her mouth tips up into a shy smile. She clears her throat, breaking eye contact, and I can detect a blush creeping onto her cheeks. "I'm guessing you have Professor Willford for biology?" she asks after composing herself.

"Yeah, how did you—"

"The man loves birds." She laughs, tucking some hair behind her ear. "I had him a year ago, and trust me, this isn't the last time you'll hear all about birds."

"Good to know." I chuckle. "Come to think of it, the man kind of looks like a bird himself. Have you seen his nose?"

She brings her hand up to her mouth, trying to mask her giggle. "Stop it, Professor Willford is a really nice guy."

"You're not denying it," I tease.

She stops laughing, smashing her lips together tightly to try to act serious, but it's no use. She cracks, falling into another fit of giggles. "Okay, I'll admit, he does kind of look like Nigel from *The Wild Thornberrys.*"

"Who?"

"Nigel from *The Wild Thornberrys.* Didn't you watch that show growing up?" she asks.

I shrug. "I guess not."

Growing up, I had limited access to TV. I had limited access to a lot of things since my mom preferred to blow her money on drugs instead

of bills for basic utilities and necessities. Half the time—between living in trashy apartments owned by her drug addict boyfriends and me living in foster homes—we squatted in run-down, abandoned houses on the outskirts of town just to have some sort of roof over our heads.

"Oh, well, the guy has a huge nose." She laughs. "Hey, were you able to get a lab manual for his class? I heard the bookstore messed up and only had enough in stock for about half the class. Supposedly they ordered more but they're on back order for, like, three weeks."

I let out a bitter chuckle. "No, they were already out by the time I picked up my books. Not even my lab partner was able to get one, so I guess we're screwed for the next couple of weeks."

Chase just so happens to be my lab partner for Willford's class. We plotted out our schedules so we'd have as many classes as possible together this semester.

"Well, if you need one, I think I still have mine somewhere. Just let me know and I can find it and lend it to you. Fair warning, though, it has some highlighting and writing in the margins. Hopefully you don't mind."

"Not at all." I grin. "Thanks, Finch."

She blushes. "No problem."

Professor Hobb walks in, her clogs clacking against the linoleum floor. "All right, class," she begins, silencing everyone. "Did we all read those poems that were assigned the other day?"

Olivia glances at me curiously, teasingly.

I flash her a thumbs-up before tapping my temple, signaling to her that I have them memorized, earning me a smile.

>> <<

"Are you coming to the game this weekend?" I ask Olivia as we walk of the language arts building after class.

She shakes her head. "No. I promised Delilah I'd go shopping with her to pick out a dress for her cousin's wedding."

"Oh, that sounds fun," I say, trying to hide the disappointment in my tone.

She lets out a huffed laugh. "You've clearly never been shopping with Delilah, then. Sometimes, I think I'd rather experience a root canal than spend hours on end trying to help her settle on a dress. Plus, I've never actually been to a college football game before."

I stop in my tracks for dramatic effect. "You've never been to a game?" I ask, shocked. "It's your senior year and you're telling me you've never been to a football game? Not even during homecoming?"

She shakes her head, her cheeks tinging pink. "I know nothing about football, why would I go?"

"Finch, Finch, Finch." I *tsk*, shaking my head. "It's part of the college experience! That's it, it's official, you're going to a game this season, even if I have to drag you kicking and screaming."

She looks at me doubtfully. "I'd have no clue what's going on."

I drape my arm over her shoulders. "What did I tell you the first day we met? I'll teach you. If you can ace every science class on this campus, you can pick up football."

Again, she looks at me with doubt. "We'll see."

"Have some faith in me, Finch." I chuckle, walking her to the parking lot to find Delilah so she can get a ride home.

Scan the QR code to discover what Olivia is feeling right now.

SIX

Home

I wake up around noon, skipping my Monday morning classes and even lunch to sleep in. The game Saturday night was brutal but we ended up pulling out a win for the first game of the season. Then the parties afterward were even more brutal, and my head throbs as soon as I sit up in my bed to rub the sleep from my eyes.

After much procrastination and a heavy sigh, I force myself to get up. Finding some aspirin sitting on top of my desk, I down two pills with a bottle of water before grabbing my towel and shower caddy, and dragging ass down the hall to the showers.

I spend about ten minutes in the shower, half that time spent just standing under the hot spray of water to try to soothe my aching muscles. Once I'm out of the shower, I slip into a pair of jeans and a T-shirt, shrug on my backpack, and head toward the language arts building.

On my stroll over, I get a number of congratulations and pats on the back for my performance Saturday night.

I walk into the building with my head held high and ego boosted. Rounding the corner, I immediately spot Olivia sitting in her seat, writing in her planner. "Hey, Finch," I greet her, walking into the classroom and taking my seat next to her.

Her head perks up at the sound of my voice, her eyes finding mine. "Hey," she says, flashing me that smile of hers. "I heard you had a good weekend."

"Yeah." I chuckle, still riding my high, especially after she personally bid me congratulations. "Thanks, we really kicked ass. How was shopping with Delilah?"

Her face falls, a look of agony washing over her features. "Remember how I told you sometimes I think a root canal would be more fun? That was one of those times."

"Ouch. Sorry. You should have come to the game instead," I jab playfully.

Her lips turn up into a half smile, and she shoots me an apologetic look. "Maybe next time."

"I'm going to hold you to it."

Once class is dismissed, I wait for Olivia to finish packing up her things and walk out of the classroom with her. As soon as we make it to the hallway, Olivia pulls her vibrating cell phone out of her pocket, checking the caller ID before answering.

"Hey, Dee," she greets her friend. Even with the buzz of the hallway I can slightly pick up Delilah's frantic, apologetic voice coming from the other end of the line, making Olivia's brows knit together.

I watch Olivia's shoulders deflate, a small frown pulling at her lips as she listens to Delilah carry on.

When we reach the front of the building, I hold the door open for her, letting her walk out first, and she mouths me a quick thank-you.

"No, it's okay," Olivia says, trying to hide her wounded tone, prompting Delilah to spout out what sounds like more apologies. "Dee, it's really no big deal. I can find another ride home or wait for my mom to finish teaching her last class." Delilah speaks and Olivia looks at her watch, slightly cringing. "It ends at five." Three hours from now.

"Delilah, really, I'm fine." Olivia giggles, trying to assure her friend by taking on a light, airy tone. "Go knock their socks off." A genuine smile touches her lips. "I'll see you tomorrow."

With a few more words from Delilah, and a few more reassurances from Olivia, the two say their goodbyes and hang up. Olivia shoves her phone back into her pocket, letting out a small sigh.

"Everything okay?" I ask.

"Oh, yeah." Olivia waves her hand dismissively. "Dee was just calling to tell me she can't drive me home today. Apparently word just spread that the president of the debate club is stepping down and the officers are having an impromptu meeting to select a new one. It's been Dee's dream since we started college to get that position."

"So you don't have a ride home?" I ask.

Over the past week I've gathered that she rides home with Delilah, since her house is on the way to Delilah's apartment.

She shrugs. "My mom gets off at five. I'll wait for her to pick me up."

I frown. "That's three hours from now."

"I can just sit in the library. I've got some homework to do anyway."

"It's the second week of classes. You don't have that much homework," I point out. "I'll drive you home."

Her eyes widen in surprise at my offer. "Bronx, you don't have to do that. Really, I have no problem waiting in the library."

"And I have no problem giving you a ride home," I state. "Coach canceled today's practice to give us a break after this weekend, so I have nothing better to do. Plus, maybe I could get that lab manual from you for Willford's class."

"Oh shoot," she mumbles. "Sorry, I totally forgot about that. Yeah, I can give it to you." She worries her lip, looking hesitant. "Are you sure you want to drive me home?"

"It would be my pleasure," I say, a feeling of excitement surprisingly bubbling up in my chest. "I just have to grab my keys, and we can get going."

Olivia and I walk across campus to my dorm room, and I unlock the door, mentally cursing myself for not making my bed. Then there are a few items of clothing scattered on the floor, most of them Chase's. Our room isn't a complete wreck, but it's not tidy either.

Speaking of Chase, he's lying on his bed shirtless, one hand behind his head while the other hand is holding the remote, pointing it at the TV to flip through channels.

"Shit, sorry, it's a mess in here," I apologize to Olivia, suddenly feeling a rush of embarrassment at having her see my room and roommate like this.

She gives me a reassuring smile, waving her hand dismissively. "It's not that bad."

"Uh—hi," Chase says, sitting up in his bed, his brows nearly to his hairline. Chase knows I never bring girls to our room. Not even to hang out.

"Chase, this is Olivia. Olivia, this is my roommate, Chase," I say, giving them a rushed introduction as I stride over to my desk, picking up one of Chase's shirts from the floor along the way and quickly tossing it at him. It hits him in the chest and lands in his lap.

Chase just stares at Olivia in confusion as she stands in the doorway, waiting for me.

"Hi." She gives him an awkward wave, probably wondering why he's staring at her like she has two heads.

"Dude," I hiss, wishing he'd stop staring at her as I throw my backpack on my desk chair.

Chase snaps his head in my direction, giving me a *what the fuck* look.

"Can I borrow the truck?" I ask, already reaching for the keys on top of his desk. In the past, Chase has let me borrow his truck if I need it, since the only vehicle I have is a motorcycle that I let him borrow in exchange.

"Uh, sure," he says slowly, still beyond confused.

"I'm giving Olivia a ride home," I explain. I know there's probably no way in hell she would let me drive her home on the motorcycle.

"I hope that's okay," Olivia says politely, looking at Chase.

Chase shakes his head, seemingly clearing his mind and sobering up. "Yeah. Yeah, that's fine, uh, it was nice meeting you," he says as I snatch the keys from his desk and usher Olivia out of our room.

"You too. Thank you," she calls over her shoulder as I close the door behind us.

"Sorry about him," I apologize, mentally shaking my head at Chase for making that so damn awkward. Sure, I may never let girls into our room, but it wasn't like I had her draped over my shoulder, ready to throw her onto my bed and toss her around in my sheets—something he's fond of doing himself. He lets girls come and go as he pleases, not finding that concept as messy as I do.

Olivia and I walk to the parking lot and hop into Chase's truck. She gives me directions to her house, which is fifteen minutes away from campus, and I'm not surprised when she tells me to turn into a nice subdivision and pull into the driveway of a beautiful home.

It's a sizable split-level house with light-gray siding, white trim, and shutters. With the colorful flowerbeds, careful landscaping, and literal white picket fence, it looks like it could grace the cover of a home magazine.

"This is it," Olivia states, reaching for her backpack on the floorboard. "Would you like to come in? It may take me a minute to find that lab manual for you."

Again, unexpected excitement bubbles up in my chest. "Sure."

We climb out of the truck and she leads me up the sidewalk to the front door. Pulling her keys out of her backpack, she unlocks the door, which has one of those decorative wreaths with a large *M* on it, and leads me inside.

Stepping into the foyer, I note that her house is just as beautiful inside as it is outside. With a relatively open floor plan, the space is homey, filled with soothing neutral colors. Nothing is too modern or dated, everything seemingly designed to show that it's a well lived–in family home.

"Dad?" Olivia calls, dropping her keys on the table next to the door.

"Hi, honey," an older male voice calls, followed by the sound of footsteps. A man, who I'd guess was in his late forties, comes into view. His dark hair is starting to gray, as is the well-groomed, full mustache resting above his top lip. "Oh, hello," he says, momentarily surprised to find someone else in his home.

"Dad, this is Bronx, we go to school together. And, Bronx, this is my dad, Stan," Olivia introduces us.

I politely extend my hand. "It's nice to meet you, sir. Bronx Miller."

He gives me a warm smile, removing the reading glasses from his light-blue eyes before placing his hand in mine, giving me a firm handshake. "Trust me, son, I know who you are. You sell me a lot of jerseys."

It takes me a long moment before I get it all to click.

McCausland.

As in, McCausland Sporting Goods.

I nearly smack myself for not realizing it sooner. McCausland Sporting Goods is the largest local sporting goods store. They sell and make the team's jerseys and apparel. Stan must be the owner.

I let out a soft chuckle. "It's my pleasure."

"I'll tell you, son, I've seen you play a handful of times. With how good you are, I wouldn't be surprised to find your name printed across the back of an official NFL jersey in a couple of years," he states, clearly impressed by me.

I can't help but grin. "That's the plan, sir."

Her father launches us into a full-blown conversation about football, and I feel bad for Olivia, since she can't really engage in the conversation. She stands patiently, though, listening to us talk about previous seasons and tactics. If this was anyone else, I'd blow them off in a heartbeat to give my attention back to her, but I'm definitely not about to do that to her father in his own home.

Once the conversation dies down, Olivia cuts in to let her dad know that I came here to drop her off and grab something for class. As soon as I say goodbye to her father, she leads me up the stairs to her bedroom.

Her bedroom is almost as I pictured it. Neat and tidy with white walls and furniture, and a powder-blue bedspread that matches her backpack.

She drops her backpack at the foot of her bed before walking over to a large bookshelf and skimming the books. "It should be in here somewhere," she mutters to herself.

I walk over to her desk, where her current textbooks are neatly stacked in one corner with a lamp resting in the other. Tacked to the wall behind her desk are some personal pictures of her with family and friends, making me smile.

"Found it," she calls, making me look over my shoulder at her. I watch as she stands from a sitting position on the floor and pulls a book from the bottom shelf. She quickly flips through the pages before extending the lab manual to me. "Again, I hope you don't mind that there's some highlighting."

"Not at all. Thanks, Finch," I say, quickly flipping through the pages myself, spotting numerous words highlighted in different colors. I tuck the book under my arm, scanning her room further. "Nice room."

She blushes a bit. "Thanks."

"A lot cleaner than mine."

She lets out a laugh, unable to deny that fact. "It looks like my dad really likes you," she points out, a small grin on her face.

"Yeah," I huff out in a laugh. "Sorry about all that football talk, by the way."

She shrugs a shoulder nonchalantly. "It's all right. He doesn't have too many sports chats with two girls who aren't really interested in the house."

"You don't have any siblings?" I ask out of curiosity.

"Nope." She takes a seat at the end of her bed. "It's just me, myself, and I. What about you?"

I walk over and cautiously take a seat next to her, watching her demeanor to make sure I'm not crossing any boundaries. She doesn't show any signs of protest. "Same. Only child."

"Ah, so you have a membership to the lonely club," she jokes.

"It's not so bad." I chuckle. "Sometimes I think I prefer it," I admit honestly, but in reality it's because I don't think I could stomach my mother having another kid and putting them through the hell I went through.

A soft knock comes from her already open door, and we both look up to find her dad standing in the doorway. "Hey, Bronx, how would you feel about staying for dinner? I'm making my famous lasagna," he says, his tone persuasive and enthusiastic.

"I don't want to intrude," I say, trying to be polite.

"Nonsense," her dad insists.

I glance over at Olivia to detect any signs of protest, but, again, I can't find any.

She catches my gaze, giving me a soft smile. "It's really good lasagna."

"All right, I'm sold," I declare, unable to pass up a home-cooked meal or the chance to hang out with Olivia outside of class.

Olivia and I head down to the kitchen to help make dinner. Honestly, I can't even remember the last time I helped in a kitchen or had a home-cooked meal.

Around a quarter to six, the lasagna is out of the oven and Olivia is placing the last set of silverware on the table when the garage door breezes open. A shorter blond woman rushes through.

"Sorry I'm late," she announces, out of breath, setting her stuff next to the door before walking over to Stan, leaning up on her toes to press a kiss to his cheek. "It smells amazing in here, honey."

"Lasagna just got out of the oven," he informs her with a loving smile.

"Perfect." She smiles and her eyes sweep the dining room, where she finds me, a look of confusion passing her face. "Oh, hello," she greets me.

"Mom," Olivia speaks up. "This is Bronx, a classmate of mine. He's going to be joining us for dinner."

"Oh, lovely." Her mother lights up. "It's nice to meet you. I'm Monica," she introduces herself with a friendly smile.

"You as well," I say.

Her gaze flicks over to Olivia and a flash of worry sparks in her eyes. "Olivia, aren't you supposed to be meeting with Cora?" she asks, looking at her watch.

"Mom, it's Monday," Olivia says blandly, but there's humor dancing behind her eyes.

"Oh, goodness me," her mother says, shaking her head. "I'm sorry, my head is—" She flails her hand above her head with a tired huff. "It is Monday." She laughs. "You'll have to excuse my jumbled brain."

After her mother washes up, we all sit down for a nice dinner where I end up going in for seconds because the lasagna is just that good. I even stay after to help Olivia do the dishes and sit around with her and her family in the living room.

I don't leave until after nine thirty, surprised at how much fun I had sitting and watching the local news with them, something I haven't done in forever. I can't even remember the last time I felt like I was in a real home, enjoying other people's company.

Their house is so warm and inviting, and their family dynamic is unlike any other. I can tell they're not putting on a show for appearances or to impress others. They're just genuinely a down-to-earth, wholesome family. And damn did it feel good to be a part of it for just a moment.

I've been in many houses—"homes"—throughout my life. Being in foster care, I was passed from home to home, no one willing to stick with me for the long run. But I guess that was partially my fault. I was an angry, unpleasant kid who didn't necessarily make it easy for my foster parents. I was too consumed with being angry about not having my real mother care for me that I didn't necessarily appreciate what others were trying to give to me. Regardless, they tossed me to the side when they got the chance, and no place I entered ever felt like a real home. They always felt a bit staged.

"It was nice meeting you," I say to Olivia's parents before I head for the front door. "Thank you for letting me stay for dinner."

"It was no problem." Her mother beams, walking up to me with her arms stretched wide then wrapping them around me in a hug. "Come back over any time you like."

I momentarily freeze, not used to being hugged like that. I wasn't necessarily expecting the gesture, but I guess I should have been, considering how kind her family is.

"Thank you," I repeat, managing to reciprocate.

"It was nice meeting you." Her father steps up to me, shaking my hand and patting my shoulder.

"Likewise."

I look over at Olivia and she smiles. "I'll walk you out."

With one final goodbye to her parents, I make sure to grab the lab manual before I head out the front door with Olivia. She walks me over to Chase's truck in the driveway, and I lean against the hood, facing her. "Thank you for tonight."

"It's no problem. I hope my parents weren't too much." She slightly cringes.

I laugh. "Not at all, they were great. So was the lasagna."

"Glad you thought so. Dad really prides himself on that."

"As he should," I state.

A short but comfortable silence lingers around us, and I find myself not wanting to leave.

"I hope your mom was serious about that offer, about coming back over sometime," I say after a while.

A soft smile graces her lips. "Anytime."

I smile, pushing off the hood of the car. Shoving my hands in my pockets, I scuff the bottom of my right shoe over the concrete of her driveway a few times before walking backward to the driver's-side door. "I'll see you tomorrow."

"See you tomorrow," she confirms, and I hop into the truck, roaring the engine to life before reluctantly backing out of her driveway.

SEVEN

Leftovers

I make my way to the science building for our anatomy lecture nearly twenty minutes early so I can secure my seat next to Olivia, because I know Rat Boy will try his hardest to make it to class before me and take my seat. I'm relieved when I walk into the large lecture hall and hardly anyone is there, only a handful of people.

I take a seat in the same spot as last time, making myself comfortable in my chair while waiting for Olivia to walk through the door. Not even five minutes later, Olivia enters through the large double doors with Delilah, both girls giggling about something.

"Hey, Finch." I smile, pulling out her chair for her.

"Hey." She smiles warmly, thanking me while shrugging off her backpack.

Once Delilah and Olivia are in their seats, Delilah leans over the desktop to look at me. "I heard Olivia found another ride home yesterday," she says, eyes gleaming with interest.

"Yeah. I couldn't have her sitting in the library for three hours bored out of her mind," I tease.

"So you guys ended up having a lot of fun last night?" Delilah continues, her voice playfully suggestive and eyes sparkling with mischief.

"Delilah," Olivia scolds her friend in a low, warning tone, shooting her a look that doesn't seem to faze Delilah one bit.

I chuckle. "Yeah, her dad makes a mean lasagna."

Olivia gives me an appreciative smile for not taking Delilah's teasing implication to heart.

"Wait," Rat Boy cuts in, stopping as he pulls out his chair. "You two hung out last night?"

"Yeah. I drove her home and stayed for dinner," I inform him, trying my best to hold back the smug tone in my voice.

He shoots me a glare before swinging his gaze to Olivia. "I could have driven you home yesterday. Why didn't you call me?" he asks a little too sternly, making me involuntarily clench my fists. Who the fuck does he think he is?

Olivia shrugs. "Bronx was right there and offered first."

His beady little eyes turn to slits, as he's clearly displeased with her answer. "Why didn't you drive her home?" he snaps at Delilah, his tone accusing.

Still unfazed, but now slightly irritated, Delilah turns to him with a bland expression. "I had something come up last minute," she explains vaguely, pissing him off further.

"Next time you need a ride, call me," he tells Olivia, his tone more of a demand than a polite request.

I drape my arm over the back of Olivia's chair, hoping to give this kid an aneurism since he's being a total possessive asshole. "She can call whoever she wants," I shoot back calmly, despite feeling anything but calm, irritation vibrating in my veins.

This kid is getting on my last nerve. I get that he probably has a huge crush on Olivia, but that doesn't give him the right to act like he owns her. Unless he's her boyfriend. I never really considered that a possibility. But based on how they interact, I highly doubt it. And even if he was her boyfriend, she can do whatever the hell she wants.

Olivia gives me an appreciative glance as Rat Boy huffs, unable to come up with a logical comeback, then takes a seat on the other side of Delilah.

The legs of the empty chair next to me screech as they scrape against the floor. I turn my head to catch a flash of raven hair, the curtain of long silky strands being flicked over a bare sun-kissed shoulder to expose a sharp smile and smoldering green eyes I know all too well.

"Hi, Bronx," Adrianna says in a sickeningly sweet, flirty voice, as she and her posse slip into our row.

"Adrianna," I say curtly, a new sense of irritation surging.

"These seats aren't taken, right?" she asks, her smile venomous.

Before I can say anything, the professor strolls into the lecture hall, wasting no time turning on the projector and starting the presentation.

Ten minutes into the lecture, I feel a hand land on my right knee and my body involuntarily stiffens. I snap my head toward Adrianna, only getting a glimpse of her profile. She carries on taking her notes, acting innocent, but I can tell she's trying to bite back a smirk.

Not wanting to cause a scene, I let it slide. That is until her hand travels upward.

Abruptly, I drop my pen and slip my hand under the table to capture her wrist, halting her actions. I snap my gaze in her direction, once again only getting a glimpse of her profile as she pretends to be focused on her notes. But this time she doesn't even try to hide her smirk.

I lean over in my chair, my lips inches from her ear. "You better knock it off," I warn quietly, only causing the smirk on her face to deepen, and I know she sees my threat as a challenge.

A few moments later, when I'm sure she's not going to try anything, I slowly let go of her wrist and pick my pen back up, scrambling to scribble down the notes I missed. Not even a minute later her hand brusquely travels from my midthigh to grip me through my jeans. I nearly bolt up from my chair, the action catching a few people's attention.

I cough awkwardly to try to mask my outburst, rushing to grip Adrianna's wrist and push it away, all the while trying not to cause more of a scene with my frantic movements.

I glance over at Olivia to find her already staring at me. Her brows are pinched together, and her head is tilted to the side in a silent question.

I give her a forced smile. "All good," I whisper to assure her. "Just had something tickle my throat," I explain lamely, trying to cover up what really just happened. Because god, if she knew . . .

She looks at me skeptically, concern still etching her features. I flash her another reassuring smile, and even though I can tell she doesn't believe me, she lets it go, reluctantly returning to writing down notes on the lecture.

Blood boiling, I quietly excuse myself and slip out of the lecture hall and into the long hallway, finding the nearest bathroom. I walk in, restlessly pacing the empty room while tugging at my hair. I kick a stall door, causing it to swing back and slam against the adjacent wall with force.

Damn it, Adrianna.

I can't believe she's starting this shit. I'll admit, freshman year it was sort of flattering having the hottest girl on campus crazy about me, but now it's just fucking annoying because she doesn't know when to quit. I've told her since the beginning, I never wanted anything serious. She's played along, but she always gets possessive, always wants something more from me. We keep going around and around. She acts cool with just hooking up, but then she starts hounding me for something more, so I cut her loose, trying to be the nice guy, but she always comes back. The cycle is never ending.

We can't keep going like this.

Reeling in my anger, I unclench my fists, roughly wiping my palms on my jeans and exhaling. Feeling more composed, I exit the bathroom to find Adrianna leaning against the wall, waiting for me, looking damn pleased with herself.

"Fucking hell," I growl under my breath. Knowing it's best to ignore her, I keep my head down, briskly walking back to the lecture hall, but her hand grips my bicep to stop me. "Don't," I warn her, refusing to turn around to look at her.

She saunters around me, stopping right in front of me, her face as charming as a snake's. "What's the matter, Bronx? Did I get you flustered?" She runs her hand up and down my arm seductively. "I can finish what I started with you in the supply closet."

"That won't be necessary." I take a step back only to have her advance. Knowing she's not going to ease up, I grip her by her shoulders to literally keep her at arm's length. "Adrianna, stop."

As fast as a flash of lightning, her charming, flirty face morphs into an angry pout I know all too well. "Bronx—"

"No, Ads," I cut her off. "I can't do this with you anymore. I can't give you what you want," I remind her for the hundredth time. I let go of her shoulders, backing away, and when she comes after me, I lift up my hand to stop her. "Don't."

With one final look, I turn around and head back to the lecture hall.

>> <<

Running off the field to the sidelines, I find my hand towel and wipe the sweat pouring down my face. It's hot as hell out today. Grabbing my water bottle, I take a long drink before placing my hands on my hips to catch my breath. When my lungs cease burning, I pick my water back up, guzzling down the remains. I gaze over the rim of the bottle, spotting a number of kids walking by. Probably from a class that just let out.

Scanning the pack, I spot a slender brunet with a powder-blue backpack talking to a curly-haired girl.

Finishing my water, I drop the empty bottle on the ground next to my things, and wipe my mouth with the back of my hand before jogging over to the pair. I realize Olivia's eyes are already trained on me, a smile curving her lips.

"Hey, Finch," I say. "Hey, Dee." I slow my jog and stop a few feet in front of them.

"Hey," they say in unison. Olivia flashes me that sweet smile of hers while Delilah clearly checks out my abs and chest, which are glistening with sweat.

"Looks like you're feeling better," Olivia notes, giving me a cautious once-over, trying to detect if anything is still wrong.

After my confrontation with Adrianna, I walked back into the lecture hall and gathered my things, knowing I couldn't sit and listen to the rest of the lecture with all the awkward tension hanging in the air. I said a quick goodbye to Olivia before I walked out, telling her I wasn't feeling well. She understood, and offered to lend me her notes later.

"Yeah, a bit better. I may be suffering from heat exhaustion now, but I'm better," I reply with a grin.

"Yo, Miller!" Brennen yells, and I look over my shoulder at him. "Stop flirting with girls and get your ass back on the field!"

I flip him the bird before twisting back around to face Olivia and Delilah.

"Nice tat," Delilah notes, having caught a glimpse of it when I turned around.

"Oh, thanks," I say, instinctively reaching my arm up and around to massage the top of my back, right below my shoulder where my tattoo ends. "So, Finch, any leftovers from last night?" I tease, although I wouldn't be opposed if she actually suggested I come back over and have dinner again.

She lets out a small laugh. "I think so. You're more than welcome to stop by and see if my dad's home and willing to share some with you. I'm sure he'd love to talk football some more. Don't know if my mom would like sitting at a table with just two men talking about football, though."

"You're not going to be home tonight?" I feel slightly disappointed for some reason.

"Don't even think about hanging out with Liv on Tuesdays," Delilah says. "Getting her to hang out on a Tuesday evening is like having the pope show up to your birthday party. Impossible."

Olivia flashes her friend a dry look, rolling her eyes. "Sorry, I just have a commitment. I meet up with a friend every Tuesday night for dinner," she explains, giving me an apologetic look.

I vaguely remember her mom freaking out last night when she thought it was Tuesday and Olivia was home for dinner.

"It's no biggie," I assure her. "I can take a rain check."

She smiles before her eyes grow wide in realization. "Oh, I have those notes from lecture today if you want to copy them," she says, starting to shrug off her backpack.

"That's okay." I stop her. "I'm kind of gross right now," I say, flashing her my sweaty palms. "I don't want to ruin them. Or possibly lose them. Any chance I can copy them tomorrow? Maybe we can do lunch together?" I ask hopefully, realizing we both have a lunch break between lab and our English class tomorrow.

"Uhh." She thinks about it for a moment, hesitating. Delilah nudges her with her elbow, and the two girls share a look before Delilah gives an affirmative nod. Seeming settled, Olivia turns back to me, smiling. "Sure, that works."

I flash her a grin before backing away slowly, knowing I need to get back to practice. "All right, I'll see you then," I confirm before turning around and jogging back to my teammates, feeling excited about tomorrow.

EIGHT

Dissect

The strong scent of formaldehyde hits my nose as soon as I set foot inside the anatomy lab. I take a look around and find dead rats sitting in trays at the center of every table. I scan the faces of my classmates, their expressions varying drastically as they all stare at the dead animals.

I turn my gaze to my table. Delilah is leaning in to get a better look at the rodents, observing them with interest. Pale Rat Boy is slumped back in his seat with a look of indifference, but I can detect some disgust in the seemingly permanent scowl on his face. Probably realized one of them is a distant cousin of his or something. Then I spot Olivia, looking at the cadavers with indifference. She's not totally disgusted or freaked out like most of the class, but she's not freakishly thrilled like some of our classmates either. She just stares at it with curiosity.

"Hey, Finch," I say, drawing the attention of everyone at our table.

She pulls her gaze away from the formaldehyde-soaked animals and flashes me a smile. "Hey."

"Finch?" Rat Boy asks, his nose scrunching in distaste.

"It's a nickname," I explain dryly, seriously restraining myself from following up my statement by calling him Rat Boy to his face.

He lets out a small *hmph* in response, scowling at me with revulsion.

I sling off my backpack and set it on the floor before slipping into my seat. "Ready to crack this bad boy open?" I ask Olivia, feigning excitement to lighten the mood, rubbing my hands together impishly.

She laughs. "As ready as I'll ever be, I guess."

"You guess? You're trying to make it into a profession where you crack people's chests open and mess around with their most vital organ," I say. There's no way she can be squeamish with a career plan like that.

"Yeah, with *people*," she emphasizes. "Not dead, smelly lab rats." She scrunches her nose adorably.

Ah, good to know she doesn't like rats.

"Good morning, class," our TA says, all too chipper while walking into the room. Tracy's cheerful mood has no undertone of malice, despite throwing us into the deep end by having us do a dissection for our first lesson.

Tracy drops her thick lab manual on top of the front desk before grabbing a marker and writing on the whiteboard. She makes a list of internal organs before calling out a page number, instructing us to open our lab manuals.

Making herself comfortable, Tracy grabs her chair and rolls it to the front table, plopping into it. She snaps on some latex gloves before turning on the projector, one half of the whiteboard now glowing with the image of a dead lab rat, much like the ones at our tables.

"Everyone needs to slip on some gloves, and each pair of partners can grab a rat from the center of your table," Tracy instructs.

I reach for the glove box at our table, pulling out two pairs and handing one of them to Olivia. She gives me an appreciative smile, but I can detect the apprehension behind it.

"Hey, we got this," I assure her with a nudge of my elbow, even though I don't feel quite as confident myself about this whole dissection thing.

She nods, reaching back to tie her long caramel-colored hair into a ponytail with the band around her wrist. She tugs it tightly into place and tucks some loose tendrils behind her ears. Slipping the gloves on, she reaches over our side of the table to slide one of the trays in front of us.

"Let's do this," I say, dramatically snapping on my gloves, causing her lips to twitch. "Who should do the honors?" I ask, grabbing the scalpel out of the tray. I'm willing to do the initial cut if she doesn't want to, but I don't want to just assume and take over.

She lets out a deep breath. "I'll do it."

"You sure? 'Cause I can do it if you want."

"No, I'll do it," she insists with a reassuring smile. "I've got to start practicing sometime."

I return her smile. "M'lady," I state, carefully offering her the blade.

She grips the scalpel securely in her hand just as Tracy starts giving instructions. With immaculate focus and precision, Olivia cuts. She slices slow and steady, doing just as Tracy instructs. When she's finished, she sits up straight, breathing out a sigh of relief and admiring her work.

"Great job, Finch," I praise her. "Now the worst part is over."

Tracy makes laps around the room, observing and helping groups when needed. She spends the most time at Adrianna's table. She and her friends are too repulsed to even touch the rat.

"Very good job," she compliments us over Olivia's shoulder as she stops by our table. "Good." She tosses out a quick approval to Delilah, who did the cutting, and Rat Boy.

For the next hour we poke around inside the rats, identifying different organs and learning their functions. Not exactly how I'd like to spend my time with Olivia, but I have to admit, I can't wait for our unofficial lunch date—even though my appetite isn't what it normally is, after digging around in a rat for nearly an hour.

"Don't forget, you'll be quizzed about what we learned today next week! So remember to study, and if you need any help there's open lab on Tuesdays and Thursdays. You can stop by and ask me questions, as well as study," Tracy yells before dismissing the class.

As we peel off our gloves and gather up our things, I begin to ask Olivia, "Ready for lun—"

"Hey," Delilah says loudly, suddenly cutting me off. "We'll catch you later, Liv." She shrugs on her backpack, walking away slowly and looking expectantly at Rat Boy, seemingly waiting for him to follow. "Have fun at your lunch meeting with Professor Cooper," she says, and shoots me a look I can't quite decipher. "Let's go, Quinton," she says, guiding him out of the room.

"You have a meeting with Professor Cooper?" I ask when they walk out, suddenly feeling disappointed.

She lets out a nervous laugh, freeing her hair from her ponytail. "No, not exactly. I'm still game for having lunch together if you are. I do have to drop some papers off in Professor Cooper's mailbox, though, first, if you don't mind."

"Not at all." I extend my arm to the door, gesturing for her to lead the way.

We walk down the hallway to the main office together, and Olivia ducks in to slip some papers into a mail slot, politely sharing friendly greetings with the secretary.

"Ready?" I ask once she exits.

"Ready."

We walk across campus to one of the many dining halls. I decide not to take her to the one I usually go to with my teammates, afraid they'll give me too much shit about having lunch with a girl and scare her off.

"So," I start, unable to hold back my curiosity, hooking my thumbs beneath the straps of my backpack as we walk. "What was that whole situation about?"

"What situation?" Olivia asks, doing that cute thing where she pinches her brows together and slightly tilts her head to the side in confusion.

"The one at the end of lab. Delilah was acting weird, and then she said you had a meeting with Professor Cooper. Why did she think that?" I ask, not in an accusatory way, but casually. I know Delilah knew about our lunch plans, since she was right there when I made them with Olivia. It doesn't make sense that she'd think Olivia had other plans, or that Olivia would tell her otherwise.

Olivia flushes and cringes in embarrassment. "She didn't . . . it was her idea to say that I had a lunch meeting with Professor Cooper instead, actually."

"All right, I'm going to need you to explain."

"Well," Olivia drawls, looking pensive. She exhales, her lips vibrating together. "I guess you could say Delilah and I sort of made up a plan to act like I had a meeting with Professor Cooper."

Now it's my turn to pinch my brows together in confusion. "I'm still not following."

She sighs, her shoulders slumping as she looks guilt-ridden. "We both kind of lied so I could have lunch with you. Alone."

"Oh." It's starting to make sense.

Olivia groans, hiding her face behind her hands in a mix of embarrassment and frustration. "I'm sorry. I was just afraid if Quinton knew he'd want to tag along, and I don't know. I just had a feeling it wouldn't be as nice if it wasn't just the two of us, because I know he can be a bit unpleasant sometimes."

I huff out a laugh. "I've caught on."

She shoots me an apologetic look, and I hold open the door to the cafeteria for her, the cool air-conditioning welcoming us as we step inside.

We both grab some food and pay, sitting at a vacant table with our trays.

"So, is—" I blank, almost slipping up and calling Rat Boy by his nickname. I scramble to think of his real name. "Quinton. Is Quinton your boyfriend?" I ask, unable to bite back my curiosity.

I can only assume there's no romantic relationship between them, but I have to ask. The question has been gnawing at me since the other day. She doesn't seem to be interested in him—at least not as interested as he is in her. But who knows, she could be attracted to him. Some girls tend to like that whole pale as hell, dying, creepy vampire look.

Olivia chokes on a sip of her water, quickly pulling the bottle away from her lips and capping it. She clears her throat before answering, "No. No, definitely not."

Relief floods my chest. "Was he ever your boyfriend?"

"No, never." She shakes her head. "He, Delilah, and I all met freshman year. Initially, we were assigned to be lab partners in one of our science classes, and then with our degrees being similar, we had all the same classes throughout the years. Naturally, we grew close and became friends. But Quinton . . . Quinton's a very closed-off person. He never really makes an effort to make new friends. I think Dee and I are the only friends he has here," she says, her voice softening with pity.

I nod. "He's got it bad for you, though." I state the obvious.

She lets out a groan, looking at me with agony. "That's what Delilah says."

"But you don't have feelings for him?" I confirm.

She bows her head in shame, shaking it.

"Does he know that?"

"Yeah, I told him once a long time ago that I didn't have feelings for him. He took it hard," she confesses. "I just feel so bad. I didn't want to be mean to him or embarrass him further, so I told him we could still be friends. But I'm scared I'm leading him on by doing so."

I shake my head and reach over the table to place my hand on top of hers, my heart aching for her. She looks wrecked over it. "You have nothing to feel guilty about. You should never feel bad for not reciprocating someone else's feelings. You were honest with him, and that's what matters. No one can fault you for being honest. Especially when you were nice to him about it. If he's the one struggling with just being friends, then it's his job to walk. He shouldn't stick around, hoping you'll change your mind when it's clearly made up."

She looks up at me, appreciation in her eyes, but I can still detect the sadness that lingers behind them over the sore subject.

We sit in silence for a moment, my hand still resting on top of hers for comfort. I catch her gaze sliding down to our hands, mine following. A form of intimacy hums between us, even in the middle of the bustling cafeteria.

"Do you have feelings for anyone?" I ask, hoping she might insinuate she has mutual feelings for me, or that she has a boyfriend. Hopefully it's not the latter.

Her brows pinch and her head tilts to the side. "What do you mean?"

"Do you have a boyfriend?" I ask, suddenly dying to know the answer.

She shakes her head, a small blush blooming across her cheeks. "No."

Silence floats between us, and I brush the pad of my thumb over the backs of her fingers.

"Do you think you could have feelings for me?" I ask, suddenly feeling confident after our little moment. She may not have felt it as strongly as I did, but I know she at least feels something—whatever it is—undeniably flowing between us.

Her brown eyes snap up to mine, her cheeks burning red. She bites the inside of her cheek, deliberating, slowly pulling her hand from mine and sitting up straight. "I don't know if that's an appropriate question for me to answer when your girlfriend is a few feet away," she says, nervously looking over my shoulder.

My face contorts in confusion. "Girlfriend?"

What the hell is she talking about?

Following her gaze, I look over my shoulder to find Adrianna sitting a few tables away, her eyes shooting daggers.

I let out groan. "She is definitely not my girlfriend," I say.

Olivia looks at me skeptically.

I let out a sigh, deciphering how I can gently break down my relationship with Adrianna to Olivia without me sounding like a complete asshole.

"Adrianna is like my Quinton," I state. "She likes me and wants me to be her boyfriend, but she knows I can't make that type of commitment to her."

Olivia's eyes soften in understanding, and she nods, looking a bit embarrassed. "Oh, I'm sorry. I just assumed with how . . ." She trails off, unsure of how to describe Adrianna's multiple bold, possessive actions toward me. "Comfortable she is with you."

"No, I understand how you might have misunderstood. Adrianna can be a bit unpleasant sometimes too," I say, quoting Olivia's earlier statement, when she was describing Rat Boy.

Olivia lets out a small laugh, some brightness coming back to her eyes, and any lingering tension dissipates.

We carry on with our lunch, conversation flowing easily and naturally. When I'm finished with my tray I push it aside and she lends me her notes to copy what I missed from lecture the other day, as promised. Afterward, we walk to English together, going over some new poems Professor Hobb assigned.

NINE

Okay?

The next week flies by. Between classes picking up and football practice, I'm beyond exhausted. But aside from exhaustion, the week hasn't been so bad. Olivia and I see each other every day in class and walk together when we can. We haven't had another lunch date or dinner, and I haven't pushed her any more about possibly having feelings for me.

The only day I didn't see Olivia was yesterday—Monday—because the game over the weekend kicked my ass. I ended up skipping English, wanting to save my energy for the team's ninety-degree weather practice in the afternoon. I felt bad for skipping, even more so for ditching her—not that she needs me in our English class. Regardless, I apologized during our anatomy lecture today, and of course she was nice about it. I even ended up scoring her number so I can text her to let her know if I'm going to be late to class or to ask her any questions.

Like I said, the week was going pretty well. That was until Chase took a particularly hard hit and fall at practice tonight.

"Fuck, dude. What if it's broken?" Chase worries as he gingerly holds his wrist to his chest.

"It's not broken," I say, praying my words are true. Because if it is broken, he's fucked.

"But what if it is? Then I'm fucked for possibly the rest of the season," he says, seemingly reading my mind. He groans, his head falling back against the headrest in agony.

"It's not."

I make a left into the hospital's ER parking lot, dropping Chase off at the door to check in while I try to find the nearest parking spot. I pull his truck into the first space I see and hop out.

As soon as Chase took the hit and tumbled to the ground with a painful scream, we all knew something was wrong. Coach immediately had me drive him to the nearest hospital; Chase couldn't hand me the keys to his truck fast enough.

I meet Chase in the waiting room, and we sit around for about twenty minutes before he's taken back for vitals and X-rays. Instead of waiting—knowing he's going to be a while—I take a walk, finding the cafeteria.

After looking around for five minutes at the limited, unappetizing selection of food, I finally settle on two granola bars and a Gatorade.

As I walk into the dining area once I'm finished paying, a flash of caramel catches my eye. I look to my left to find Olivia sitting at a table with an older woman who looks to be in her late forties. The woman is dressed in scrubs, telling me she's a hospital employee of some sort.

There's a tray of food between them on top of the table. But they're not eating.

The pair of them sit with their chairs pulled close, their knees almost touching as they face each other. They're both sitting up straight with their heads bowed a little, their eyes closed, looking somber. The woman has her stethoscope out, listening to Olivia's heart. She's deeply focused.

I stand and watch for a few moments, confused.

Why is Olivia at the hospital? Why is a lady listening to her heart in the middle of the cafeteria?

So many questions filter through my head, and then I remember something.

Taking my phone out of my pocket, I glance at my home screen, checking that it is in fact Tuesday evening. Olivia mentioned that she had a commitment on Tuesday nights to meet up with a friend for dinner. Even Delilah confirmed how religious Olivia is about this.

This must be the friend she was talking about.

Curiosity getting the best of me, I quickly dart behind a large pillar to observe the pair a bit longer.

After a few moments, the woman reluctantly pulls her stethoscope away with a shaky breath, giving an almost grim smile. Olivia lifts her head and mirrors the woman's actions, looking just as subdued.

The two seem to collect themselves, then they ease into an apparent natural, comfortable conversation. Suddenly, it feels inappropriate to watch them, and I slowly back away, sneaking out of the cafeteria, praying Olivia doesn't spot me.

I return to the waiting room and take a seat. I peel open the wrapper of my granola bar, munching on the honey-flavored oats while mulling over what I just saw.

Thirty minutes later, my mind still wandering, I hear a pair of doors open and look up to spot Chase walking out of the ER wing. His injured wrist is wrapped, resting against his chest, while his other hand holds two pill bottles and some papers.

He looks up at me and lifts his right hand, shaking the pills and flashing a tired smile. "Good news, it's not broken. Bad news, it's sprained pretty bad, and I'll have to sit out for at least two weeks. Possibly four if it doesn't heal properly."

I let out a relieved sigh, standing up and dusting off some of the crumbs that fell onto my shirt. "Thank fuck."

If it was broken, there's a good chance the season would be over for him, or at least a large chunk of it.

"Right." He lets out a breath. "Hey, you going to eat that?" he asks, nodding at the other granola bar sitting on the chair next to mine.

I roll my eyes, grabbing the granola bar, the Gatorade, and his keys. I almost toss the granola bar at him but think better of it since his good hand is already full.

>> <<

The hot water of the shower sprays my back, and I turn to let it run down my face, willing myself to wake up.

After my shower, I lazily slip into a pair of jeans and shoes, tugging a simple T-shirt over my head. With great effort, I sling on my backpack and trudge to the science building.

When I round the corner to the anatomy lab, I find the majority of the class waiting outside, the door to the lab closed. Most of my classmates are sitting on the floor, their lab manuals in their laps as they study. But one brunet in particular catches my eye.

Olivia sits on the floor sandwiched between Delilah and Rat Boy as they all look over their lab manuals.

I walk over to them, standing in front of Olivia. Gently, I tap the toe of my shoe to hers to gain her attention. "Hey, Finch." I smile once she looks up at me.

She flashes me that beautiful smile of hers. "Hey."

I kneel down to be at eye level with her. "Whatcha doin'? Why is everyone out in the hallway?"

"Tracy is setting up for our quiz," she informs me.

"Shit." I completely forgot about the quiz.

Falling back on my ass, I take a seat, struggling to rip off my backpack and pull out my manual.

I hear Rat Boy let out a judgmental scoff, and I quickly flip him off while Olivia's face is buried in her book.

For the next ten minutes I sit in the middle of the hallway, trying to cram all of what we went over last week into my brain. Kids come and go, brushing past me as I sit nearly in the middle of the hallway. I scoot forward as much as I can, my knees inches from Olivia's as we sit crisscross, facing each other.

"All right, everyone," Tracy says in her usual chipper tone, opening the door. "Ready?"

Everyone lets out grumbles, getting up and heading to the door to go inside.

"Manuals away!" Tracy orders before anyone can sneak into the room.

I gather my things and stand, extending my hand to Olivia to help her up. She accepts, her small hand fitting in mine as I tug her up. I keep hold of her hand until I'm sure she's stable, fully standing, and catch a look at her warm brown eyes.

Someone loudly clears their throat from the floor, and we tear our gazes away to look down at Delilah. She looks at me expectantly, jutting her hand out to me.

With reluctance, I let go of Olivia's hand and extend my hand to Delilah, helping her up from the floor.

"Thanks, Bronx. You're a peach," she says, patting my shoulder before brushing past me to head into the classroom.

I look over at Olivia, whose eyes are laughing at the whole situation.

My lips curve and I extend my arm, gesturing for her to lead the way. I follow her to our table, the smell of formaldehyde strong. Rats are placed on every table, little stakes with numbers sticking out of them punctured into some of their organs. A piece of paper lies on the table at every seat, a quiz of about ten questions.

Taking my seat, I mentally groan, knowing I'm not prepared for this.

"Be sure to write your name at the top and answer all the questions,"

Tracy instructs. "Some are basic questions, and some will have you identify different parts of the cadaver, so pay attention."

I stare at the questions blankly, not knowing a handful of them. Damn, I should have remembered to study.

Discreetly—guiltily—I strain my eyes to try to glance at Olivia's paper, but her long hair creates a curtain as she leans forward to write, shielding her answers. I sneak a peek across the table but Delilah has her forearm on top of her paper, and Rat Boy is clearly hiding his answers by using his tiny hand as a shield. Asshole.

"Five more minutes," Tracy announces.

I stare at the dead rat in front of me, trying to decipher what red-gray organ is being staked as number four. Everything looks the damn same, all blending together. Then I forget what the hell the function of the liver is.

Yep, I'm screwed.

For the remaining questions I don't know the answers to, I write down random answers, taking a shot in the dark with the limited time we have left.

"Time's up! Pencils down." Tracy quickly walks around the room, collecting papers. I reluctantly hand her mine.

"That wasn't bad," Delilah says matter-of-factly.

Rat Boy agrees, arrogantly declaring that it was easy, and Olivia shrugs casually. I mirror Olivia's action, trying to feign indifference and confidence even though I feel like I knew jack shit.

For the next hour and a half Tracy pulls out the model brains and we go over the different parts and hemispheres.

>> <<

"Fuck it's hot out," I say absentmindedly as Olivia and I walk out of the science building, the hot summer air smacking us in the face.

She lets out a small giggle at my blunt observation. "It is pretty hot out here," she agrees, reaching back to tie her hair into a ponytail to get it off her neck.

I watch shamelessly as her slim, delicate fingers twist the hair band around to pull her hair back, exposing the lines of her long, smooth neck. The tendrils of hair that frame her face brush against her cheeks as a light breeze rolls through. I blatantly admire her subtle, self-undermined beauty.

I suddenly remember her last night, sitting in the hospital cafeteria with that woman listening to her heart, the pair of them wearing somber expressions. Slight worry knots my stomach, and I can't help but let my eyes slowly rake her from head to toe. Not in a caveman-like, perverted way, but in a concerned manner, trying to detect if anything is wrong with her. Is she sick? She doesn't look sick. But that's how it always is; looks can be deceiving.

Her eyes meet mine, probably sensing my lingering gaze. Now it's her looking at me with concern after catching me staring at her. "Bronx?" she asks when I don't steer my gaze away.

"Are you okay?" I ask abruptly, unable to bite back my curiosity.

Her head jerks back in surprise and then she does that cute little head tilt thing she always does when she's confused. "Huh?" she asks, looking down at her body to self-assess. When she doesn't detect anything wrong, she swipes at her face self-consciously. "Is there something on my face?"

"No." I can't help but let out a small chuckle, but I sober up quickly, turning serious. "I—" How do I tell her without sounding like a creep? I let out a breath, my lips vibrating together before continuing. "I saw you at the hospital last night."

"Oh." Her eyes widen with surprise.

"I'm sorry. I promise I wasn't spying on you or anything weird like that. Chase sprained his wrist at practice last night and I had to drive him there. When I was waiting for him, I took a trip to the cafeteria and saw you with some woman. She was listening to your heart and you both looked . . . it just had me worried, that's all," I admit, shoving my hands deep in my pockets.

Her eyes soften and then she looks away, almost embarrassed. She clears her throat before speaking. "Yeah, that was Cora. She's a nurse at the hospital, and I shadowed with her in the OR over the past few summers. We became pretty close," she says, lifting her shoulder in a casual shrug. "She doesn't really have any family, so I have dinner with her on Tuesdays when she has to work the night shift. I can imagine how lonely it must be not having much family around, and she's good company."

"So you're okay?" I confirm.

She lets out a small laugh. "Yeah, she was just checking her stethoscope. She thought it wasn't working properly earlier and decided to try it on me."

I mentally breathe out a sigh of relief. "Okay, you had me scared there for a minute," I admit with a shaky laugh.

Her eyes soften with appreciation and a hint of affection. "No worries, I'm all good," she assures me.

I nod, grabbing the door of the language arts building for her. "I wonder what crazy outfit Professor Hobb will be wearing today?" I ask, referring to our English teacher's fondness for '70s attire and chunky jewelry, which she tries her best to make look business casual.

Olivia's mouth curves. "I feel like you pay more attention to her outfits than what she's teaching."

"You're not wrong," I admit honestly, earning me a melodic laugh. "What? You have to admit her outfits are a little distracting."

Olivia shakes her head in amusement. "Maybe she'll let us write our final paper on whatever we want, and you can critique her fashion choices over the semester."

I laugh, flashing her a razor-sharp smile. "That's actually a good idea, Finch. I'll be sure to give you credit for it."

She rolls her eyes at me good-naturedly, taking her seat. "Fiend," she mutters.

Minutes later Professor Hobb walks in, her clogs rapping against the linoleum floor, dressed in black bell-bottoms and a puffy-sleeved shirt with bright multicolored jewelry as accents.

I shoot Olivia a knowing stare and she tries her best to glare back at me, but her pursed lips give away her desire to laugh.

TEN

Tests

I walk into the anatomy lecture hall to find everyone either anxiously talking among themselves or frantically flipping through their notes, trying to soak in every last second to study.

Four weeks into the semester and it's our first test. Around this time, almost every class is handing out tests, and it fucking sucks.

You know what else fucking sucks? Rat Boy is in my damn seat. For the past four weeks the little twerp has been trying to steal it from me to be closer to Olivia, but I always try to get to class early to claim it. Only twice has he beaten me to class.

Olivia, Rat Boy, and Delilah are all looking over their notes. I walk up to our row and resist the urge to smack Rat Boy in the back of his head as I pass. Walking past Olivia, I glide my fingertips across the back of her upper arm, across her back, and to her other arm, catching a strand of her long, silky caramel-colored hair. I twirl it around my finger and let it naturally unravel itself.

Olivia twists around in her seat, smiling when she realizes it's me.

"Hey, Finch," I greet her, placing my hand on the back of her chair.

"Hey," she greets me quietly, trying not to disturb those around us. "Ready?" she asks, her tone and her face portraying her nerves.

"Ready to get it over with," I admit.

She gives me an understanding smile.

"Take your seats and put away all study materials," our professor announces, walking into the room with a stack of tests.

Good luck, Olivia mouths.

You too, I mouth back, even though I'm sure she doesn't need it, and take the seat on the other side of Delilah.

Our professor rattles off instructions before passing out the multiple-choice tests. As soon as the paper lands in front of me and I read the first few questions, I know I'm fucked.

Is it A or C? It has to be C, right? I question myself. *Or could it be D?*

Fuck.

You have C for four questions in a row! That can't be right, there can't be that many in a row, I realize, scolding myself for being such a fucking idiot and not studying as much as I should have.

Not even thirty minutes in the legs of the chair next to me scrape against the floor, and Delilah stands confidently with her test in her hands, turning it in before exiting the classroom. How the hell can she be done so fast?

Five minutes later Rat Boy stands and turns his in, just as confident as Delilah and even a bit cocky. Olivia is still in her seat, randomly flipping through pages to double-check her answers, but eventually she stands ten minutes after Rat Boy leaves to turn in her test. I catch her eyes just before she goes, and she flashes me a reassuring smile. If only that smile could help me get a better grade than I'm sure I'm going to get.

When the teacher announces that there's only five minutes left, I throw in the towel, giving up. If I don't know now, I won't know it five minutes from now either. Defeated, I get up and reluctantly hand my test in to the professor and walk out. There are only a few other kids left struggling.

Less than confident, I step into the hallway to find Olivia sitting on one of the benches, reading a textbook. She looks up at the sound of the door shutting behind me and gives me an anxious smile. "How did it go?" she asks.

I stop in my tracks. I hadn't expected her to be waiting for me. I know she means well, but now I feel like even more of an idiot by having her know I ate up all the time while she and her friends didn't spend nearly as much and even walked out with confidence. I'm not usually one to feel embarrassed by not doing well on a test, but this one is different. Having her know I spent so much time on it is humiliating.

Playing off my bruised ego, I let out an overdramatic groan in response, plopping onto the bench next to her.

She lets out a giggle and, surprisingly, pats my thigh in sympathy. "Yeah, some of them were a little tricky," she says genuinely, although I'm convinced that she's just trying to spare my feelings.

"You waited for me, Finch?" I ask, my voice slightly teasing, although deep down I can't deny the fact that she waited for me actually makes me feel a bit giddy.

Her cheeks heat up. "Not necessarily. I have some time before my next class starts, and the study lounges are usually packed this time of day."

"Mh-mm. Just admit you're obsessed with me," I tease, bumping my thigh with hers.

She rolls her eyes, closing her textbook and stuffing it into her backpack. She stands, slinging her bag over shoulder before looking down at me expectantly.

I stand. "How long do you have until your next class starts?"

She looks down at the dainty silver watch on her wrist. "About forty minutes."

"Have you eaten lunch yet?"

She shakes her head. "No, I was too nervous to eat before the test."

Now it's my turn to roll my eyes at her. "Finch, you're a genius. You have nothing to worry about," I assure her, slinging my arm over her shoulders and guiding her toward the cafeteria.

She gives me side-eye, scoffing humbly. "I am *not* a genius."

"Whatever you say, Einstein Junior," I taunt. "Just add a mustache and—"

She gasps, offended, and lightly swats me in the chest.

I laugh, catching her hand and holding the back of it to my chest for a few seconds longer. "I'm just teasin', Finch. You're way too pretty to be compared to Einstein. Physically at least."

She blushes, shyly darting her gaze away from mine as we walk the rest of the way to the cafeteria.

>> <<

"Time's up!" Tracy announces, scurrying around the classroom to pick up our quizzes.

I hand in my quiz more willingly this time, feeling a bit more confident after actually studying for this one. I know I didn't get 100 percent or anything like that, but I know I did better than the previous quizzes.

Once Tracy is finished collecting papers, she places them on her desk and grabs another pile sitting there. "Good news, class. Your professor has finished grading your tests from last week, and I can hand them back to you now," she says, calling out names to have us come collect them.

"Olivia McCausland," she calls, and Olivia stands, walking up to Tracy to grab her test. "Good job," I hear Tracy say as she hands Olivia her test, smiling.

Olivia scans her test on the way back to her seat, sitting down and placing it face down on the table.

"What did you get?" Delilah asks, stretching over the table and snatching Olivia's test. Olivia lunges to prevent her from doing so, but Delilah is too quick for her.

"Delilah!" Olivia scolds.

Delilah's eyes grow wide, and then her brow furrows in confusion. "How?" she breathes out in disbelief and aggravation. She picks up her own test, frantically flipping through the pages, scanning and comparing her test to Olivia's.

While Delilah is messing with the tests, Rat Boy gets called up and scurries back with his own test, looking pissed. He scoots close to Delilah to search Olivia's paper, intently comparing answers. Between all the page swapping, I manage to see that both Delilah and Rat Boy got a 95 percent while Olivia achieved a 100.

"Bronx Miller." Tracy calls my name, and I pop out of my seat to grab my test from her, expecting the worst. By the grim look on Tracy's face, I know it's not good.

I grab my test and immediately frown at the D+ scribbled in red ink staring back at me. Fuck.

Beyond frustrated with myself, I rid my face of any emotion when I return to my seat, not wanting to give away my horrible test score to my brainiac tablemates, feeling uncharacteristically embarrassed and ashamed. I can only imagine the shit Rat Boy would give me if he knew my test score. And Olivia . . . she'd probably think I'm the biggest idiot alive.

When I return to the table I take my seat and immediately shove my test into my backpack to hide it from any wandering, curious eyes.

"How did you do?" Delilah asks curiously, looking up at me from the pages in front of her.

"Well," I lie, giving a casual shrug.

"Define *well*," Rat Boy presses, almost knowing.

"Can I have my test back now?" Olivia cuts in, unamused that her friends are fawning over her perfect test.

Delilah scowls, reluctantly handing Olivia back her test, but not before asking her numerous questions, wondering how she got some answers wrong. While the girls debate, I feel Rat Boy's beady gaze on me, staring me down. There's a hint of a malicious smirk tugging at his lips, like he knows how poorly I did on the test and is criticizing me for it.

You're so stupid, Bronx! You'll never amount to anything!

My eyes snap to Olivia, but she doesn't say anything. She's still explaining concepts to Delilah.

What the hell?

Shaking my head, I try my best to clear my thoughts, but the negative judgments keep crawling to the forefront of my mind. The whole lab period I fight with the voice swirling around my head, and Rat Boy's shrewd smile and stare aren't helping one bit.

"Bronx?"

I swing my gaze to Olivia to see that she is, in fact, speaking to me this time.

"Are you okay?" she asks, looking at me with concern.

"Yeah. Yeah," I lie, realizing I've totally been zoning out on her this whole lab period.

She looks at me skeptically, but before she can confront me further Tracy dismisses the class.

"I'll see you later," I tell Olivia, ducking out the door in the opposite direction of her and her friends.

I walk down the hall, pacing at the end of it, trying to release some of the pent-up anger and irritation vibrating through me.

"What's the matter, Bronx?" someone asks, feigning concern. I'd know that condescending voice anywhere.

I look over my shoulder to spot Adrianna standing behind me. She's managed to squeeze her curves into the tightest pair of jeans, and her breasts are almost popping out of her ribbed black tank top.

Those piercing green eyes stare back at me, practically begging for a challenge.

Without a word, I charge her, gripping the back of her head and forcing her with my body to take a few steps back into a nearby empty classroom. As soon as we step inside, I kick the door shut behind us and Adrianna pushes me against the door before sealing her lips to mine.

Instinctively, I let out a groan, loving the feel of her plump pink lips and how her tongue swirls around mine. I know I shouldn't be doing this, but I can't stop. As much as I can't stand Adrianna most of the time, I have to admit, she's one hell of a distraction and an immediate ego boost.

Adrianna roughly rakes her fingers through my hair and jumps, wrapping her legs around my torso. With one hand supporting her back, I walk forward and blindly find the nearest desk, setting her on top of it. With one swift movement, never breaking my lips from hers, I roughly shove the desk with her on it over to the door, blocking it to prevent anyone from coming in.

She giggles against my lips, momentarily breaking contact. "Eager, huh? I guess someone really missed me," she taunts, and before she can say more to put me off, I slam my lips to hers to prevent her from saying anything else.

>> <<

I practically sprint to English, running late after my little lunch hookup with Adrianna.

The AC greets me as soon as I get inside, and I pause right around the corner. Running my hands through my hair, I try to make myself seem as put together as possible, despite feeling anything but.

While my hookup with Adrianna was an impulsive decision that made me feel good in the moment, I feel disgusted now.

Once I compose myself, I walk into our English class with my head held high, masking my shame to save face in front of Olivia.

"Hey, Finch," I say, plopping into the desk next to her.

"Hey." She looks over at me, giving me that signature smile, but it falters after a few seconds.

I watch as a handful of emotions scroll over her face, her expression eventually landing on suppressed surprise.

"What's up?" I ask hesitantly. I know my face is probably still flushed from my lunch break activities, but that can easily be excused as the heat outside.

"Uhh," she stutters, chewing at the corner of her lip, debating whether to tell me or not. It's then I realize she's staring at my neck.

"Yeah?" I softly urge her, already swiping at my neck.

"You, uh, have something—" She pauses, pointing at her neck, just below her ear, to signal to me.

I swipe higher on my neck and peer at my fingers, finding a faint pink sparkly tint smearing them.

Fucking hell.

I let out an uneasy laugh, then excuse myself to the restroom to wash off Adrianna's lingering lip gloss, damning everything to hell.

ELEVEN

Tutor

I walk into the anatomy lecture hall to find just Delilah in her seat. There's about ten minutes until class starts, and I'm sort of relieved that Olivia isn't here yet. After she noticed Adrianna's lipstick on my neck, I could sense the lingering, awkward tension between us. I've been mortified ever since.

I almost didn't show up to class today, but I figured that was the cowardly thing to do, and it could potentially worsen the situation.

"Hey, Dee," I greet Delilah, who has her nose shoved in a textbook.

"Hey," she says, peeling her eyes away from her book to greet me properly. "How are you?"

I give her a shrug of indifference. "All right."

She frowns. "You didn't do so hot on the test, did you?"

I'm taken aback by her blunt question. "Uhh," I stall awkwardly, scratching the back of my neck. "Not the best, I guess."

She nods. "Quinton was pretty insistent about it, and you quickly shoving your test in your backpack was kind of a giveaway," she says with a wry smile.

At the mention of Rat Boy my fists involuntarily clench. I knew he would be an asshole about it.

"So, how bad was it?" Delilah asks cautiously, surprisingly not in a condescending way. She asks out of genuine concern, like a friend would.

I let out a groan of agony and contemplate if I should tell her or not.

Sensing that I must be on the fence, she speaks up. "You don't have to tell me if you don't want to, but just know I won't tell anyone," she says sincerely. "Especially not Quinton. I can tell you two don't exactly get along."

"You got that right," I mumble. After a few beats, I let out a sigh. "It wasn't necessarily a complete crash and burn, but let's just say there were some major damages," I confess, willing to trust her.

She purses her lips together and nods. "Well, you know who's a great tutor? Olivia." A small, knowing smile spreads across her face. "Just ask and she'll be more than willing to help you."

I try my best to suppress a smile. While that does seem tempting, a part of my ego is telling me not to ask Olivia. But then again, it would be a good excuse to spend more time with her . . .

"I'll think about it," I tell Delilah, and she flashes me another knowing smile, one that says she knows I'll eventually cave and ask Olivia to tutor me.

We sit in silence for a few moments, more students filing in. I know I only have moments left, and something inside me can't bite back my curiosity, so I just come right out and say it. "Can I ask you something?"

She carelessly shrugs a shoulder. "Go for it."

I twist in my seat to face her directly, one elbow resting on the back of my chair while the other is planted on the desk. "What's up with Ra—Quinton?" I quickly correct myself.

Delilah doesn't even flinch at my question; it's almost as if she's been expecting it. With a sigh, she looks over both shoulders before leaning in to whisper to me. Instinctively, I lean in to hear her and give her my undivided attention. Her lips twist to the side as she contemplates how to begin. "Quinton has a pretty big crush on Olivia."

"I've gathered that much," I mutter, and she shoots me a look that tells me to shut up and listen.

"He's had a crush on her since freshman year, but Olivia has never reciprocated those feelings." She pauses, looking contemplative. "When Olivia told him she couldn't be with him, he took it really hard. At one point I honestly thought Olivia was going to cave and just date him because she felt so bad, but I told her that would only make the situation worse. Not to mention make her miserable."

My fists involuntarily clench. From what Olivia told me that day in the cafeteria, I already knew Rat Boy hadn't taken her rejection well and that she felt guilty about it, but I didn't know how bad the situation really was.

Delilah opens her mouth as if to say more but quickly snaps it shut as her eyes dart to the door.

I look over my shoulder to spot Olivia walking into the classroom. Her hair tie is trapped between her teeth as her hands work to quickly scoop up her hair to redo her ponytail. Once her hair is secured, her eyes travel up to meet mine. I take in a sharp breath, staring into those sweet, warm brown eyes that have imprints around them from lab goggles.

A small blush makes its way to her cheeks, and she slowly walks up the stairs to her seat.

"Hey, Finch," I say softly, treading lightly after yesterday.

"Hey." She gives me a small smile as I pull out her chair for her.

After the information I just found out, I can't help but stare at her, my heart hurting for her. I can't say I completely understand her situation—I don't feel guilty for constantly rejecting Adrianna. It's her fault that she can't accept the fact that I'll never be with her in the way that she wants. But Olivia is too sweet to have someone treat her that way and make her feel so guilty. That's why I have to seriously restrain myself when Rat Boy walks in.

The lecture goes by with a breeze, but I can tell something is wrong with Olivia. I can sense her gloomy mood. And it's not just the lingering tension from yesterday.

When our professor dismisses class and we all begin to pack up, Delilah speaks up. "Hey, Liv, you're still willing to tutor people, right?" she asks, shooting me a secretive glance.

"Hmm? Oh, yeah. Who needs help?" Olivia asks, looking up from shoving her binder into her backpack.

"Oh, just someone I know. I'm not totally sure if they're set on a tutor yet, but I'll let you know," Delilah says, flashing me another discreet look.

"Yeah, just let me know," Olivia says, slinging her backpack on. I can see it in her eyes that something is bugging her; her voice is a bit dejected as well.

We all walk out of the lecture hall together, and eventually Delilah and Rat Boy have to veer off to their next class. Olivia and I walk together in silence, and I glance at her frequently, able to tell she's mulling over something in that pretty little head of hers.

"Hey." I gently grab her elbow, stopping my stride. She spins around to face me. "Are you okay?"

"I'm fine," she states, giving me an unconvincing smile.

"Finch," I begin.

"No, really, I'm fine," she says all too quickly, refusing to meet my gaze.

I sigh and silence floats between us.

A warm breeze passes, causing the tendrils of hair framing her face to wisp across her cheek. Without thinking, I reach up to tuck them behind her ear. It's then those big, vulnerable eyes peer up at me, nearly knocking the air out of my lungs.

"I wish you would tell me what's wrong," I whisper honestly, swiping my thumb across her cheek.

Surprisingly, she leans into my touch. Her eyes flutter closed for a moment as she slowly exhales through her nose. Those warm honey eyes open, the sun hitting them just right.

"It's just been a really rough day," she admits, voice tired. "The lab assistants didn't wash the test tubes so I couldn't do the original lesson I'd planned for today, leaving me to scramble to come up with a new plan. Then I'm teaching all freshmen who are still so immature. One kid started playing with the Bunsen burner and nearly set the lab on fire," she says, getting more and more worked up with every word that passes her lips.

She presses her fingers to her eyes, clearly overwhelmed.

"Hey," I coo, immediately wrapping my arms around her and pulling her into my chest. I run my hand up and down her back in a soothing manner, wishing there was something I could do, something I could say, to make her feel better.

I rest my chin on top of her head, just holding her close, loving the feel of her in my arms.

"Want me to beat that kid's ass?" I ask in all seriousness, and I feel her shoulders shake.

I immediately think she's crying, and pull away to assess her. When I finally see her face, I realize she's laughing.

"No," she says, through a string of silent giggles, her eyes sad but shining with appreciation and hilarity. "Thank you, though."

"Are you sure?" I ask, running my hands up and down her arms. "I have a whole football team behind me to take care of the little shit for you."

She holds back a laugh. "If I ever need your assistance, I'll let you know," she assures me, and I can't help but smile at the light coming back to her eyes.

"Come with me," I say, grabbing her hand and linking our fingers together.

Her footsteps are hesitant at first, but eventually her stride matches mine. "Bronx, where are we going?" she asks, slightly gawking down at our joined hands.

"You'll see," I say, leading her across campus.

My hand tingles, and I'm mesmerized by how good it feels to have her hand fit in mine so perfectly.

We finally reach the coffee shop, and I hold the door open for her, making it a point to not let go of her hand just yet. The strong scent of coffee hangs in the air, and thankfully it's not too busy in here.

I lead us to the end of the line and look down at her quizzical face.

"Pick out whatever you want. It's my treat," I say, giving her hand a small squeeze.

Her eyes soften, looking at me for a few beats before darting to the menu. She cringes, her expression flooding with guilt. "I'm not really a coffee drinker," she timidly admits.

"That's okay. The pastry selection here is amazing. Girls love sweets when they're having a bad day, don't they?"

Her bottom lip pokes out in an adorable pout. "Bronx, really, you don't have to do this," she insists.

"Hey." I give her hand another squeeze. "You had a bad day. I want to make you feel better. Now what would you like?" I ask as we get closer to the counter and stand in front of a display case, which showcases numerous pastries.

"Bronx," she protests again.

"Sorry, I'm not on the menu, sweetheart, but if you really want a taste of me—ow!" I feign hurt, rubbing the center of my chest where she playfully hits me with her free hand.

"Hi, what can I get you?" the barista behind the cash register greets us as soon as the person in front of us moves.

I look down at Olivia expectantly, and she shoots me a glare despite the grin trying to break across her face.

"I'll take a blueberry muffin," she tells the cashier.

"And I'll take a small cold brew with a double chocolate brownie," I say, knowing I'll need the coffee to get through practice later.

The cashier rambles off the total and I'm a bit bummed when I have to let go of Olivia's hand to take my card out of my wallet. Once I'm finished paying, I have Olivia go find a table while I wait for our orders.

"You don't like coffee?" I ask as soon as we get settled, taking a drink from my cup.

She shakes her head. "Not really. Plus, I've seen how wired it can make Delilah, so I don't know if my heart would be able to handle all the caffeine if I drank it frequently," she laughs.

I nod, pinching off a piece of my brownie as she nibbles on her blueberry muffin.

"Speaking of Delilah," I mention casually. "Were you serious when you said you'd tutor one of her friends?"

"Yeah."

I nod, suddenly finding interest in a chocolate chip that falls out of my brownie.

Come on, Bronx. Do it. Ask her!

I bite the inside of my cheek, my pride clawing at me to keep quiet.

Just do it, you pussy!

How is it I can ask any girl to sleep with me, but the one girl I actually like I can't even ask to tutor me?

Just think of all the extra time you'd get to spend with her, I try to persuade myself.

"Finch?" I ask.

"Hmm?"

"Would you tutor me? In anatomy."

God, I sound so pathetic.

"Sure," she says, taking the final bite of her muffin.

Sure?

Really? It was that easy?

"Really?" I ask.

"Yeah." She shrugs. "It'll be nice to have someone to study with."

I lean back in my chair, nodding. "All right, then. We're officially study buddies. Put it there, partner," I say, extending my hand to her across the table.

She lets out a small laugh, her hand fitting in mine once more to give me a firm handshake.

TWELVE

Bet

"Have a good weekend, class," Professor Hobb dismisses us.

"Ready to get this wild Friday night started?" I ask Olivia, slinging on my backpack.

"I don't know. You think you can handle it?" she teases.

"Try me, Finch." I smirk.

A blush blossoms on her cheeks. "Don't worry, I'm sure you've had much wilder nights."

"That may be true," I muse. I place my hand on her desk, leaning in to be eye level with her, inches away from her face. "So I guess I'm down for anything," I say, giving her a wink, my voice low and playful.

Her cheeks turn red and she pulls her gaze away from mine, quickly stuffing the rest of her belongings into her backpack. I can't help but chuckle, pulling away and leaning back against my desk to give her some space.

"Ready?" I ask as soon as she's finished packing her things.

She nods, still clearly bashful after my forward flirting.

We walk out of the language arts building and into the late summer heat. Olivia's dressed in her usual T-shirt and jeans combo. Today her shirt is as yellow as the sun, and I have to admit, yellow looks good on her. The color really complements her hair and eyes.

"What?" I hear her ask, her voice shy, and I realize she's looking at me.

Damn. She must have caught me staring.

"Yellow's your color," I admit honestly, causing her to blush once more. "I know powder blue is your favorite color, but yellow looks really good on you."

Her brows furrow and she briefly stops in her tracks. "How do you know that's my favorite color?" she asks, doing that adorable little head tilt thing.

"It's kind of obvious, Finch. Your backpack, your room, just little things."

Her head jerks back in surprise, an emotion washing over her face that I can't quite decipher. After a moment, a smile tugs at her lips and she bows her head to hide it from me, brushing past me to lead us to the library.

We jog up the building's stairs, and I make sure to grab the door for her. The place is fairly empty, given it's a Friday and pretty much everyone wants to get the hell out of here after their classes are over. Normally that would be me, but Olivia suggested we have our first study session, and I didn't have the heart to tell her no. She's already accommodating me enough, working around my crazy football schedule.

She leads us to a back table, walking confidently, like she's been here a million times before. I've only been here once, *maybe* twice my whole college career.

She takes a seat across from me and pulls out her books. "Do you want to start with the lab material first or lecture?"

"Lab is fine," I say, hoping I can remember some of the material from Wednesday so I don't look like a complete moron.

"Okay," she says, grabbing her lab manual and flipping the pages to this week's lesson. "I'll let you study the figures for a few minutes and then quiz you on them."

I nod, getting to work.

For about ten minutes she lets me look over the material—bones of the hand and arm as well as muscles of the arm. She uses Post-it notes to hide the answers from me, pointing at the figures and having me name what she's pointing to. She starts out easy and then it gets more difficult.

"Triquetrum."

Shit, where is that again?

I look at the figure, blanking. I look down at my own hand, thinking maybe somehow that will help. When I don't know it, I take a wild guess.

"Not quite," Olivia says, correcting me. "Abductor pollicis longus."

The what now?

I look at my arm, trying to envision where the hell it would be. When I come up short, I look up at her helplessly. "I have no clue."

She bites the inside of her cheek, looking pensive as her eyes shift from mine to my arm. "Can we try something?" she asks.

"Is this where our Friday night starts to get wild?" I tease with a grin.

She shoots me a bland look, but I can tell she's biting back a laugh. Grabbing some highlighters and a pen, she stands and walks over to my side of the table. She takes the seat next to me, pulling her chair closer to mine, and tucks one leg under her.

I'm suddenly hyperaware of her presence, how close she is to me. I get a whiff of her vanilla perfume when she loops her arm through mine, using both of her hands to position my arm. When she has my hand flat on the table, she grabs a pen and starts drawing and writing on my hand.

She looks up at me through her long lashes, her face so close to mine I can almost feel her breath on my skin. "Is this okay?" she asks, her voice small and sounding almost nervous.

"More than okay."

She gets back to drawing on my hand and eventually moves up my arm.

When she's finished with the bones, she flips my arm over to start on my forearm. Pink highlighter starts at my wrist, slowly traveling upward, but then she stops.

I look down to see that she's stopped at a small, pink, risen circular scar on my arm, and my blood instantly turns cold.

I have similar scars scattered all up my arm from one of my mom's ex-boyfriends. He was a drug addict and a drunk who didn't like it much that my mom had a kid. He despised me, and whenever I would act up, or when he was just angry in general, he would grab me by the back of my shirt, hold me down, and stub his cigarettes out on my arm.

Just thinking of the pain makes my hand involuntarily clench into a fist.

Olivia stares for a moment, a flash of sadness and knowing in her eyes.

Normally, whenever I catch someone staring at my scars, I get angry, defensive, but with her I feel ashamed. I don't want my miserable past to tarnish her image of me.

I'm used to people staring at my scars and asking about them, and every time I snap or immediately shut them out. It's not like they care. They just want to know the sob story behind them so they can rub it in my face and belittle everything I've fought to overcome to get to where I am today.

But with her, somehow, deep down, I find myself wanting her to ask, to care, even though I don't want her to know the truth.

Olivia blinks slowly a few times, composing herself before running the highlighter up and over the scar, like it's not even there, passing all the others just the same.

When she's finished labeling my arm she silently stands and moves back to her seat across from me.

"All right, let's get started," she says, and just like that, it's like my scars are forgotten.

Weirdly enough, I can't tell if I'm more relieved or disappointed that she didn't ask about them.

>> <<

I let out a low whistle. "I think that's one of the wildest Fridays I've had in a long time," I joke, stuffing my hands in the front pockets of my jeans as Olivia and I walk out of the library together.

Olivia laughs, pulling her phone out of her back pocket and typing out a quick text.

Our first study session went really well—aside from the whole scar situation. I actually ended up learning a lot, Olivia putting concepts in perspective for me by using my own body as an example.

"So are you going to keep the party going?" she asks, stuffing her phone back into her pocket.

I shrug. "Dunno. Why, you got something in mind?" I smile.

She laughs, and just as she's about to answer, a black Chevy Equinox pulling up to the curb steals her attention. The passenger-side window rolls down and her mom comes into view.

"Hi, Bronx," she greets me, giving a wave.

I walk Olivia over to her car. "Hi, Mrs. McCausland. How are you?"

"Good. Did you kids have fun? Well, as much fun as you can while studying."

I chuckle. "Yeah, Olivia's a great teacher," I say, shooting Olivia a smile, making her blush.

"Any plans for the weekend?" Mrs. McCausland asks, making small talk.

"Not really, just football."

"Any big plans for tonight?" Olivia asks.

"Not really, no," I admit. There's probably some sort of party going on, but I've been there, done that a hundred times.

"Well, if you want, Dad is firing up the grill tonight and there will be more than enough food," she says, shifting her weight from one foot to the other, appearing nervous.

"Oh, what a wonderful idea!" her mother says, beaming from the car.

"Are you sure?" I ask Olivia.

"Yeah. You must be sick of eating cruddy campus food all the time."

"You got that right," I say.

"Perfect! I just have to make a quick grocery run before I go home. I don't know if you kids want to go with me or . . ." Mrs. McCausland trails off.

"That's okay," I say. "I can drive us so you can get your shopping done."

"Are you sure you don't mind?" she asks, looking guilty.

"Positive." I smile.

"We'll meet you at the house," Olivia says, waving goodbye to her mother.

When the Equinox pulls away, I lead Olivia across campus to the parking lot, where we hop into Chase's truck.

>> <<

"I had a lot of fun tonight," I tell Olivia, leaning against Chase's truck, which is parked in her driveway. I just got done saying goodbye to her parents after having dinner and watching the game with her dad, and Olivia offered to walk me out. It's almost ten now and I figure I better get going.

"I'm glad." She smiles, crossing her arms over her chest to ward off the cool evening breeze. "And it's nice seeing my dad talk to an actual person instead of the TV while watching a game." She giggles.

"You still haven't learned much about football, have you?"

She gives me a sheepish look.

"Finch, Finch, Finch." I *tsk*, shaking my head. It's then I come up with an idea. "Come to my game tomorrow," I say.

She looks at me hesitantly. "I don't know . . . maybe."

"That doesn't sound convincing." I am determined to get her to at least one of my games this semester. "What do you say we make this tutoring thing a bit more interesting?" I suggest, smirking and leaning farther into the truck, crossing my arms and ankles.

Her brows pinch together. "What do you mean?"

"How about we make a bet?"

She looks at me skeptically. "And what kind of bet are you thinking about?" she asks, a hint of a challenge in her voice.

"If I do well on this next test, you have to go to the homecoming game."

She purses her lips thoughtfully, nodding. "Define well."

"I have to get a C."

She shakes her head. "C plus," she counters.

"Fine," I agree. "C plus and you come to the homecoming game . . . and wear my jersey."

Her eyes nearly bug out of her head. "No way."

"Aww, c'mon, Finch," I plead, laying the charm on thick and giving her my best puppy dog pout. I push up off the truck and take two steps to be toe-to-toe with her. "You'd look really good in my jersey," I say softly, almost seductively.

I hear her sharp intake of breath, and she takes a step back. "Bronx . . ."

"Please," I beg, batting my lashes.

She nervously chews the bottom corner of her lip. "Okay," she says slowly. "Fine." But before I can victoriously pump my fists in the air she cuts in and adds, "Only if you get a C plus on the test *and* a C on every lab quiz until then."

I feel myself deflate, shoulders slumping. I'm about to negotiate, but the look she shoots me says her decision is final.

I sigh. "You drive a hard bargain, Finch, but you got yourself a deal." I stick my hand out to shake on it, and before she can let go, I playfully jerk her forward and she stumbles into me. Her palms land flat on my chest to stabilize herself. "You're going to look great in my jersey," I whisper huskily into her ear.

Those honey-colored eyes widen in shock as they look up at me, and her cheeks burn red. She quickly regains her balance and takes a step back, clearly flustered, making me chuckle.

She clears her throat, tucking some hair behind her ear. "Don't get too cocky," she says, trying to humble me.

"Don't act like you're not dying to wear my jersey," I tease, advancing on her.

Her eyes widen and she takes a step back, ready to bolt.

In a playful mood, I lunge forward, and a surprised squeal escapes her lips. On bare feet, she turns and runs up the pathway to her front door. Before she can reach the porch, I wrap my arm around her waist, pulling her back into my chest and lifting her off the ground.

"Bronx!" she yells, laughing uncontrollably.

I can't help but chuckle, setting her back down on the porch. She turns around, almost eye level with me now that she's a step up.

"Good night, Finch," I say, backing away slowly to the truck.

"Good night," she says, smiling. "Get back safe."

"Yes, ma'am," I say, taking the keys out of my back pocket and spinning them around my finger. "See you Monday."

"See you Monday. Feel free to study," she calls, making me laugh.

She stands on her porch until I've backed out of her driveway, giving me one final wave goodbye.

As soon as I'm about to pull out of her subdivision my phone chimes with a text. I quickly glance at the screen to see it's from Chase.

Chase: Yo, you coming to Goldman's party or what?

I quickly type back that I'm on my way, and pull up to Goldman's ten minutes later. I make sure to lock the truck before I walk up the steps and into a house that's thumping from the bass of the speakers.

Walking into the kitchen, I grab a beer from the fridge and make my way to the dining room, knowing I'll find Chase and some of the guys at the beer pong tables.

"Hey, man." I clap hands with Chase as soon as I find him.

"Dude, what the fuck is all over your arm?" he asks, staring at all the ink on my arm.

I can't help but smile, taking a swig of my beer. "Anatomy."

THIRTEEN

Bad Liar

I walk down the empty hallway of the science building, wandering aimlessly to pass the time I have between classes.

Passing a classroom, I faintly hear an all-too-familiar voice.

I stop in my tracks and take a step back to look through the small rectangular window in the door. Sure enough, Olivia is standing at the front of the classroom, talking to the students while writing on the whiteboard.

I step closer, watching her teach a small group of kids sitting at lab benches. Microscopes line the tabletops, and the students mess around with them, observing different slides.

I hear Olivia's voice drift off and swing my gaze back to her, watching her cap the dry-erase marker. She turns around and her eyes meet mine through the window. I grin as her eyes widen in surprise.

What are you doing here? she mouths discreetly.

I point to her class. *Who do you need me to rough up?* I mouth, jokingly pounding my fist into my opposite palm. I remember her telling me about the immature freshmen who gave her trouble last week.

Her eyes sparkle with humor as she fights to keep a stern face. Eventually, she cracks a smile, shaking her head before returning to teaching her lab.

I take a seat on the bench adjacent to her door and wait for her to finish up.

Twenty minutes later the door to the classroom opens and the students file out. I walk into the classroom when there are only a couple of stragglers left.

Olivia is erasing the whiteboard as I walk up behind her and hop onto the bench at the front of the room. I take a seat and let my feet dangle a few inches above the floor. She glances at me over her shoulder, flashing me a smile.

When she's finished, she turns around and stands next to me, her binder and papers scattered to my right.

"What are you doing here?" she asks, collecting her papers and neatly placing them into her binder.

I shrug. "I was walking down the hallway and thought I heard your beautiful voice. Stopped in my tracks and had to turn around to make sure it was you, and that no freshman was giving you shit."

She lets out a soft laugh, looking down and shaking her head. I can tell she's embarrassed by my compliment.

"So . . ." I drawl, cracking my knuckles. "Anybody's ass you need me to kick?" I joke.

"No," she says emphatically, shooting me a look before shrugging off her lab coat and neatly folding it. "I don't need you to kick anyone's butt."

"Butt? What's the matter, Finch? Can't say *ass*?" I tease.

She rolls her eyes, shoving her things neatly into her backpack.

"C'mon, say it," I urge playfully.

This time she laughs. "No."

"Aww, come on," I beg. "You can even use it in a different sentence, like, Bronx has a really nice a—ow!"

She playfully smacks me on the thigh, her jaw dropping and eyes wide with shock as well as amusement.

"All right, all right," I say, feigning hurt, rubbing my thigh where she hit me. "I won't make you say it now, but maybe that can be a part of our next bet."

"You'd have to get a perfect score in order for that to happen," she claims, slinging on her backpack and walking to the door.

"It's not that hard to say, Finch! It's a fact," I call after her, hopping off the counter and lightly jogging to catch up to her.

I get a few steps in front of her, then stop. I twist at the waist to look back at my ass, slightly lifting the hem of my shirt to fully show off my assets, my black boxers peeking out from the top of my jeans.

"See," I say, smirking.

"Oh my god." She laughs and playfully shoves me out of her way.

"You're just jealous," I tease smugly, falling into step with her.

She shakes her head. "You're in a good mood. Still partying on from Friday night?"

"Something like that." I chuckle. "Sorry if I woke you by the way," I apologize sincerely, cringing while awkwardly scratching at the back of my neck.

Friday night after I left her house and went to Goldman's, I may have had more to drink than I intended and ended up drunk texting her. I sent her multiple selfies and pictures of the arm that she drew on, letting her know that her diagram was a huge hit at the party. Honestly, I was a little sad when I took a shower the next morning and all her writing washed off.

I may have also texted her that night that I really, *really* can't wait to see her in my jersey . . .

Jesus.

Someone needs to take my phone away from me when I'm drunk.

She laughs, her cheeks heating up. "It's okay. I was up reading, so you didn't wake me."

I let out a sigh of relief. I would have felt awful for not only annoying her with my drunk texts but waking her up as well.

"Are we still down for a study session after English?" I ask hopefully.

"Sure thing. Let me just text Delilah and let her know I'm going to be skipping MCAT prep, then," she says, taking her phone out of her back pocket.

"You don't have to. If you have other plans, don't let me stop you," I say, guilty she's rearranging her plans just to tutor me.

She waves her hand dismissively. "It's no big deal. I wasn't really up for it anyway."

"You sure?" I ask, my heart warming at the thought of her giving up her original plans just to spend time with me instead.

"Yeah, Delilah's always lecturing me anyway about how she thinks I don't even need to be there or take the test again," she says with a slight eye roll.

"Let me guess, you got a really good score the first time?"

Olivia shrugs. "I did well enough," she says, and I know that's her humble way of saying she fucking aced it.

"All right, smarty pants." I snicker.

"Whatever," she mumbles, bumping me with her shoulder. "I'll see you later in English?" She slowly veers off, probably going to her next class.

"I'll see you there," I confirm.

>> <<

When Professor Hobb dismisses us for the day, Olivia and I pack up and head to the library.

The weather is actually really nice today, the heat mild as fall rolls in. Olivia and I are strolling across campus chatting about our day when we come up on one of the practice fields, where pop music is blasting from some speakers.

I look up to see the dance team practicing one of their routines, and I mentally groan when a pair of piercing green eyes meet mine.

Adrianna smirks wickedly, calling for someone to cut the music and telling the girls to take five. Her eyes are set on me, and I can tell from her stride that she's determined on us crossing paths.

I try to quicken my pace to dodge her without tipping off Olivia, but Adrianna is persistent and manages to step right into our path.

"Bronx," she says in a sickeningly sweet tone, her smile razor sharp as she stops us. "What have you been up to?" she asks, her eyes scanning me from head to toe while she places her hand on my bicep, squeezing possessively.

I chuckle uncomfortably. "Nothing much."

"Hey, why don't we have dinner tonight," she suggests, her hand running down my arm and grabbing my hand. "I mean, I have to shower first." She laughs flirtatiously, gesturing to her body, which is covered by a black sports bra and tiny gym shorts.

I clear my throat, awkwardly pulling my hand out of hers. "Sorry, Ads. I'm busy."

Adrianna's eyes darken and flick over to a very uncomfortable Olivia. "And who is this?" she asks me, folding her arms over her chest, clearly displeased.

"This is my tutor, Olivia," I say, not even willing to introduce them.

"Tutor?" Adrianna practically laughs. "What do you need a tutor for?"

"She's just helping me with anatomy," I say, dying to end this conversation.

Adrianna's eyes narrow and turn a wicked shade of green. "But you know all about anatomy, don't you, Bronx?" she says, her voice packed with meaning.

"Adrianna," I practically hiss in warning.

"Olivia?" someone calls from behind us.

I turn to see Rat Boy heading our way, Delilah behind him with slight panic in her eyes.

As if this situation couldn't get any worse if it tried.

"I thought Delilah said you were skipping MCAT prep because you weren't feeling well and your mom was going to take you home instead," Rat Boy says, standing next to Olivia.

Delilah stands behind him, her eyes wide behind her thick glasses as she slightly shakes her head, desperately trying to silently communicate with Olivia without him knowing.

Olivia stares helplessly at her friend, trying to read her mind.

"Yeah, I'm actually going to go meet up with her now. My head has been killing me, so I think it's best if I just go home with her and get some rest," she says, following up her statement with an awkward, uneasy laugh.

She's such a bad liar.

Why can't she just tell him the truth, that she's spending time with me? The obsessive little twerp is just going to have to accept the fact that he doesn't own her and she can hang out with whomever she pleases.

I look at Delilah, and she looks like she mentally wants to hit her face with her palm.

"Really?" Rat Boy says, raising a dark brow in challenge. "Because we just ran into her, and she said she was in a rush because she has to attend a mandatory staff meeting."

Busted.

Olivia's eyes widen. "Uh, I—" she stutters, stalling, trying to think of another lie.

"Yeah," she says eventually, clearing her throat and evening her voice. "She forgot, and I'm on my way to pick up the keys from her now to drive myself home."

"Then how is she going to get home?" he counters, clearly unconvinced.

"A colleague said they can drop her off," she says, voice still a bit shaky.

"Oh, yeah, doesn't Ms. Tillman live in your neighborhood?" Delilah cuts in, trying her best to save her friend.

"Yeah, yeah, Ms. Tillman is going to drive her home," Olivia says.

Rat Boy looks at them both suspiciously.

"Wait," Adrianna says, her eyes shifting from me to Olivia. "I thought you said she was going to tu—"

"Hey, Ads," I abruptly cut her off. "Why don't we take a rain check on that dinner," I say, trying to distract her and divert the conversation so Olivia doesn't end up in an even bigger hole.

Adrianna's eyes sparkle in victory.

"I better get going," I hear Olivia say, scurrying off to avoid further questioning, while Adrianna begins to talk my ear off. I almost go after her, but I don't want to blow her cover.

Once Rat Boy and Delilah leave, and I tell Adrianna that I'll do dinner with her sometime, I feel my phone vibrate in my pocket with a new text. It's Olivia, telling me to meet her in the back corner of the library.

"You're a really bad liar," I tell her once I find her. "You really dug yourself into a hole back there."

She lets out a groan, hiding her face behind her hands.

"Why don't you just tell him the truth?" I ask gently, taking a seat across from her.

She sighs, removing her hands and shaking her head. "It's more of a hassle than it's worth," she admits, defeated.

"Finch, you can't just tiptoe around him forever."

"I know, I know," she whines, massaging her temples, looking like a real headache is starting to come on.

Feeling bad for her, I decide to let it slide for the time being, wanting her to smile instead.

"I have to admit, this whole situation is very Romeo and Juliet, though. What next? You going to start throwing rocks at my window and professing your feelings for me?" I tease.

She shoots me a glare, standing up and grabbing her pens and highlighters before taking a seat next to me, scooting close. "Just shut up and give me your arm."

FOURTEEN

Jersey

I walk into the anatomy lecture hall feeling nervous. Like last time, there's a low murmur over the classroom, students quizzing each other and quickly scanning their notes one last time.

I look up a few tiers and spot Olivia sitting next to Delilah, an empty seat between them as they each review their notes.

As if feeling my gaze on her, Olivia lifts her eyes to meet mine, and she gives me a soft smile.

I jog up the stairs to our row and take a seat one away from Olivia. It's protocol to leave a seat open between each student on test day to prevent cheating.

"Hey, Finch."

"Hey. Ready?" she asks, looking anxious.

"I hope so," I admit nervously. "But I had a great tutor, so I'm pretty confident," I say, causing her to blush.

For the past month I've met up with Olivia a few times a week to study, and I can only hope all of our time together will pay off. I'm almost positive it will. She's truly a great teacher, but my old insecurities can't help but creep in.

What if I fail? Then I've wasted all of her time for nothing, and I'll feel absolutely awful.

No, Bronx, I tell myself. *You're going to ace this fucking test and she's going to look damn good in your jersey at the homecoming game this weekend.*

Suddenly feeling very determined, I'm ready for the professor to walk through the door and hand out the papers so I can get this over with. Adrenaline is pumping through my veins the way it does before a big game, and I know I'm ready to tackle this head-on.

When the professor eventually walks in, I can't get started fast enough.

Staring at the first question, I'm surprised at how fast I can answer it, and with confidence. I seem to be breezing right through the test with only a few answers stumping me.

Olivia, Delilah, and Rat Boy all finish before me, but I make sure not to let that stress me out. I take my time, double- and even triple-checking my answers. When I feel confident enough, I get up and turn my test in, praying I didn't flunk.

I'm almost certain I didn't fail. I felt way too sure about some answers, whereas last time I felt like I didn't know anything. That has to be a good sign, right? At least an improvement?

Trying not to overthink it, I return to my seat and pick up my stuff, slinging my backpack over my shoulder and walking out of the room.

When I make it to the hallway, I'm greeted by a familiar sight.

Olivia is seated on the bench across from the door, the same bench she was sitting on when I found her after our first test, now staring down at her phone. When the door closes behind me, she lifts her head to meet my eyes, staring at me with anxious curiosity, dying to know how I thought it went.

"Well?" she asks impatiently.

I let out a sigh, plopping down next to her on the bench. Closing my eyes, I rest my head back against the wall.

I feel Olivia shift, bending her knee up on the bench between us to face me. Sensing her intense gaze, I peek one of my eyes open to look at her. She's staring at me with wide eyes full of worry, and my lips involuntarily twitch up at the corners due to her adorableness.

"Bronx!" she whines, shoving my shoulder.

I can't help but laugh, sitting up straight. "I don't want to jinx anything," I confess, "but I think I did pretty well." I grin, turning to look at her expression.

"Really?" she asks excitedly, eyes sparkling.

"Like I said, I don't want to jinx it," I say, standing and stretching. "So don't get too excited about wearing my jersey just yet," I tease with a wink.

She rolls her eyes good-naturedly, then stands and grabs her backpack. Brushing past me, she walks down the hall and I fall into step with her.

"But for now," I muse, "we could have a celebratory lunch date?"

She nods, blushing at the word *date*. "Yeah, we can do that."

"Good." I grin, leading her to the cafeteria.

"So you really think it went well?" she asks cautiously, hopefully, looking up at me with those big, innocent eyes.

"I think so," I admit earnestly. "So should I give you my jersey now or . . . ?" I trail off, grinning.

She laughs, shaking her head. "We'll just have to wait until we get our results tomorrow in lab."

>> <<

I get to lab just as Tracy opens the door and instructs everyone to put all study materials away for the quiz. Everyone begins shoving things into their backpacks and filing into the classroom.

I find Olivia sitting on the floor of the hallway between Delilah and Rat Boy, packing up.

"Hey, Finch," I greet her, extending my hand to help her up, earning me a glare from Rat Boy.

"Thank you," she says, brushing off the back of her jeans.

Before she can lean down to pick up her backpack from the floor, I swoop down and grab it for her, proceeding into the classroom with it.

"Bronx," she hisses, giggling while chasing me into the room, trying to grab her backpack from me.

"What a gentleman," I hear Delilah coo behind us, followed by a disgusted noise from Rat Boy.

When everyone is seated, Tracy passes out the quizzes over last week's material. I surprisingly breeze through it, confident I'm still going to hold up my other end of the bet by getting a C or better on the lab quizzes. Now all I have to worry about is what I got on the test yesterday.

After Tracy collects the quizzes, she reaches for the large stack of papers on her desk that I already know are our tests from lecture.

"I have your tests," Tracy announces. "When I call your name, please come and grab it from me," she instructs.

I wait impatiently as she calls name after name. Olivia, Delilah, and Rat Boy all get their tests before me, and look pleased. It isn't until Tracy has the last test in her hands that she calls my name. Of course.

I walk up to her, my heart thudding nervously in my chest.

"Here you go, Bronx." Tracy hands me my test, her face neutral.

I immediately stare at the red ink scribbled at the top of my paper, my heart faltering for a moment. Swallowing hard, I quickly regain my composure and walk back to my desk. I feel Olivia's eyes burning into me but I refuse to look at her, taking my seat and shoving my test into my backpack before anyone can see.

"What? Fail again?" I hear Rat Boy snicker maliciously, and it takes everything inside of me not to lunge over the table and break his fucking nose. Along with his jaw. See if he can make any more smartass comments after that.

Olivia quickly shoots him a glare, and for a split second I see a flash of regret cross his face. He's only guilty because he upset her; he couldn't give his own kind's ass if he hurt me or not.

Olivia's eyes eventually swing to me, softening, full of questioning and worry. I can tell she's dying to know about my grade, but she's too polite to flat out ask me.

I only shake my head, grabbing my lab manual as Tracy begins teaching this week's lesson and shoving my nose into the book.

The rest of the lab I try my best to focus, acting as neutral as possible. I can tell Olivia is trying to walk on eggshells around me, worried about my reaction, or lack thereof, after getting my test back.

When Tracy dismisses us, I can't pack up my stuff fast enough and head out the door. I make it halfway down the hallway before I hear footsteps running up behind me.

"Bronx! Bronx, wait!" I hear Olivia call after me, her footsteps nearing closer.

"Bronx," she says breathlessly, catching up to me and grabbing my bicep.

I stop in my tracks, and she cautiously walks around me to stand face-to-face. Those warm brown eyes search mine, worry marring her forehead.

"Bronx?" she says softly, still desperately searching my eyes for some sort of answer.

I let out a sigh, closing my eyes and pinching the bridge of my nose. When I finally look up, I watch her face fall and shoulders deflate.

"How bad?" she whispers carefully.

Instead of answering verbally, I shrug off my backpack and reach inside it to pull out my test. I hand it to her, restlessly shifting on my feet.

Slowly, hesitantly, she grabs my test from my hands, her eyes immediately landing on my score. I watch as a handful of emotions scroll over her face. Her brows pinch together in confusion for a few moments before smoothing over, and she blinks a few times.

Confused, she frantically flips through the pages, eyes scanning my answers. She eventually makes her way back to the first page, her eyes trained on the red ink once more.

Her eyes snap up to mine, widening in shock and surprise. "Bronx."

I can't help but grin, gently grabbing my test back from her. My smile widens as I stare at the 82% and the B- written at the top of my paper in red ink.

"You did it," she breathes in disbelief, a slow smile making its way onto her face.

I nod, my grin almost splitting my face. "I did it."

"You did it!" she exclaims excitedly, throwing her arms around my shoulders, hugging me.

I immediately wrap my arms around her waist, picking her up a few inches off the ground and spinning her around a couple of times in the middle of the hallway. She lets out a melodic laugh, taking a step back to look at me when I set her back down.

"You scared the heck out of me!" she cries, shoving my shoulder.

I can't help but chuckle, placing my hands on her shoulders and running them down her arms until I capture her hands in mine. "You can say *shit*, Finch," I tease. "And come on, did you really think I'd fail with you as my tutor?"

She shyly tears her gaze away from mine, humbly shrugging a shoulder.

"I passed all because of you, Olivia," I say, dipping my head to meet her eyes. "Thank you."

She blushes. "You're welcome."

"How about we have an official celebratory lunch?" I ask, smiling.

Her face falls, and a slight pout forms on her lips. "I would love to, but I actually have a lunch meeting with Professor Cooper."

I feel my shoulders deflate. "Do you really, or are you just trying to get out of lunch with me?" I joke, chuckling lightly, praying she really does have a meeting, instead of trying to use that excuse to ditch me like she did with Rat Boy.

"I promise you I *do* actually have a meeting with Professor Cooper," she says, laughing lightly, actually seeming disappointed. "How about dinner instead?" she asks hopefully.

I sigh, using my thumbs to rub circles into her palms. "Can't. I have practice," I say sadly.

She frowns, looking just as disappointed.

"Rain check?" I ask hopefully.

Her lips twitch upward. "Sure."

"All right." I sigh dramatically, causing her to laugh, then reluctantly let go of her hands. "Have fun at your lunch meeting."

"Loads," she says sarcastically, giving me an apologetic smile. "I'll see you in English."

She gives me a small wave goodbye before walking away, heading toward Professor Cooper's office.

"Finch, wait!" I call, reaching into my backpack.

She spins around, looking at me expectantly.

"For Saturday," I inform her, throwing a maroon article of fabric at her.

She fumbles to catch it, caught off guard, the fabric nearly slipping from her fingers and falling to the floor. I watch as she unfolds it and holds it out in front of her at arm's length to inspect, my last name and number staring back at her.

"You're going to look really good in it," I tell her, grinning.

She laughs, and shakes her head in disbelief before draping my jersey over her arm and heading back down the hallway, smiling at me over her shoulder.

FIFTEEN

Homecoming

The sound of lockers slamming echoes off the walls as Coach calls us in for a group huddle. Everyone gathers around to form a circle, all eyes on him.

"Boys, I don't have to remind you how important this game is," he says, his eyes, almost hidden by the brim of his cap, sweeping over every single one of our faces. "We've been busting our asses for weeks to prepare for this. Now let's go out there and win this thing!"

Cheers erupt throughout the room, everyone getting pumped up and putting their game faces on. Shortly after we all file out of the locker room and into the tunnel that leads to the field.

Coach stops me just at the door, gripping my shoulder.

"Kick ass, Miller," he tells me quietly, his eyes stern and proud.

"You got it, Coach."

He slaps me on the shoulder and follows me out to the tunnel, where I find my teammates jumping up and down or restlessly moving around on their feet, getting hyped up for the homecoming game, which just so happens to be against our biggest rivals.

I scan the group for Chase, finding him toward the front of the pack. His arm healed just in time for the big game but Coach is still going to ease him back into it, not giving him much field time. I know Chase is bummed about it, but it's a miracle he's getting to play at all.

I lock eyes with him. He stares back at me with intensity and gives me a nod, determination written on his face.

I make my way to him, smacking hands and bumping helmets before heading to the front of the line, adrenaline coursing through my veins.

I crack my knuckles, stretching a bit while I anxiously wait for the announcer to call us. As soon as he does, the crowd erupts and we run onto the field, busting through a banner to hype up the crowd.

We gather on the sidelines, and my eyes immediately scan the crowd for a particular brunet. I find her almost instantly, ten rows back on our team's side of the field, in the center of the packed stadium. Although I was afraid I'd lose her in the sea of maroon, I know I'd eventually find her in any crowd. Her text telling me where her seats were beforehand just helped.

Our eyes lock, causing me to smile instantly. But my smile quickly fades almost as fast as it came when I realize she's sandwiched between Delilah and Rat Boy.

My mood instantly plummets. Why in the hell is he here?

My hands curl into involuntary fists at my sides, my skin heating with anger despite the crisp October air. He looks bored, like he'd rather be anywhere else, and damn I wish he was. He probably only came here to keep tabs on Olivia, the obsessive little rat.

To make matters worse, when my eyes flick back to Olivia I find her not in my jersey. Instead, she's wearing a maroon Garner University pullover.

I instantly frown, crossing my arms over my chest, irritated.

Sensing my bad mood, she pinches her brows together in confusion, and she does that adorable little head tilt.

"Where's my jersey?" I yell, even though it's impossible for her to hear me over the crowd.

"What?" I see her yell, her brows pinching even closer together and eyes squinting, trying to decipher what I'm saying.

I take off my helmet.

"Jersey!" I yell, gripping the collar of the jersey I'm wearing between my thumb and forefinger, tugging at it to signal to her.

Her eyes clear in realization, and she straightens. Reaching down, she grabs the hem of her pullover and tugs it up to flash me my jersey, which she's wearing underneath.

I bite the inside of my cheek, trying my best not to smile at seeing her wear it. But I wanted to really see her wear it, loud and proud. Not under some damn pullover.

I shake my head, crossing my arms back over my chest, my stance firm. "Uh-uh."

Her lips form into a cute, confused pout, and damn does it make it hard for me to be mad at her.

"Over the pullover!" I instruct.

Her pout becomes more prominent. "Then I have to change," I'm almost positive I see her mutter. She also adds something about it being cold out.

I shake my head, not letting up. A bet is a bet, and I'll be damned if she doesn't hold up her end.

"Over. The. Pullover." I point sternly to the restrooms where she can go change.

I watch as she heaves out an exasperated sigh, arching a dark brow as if to ask *Really?*

I don't back down, staring at her intently. She's crazy if she thinks I'm going to let this slide.

After a few moments she realizes I'm not going to give up, and our little showdown ends. Shoulders sagging in surrender, she taps Delilah on the shoulder, asking to get by. She shimmies her way down the row past people to the stairs.

When she reaches the bottom of the stairs she flashes me an exasperated, but fond, good-natured look, childishly sticking her tongue out at me.

Two can play at this game.

Smirking, I pucker my lips and blow a kiss at her.

She falters a bit, her eyes widening and cheeks burning an undeniable shade of red, making me laugh. Adorably flustered, she hightails it to the restrooms, her long ponytail swishing back and forth behind her as she practically sprints.

Amused, I turn my attention back to the field, watching all the pregame activities go down. I turn back around just in time to just catch Olivia coming back from the restrooms, my jersey on full display over the pullover.

My heart seems to do a backflip in my chest.

They say one of the hottest things ever is when a girl wears your clothes, especially your jersey, and with her . . . *fuck*.

The maroon fabric hits her midthigh, loose and flowy on her tall, willowy frame. Damn, what I would give to see her in it and nothing else. I can only imagine how long and lean her legs would look peeking out, maybe her hair a bit tousled around her shoulders as she sits on my bed. . . . But for now I'll have to settle for her wearing it with dark jeans and a pullover underneath.

Halfway to the bleachers, she lifts her eyes to capture mine. She gives me that slow, shy smile, and it takes everything in me not to run to her. To grab her face in my hands and kiss the absolute hell out of her. But I know I can't do that. Not here. Not now. That would be too aggressive. I'd want to take my time with her, savor every precious moment.

One day, I think.

All hot and bothered, I turn my focus back to the field, trying not to let my eyes drift over to her too much.

After the coin toss and accurately calling heads, I jog back over to the sidelines, stealing a quick glance at Olivia to find her back on the bleachers between Delilah and Rat Boy, eyes glued on me.

I throw her a grin, and shortly after I see someone approaching me from my peripheral vision.

"Hey, Bronx."

I turn my head just as Adrianna's fingertips graze my bicep, running down my arm to squeeze my forearm. Those piercing green eyes sparkle with mischief and a hint of trouble.

"Have a good game," she says, purposely making her voice low and raspy to sound seductive. She stands on her tiptoes, planting her lips on my neck as high as she can manage with my helmet on. Her lips lightly suck at the skin, her tongue poking out to softly lick.

I quickly recoil, taking a step back.

She lets out a soft chuckle, a naughty smirk on her plump, glossy lips. "I'll catch up with you later to celebrate," she promises before sashaying away, back to the dance team.

Cursing under my breath, I bring my hand up to where she kissed me and try to wipe away the lingering burn of her lips. And it isn't the good type of burn. Not anymore.

I quickly glance over my shoulder to look at Olivia. Her eyes are cast down, her shoulders slumped while Rat Boy's beady little eyes seem to glitter in delight. I lock eyes with Delilah, and she looks disappointed, frowning at me. I give her a helpless look, not knowing what else to do. It wasn't my fault, and I certainly didn't reciprocate Adrianna's actions.

Beyond frustrated, I'm relieved when the whistle blows and I have to get my ass out onto the field, where I can blow off steam.

Game on, I think.

The game goes as expected. We have to put in the maximum amount of effort to stay ahead of the other team, giving the crowd quite a show to hopefully pull out a win.

With less than twenty seconds on the clock, the score tied, I'm hiked the ball. I catch it with ease and my eyes immediately dart to my teammates, calculating. Everyone is blocked, but there is a small break straight to the end zone. With no choice, I rush the ball, and the crowd goes absolutely nuts.

Approximately ten yards away from the end zone, one of the opposing players breaks free, blocking my path. I try to dodge him but he lunges, his shoulder ramming into my side and throwing me off balance. But somehow I'm able to maintain my footing; that is until another player dives, catching me by the ankle. I stumble forward, stretching as far as I can, and manage to land the ball over the line for a touchdown, solidifying our win.

Everyone erupts into cheers, and suddenly, like magic, before I'm even fully back up on my feet, a cooler full of Gatorade is dumped over my head, soaking me. Everyone seems to attack me all at once with back slaps and chest bumps, and sometime during the mix, my teammates lift me onto their shoulders, chanting. I take the opportunity to scan the crowd, finding the one person I'm looking for. I point to her, grinning uncontrollably.

Olivia smiles, looking excited and proud, clapping. Delilah stands beside her, cheering us on, while Rat Boy looks like he wants to drag the both of them out of here as fast as he can.

Too bad.

"Wait for me!" I call to Olivia as the team heads to the locker room with me still on their shoulders, leaving me no choice but to go with them.

After a record-speed shower and some more congratulations from the team, as well as Coach, I'm finally able to sneak out of the locker room and back out to the field where people are still hanging out, celebrating.

I spot Olivia and her friends near the stands. I saunter over to them, and Rat Boy's beady little eyes home in on me, turning to slits. Her back is to me, and I walk up behind her, casually slinging my arm over her shoulders.

"Hey, Finch."

She tips her head back, looking up at me through her lashes, smiling. "Hey, congratulations!"

"Thank you." I smile down at her.

"Great play," Delilah comments, the bright field lights reflecting in the lenses of her glasses and her dark curly hair blowing in the breeze. "Way to show those preppy assholes they'll never beat us, no matter how hard they try."

I chuckle. "Thanks, Dee."

A sharp gust of cold October air rushes through, sending a zip down my spine as it whips through my still-damp hair. The cold air bites into my skin, especially the tips of my ears, and I tug at the back of my hoodie, pulling the hood up and over my head.

I feel Olivia shiver, and she wraps her arms around herself, trying to ward off the cold. I pull her closer to me, trying to huddle and share body heat, and earning a glare from Rat Boy.

Delilah rubs her hands together for warmth. "Let's go over by the fire, shall we?" she asks, already heading for the large bonfire set up at the far end of the parking lot.

"Or we could just go home," Rat Boy mutters not so quietly under his breath.

We all walk out of the stadium and over to the fire, my arm still hooked around Olivia's shoulders. There's a crowd around the fire, everyone trying to seek warmth in either the flames or the red Solo cups of liquor being passed around.

"Shots?" Some random frat boy approaches us, offering up the red Solo cups in his hands.

"You still driving?" Delilah asks, looking over her shoulder at Olivia.

"Yeah," Olivia replies. "Go ahead, Dee, I'll drive you home."

"You're the best," she says, grinning. "Don't mind if I do." Delilah accepts the cup, downing the liquid inside. She reaches for the other cup in the guy's hand and offers it to Rat Boy. "Here, Quinton, you could stand to loosen up."

I choke back a laugh.

"I'm fine," Rat Boy spits, indicating he's anything but fine, his jaw tight and ticking in frustration.

"Sure," Delilah drawls dryly. Not letting the shot go to waste, she downs that one as well.

"You guys want anything?" the frat boy asks, looking at Olivia and me expectantly.

"No, thank you," Olivia replies.

He gives her an understanding nod. "Miller?"

"Nah, man. I'm good," I say, not wanting to drink around Olivia when she's going to be sober.

"You sure? You were the MVP out there tonight, you deserve it," he presses.

"No, thanks, man," I insist.

"All right," he says, lingering for a few more moments, thinking I'll change my mind, before heading to the next group.

Another harsh gust of wind comes through, causing the flames of the fire to whip around and a shiver to run down Olivia's spine.

"Cold?" I ask, running my hand up and down her arm, trying to provide her warmth.

The light of the fire dances across her face, and I can see the tip of her nose is starting to turn red from the cold.

"I'm okay," she lies, just as another shiver racks her thin frame.

"Come on, Finch, I have an extra hoodie in the truck," I say, grabbing her hand and lacing our fingers together, then pulling her toward the other end of the parking lot.

"Where are you going?" I hear Rat Boy ask.

"We'll be back," I say, not even bothering to look over my shoulder at him.

Halfway across the parking lot I find Chase talking to a redhead from the cheerleading squad, both of them looking a bit intoxicated and very flirty.

"Hey, man, can I have the keys?" I ask, interrupting their flirt fest.

"Sure thing," he says, struggling to dig them out of his pocket, then throwing them at me. I have to dive to the left a bit to catch them.

"Hey, Olivia, right?" he asks, pointing at her, remembering her from that one time I brought her to our room. His eyes home in on our intertwined fingers, and a wicked grin splits his face. "So are you going to be coming back to the dorm late tonight?" he asks me suggestively, basically asking if I'm going to have sex with her, knowing I never bring girls back to our place to hook up.

I mentally groan, wanting to punch him in his face. "No," I almost growl in response.

"So, what time do you think you'll be back to the room?" he asks quizzically, and I already know he's planning on taking Red back to our room.

"I don't know, I'll text you," I say, avoiding adding *to see if the coast is clear*.

He gives me a lazy, drunken smile. "You're the best."

"Whatever," I mumble under my breath, walking away and leading Olivia to the truck.

I let go of her hand to unhinge the tailgate, then hop into the bed of the truck and walk over to the large toolbox attached to the back, using the key to open it. Among all the stuff Chase keeps in there I find the old hoodie I stashed away in case of an emergency. I pull it out and lock the toolbox back up, turning around to see Olivia sitting on the edge of the tailgate, her legs swinging about a foot from the ground.

"Here, Finch," I say, jumping onto the concrete to stand in front of her.

I hand her the hoodie, then help her put it on. When she has it pulled over her head and down her torso, I reach back and pull her ponytail out, draping her long caramel-colored hair over her right shoulder.

"Thank you." She blushes, shying her gaze away from mine.

I place my hands on her thighs, spreading them apart so I can slot my body between them. It was meant to be a fairly innocent move, until I hear the little hitch in her breath.

"Thank you for coming tonight," I say sincerely, trying to find her eyes. "Look at me, Finch," I demand softly, running my hands up and down her thighs soothingly. I look down, loving how large my hands look on her body. The hem of my jersey peeks out from beneath the hoodie a few inches, putting a smile on my face. I lean forward, my lips close to her ear. "I told you you'd look great in my jersey."

Her body tenses, and I shift my gaze to see the pulse in her neck jump.

I run my hands a little higher on her thighs, the hem of my jersey starting to drape over my thumbs. Startled, she grabs my wrist with one of her small, cold hands while the other lands on my shoulder, not to push me away, but more to brace herself, her spine straightening. Her legs gently squeeze a fraction around my hips.

"Finch?" My voice comes out low and gravelly as I pull away to look at her face to find her still shyly casting her eyes down. I raise my hand, hooking a finger under her chin to lift her eyes to mine.

When those warm honey–colored eyes lock on mine, my heart does this long, slow jump in my chest. Her gaze is so soft yet intense, and for a moment I swear it drops to my lips, a look of yearning flashing across her face.

Just as my hand slides up, my palm coming to rest on the side of her neck as my thumb strokes her jaw, her hand on my shoulder slides down to my chest. Her long, thin, delicate fingers toy with one of the strings from my hoodie, and her eyes bounce from her fingers, lingering on my lips before sliding up to my eyes.

Instinctively, I lick my bottom lip to moisten it, leaning in to test the waters. When she doesn't pull away, I lean in closer, until our breath mingles, my heart pounding in my chest.

"Olivia!"

She jumps, and a frustrated growl crawls up the back of my throat. I shoot my gaze over my shoulder to see Rat Boy stomping toward us, Delilah running after him, stumbling over her feet to catch up. His tiny hands are bunched into fists, to the point where I'm sure his knuckles are turned white, and I can practically see steam coming from his ears.

"Let's go," he demands, like an overbearing father.

"Don't talk to her like that," I snap, removing myself from Olivia and walking toward him.

He puffs out his chest, trying to seem intimidating, but his eyes give him away. I can see deep down he's scared shitless, and he knows he would never be able to get a swing on me.

Delilah stops in her tracks, knowing there's nothing more she can do. She knows he's fucked. All she can do now is watch helplessly.

When there's less than ten feet between us, I feel a pair of hands grab my forearm, stopping me from going any further.

"Bronx." Olivia's voice is soft and strained. She moves in front of me, placing her hands on my chest to prevent me from bashing his face in. She looks up at me helplessly, practically begging me with her eyes not to.

"Dee, take Quinton to the car, I'll be there in a second," she says, never taking her eyes off mine.

"Oliv—" Rat Boy tries to cut in.

"I'll meet you at the car," Olivia says, her voice small but stern.

I quickly tear my gaze away from hers to look over her shoulder. Rat Boy is staring at me with a look that could kill, and his jaw is clenched so tight I wouldn't be surprised if he cracked some teeth.

Delilah reaches for his arm, and he rips it out of her grasp like a spoiled child, spinning on his heel and marching to the other end of the parking lot to throw a fit. Her eyes meet mine and she gives me a tired, apologetic look before going after him.

Olivia hesitantly grabs my chin, her touch gentle but firm, urging me to look at her. She searches my eyes, seemingly looking for something in them, in me.

Letting out a long sigh, she briefly closes her eyes, looking worn out and miserable, causing me to temporarily leash my anger. When she opens her eyes, it looks like she's trying to hold back frustrated tears.

"I should go," she whispers sadly, taking a step back, and I instinctively reach for her. "I'll see you Monday."

"Finch," I call for her, desperation in my tone.

She shakes her head, giving me a sad, strained smile. Her hands reach down, grabbing the hem of my hoodie.

"Keep it," I insist, before she can take it off to give it back to me. Her movements halt and she hesitates, looking conflicted. "Keep it, Finch," I urge her.

She nods, her eyes casting to the ground. "I'm sorry," she says, her voice barely above a whisper. "This is supposed to be your night, and I completely messed it up. You should be celebrating, partying."

I close my eyes, exhaling through my nose. "You didn't mess up anything." I take a step toward her, planting my hand on her waist. "But just promise me for the next bet he won't tag along," I tease, trying to lighten the mood.

She lets out a soft laugh. "Who says there'll be another bet?" She looks at me skeptically, smirking a bit. When I don't respond, her expression sobers, and she lets out a disheartened sigh. "I'll try my best," she promises. "He wasn't supposed to come tonight but—" She shrugs miserably. "Somehow he figured it out and tagged along."

Of course he did; he probably stalks her every move.

Somewhere off in the distance, a car horn blares, and I nearly lose it.

"It's not him," Olivia insists, reading my mind. She pulls her car keys from her back pocket, some humor shining in her eyes. "I have the keys."

I let out a relieved breath, allowing myself to laugh a little.

"I should get going, though," she says reluctantly, chewing at her bottom lip. "You really did do amazing tonight. Now go have fun, Bronx. You deserve it."

I shake my head, trying my best to hide my smile. Stepping forward, I extend my arms, and she willingly walks into them. I hug her tightly, and before I pull away I plant a kiss on her cheek, watching it turn red seconds after.

Olivia tucks some loose tendrils of hair behind her ear, blushing madly as she backs away. Walking away toward her car, she flashes me one last longing look over her shoulder. "Bye, Bronx."

"Bye, Finch," I say, disappointment filling my chest as I watch her go.

Scan the QR code to discover what Olivia is feeling right now.

SIXTEEN

Up the Ante

Monday morning, my alarm clock goes off and I hit the snooze button at least seven times, missing my first class.

After the homecoming game, and after Olivia was rudely whisked away thanks to Rat Boy's temper tantrum, I may have celebrated our win just a little bit. Or a lot. All weekend long. And I may or may not have a mild hangover currently.

I'm almost tempted to skip my second class, but I think better of it. It's already halfway through the semester and I'm not sure how many classes I can afford to skip anymore with finals slowly approaching.

Half awake, I drag my ass out of bed and shuffle to the showers. After a quick shower, I get dressed and sling my backpack over my shoulder, heading to the nearest coffee shop on campus, in dire need of a caffeine fix to get myself going.

I walk into the sleek, modern space filled with students, the strong scent of coffee wafting in the air, tingling my senses. Standing in line, I look around and notice Delilah sitting near the windows, chatting with someone. As if sensing my gaze, she turns her head, and we lock eyes. She gives me a smile and a wave, and I reciprocate the gesture just before I'm up next to place my order.

After ordering my coffee, I stand off to the side and wait for the barista to call my name. It only takes a few minutes for them to make my drink and I'm out the door, walking toward my class.

"Miller!"

I look over my shoulder to see Delilah jogging to catch up with me, her dark curls bouncing with each step. I stop and wait for her.

"What's up, Dee?" I ask, taking a sip of my coffee.

She takes a moment to catch her breath, adjusting her glasses and the emerald-colored cardigan she's wearing with a white top and dark plaid pants. "I just wanted to apologize for the other night."

I furrow my brow, not quite understanding what she has to be sorry for.

"Quinton," she says. "I realize I'm the one who accidentally spilled the beans that Olivia and I were going to the homecoming game," she clarifies.

"Originally, I was texting my cousin, and I guess I wasn't paying too much attention. A text came through asking me what I was doing that night, and me thinking I was still texting my cousin, texted back that I was going to the homecoming game. I didn't think anything of it, but then the next thing I know it's an interrogation about who I was going with, what time, etcetera. Before I realized it wasn't my cousin I was texting with anymore, it was too late." She cringes, looking guilty.

Ahh, that explains it.

"From there, Quinton called me, and I couldn't really lie at that point. He came over just as Olivia was picking me up and he tagged along. I'm sorry," she apologizes sincerely.

I shake my head, dismissively waving my hand with the coffee in it, the ice clanking against the side of the cup. "It's all right, Dee. I'm sure he would have found some other way to crash anyway," I admit bitterly.

Her lips purse ruefully, and she nods. "Still. And I'm sorry I couldn't hold him back when you guys went to the truck. You two looked pretty preoccupied when he stormed over," she says, her lips twitching into a knowing grin.

I huff out a laugh, shoving a hand into the front pocket of my jeans. "Yeah, the guy has got great timing."

She lets out a laugh, expression sobering after. "You were going to kiss her, huh?"

I take a sip of my coffee, trying to hide any emotions on my face. "Maybe," I muse.

She grins, eyes twinkling. "I knew it."

"Did she say anything about it?" I ask, figuring I may have a chance of getting some dirt on Olivia from her.

She tries to smother her grin, failing. "She's my best friend, you know I can't rat her out," she says, and I can't help but frown.

"But." Delilah looks over both of her shoulders, making sure no one is lingering, eavesdropping on our conversation. "Let's just say she was pretty bummed to have to go home early," she says, keeping her voice down.

She flashes me a smile, purposefully bumping her shoulder with mine as she brushes past me, walking away. I spin on my heel and follow her, matching her strides.

"Really?" I ask, a huge grin forming on my lips. I was hoping there was a possibility she wanted to kiss me back. If not, that would have been awkward as fuck and I would have felt awful.

"Mh-mm," she hums, taking a sip of her iced caramel macchiato. "That was a smart move, you know? The bet. Although next time I'd really up the ante." She grins mischievously. "The jersey was cute, but you can do better."

I match her grin. "Oh, I plan to."

>> <<

After English, I follow Olivia to the library to study. We walk across campus, the air chillier now that fall has arrived. The trees have just started changing colors, and leaves are falling and swirling around in the breeze.

With the temperature change, Olivia has exchanged her staple T-shirts for sweaters, looking adorable and cozy. She's wearing a cream-colored one today paired with black jeans and tall brown boots, and her long caramel-colored hair is tied back in a braid.

"You know," I say as we walk up the library steps, "you could have worn my hoodie today."

"Shoot, I forgot to bring it in to give it back to you," she says worriedly.

"Don't worry about it," I assure her. "I don't want it back. The jersey, though, as much as I'd love for you to keep it, I don't think Coach would be too happy to have a jersey missing."

"I'll get it back to you," she promises.

We walk into the library and grab our usual table tucked away in the back corner. She pulls out all of her study materials, getting everything set up.

Flipping through pages of the textbook, Olivia sketches out a quick outline of topics to go over, referring back to our notes. I watch as she scribbles and highlights, my mind running a little wild whenever she pauses to think, pressing the end of her pen to her bottom lip.

Those lips. They look so soft, so inviting.

My mind wanders back to the other night, how it felt to be standing between her thighs, my hands running up and down them. How it felt to have her hands on my body. And when her breath mingled with mine at one point . . .

Damn. I want those lips on mine. To sink my teeth into her bottom lip and suck, letting my tongue—

"Bronx?" Olivia's voice pulls me out of my thoughts. I look up to see her looking at me expectantly.

I clear my throat, adjusting in my seat and sitting up straighter. "Yep?"

She looks at me tentatively. "Ready to get started?"

Kissing? Yes.

But then I glance down at all the books in front of her.

Studying. Right. Not really, but I nod anyway.

I try my best to focus on what she's saying, I really do, but it's so hard to concentrate with all the wildly inappropriate thoughts running through my head.

Finally, I lean forward, placing my elbows on the table. "Finch," I say, cutting her off and nudging her foot with mine under the table.

She looks up from her textbook at me. "Yeah?"

I bite my lower lip, trying to suppress a grin. "We never discussed the wager for the next test."

She blinks, looking perplexed. "You want to make another bet?"

I lean back in my chair, folding my arms over my chest and giving a casual one-shoulder shrug.

She gives me a pointed look. "Depends. What are you thinking?"

"Hmm," I hum, thinking of a way to make this interesting. I've been thinking about it pretty much nonstop since Delilah and I talked this morning, and I think I've come up with the perfect plan. "If I pass the next test, you have to go to The Library with me."

Her face screws into a cute, confused expression. "But we're already in the library . . ." She trails off, acting like this is some sort of riddle or trick.

I can't help but chuckle. "Not this library, Finch. *The* Library."

It takes her a moment but eventually it clicks, and her eyes grow wide in realization. She shakes her head. "No, Bronx, I can't. I've never been to *that* library," she sputters adorably.

"There's a first time for everything." I grin.

The Library is the local nightclub that's popular among the college crowd, and I'm not surprised she's never been there. Which is exactly why I want to be the first one to take her.

She shakes her head again. "That library's not really my scene," she admits, her nose crinkling adorably.

"And you think *this* library is my scene?" I tease playfully. "Come on, Finch, it'll be fun," I try to coax her.

She gives me a tentative look, anxiously nibbling at the corner of her bottom lip.

Damn, those lips . . .

"You'd have to get a nearly perfect score for that to happen," she says.

"Fin—" I begin, planning to persuade her, but she holds up her hand, silencing me.

"A ninety percent or above."

"B plus," I counter, knowing there's no way in hell I'll be able to pull off an A.

She shakes her head. Now she's the one leaning back in her chair, arms folded over her chest, looking uncompromising. "I'll accept nothing less than an A."

I mull it over, trying to think of some sort of compromise, but she doesn't look like she's going to budge.

I lean over the table. "You know, you're pretty sexy when you take charge."

Flustered by my boldness, Olivia lets her authoritative mask slip for a moment. But she composes herself by sitting up straighter, her folded arms tightening across her chest. "Those are my terms," she says with finality, only the tiniest nervous wobble in her voice.

I grin, leaning back and getting more comfortable in my chair. "You drive a very hard bargain, Finch. You must really not want to go with me."

I watch her features soften a fraction, a look of guilt flashing across her face. "It's not that," she mutters so low I almost don't hear her.

Damn, now I kind of feel like a jackass for making her feel bad. I only meant it as a joke.

Before I can ask her what it is like, my phone rings in my pocket, and I quickly grab for it, silencing the ringer. I glance at the screen, mentally groaning. This is the third time I've gotten this call in the past week, so I know something must be up. I just don't have the time or the mental capacity to deal with it right now.

Stuffing my phone back into my pocket, I look up at Olivia. "Like I said, Finch, you drive a hard bargain, but I'll have you know I thrive under pressure. And with the stakes this high"—I let out a low whistle—"I may even get a hundred."

That puts a tiny smile on her face.

"I'm going to have to work my ass off in order to get that grade," I admit. "So I guess I'll have to spend even more time with my tutor," I say, giving her a hopeful, lopsided grin.

She bites back a smile, sitting up straight in her chair and flipping a page of her textbook. "I think she can squeeze you into her schedule."

SEVENTEEN

Explode

My phone at the edge of the table lights up with an incoming call. I quickly glance down at the screen to see a number I've been dodging for some time now. Instinctively, I hit the Decline button and flip my phone over, face down on the table.

I look up and just so happen to catch Rat Boy's beady little gaze on my phone from across the table. Nosey motherfucker.

Snatching my phone, I stuff it into my pocket, flashing Rat Boy a *what the fuck* glare. His gaze quickly snaps back to the dead relative in front of him.

I turn my attention back to Olivia, getting a large whiff of formaldehyde from the actual lab rat sitting between us as I do so. The little rodent is cut wide open, its internal organs on full display. With gloved hands Olivia pokes and prods around inside the little guy, glancing back at our lab manual for reference every now and then as she rambles off the different parts we're going to be quizzed on next week.

"I think this is the adrenal gland," she mutters uncertainly under her breath. Squinting and angling her head to get a better look, she points with her pinkie at some bland-colored tissue inside the rat.

I scoot closer, tilting my head to hover over the rat, my cheek inches away from hers.

"Hmm, I don't know," I say, my gaze swinging back and forth from the live—not so live—rodent in front of us and the one in our lab manual for reference. "I think this might be it." I point just above where she's pointing.

Her lips twist to the side in contemplation. "No, I really think this is it," she says, still pointing to the same spot with her pinkie.

Hell if I know. Everything is so tiny and pretty much the same bland color, it's hard to tell what's what. But I'm fairly certain I'm right, though.

"I don't know, I think I'm right. Maybe your genius has finally rubbed off on me and now you need me as your tutor," I tease.

Olivia grins. "You wish," she says, and we fall into a playful banter of who's right.

"Olivia's right," Rat Boy cuts in from across the table matter-of-factly.

How the hell does he know that? There's no way he can see what she's pointing to from that far away. Hell, I'm sitting right next to her and even I have to squint to see. So either this rodent-faced asshole has superhuman, laser-sharp vision or he's just trying to spite me. And I know it's the latter.

I flash him a glare, clenching my jaw to prevent myself from chewing him out. "Focus on your own rat," I instruct him curtly.

His dark beady eyes narrow, glaring back at me.

"What are you guys looking for?" Delilah asks, peering at us over the rim of her glasses from the other side of the table, where she hovers over her own dead rat.

"The adrenal glands." Olivia sighs, sulking back in her chair, mildly defeated and slightly irritated.

"Let me take a look." Delilah stands up and walks over to our side of the table, wedging herself between the two of us. She leans in over our shoulders, observing. "Hmm, it's hard to tell," she says, pulling away and using her wrist to push up her glasses.

Looking over her shoulder, Dee flags down Tracy, who skips over to our table.

"What's up, friends?" the bubbly TA asks, more than ready to help.

"We're trying to find the adrenal glands," Olivia informs her.

"All right, what were you guys thinking?" she asks, prompting us to show her our ideas, probably wanting to make this some sort of teaching moment instead of just giving us the answer.

"I think one is here," Olivia says, pointing with her gloved pinkie again.

"Bronx?" Tracy prods, and I show her where I think it is.

"Sometimes, those tiny parts are a little hard to identify with these guys. They're definitely not as clear cut and defined as the manual makes them out to be, and these rats get roughed up after being used all week, so they're by no means in prime condition. But, Olivia, I think you're right. Right here"—Tracy points to where Olivia was moments ago—"is a gland. Then the other is over here." Tracy points to the one on the other side. "Like I said, sometimes it's very hard to tell, but you were really close, Bronx," she says encouragingly.

"Told you," Olivia says smugly, playfully sticking her tongue out at me. I know it was a good-natured, poke-fun gesture, but somehow it rubs me the wrong way.

"I told you she was right," Rat Boy states not so pleasantly, really making my blood boil. I muster up a great deal of restraint and hold myself back from leaning over the table and punching him square in the face.

Then my phone buzzes in my pocket. Again. Making me even more irritated.

"You all think you're so smart, don't you?" I explode, feeling like a balloon filled up with too much air. I abruptly stand up from my chair, the legs screeching against the floor.

Everyone in the class snaps their attention to me, the room falling silent.

Olivia jerks her head back, stunned. A flash of hurt and confusion flickers in her eyes as she stares up at me from where she's still sitting. "Bronx," she says softly, reaching out to touch my arm, but I jerk away.

"Don't," I instruct firmly.

She draws her hand back, limply placing it in her lap as she looks away, her hair creating a curtain to hide her wounded expression. A pang of hurt shoots through my chest.

"What the hell, asshole?" Rat Boy sneers.

I clench my jaw, peeling off my latex gloves. "I'll show you asshole," I say, taking a few quick strides to round the table. He scurries back, pure fear in his eyes.

"Bronx!" Tracy yells, her voice surprisingly stern and anything but bubbly now. She quickly grabs my bicep to prevent me from going any further. "If you're going to act like this, out of my lab. Now."

"Gladly," I bite out.

In a blur I snatch up my things, flinging my backpack over my shoulder and storming out of the classroom. Shortly after, I find myself barging into my room, throwing my stuff down next to my desk.

"Damn, Tasmanian Devil," Chase comments from his bed. He stops throwing his football up in the air and catching it, hugging it to his chest. "What's got you all riled up?"

"Don't start," I grumble, snapping open my dresser drawer and pulling out a pair of gym shorts and a muscle tank.

His brows pinch together. "What crawled up your ass and died?"

Wordlessly, I change clothes and shove my AirPods into my ears, turning the volume all the way up to max.

"Wow, I love this song!" Chase yells, just to be a dick, and bobs his head to the beat.

I flip him off and grab a water from the fridge.

"Love you too!" he yells just before I slam the door behind me.

I take a few laps around campus, needing to blow off some steam. Once my calves and lungs are burning, I stop at the gym on the south side of campus. Scanning my student ID, I walk past the front desk and go over to the weights. Finding an empty bench press, I load on the weights accordingly and take a seat, reclining back. Gripping the bar, I ease the weight off the rack and do a couple of reps before placing the bar back with a *clank*.

Sitting up, I take a few breaths, then lift the bottom of my tank to wipe my sweaty brow. Reaching down, I find my water bottle and take a few swigs as I scan the gym.

Out of my peripheral vision I catch a flash of neon pink. I turn my head to see Sasha Allen sashaying over to the row of treadmills, her high, bleached-blond ponytail swinging behind her. She's dressed in all hot-pink gym attire: leggings, sports bra, tennis shoes, and even her water bottle is pink.

I watch as she hops onto a treadmill, working her way up to a jog. While her leggings are a bit too loud, I have to admit they look fan-fucking-tastic on her, shaping her ass and legs perfectly.

My mind wanders to Olivia and how great she would look in a pair. Maybe not hot pink—I doubt she'd ever wear that color—but I could picture her in a powder-blue pair, her favorite color. Now that fall has started, Olivia's worn black leggings occasionally. Hers fit a little less scandalously, and usually she has them paired with a long sweater or cardigan so you can hardly see her shape. She doesn't even wear shapely, skintight jeans, but I can tell she has a body under her conservative clothing.

After fantasizing about Olivia in those tight leggings—my mind even taking a detour to her in my jersey for a bit—I find myself back down on the bench. Worked up, I pump out as many reps as I can, still not feeling satisfied or settled.

I let out a growl of frustration, setting the bar back into place with wobbly arms. Irritated, I get up and walk over to the locker rooms, hoping a cold shower will do me some good and get my mind out of the gutter.

Passing the girls' locker room, I run smack-dab into Kenzie Jones. Literally. Her petite body collides with mine, and I nearly bulldoze her over. I must not have seen her due to the height difference—that and the fact that I probably wasn't paying any attention.

"Oh!" Kenzie lets out a startled noise, stumbling a few steps back. She opens her mouth, probably to curse me out, but quickly closes it when she realizes it's me. Her eyes dance with excitement. "Bronx."

"Uh, sorry, Kenz," I reply lamely, trying to skirt around her.

"Long time no chat," she says, placing a hand on my bicep and flashing me a flirtatious smile. She tucks a strand of dark-blond hair that fell out of her bun behind her ear.

You mean long time no fuck, I think.

I've hooked up with Kenzie once or twice at some random frat party over the years. From what I remember, she was a good lay, but we never really talked.

Come to think of it, I haven't had sex in over a month. Probably a record for me, I think. The last time I hooked up with someone was after the first anatomy test when I dragged Adrianna into that classroom and we had a quickie. Since then, nothing. I've been too busy with football and tutoring with Olivia.

Beyond sexually frustrated and needing a fix, I look down at Kenzie, who is already giving me bedroom eyes. Dipping my head, I brush my lips up against the shell of her ear. "Do you really want to chat?" I ask, my voice low and suggestive.

I pull back to see her teeth sinking into her bottom lip. She shakes her head, biting back a smile. "Not really."

I grab her hand and walk over to the large spin classroom. The lights are out, and no one is inside. Reading the schedule posted on the wall, I realize there won't be any classes for another two hours. I push open the door and Kenzie happily follows me in, and I flip the latch of the lock, ensuring our privacy.

I spin around, backing her into a dark corner where no one will be able to see us. Placing her hands on my shoulders, she jumps, wrapping her legs around my waist with ease. I press her up against the wall and she grips the back of my neck, pulling my lips to hers. Our lips crash together in a rough, desperate kiss.

She claws at the back of my tank, pulling it up and over my head, then discarding it somewhere on the floor. Her hands settle on my chest while mine roam her body, a lot of skin already on display since she's only wearing shorts and a sports bra.

Slowly, leisurely, torturously, I grind my still-clothed hips against hers, building friction. A small moan comes from the back of her throat, and I slide a hand up the nape of her neck, tugging at the roots of her blond hair.

I imagine running my hands through long caramel-colored locks, the sweet little sounds Olivia would make if in Kenzie's position.

Holy hell.

Tugging at the roots of Kenzie's hair, I angle her face more to the side, deepening the kiss. Her thighs tighten around my waist in a viselike grip, and all I can seem to think about is when Olivia's thighs were pressed against my hips when I almost kissed her as she sat on the tailgate of the truck after homecoming. How good it felt. Even when it was innocent.

Fucking damn it.

Awareness tears through me like a bullet. All I can think about is Olivia.

Suddenly, everything feels wrong. So, so wrong.

Breathless, I break away from the kiss and hastily drop Kenzie to the floor, where she safely lands on her feet. She looks up at me, giving me a *what the fuck* look for stopping so abruptly.

"I can't, Kenz. I—" I fumble around, looking for my shirt. "I gotta go."

Guilt forms in the pit of my stomach. Finding my shirt, I pull it on and walk out of the gym, heart pounding.

EIGHTEEN

Girl Troubles

The next day, guilt is still settled deep in the pit of my stomach, eating away at me like acid after my little gym mishap. Ashamed and mortified, I refuse to leave my room in fear of running into Olivia.

I purposefully skip our anatomy lecture to avoid her and those in the class who witnessed my outburst in our lab section. I couldn't care less that anyone else witnessed it, but her . . .

I could tell that I startled her with my behavior. Why wouldn't she be startled when I completely blew up out of nowhere? Then the hurt on her face when I jerked my arm away from her and stormed out like a child kills me inside, thinking back on it now. And the whole gym mishap . . .

God I'm such an idiot.

I know my actions were just hormones and pent-up sexual frustration, but I never should have let it go that far. I was angry and needed a release that the gym couldn't give me, and Kenzie was the first thing that stumbled into my path that I thought would help. It was stupid and impulsive, and three months ago I would have followed through, but then Olivia kept popping into my head and I just couldn't.

Letting out a groan, I roll over on my uncomfortable dorm mattress and stare up at the popcorn ceiling, thinking.

What the hell is wrong with me? It's not out of the ordinary for me to skip class, but to skip class in order to avoid a girl because I'm embarrassed is out of character. Normally I wouldn't bat an eye or give a fuck if I hurt someone's feelings, and I certainly wouldn't go out of my way to avoid a girl—especially one I like.

What the hell are you doing to me, Finch?

>> <<

I force myself to take another gulp of the cheap, lukewarm beer in my cup, hoping the alcohol will help take off some of the edge—since working out, an almost hookup, a cold shower, and my hand clearly didn't do it for me. But all it seems to do is sit uncomfortably in my stomach.

God I'm pathetic.

Still, I nurse my beer, my eyes scanning the crowd before me as I sink deeper into the old, worn couch. I thought it would do me some good to get out and try to clear my head, so I tagged along with Chase and most of the team to another frat party. I feel like I've cut back on my partying a lot lately, and it was time to go out and have some mind-numbing fun with the boys.

Although I seem to be having anything but fun.

"Why so glum, chum?" Brennen asks, plopping down next to me.

I jump slightly, some of the beer sloshing out of my cup and onto my shirt as I was midsip. "It's nothing," I grumble bitterly, aggressively swiping at the liquid on my shirt.

"Doesn't sound like nothing," Brennen taunts.

"Fuck off."

Brennen's thick brows shoot up to his hairline. "All right, someone's testy."

Silence, aside from the party raging around us, falls.

"Is everything all right between you and Liv?" he asks quietly, genuine concern in his voice.

I snap my head in his direction. Man, he really knows how to hit a guy where it hurts, huh?

"Why do you ask?" I retort a little too harshly.

His lips purse into a thin line, hazel eyes sympathetic. "I heard about your little blowup in lab the other day."

Great. My blowup has become *news* and is spreading around campus. Fucking fantastic.

I groan, pinching the bridge of my nose in annoyance.

"Look, man, I know you like her—"

"How do you know I like her?" I cut in quickly, probably too quickly.

He gives me a knowing smile, and I avoid his gaze, pretending to be interested in a hangnail on my thumb. "It's pretty obvious. You making her wear your jersey to the homecoming game, spending a lot of time with her, the way you look at her—"

I sigh in response. No point in denying it.

"Well, it doesn't matter anyway. I fucked up."

"Doesn't mean you can't un–fuck it up," he counters.

I shrug pathetically, sulking.

Brennen places a strong, comforting hand on my shoulder. "You had one minor blowup. Nothing an apology and explanation can't fix."

"Yo, Brennen!" a deep voice booms from the dining room, where the beer pong tables are lined up. Brennen and I look up to see Bodie from the basketball team eagerly waving him over.

"Wanna play?" Brennen asks me, hopeful.

"Nah, man. I'm going to pass."

He gives me a look of understanding and squeezes my shoulder again before getting up and striding over to the tables.

I sink farther into the couch, forcing myself to sip the beer in my cup as I watch. Once my cup is empty, I struggle to get up and walk over to the kitchen for another beer, starting to feel light on my feet from the four I've already had.

As I'm about to slip through the entryway of the kitchen, a slender tan arm shoots across it, a well-manicured hand with black nail polish landing on the door frame to block my path. My gaze travels up the arm and over a bare shoulder to meet a pair of familiar wicked green eyes.

"Hi, Bronx," Adrianna says with a vicious smile.

I sigh. "I'm not in the mood, Ads."

Her hand stays planted on the door frame, preventing me from entering the kitchen. "Your little blowup in lab the other day was pretty Oscar worthy," she comments. "Left those nerds at your table stunned."

My jaw ticks. "Move," I demand, my voice hard. I debate ducking under her arm to slip by, but I don't think our height differences—or the alcohol in my system—will allow me to limbo under her arm gracefully.

Adrianna stays put, a grin spreading across her face. "And you thought you had her fooled."

My blood boils, and before I can have another public blowup—something Adrianna would *love*—I turn on my heel and shove my way through the crowd to get the hell away from her. I head straight for the backyard, needing some fresh air. I'm not going to stand around and play cat and mouse with her all night. I came to this party to try to relax and forget about everything.

Shoving past numerous sweaty bodies, I finally reach the back door and head outside. The night air is chilly, probably colder than I actually think it is, but the alcohol and the anger coursing through my veins seems to keep me comfortable temperaturewise.

I scan the backyard, finding a handful of people occupying the space. Most of them are smoking, actually having the decency to step outside instead of doing it in the house. A few are standing around drinking, talking and laughing obnoxiously. Then there's one couple practically getting it on near the bushes lined along the back fence.

With the temperature dropping, I opt to sit near the fire pit crackling in the center of the yard. Daringly, I take a seat on one of the old, dry rotted lawn chairs, praying it holds my weight. It makes a god-awful noise but manages to stay in one piece.

I recline, the chair making another sound that makes me cringe, and watch the flames dance around in the light breeze that's causing goose bumps to form on my bare arms. I debate trying to find Chase so I can get the keys to the truck to grab my hoodie, but my stomach drops in realization that my hoodie is no longer in his truck. I gave it to Olivia at homecoming.

Has she worn it since that night? I wonder childishly. *Or has she tossed it in a fire and watched it burn with satisfaction after I acted like a complete ass?*

Because I would.

God I could really use another drink.

Before my mind wanders too far down the Olivia rabbit hole, I feel my phone vibrate in my pocket. I pull it out to see a new text message from Adrianna. Stupidly, I open it.

Adrianna: Come find me when you're done with your hissy fit. The attitude doesn't suit you

Now I could really use a drink.

Riled up and fuming, I sit up, leaning forward to place my elbows on my thighs as my thumbs tap away at my phone screen. Instead of replying, I go straight to my contacts, Adrianna's name the third on my list—right after Abbi and Abby. I click on her name, and without thinking twice hit Delete Contact, watching her name disappear from the list, a weird sense of satisfaction and relief running through me.

On some weird high, full of spite and anger, I go down the list, deleting every girl's name from my phone—including Abbi and Abby. When I get to the Fs my heart drops. My thumb hovers over the name *Finch* for a long time, a weird feeling settling deep inside my chest. I swallow thickly before eventually scrolling past her name. Hers is the only female contact I have in my phone by the time I'm done.

I hear the chair next to me groan in protest under someone's weight. Turning my head, I catch Ciara reclining, a cloud of smoke swirling around her as she exhales, a joint lazily dangling from her fingers. "You look like you could use this," she says, extending the joint to me, her voice only half teasing.

I shake my head. "No, thanks."

Ciara shrugs, taking another hit. "What's got you down?"

"Nothing."

"Girl troubles?" she jokes, knowing I don't date.

I stay silent, avoiding her gaze.

"Wait," she says in disbelief. "Holy shit, is it a girl?"

I sigh, scrubbing a hand down my face.

"Who is she?" Ciara presses.

"You don't know her."

"So?"

"She's just some girl from my class."

"And?"

"And I fucked up, okay?" I spit bitterly.

Ciara studies me, her lips pressed into a firm line. "Damn. I always knew you'd settle down eventually, I just thought it would be long after college." She chuckles softly, throwing me a sympathetic smile.

"Yeah, I get it, Bronx is pussy-whipped," I mock self-deprecatingly, thinking she's teasing me.

Ciara frowns. "That's not what I'm saying at all. I'm actually really happy you found someone you genuinely like. I wish I could do that," she says, sinking back into the chair, making it groan.

I look at her quizzically. "But you've had boyfriends and girlfriends."

A hint of a sad smile crosses her face. "Yeah, but they've never been anything serious. That's the difference between you and me. I'm willing to 'date,' put a meaningless label on relationships I know won't go anywhere, but at least you're honest and let them know you're only in it to fuck instead of desperately searching for something that isn't there and stringing them along, like me.

"I know I won't settle down anytime soon, not until I find 'the one' or whatever clichéd bullshit fairy tales make you believe. But, hey. If you really like this girl, go for it. No girl has ever left you like this." She gestures at me up and down. "So she must be worth something. Maybe she's your one."

I swallow thickly, trying not to think about her words too hard.

She sits forward in her seat, taking a long drag from the joint and exhaling a large cloud of smoke. "My advice," she says, standing and looking down at me. "If you really do like this girl, don't let her go."

Ciara flicks her joint to the ground, stubbing it out with the heel of her shoe before walking away, back inside the house.

Her words swirl around in my head until I'm restless enough to stand up, and I find myself crossing the lawn and leaving through the back gate.

I walk down the street, past all the cars lined down the block for the party, until I hit the main road. Campus is about three miles from here, so I can manage the walk back and hopefully use the time to clear my head. However, the farther I walk the more my thoughts land on Olivia, making my chest heavier and heavier.

As if the universe can detect my shitty mood, it begins to rain.

What kind of Steven Spielberg shit is this?

I cross my arms over my chest, the rain coming down heavier and hitting my skin like ice. My feet pick up the pace as I jog across a crosswalk, planning to duck into the next available store to seek shelter, but most of them are closed.

I groan in frustration, and out of the corner of my eye I see some activity on the other side of the street. Hopeful, I whip my head in the direction, ready to bolt across to the only store with some lights on, but I stop dead in my tracks.

Across the street is McCausland's Sporting Goods, and my heart nearly tumbles out of my chest when I spot Olivia through the large glass windows. She's inside, stocking shelves. I know she occasionally helps her dad out at the store, but I definitely wasn't expecting to see her tonight.

Feet rooted to the ground, I stare at her like a total creep, unable to look away. As far as I can tell, Olivia is the only one inside, and in the dim lighting I can make out the sad look on her face. My stomach tightens at the thought that I'm the reason for it.

Her movements are slow, sluggish, as if she's lost in her own thoughts. I continue to watch as she finishes stocking the shelf, then breaks down the empty cardboard box and disappears into the back. She reemerges with a large box in her arms, seemingly struggling with the weight of it as she stops halfway to her destination, balancing on one leg so that her other thigh can push up the box slipping from her arms. It takes everything inside of me not to run over to help her.

Once she reaches a nearly empty clothing rack she drops the box with a huff, resting her hands on her hips for a moment. When she catches her breath, she bends down to open the box and pulls out a maroon-colored T-shirt, my name and number printed on the back.

The beer in my stomach churns uncomfortably as I watch her slowly turn the shirt around to stare at my last name, an emotion crossing her face that I can't quite gauge. She stares at it for several moments before grabbing a hanger and placing it on the rack. One by one she takes out each jersey, places them on hangers, and hooks them on the rack, that sad look on her face seemingly intensified.

As if to punish me, a strong burst of wind barrels down the street, a sheet of rain coming along with it, pelting me like a hundred tiny needles. I break out of my trance and hightail it to campus, forcing my clenched, frozen limbs to push forward.

NINETEEN

Explain

Friday, I sit at my old wooden desk in English, anxiously toying with the stupid little teddy bear holding a heart in its paws that reads I'M SORRY in my hands.

Last night I decided it was time to face the music and actually go to class today to see Olivia. Somewhere in my dysfunctional brain, I thought it would be a good idea to show up bearing gifts along with my apology, which led to a midnight CVS run where I picked up the teddy bear to try to win her over. Thinking about it now, it seems so stupid.

A teddy bear, Bronx, really? How lame can you be? I scold myself. *You seriously think a stupid little bear is going to show her you're sorry?*

Feeling stupid and pathetic, I rise from my chair, ready to throw the cheesy stuffed animal in the trash, when suddenly a laugh floating in from the hallway stops me in my tracks. I look up to see Olivia walking toward the classroom, animatedly talking with another girl. She looks into the room and catches my gaze, her features smoothing over. She stops at the door, saying goodbye to whoever she was talking to, and hesitates for a moment, eyes uncertainly locking with mine.

Teddy bear in hand, I slowly sink back into my seat, heart racing.

Olivia nervously tucks a strand of hair behind her ear, taking a deep breath before cautiously walking over to her seat. It's then I notice that she has the hoodie I let her have after homecoming draped over her forearm, her opposite hand anxiously clinging to some of the fabric, making my heart drop.

She's going to give it back, making me think this is a means to an end.

"Hi," she says softly, uncertainly, stopping at the edge of my desk. "Uh, I thought you might want this back." She offers me the hoodie, refusing to meet my gaze.

Fuck, if this is anything compared to what a breakup feels like, thank god I don't date.

I scramble to my feet. "No, keep it," I insist, my voice sounding more desperate than I intended. "I still want you to keep it."

She cautiously peeks up at me through her lashes, eyes questioning.

"Finch, I . . ." I fumble, trying to find the right words. "I'm sorry," I reply lamely, shoulders sagging, but I mean it. I puff out a breath, running a hand through my dark hair. "I lost my cool the other day, and I didn't mean to take it out on you. I just . . ."

I look around, noticing some of our classmates watching us. "Can we talk after class?" I plead.

Her features soften and she nods. Removing her backpack, she takes a seat before pulling out her class materials and neatly folding up my hoodie, packing it away in her backpack for safe keeping. That action puts me mildly at ease.

I take a seat, watching her, realizing just how much power she has over me. She isn't like any other girl I've come across before. Most girls go out of their way to capture my attention and compete for it, but her? She attracts it without even trying.

"What's that?" she asks, pointing to the bear still in my hands.

Shit.

"It's, uh, nothing," I lie, shaking my head, completely embarrassed.

Ready to shove the thing in my backpack, I stop when I detect the flicker of disappointment in her eyes. Reluctantly, I hand it over to her. "Actually, it's for you."

She takes it, inspecting it with curiosity. Her thumbs graze back and forth over the soft fur as she reads the message stitched onto the plush heart. She gives me an apprehensive smile. "You got me a bear?"

I groan, slumping back in my seat. "Yes. I know, it's lame."

A real smile tugs at her lips. "It's not that lame."

I flash her a look. "It's lame."

"It's cute," she corrects me, just as Professor Hobb walks in and starts class.

>> <<

After class, I'm surprised when Olivia agrees to hop on the back of my motorcycle, and we ride to a nearby park. When I ease into a parking spot, I help her off and take her helmet as she shakes out her hair, raking her fingers through it. My hoodie, which she tried to give back to me, adorns her tall, willowy frame, since I insisted that she needed another layer over her light sweater while on the bike.

Once she's settled, I silently lead her to the pond and we take a few laps around it, trudging along slowly until we sit on one of the benches, a good three feet of distance between us.

We sit in silence for a while, watching the water ripple and the ducks splash around. I steal a glance at Olivia, watching her nervously pull the cuffs of the hoodie over her hands. The tension between us shifted on the way over here. I could tell her guard flew back up after class, especially when she had to be physically close to me, her arms wrapped around my waist on the bike. And I can tell she's uncomfortable in my hoodie since things are still unresolved between us, but she doesn't take it off.

Puffing out a breath, I lean forward and rest my elbows on my thighs, trying to figure out where to start without scaring her off. I know I have to tell her, explain myself, which isn't going to be easy.

I've never told my story to anyone before, and now I'm about to spill my guts to her. I'd rather not tell her and keep that part of myself locked away forever, but I know if I don't tell her it's always going to be a wedge between us. I trust her. But I also wouldn't blame her if she ran for the hills.

With every minute I keep stalling, I feel her retreating more, both physically and emotionally.

"Finch," I breathe helplessly. "I'm sorry. I was a complete ass to you the other day. I didn't mean to be, but I just blew up."

"It's okay," she says softly, refusing to meet my gaze.

"No, it's not," I insist, turning my body toward her. "I just . . . fuck." I rub my eyes with the heels of my hands, stomach knotting. "I don't even know where to start," I admit, looking up at the sky.

"When I was a kid," I begin, swallowing thickly, "I didn't have the best home life. My mom's a drug addict and I don't even know who my dad is. Throughout my life I've bounced back and forth between my mom and foster parents because she couldn't take care of me. And when I was with her, she ran through a bunch of boyfriends who weren't great guys . . ." I trail off, cringing and looking down at the cigarette burns on my arms.

I glance over to see Olivia's worried expression. "Did they hurt you?"

"Some," I admit, unable to look her in the eyes.

"Is that how you got those?" she asks quietly, almost scared to ask.

Instinctively and self-consciously, I cross my scarred arms over my chest. "Yeah. One boyfriend used to stub his cigarettes out on me if I was acting up."

Olivia's eyes widen, horrified. "Bronx." Her voice drips with shock and sympathy, making me disgusted with myself.

"It's nothing," I say dismissively, wanting to skirt around the subject, not accepting her pity. "What I want to explain to you is why I snapped the other day. In school, I was never the smartest kid in the room. I bounced back and forth between so many schools I could never keep up with the curriculum, and it's not like I had help or support at home. Half the time, I never really had a home. My mom wasted all of her money on drugs so she couldn't afford the basic necessities. At times we had to squat in abandoned places for a while."

I steal a quick glance at Olivia, her full attention focused on me, patiently waiting for me to continue.

Suddenly, I feel nervous. No one knows this about me. No one knows about my mom, the abuse, the neglect, all the foster homes. I feel ashamed, because here she is, perfect and innocent in every way, and I feel like I'm tainting her with all my *bullshit*.

"Anyway, my grades suffered and kids—even the teachers—would always make fun of how far behind I was on the learning curve. They would purposefully belittle me and make me feel stupid. Everyone always said I would amount to nothing because I wasn't smart enough, because I was rough around the edges. So when I was wrong the other day in lab, all those memories came flooding back," I admit, ashamed.

"Oh, Bronx." Olivia delicately places her hand on my arm, eyes wide with realization and guilt. "I'm so sorry. I didn't know."

I shake my head. "How could you have?"

She frowns, shoulders slumping. "Still. I never intended to make you feel that way. I thought we were just poking fun at each other."

"We were," I assure her. "But then Quinton jumped in, and my phone starting going off with a call from my mom. It just felt like everything was hitting me at once and a wire tripped in my head, sending me spiraling down Bad Memory Lane." I shake my head. "I lost my cool, and I didn't mean to take it out on you. I know it's not an excuse, but I'm sorry."

She nods in understanding. “Your mom called?”

I blow out a breath. “Yeah, she’s been calling me all week.”

“Why?”

“Dunno,” I admit. “I’ve been dodging her calls, because whenever she does call me it’s never a good thing.”

She presses her lips together, nodding. “Where is your mom?”

I shrug. “Off with another boyfriend.”

Her eyes grow sad, worried. “Is it the one who . . .” She trails off, looking at my arm.

I swallow, nausea swirling around in my stomach. *Oh, Finch, if only you knew.*

Many men have entered and exited my life. My mother was a full-blown cracked-out carousel who only cared if they had drugs and a roof to provide her. Unfortunately for me, she didn’t care about much else, and the guy who stubbed his cigarettes out on me wasn’t the worst one.

The lowest low was when she was with this guy named Benny. He lived in a shithole apartment building, but to my mother that was luxury. Only because it had a roof and he had drugs he was willing to share. For a price.

He used to hit her all the time and would take swings at me, but again, she didn’t care. Benny was absolutely ruthless, and he was the reason I started taking football seriously.

Benny and my mom used to get into it all the time whenever they were on their binges. If I came back from school and they were fighting or fucking, I would sit outside all night on the stairs until I knew they were passed out and the coast was clear. I’d learned my lesson too many times.

Sitting outside all the time, I ran into a lot of the neighbors, who seemed to be just as sleazy as Benny, but there was one girl who wasn’t like the rest of the sketchy tenants. She actually ended up saving my life.

She was an angel in disguise, and I couldn't thank her enough for the kindness she showed me.

Her name was Lexi. She was only a few years older than me at the time and lived with her mom on the floor above Benny. We became friends and she would bring me food whenever she could, because I could tell she felt sorry for me.

Whenever Benny would rough me up pretty bad, she would help clean me up. Her mom was a nurse and always had first-aid stuff in the apartment that Lexi would sneak to me and patch me up with. But one night it got so bad that Lexi had to go get her mom to help.

We'd never gotten Lexi's mom involved before, because as much as I despised my mother, I didn't want to get placed in foster care. Thankfully, Lexi's mom was a single mother and so busy working that she didn't know much about me or my home life. But when Benny really beat me up good that night, there was no covering it up.

Benny got out of control and slammed me up against the wall so hard that I'm surprised he didn't damage the drywall. We scuffled for some time before I managed to get away. I made a break for the front door and ran down the stairs, but Benny caught up to me and pushed me down the flight of concrete steps.

Lexi found me in a small pool of my own blood sometime later, wheezing and struggling to get up. It was so bad that she called her mom, who brought me to the hospital. I'd cracked my head open, needed stitches, and broken a few ribs. At that point, Lexi couldn't cover for me anymore and her mom called child protective services. I wasn't allowed to live with my mother after that, nor did I want to.

I got swept up into the system and never got a chance to go back to see Lexi again.

I shake my head. "Nah, I never met this one. They never last long, only a few months at a time."

Olivia nods. "And you never met your dad?"

I feel my insides clench uneasily, knowing that I've just opened up a whole can of worms for her to prod into. While I may not be happy that she cracked me open and pushed her way inside, there is this weird sense of relief in finally sharing that part of my life with someone. Still doesn't mean it's any less terrifying or easy to share, though.

"Nope. My mom doesn't even know who he is. She was too drunk or high to remember."

She frowns and looks at me curiously. "Does that have anything to do with your tattoo? Unknown?"

She paid attention to my tattoo?

No one has ever really asked me about it or pieced it together. All I usually get are comments along the lines of "Sick tat, bro."

"Maybe. Do you like tattoos?" I ask with a smirk, desperate to lighten the mood and change the subject.

She blinks once, processing my mood change before blushing. She gives a weak one-shoulder shrug, pretending to be indifferent. "They're all right."

I laugh, sobering after. "So are we good?"

I watch her body physically relax and she gives me a closed-lipped smile. "Yeah, we're good."

I blow out a relieved breath. "So the bear worked?" I tease, my lips tugging up into grin.

She laughs, shaking her head. "It helped. But I think to really cover your bases you should throw in some ice cream," she says, eyes twinkling.

"You know I play football, right? See, Finch, you should have taken me up on my offer to teach you about football. There are no bases in football, sweetheart."

She rolls her eyes, playfully swatting me on the arm. "Fine," she says, standing up and crossing her arms over her chest. She begins to walk away. "I guess you're no longer forgiven." She throws me a look over her shoulder, still strutting away from me.

I flash her a sharp grin and stand up, bolting after her. She lets out a squeal, breaking into a full-out run toward the motorcycle. Just as she reaches the bike, I catch her, wrapping my arms around her waist from behind.

"If we go to that old-fashioned ice-cream place down the road am I forgiven?" I compromise, resting my chin on her shoulder, my lips dangerously close to her ear.

Her body tenses a moment before relaxing.

"Only if you get me a double scoop strawberry ice-cream cone."

I let out a dramatic sigh, gripping her hips and spinning her around to face me. "You drive a hard bargain." I reach behind her and grab a helmet, placing it on her head and buckling the strap under her chin. "But since I really am sorry, I'll even throw in some sprinkles and a cherry on top."

She scrunches her nose. "Sprinkles?"

I let out a laugh. "What, you don't like sprinkles?" I ask, amused, helping her onto the back of the bike.

She shakes her head, a mildly disgusted look on her face.

"All right, Finch, no sprinkles."

I smile, getting on the bike and putting on my helmet. Once I'm set, I roar the engine to life, grab Olivia's hands, and secure them around my waist before we take off down the road, feeling happy and content.

TWENTY

Believe in Me

I walk into the anatomy lecture hall, feeling surprisingly confident given the circumstances. Shutting out all the low, anxious murmurs, I walk past students who have their noses shoved in textbooks, cramming in a last-minute study session, and make my way to my seat.

Halfway up the stairs a pair of warm brown eyes catches mine and I smile, jogging just a bit faster to reach my seat. "Hey, Finch."

She flashes me a nervous smile. "Ready?"

"So ready." I smirk confidently. "You better start planning out your outfit for The Library."

She rolls her eyes, pressing her lips together to suppress a smile. "Only if you get an A, remember?"

"I've got this. C'mon, have some faith in me. You are my tutor, after all," I tease.

Her eyes soften, a look in them I can't quite decipher. "I believe in you," she says sincerely.

I smile. "So, what are you going to wear?" I press her, quirking a brow.

She rolls her eyes again, shaking her head in amusement. "You're impossible."

I grin, but it quickly fades when I catch Rat Boy walking in with Delilah, his beady little eyes shooting daggers my way.

"Where were you yesterday?" Rat Boy demands of Olivia as soon as he makes his way to our tier of the lecture hall.

Olivia jerks her head back in surprise. "Uh, I was too busy studying for this."

"Really?" Rat Boy asks in a demeaning tone that makes me grind my teeth. In my opinion, he might as well have just said *bullshit.* "Olivia, you know this stuff like the back of your hand, and you're telling me you blew off the Medical Honor Society meeting to study?"

He looks at her incredulously.

She gives a dismissive shrug. "You guys were only meeting up to get coffee and discuss a few things. It was more of a social event than an actual meeting. You didn't really need me there."

"But you're the president!"

"I told you, let it go, Quinton," Delilah says, sounding tired and annoyed.

He throws her a glare.

Wait, did Olivia skip her meeting to tutor me?

Yesterday afternoon Olivia and I met up in the library, cramming in a last-minute study session to prepare for today's test. Our study session lasted three hours, not including the impromptu dinner date that I may have talked her into halfway through.

Before any more questions can be asked or accusations thrown, our anatomy professor walks in and a hush falls over the classroom. Once the rules and guidelines are explained and established, tests are passed out.

I look over at Olivia and she gives me a reassuring smile. *Good luck*, she mouths, just before copies of the test are passed down our row.

>> <<

I walk out of the lecture hall feeling oddly confident. Just as I suspected, I find Olivia waiting for me, sitting on a bench down the hall. She finished her test about twenty minutes ago but I stayed back, not rushing and triple-checking my answers.

Sensing my presence, she looks up from her phone. She sits up straighter, eyes wide, anxious. "Well, how did it go?" she asks impatiently.

I let out a dramatic sigh and plop down beside her. I practically fall on top of her, purposefully sitting halfway on her lap. Not enough to crush her, though.

"Bronx!" she squeals, playfully pushing me off.

I chuckle, scooting over to fully sit down on the bench but sitting close enough so that our sides are pressed against each other. Casually, I throw my arm over her shoulders, rubbing the soft fabric of her sweater between my fingers. "So I'm thinking you should wear something strapless. Maybe tease your hair a bit and throw it up into a high ponytail," I muse. "It can get pretty hot and sweaty inside the club."

She deadpans, arching a brow, "Someone is awfully confident."

I lazily grin, continuing. "Some tight leather pants would be nice too. They're in, you know."

She gives me a bland look. "I'm a twenty-two-year-old girl going to a club for the first time, not a forty-year-old man who just bought a Harley and is going through a midlife crisis."

I laugh and give her a sharp, impish grin. "So you think you're going?"

"So you think you're my stylist?" she counters, crossing her arms over her chest, avoiding my question.

"Touché, Finch. Touché." I stand, stretching my limbs before extending my hand to her. "But I know I aced that test, so you're going."

She suppresses a smile, accepting my outstretched hand, and I help her up. "You're going to need an A, remember?"

"You believe in me, remember?" I counter, smugly throwing her words back at her.

She bumps her shoulder against mine. "Touché."

She begins walking down the hall, her grip on my hand loosening. I can tell she's going to let go of it, but I don't let her pull away. I keep my grip casual but firm, my stride cool as I walk beside her hand in hand.

I sneak a quick glance at her out of the corner of my eye. Her cheeks have a noticeable blush and she's staring at our joined hands, and I'd be lying if I said I didn't love that I have this sort of effect on her.

"Lunch?" I ask casually, shoving my free hand in my pocket.

She looks up at me, blinking once, processing. "Lunch? Uh, yeah, sure," she says, clearly flustered, but she still doesn't pull away. She shyly holds my hand all the way to the cafeteria.

>> <<

Formaldehyde hangs in the air and the dead rats on the tables are covered with wet paper towels to prevent them from drying out, making this look like a weird episode of *CSI* or some shit.

"Class, I have your tests from yesterday. When I call your name, please come up and I'll hand them to you," Tracy instructs, pulling a large stack of tests out of her colorful tote bag.

Tracy begins reading off names, and I glance at Olivia, who looks nervous.

Chairs scrape against the floor one by one as students go up to collect their tests. Olivia's name is the seventh one to be called, and she stands to go grab her test from Tracy, followed by Rat Boy and Delilah shortly after.

"Pearson," Tracy calls, and Adrianna stands to go grab her test.

As soon as Adrianna's hands grasp the paper, Tracy calls my name.

I stand up, then walk slowly to try to avoid Adrianna. But Adrianna deliberately walks slower, forcing me to walk past her. She purposefully brushes against me, sending me a flirtatious smile. You'd think after I dodged all of her texts she'd finally give up, but no.

I don't react, breezing past her to grab my test, my heartbeat nervously kicking up a notch. I take my test from Tracy, quickly glancing at my grade, and my heart sinks.

No fucking way.

My shock, disbelief, and disappointment quickly bleed into anger. Fuming, I clench my hands, wrinkling the paper a bit. I turn on my heel and trudge back to my seat, avoiding Olivia's stare. I take a seat, shove my test under my lab manual so no one can see it, and try my best to leash my temper.

"Bronx?" Olivia asks softly, hesitantly.

"Not right now, Finch," I state, refusing to look at her, and she immediately backs off. I don't mean to be so rude and abrupt, but I know if I don't have a minute to cool down I'm going to lose it.

For the rest of the lab period Olivia lets me simmer in my sour mood. She lets me be, and as soon as Tracy dismisses class I'm packing up my stuff and leaving in record time.

"Bronx, wait!" I hear Olivia call after me.

Eventually she catches up, rounding me and placing her hand on my chest to stop me. I stop, not wanting to bulldoze her over.

She looks up at me, her warm brown eyes questioning and vulnerable. "Talk to me. What was your score?"

My eyes bore into hers, and for a moment I see a glimmer of hope behind them. I can tell there's a part of her that thinks I'm faking her out—like I did last time.

Silently, without taking my eyes off of hers, I shrug off my backpack and reach inside, then hand her my crinkled-up test. She takes it, hesitantly tearing her gaze away from mine to look at my grade. I watch as a dozen emotions scroll across her face, her expression morphing from shock, to disbelief, to excitement, finally landing on confusion.

"Bronx, you got eighty-nine percent! That's amazing!" she exclaims excitedly, showing me my score, as if I misunderstood.

"Yeah, an eighty-nine," I reiterate bitterly. "Which means I'm one percent—just one fucking percent—off."

Wow, who would have thought six months ago I would be the type to get this upset if I didn't get the grade I wanted. Half the time I didn't even care if I passed or failed. As long as I could keep my grades afloat, high enough to play football, that was all I cared about.

And to miss the mark by 1 percent. One fucking percent. A part of me thinks I would be less mad if I'd absolutely failed.

Her face falls in realization, and she stares back down at my paper, as if the grade will somehow magically change. She quickly flips through my test, scanning my answers. "You still did really well," she says, trying to be encouraging, but I see the disappointment on her face. It kind of surprises me.

"Yeah, but I still came up short," I mutter.

She frowns. "I'm really proud of you, though. This is an amazing score."

I shrug one shoulder, still disappointed and angry at myself.

Olivia lets out a sigh, her eyes drifting down to my paper and back up at me. "Look, what if I make you a deal?"

I look at her skeptically. "What kind of deal?"

"If you can tell me why you got the answers wrong and correct them during our next study session, I'll go to The Library with you," she offers.

"Seriously?" I ask, my mood instantly lifting.

She gives me a timid smile. "Yes."

I break into a full grin. She basically just agreed to go with me even though I didn't quite get the grade she required.

"Admit it, Finch," I drawl teasingly, slinging my arm around her shoulders and steering her down the hallway, "you wanted to go with me all along."

"Hardly," she mutters, but I can tell she's biting back a smile.

"So I'm thinking heels. The sexy, strappy kind."

"You're pushing it," she warns in a singsong voice.

"Miniskirt?" I press teasingly.

She lets out an exasperated groan. "Don't make me regret this."

TWENTY-ONE

Sabotage

I lean against the brick exterior of The Library, watching my breath mingle with the cold November air. Shoving my hands into the pockets of my leather jacket, I observe all the cars coming and going, anxiously waiting for Olivia's car to pull into the parking lot.

I check my watch: 7:54 p.m. I told her to be here around eight.

Six more minutes.

Knowing Olivia, she's probably going to arrive at eight on the dot, not wanting to spend any more time here than she has to or scared that she'll beat me here and have to sit in her car awkwardly waiting for me.

Originally, I wanted to pick her up from her house and drive here together, but she refused. She wanted to drive herself, and as much as I hate it, I have to give her props. She's a smart girl; I should have known she'd come up with a foolproof escape plan in case things go south. Not that I plan on letting them.

At 7:58 p.m. I finally spot her little white Mazda turn into the parking lot and find the closest spot available. I jog up to her car then open the door for her.

"Hey, Finch," I greet her, suddenly riddled with excitement and anticipation.

"Hey." She gives me a timid smile, pulling her keys out of the ignition. I can tell she's nervous.

I extend my hand to her, and she takes it. Once I help her out of the car, I close the door for her and she locks it with the key fob, sliding her keys into the pocket of her white puffy coat.

I let my eyes roam over her, my heartbeat kicking up a notch. Her hair is thrown up in a high ponytail, slightly teased, and what I can see of her outfit under her winter coat is a black pair of jeans with a pair of short heeled boots. She also has on a light application of makeup—mascara and eyeliner, which make her brown eyes pop—something I've never seen her wear before. And even though she looks beautiful in simple, casual clothing, I have to admit this is a nice change of pace. She looks phenomenal.

I can't wait to see what's under the jacket.

I give her hand a reassuring squeeze and lead her to the main entrance. "Ready?"

She looks at me nervously, giving me a stiff nod that says otherwise.

When we get to the front door, the bouncer checks our IDs before letting us in the dimly lit club. Inside the music is thumping, as strobe lights and lasers dance across the walls to the beat of the music.

"This way," I instruct her, yelling over the loud music.

With her hand still in mine, I pull her through the crowd to the back of the club, finding my teammates already occupying a large seating area.

"Miller!" Brennen beams, spotting me first. Then the rest of the team bursts out in greeting.

"Hey, guys. This is Olivia," I introduce her, pulling her to my side.

She gives a shy smile, and they greet her warmly.

JC pops up from his seat, beer in hand. "Hey, Liv," he says with a fond smile.

She genuinely smiles back, probably relieved to see another familiar face. "Hey, how have you been?"

I remember JC mentioning that she was his physics lab partner last year. Trusting that he's not going to make any moves on her, I saunter a few feet over to Chase and some of our other teammates to let the two of them catch up briefly, not wanting to breathe down her neck. But I stay close enough to make her feel secure.

"Holy shit," Chase hisses. "She actually came?"

I shrug, a huge smile on my face.

Chase shakes his head in disbelief. He may or may not have heard some of my nervous rambling about whether she was going to show or not. "I for sure thought she would bail on your ass."

"Nah," I say, more confident now than I was a few hours ago. I knew deep down Olivia would never stand me up, but still, I'd be lying if I said a part of me wasn't worried.

Realizing Olivia and JC's conversation is tapering off, I make my way back over to her. Shrugging off my jacket, I drape it over the back of a nearby chair, motioning for Olivia to do the same.

Slowly, she grabs the zipper of her coat and drags it down. Once it's all the way unzipped, she slips it off her shoulders, revealing a high-neck black halter top of some sort that makes my breathing falter.

I take her in, marveling at her fair, smooth skin in the dim light of the club. She looks so delicate, so feminine, so perfect that all I want to do is drag my lips across her bare shoulder to the small sliver of collarbone showing, up to the long, smooth lines of her neck.

Fuck.

I swear, any girl could come up to me right now with less clothing and I wouldn't be nearly as impressed.

Swallowing thickly, I reach for her coat, deliberately letting my fingers graze hers, and set it on top of mine. I take a step toward her, leaning in to ask if she wants to grab something to drink, my hand reaching around to rest on her back, but I freeze as soon as my hand lands on a smooth, warm span of skin.

All blood flow to my brain seizes momentarily, my hand soaking in the feel of her soft, bare skin. A tingle runs up my arm and down my spine, and I struggle to form a coherent sentence. I clear my throat, my voice still gruff. "Do you want anything to drink?"

"I'll take a water."

I raise a brow. "That's all?"

She gives me a sheepish smile. "I don't drink," she admits.

I nod once. "I respect that. Do you want to stay here or come to the bar with me?"

She looks over my shoulder at all of the football players warily. "I'll come with you."

I suppress a smile, knowing she's still racked with nerves and isn't quite comfortable enough for me to leave her yet. Not that I want to. At all.

"Come on." I extend my hand to her and lace our fingers together, leading her over to the crowded bar.

We stand there, trying to fight our way up to the counter to place our order. As soon as a small opening becomes available, I urge Olivia forward. She slots herself between two people and leans against the bar. I'm right behind her, my front pressed against her back. I reach forward, resting my hands on the edge of the bar to bracket my arms round her, protecting her from the crowd.

I scan the staff behind the bar, and luckily my eyes lock with Toby from the basketball team. He grins, holding up an index finger to me before grabbing three shot glasses and disappearing to the other end of the bar. He's back in a flash, taking our orders.

"Two waters," I tell him, holding up my index and middle finger to signal to him.

He quirks a brow. "Two waters?" he repeats quizzically, knowing I usually order a beer or a round of shots for the guys.

"Two waters," I confirm.

"You got it, man." He disappears to grab us two waters.

Olivia cranes her neck to look back at me. "You can drink if you want to, Bronx. Don't let me stop you from having fun."

I shake my head. "I'm fine. You're here, that's all I need."

She gives me a soft, appreciative look before turning back around, her attention focused on the hustle and bustle of the staff while mine is focused on the rather large patch of her skin on full display for my greedy eyes. I observe the soft, smooth lines of her back, realizing now that the back of her top has a decently sized cutout, a delicate bow tied at the back of her neck to hold the front up. What I also realize is that with this shirt she's not wearing a bra.

Fuck me.

Damn it, Finch.

Clearing my throat, I take a step back so I'm not plastered up against her anymore, not wanting her to possibly feel anything and be scared off, but I keep my hands still firmly planted around her on the bar.

Toby comes back with two plastic cups filled with ice water. I immediately take a large gulp, needing to cool down.

"Want to dance?" I ask Olivia.

She looks at the packed dance floor hesitantly, nervously nibbling at her bottom lip. "Maybe in a little bit?"

I nod. I get it. Baby steps.

"All right, Finch. 'Cause you know you're going to have to dance with me at some point tonight, right?" I grin.

She lets out a light laugh. "I figured."

We wander back over to the team and take a seat on one of the couches, making light conversation. In no time girls flock over to our section, finding their favorite player to try to shoot their shot. A couple of girls take a seat next to me, trying to strike up a conversation, but I pay them no mind. Even with my hand resting on Olivia's knee, none of them really seem to get the hint that I'm not interested. Some of them even full out acknowledge my hand on Olivia's leg, giving her a rude, sideways glance, and making my blood boil.

By the time a fifth girl approaches me I'm thoroughly annoyed, and I can tell Olivia is extremely uncomfortable with all the unsolicited attention. Fed up, I stand, plucking Olivia's water from her hand and setting it next to mine on a table where Brennen has his feet kicked up, talking to some random chick giving him googly eyes. "Watch these," I instruct him, and he gives me a thumbs-up, flashing me his infamous pearly whites.

I turn back to Olivia, finding her also standing, alarmed.

"Dance with me." I grab her hand and lead her to the dance floor before she can protest.

Brushing past people, I pull her through the crowd to the middle of the dance floor. Finding some space, I turn around to face her and put my hands on her hips, moving to the beat of the music thumping through the speakers.

She hardly even sways, her body strung tight as her eyes dart around the club.

"What's wrong?" I yell over the music.

"Everyone's looking at us." I don't exactly hear her soft voice over the loud music, but I'm able to read her lips.

I give the room a quick once-over, noting that many people are indeed staring at us, but I'll be damned if I let them ruin our night.

"No one's looking," I lie.

"You're looking," she whispers, shyly looking away from me and down at her feet.

I lean in close, letting my lips brush against the shell of her ear. "Well, then, you better put on one hell of a show."

I hear her soft little gasp, and I can't help but grin. She grips my biceps, momentarily stabilizing herself before her body gives way to me.

Holding her firmly but gently, my hands still planted on her hips,

I draw back and give her an encouraging look. Using slight force, I sway her hips from side to side, trying to get her tense body to loosen up. It takes her a song or two, but eventually she finds the rhythm. By the third song her hips are moving freely, but I can tell she still has her guard up.

I take a step closer, our bodies brushing against each other as we move to the beat. Placing my hand on her lower back I pull her closer, and she momentarily stiffens, her hands landing on my chest. She looks up at me, her big brown eyes clouding over.

I grab her hand, twirling her around until her back is pressed up against my front, anything but friendly thoughts now entering my brain.

My eyes lock on her long, exposed neck, which glistens with a light sheen of sweat, and all my restraint flies out the window. Dipping my head, I place a featherlight kiss to her bare shoulder, skimming my lips up to her neck where I let my tongue softly poke out to taste her salty sweet skin before kissing just below her ear.

Olivia gasps, spinning around and staring up at me with a mixture of shock and fascination.

I give her a wolfish grin, then grab her hands and hook them behind my neck. My hands drag down her arms, her ribs, and land back on her hips, rocking them to the rhythm. I lean forward, resting my forehead against hers, and she looks up at me through her thick lashes, unblinking.

Suddenly, I feel a pair of hands land on my shoulders, running down my back seductively. I look over my shoulder to see Adrianna's green eyes boring into mine, her body now pressing into my back. She flashes me a malicious grin, like a black panther ready to catch its prey.

Stunned, I feel Olivia start to slip from my grasp. I snap my head back around to see her slowly backing away, dazed, eyes that were just clouded over with desire now clouding with shock and confusion.

Adrianna takes the opportunity to squeeze herself between us, her back against my front as she grinds against me. I try to move away but she raises her arms back, clasping her fingers tightly behind my neck, like an octopus wrapping its tentacles, unwilling to let go.

Olivia shakes her head, as if snapping back to reality. Mortified, she takes a few steps back before turning around and briskly walking off the dance floor.

"Olivia!" I call after her, trying to untangle myself from Adrianna.

"What the fuck, Adrianna?" I growl, having to use a bit of force to successfully pry her hands off me.

"Bronx, wait. We were having fun!" she says, catching my arm, but I yank it out of her grasp.

"Finch!" I yell, running in the last direction I saw her go.

I exit the dance floor, heart pounding, and scan the club, my eyes finally landing on her picking up her coat. Running as fast as I can, I nearly take some people out trying to get to her.

"Finch, wait," I plead, my hand gently grasping her arm. "Stay."

She shakes her head, looking frantic. "I should go," she insists, grabbing her keys from her coat pocket. "I'll see you Monday."

I watch her take off, her head bowed in shame as she fights her way through the rowdy crowd, some wandering eyes skeptically watching her.

I look over my shoulder at Chase and Brennen, who sit up straighter, giving me curious glances. Throwing a glance back over to the dance floor, I see Adrianna grinding against some random dude, dancing so raunchy that it makes me cringe in embarrassment. She catches my gaze and throws me a devilish smile, and I turn my attention back to Chase and Brennen, who witnessed the exchange. We all give each other an *Are you fucking kidding?* look.

Balling my hands into fists, I shove my way through the crowd and find the exit. The cold air smacks me in the face the second I push through the door, and I scan the parking lot to see Olivia halfway to her car.

"Finch!" I jog to catch up with her.

She stops in her tracks, turning around to face me.

"Don't go."

She shakes her head, giving me a forced smile. "Go have fun, Bronx. I'm okay, I just—this isn't my scene. In there, with you—I don't know . . ." She gives a helpless shrug, not knowing what to say.

I take another step toward her. "What?"

I see the storm of uncertainty brewing behind her eyes, and she backs away, pulling away both physically and emotionally.

"I only want to be here if you're here," I confess, taking the last few strides to reach her. My eyes bore into hers. "I know this isn't your scene and that you're uncomfortable. I get it. I'm not going to force you to go back in there, but I know there's something else bothering you. Talk to me," I plead.

She stares up at me, contemplating. Then she takes a step back, and another. "I'll see you Monday," she repeats, her voice almost a pained whisper.

You're losing her, my mind screams at me. *Do something!*

Watching her hightail it to her car, I go into panic mode.

Brain on the fritz, I check my surroundings to think of something, anything, to get her to stop. I look to my right and spot a couple of guys perched against the wall, sharing some beers. Without a second thought I snatch a bottle from one of their hands and down the remaining contents.

"What the fuck, man?" the guy yells.

Once I'm finished, I let the bottle fall from my grasp, the glass shattering as soon as it hits the concrete.

Olivia spins around, her eyes landing on me.

I steal another guy's beer, downing the contents and dropping the bottle like the last one. Then another.

Olivia looks at me, baffled. Like I'm insane.

Maybe I am.

Hell, here I am, going to drastic measures to not let her leave like this, without talking to me and telling me what else is bothering her. *I think that automatically puts you in the insane category, moron.*

But I need her to talk to me.

I stride up to her. "I need a ride home," I say, knowing she won't be able to turn me down. She won't chance letting me drive with alcohol in my system.

Her shoulders sag. "Bronx," she sighs, overwhelmed.

I know what I'm doing is manipulative and wrong, but I swear my intentions are good. I can't have her run away like this on bad terms.

"Please, Finch?"

Silently, not tearing her gaze away from mine, she hits the Unlock button on her key fob, the rear-end lights softly illuminating her face for a moment as they blink. She turns and walks to the driver's-side door and opens it, and just when I think she's going to leave my dumb ass behind, she looks over her shoulder at me expectantly, waiting.

I waste no time reaching her passenger-side door, opening it and slipping inside the vehicle. A fresh, clean scent engulfs me, and I spot the air freshener clipped to one of the air vents. I observe the rest of the interior of her car, noting how clean and pristine it is.

Olivia gets behind the wheel, turns on the engine, and cranks up the heat. Wordlessly, we both put on our seat belts and she slowly, cautiously, backs out of the parking space and turns onto the main road.

It's quiet as she drives to campus, the tension between us like a rope tied around my neck. In the intimacy of the dark, in her small car, I struggle to find the right words. I know I'm running out of time as we approach the campus at a steady pace.

"Where's your jacket?" she asks, her voice cutting through the silence, startling me.

Huh?

I look down at my body and realize I must have left my jacket back at the club, and I can't help the smile that tugs at my lips, despite the rather serious situation.

"I must have left it back at the club."

A frown etches her features, making me smile more. Only she would care about that right now.

"Finch, pull over."

"What?" She steals a glance at me, looking at me like I have three heads.

"Pull over."

No questions asked, she pulls into an empty parking lot, staring at me.

"Put it in Park," I instruct, knowing this is going to take a while.

She does as I say, throwing the gearshift into Park and then staring down at the wheel.

"Look at me, Finch."

Hesitantly, she turns her head to me, but her eyes don't find mine. I twist my frame, planting my elbow on the center console and gently grabbing her chin, angling her face until I find her eyes. "I'm sorry about Adrianna."

She shifts her eyes, and I lose her gaze. "It's not that."

"What is it?" I ask gently, patiently.

She sighs, pulling her chin from my grasp and fixing her gaze on something past the windshield, looking contemplative.

"I don't know," she says helplessly. "I guess . . ."

I reach over and place my hand on top of hers, giving it a reassuring squeeze.

"I'm not used to going to places like that, and going with you . . . I felt like everyone was staring at me, like, who's this girl hanging out with him? We've never seen her here before. Why is he giving her the time of day?"

I frown, crushed she feels this way.

"I just felt like all eyes were on me. Judging me." She takes a deep breath. "And when we were dancing . . ." She trails off, looking uncomfortable and embarrassed.

"I'm sorry, Finch, I crossed a line," I admit. "I didn't mean to make you feel uncomfortable, I just—" Now it's my turn to struggle for words. "I got too caught up in being that close to you. You look beautiful and you smell fucking awesome. I guess I just got carried away and lost control."

Even in the dark I can make out her blush. She shakes her head. "No, I guess I got lost in all of it, too, for a bit," she admits shyly, her confession so soft I almost don't hear it.

I try my best to tamp down my triumphant smile. So she didn't hate it? Did she maybe even enjoy it a little?

"I guess it's a good thing Adrianna intervened," she says, her tone kidding, trying to lighten the mood, but a flash of anger strikes me.

"Yeah," I grumble, clearly bitter.

I can't help but wonder what would have happened if Adrianna hadn't ruined the moment.

Olivia cracks a smile, eyes laughing. "She's pretty determined."

I let out a frustrated breath, raking a hand through my dark hair. "Tell me about it," I grumble. "I'm sorry tonight was ruined. I'm sorry I even made you go in the first place."

Olivia's smile softens. "You didn't make me do anything."

"Why did you come anyway? I lost the bet."

The side of her mouth quirks up. "Yeah, and you were pretty upset about losing," she points out.

"Of course I was."

She lets out a sigh, leaning back in her seat, her eyes fixed on the visor above her head. "A part of me wanted to go. Finally have a legit college experience. Delilah and even my parents tell me that I need to get out more, live life not so uptight."

"Why don't you?" I ask.

She shrugs. "I guess I'm scared."

I furrow my brow. "Why?"

She gives another meek shrug, her eyes drifting to our still-joined hands.

We sit in silence for a few moments.

"Can I propose something?"

"Hmm?" She turns her head to look at me.

"How about for the next bet, you set the wager. Come up with something crazy, something you've never done before. Anything you want, and I'll do it with you."

She smirks playfully. "And what if you don't like it? How do I know you're not going to sabotage me and purposely get a bad grade to get out of it?"

"I would never do that to you."

Her features soften. "Can I have some time to think about it?"

"Take all the time you need."

TWENTY-TWO

Lights Out

"It's fucking freezing out here," I say, speed walking with Olivia to the science building, trying to seek warmth as fast as possible.

"Well, it is below freezing," she says, her voice slightly muffled by the thick scarf that she has her chin tucked into.

"Smartass," I mumble, playfully bumping into her.

She giggles, then jogs the rest of the way to the science building. As I chase after her it begins to sleet, tiny snowflakes and frozen pellets flying all around us.

Once inside, the sweet heat engulfs us, and we begin to delayer. She peels off her gloves and unwinds the scarf around her neck while I remove my beanie and shake out my dark-brown hair, and unzip my winter coat. Looking down at my red, freezing-cold hands, I cup them together in front of my face, breathing on them while rubbing them together every few seconds, trying to regain feeling.

Olivia sniffles, shrugging off her backpack and setting it on a nearby bench to pack her winter accessories inside. I note how red the tip of her nose, as well as the tips of her ears, are from the cold.

I reach into my coat pocket and fish out my beanie, and walk up to her, placing the black knit fabric on top of her head, making sure it covers her ears.

She looks up at me with confused amusement, self-consciously reaching up to touch the fabric at the top of her head.

"Don't want your ears to fall off, Finch."

She smiles, shaking her head. "Says the guy whose fingers are almost blue."

I look down at my hands and back up at her, quirking a brow and taking a step closer. So close our bodies are almost touching, and I can faintly smell her vanilla perfume. "Want to warm them up for me?" I ask, my voice low.

Her smile fades and I watch her throat work on a swallow. She looks down at my hands, and, surprisingly, grabs them with her own. Her hands look so small compared to mine, her fingers long, slender, and dainty compared to my rough, calloused ones. She holds little heat in her own hands, but I feel a flush slide over my body just from her touch.

"Have you thought any more about my offer?" I ask, my voice raspy in the intimacy of what feels like our own little bubble.

After the club, on the car ride back to my dorm after our stop in the parking lot, I may have asked Olivia to spend Thanksgiving with me since we'll be among the few who aren't leaving town for the holiday—her since she lives here and me because I have nowhere to go, no family to see. The football team is holding a small get-together at one of the frat houses, since most of us are staying in town because we have a game that weekend. I invited Olivia but she seemed hesitant, and I guess I can't blame her. I'm not too keen on spending the holiday in a dingy frat house either.

She looks up at me through her thick lashes, seemingly lost for a moment before regaining her mental footing. "I actually talked to my parents and you're more than welcome to stop by tomorrow if you'd like."

"Hmm." I tilt my head to the side, pursing my lips and looking up at the ceiling, pretending to think. "Thanksgiving at your house, *or*"—I tilt my head to the other side, seemingly weighing my options—"at a grimy frat house with guys who have sliced deli turkey sandwiches and reek of stale beer. That's a tough call, Finch."

She flashes me an exasperated look, and playfully squeezes my fingers hard.

I chuckle, pulling on her hands and jerking her body forward the few inches between us so that she collides into me. I hear her laugh as soon as her chest presses against mine, and I can't help but grin, my teeth sinking into my bottom lip. "What time should I be over?"

She looks up at me, warm honey–colored eyes wide with surprise. "I, uh—" she sputters adorably. "Three," she finally blurts. "Three is good."

I grin, adjusting our hands to thread our fingers together. "Should I bring anything?"

She shakes her head, seemingly at a loss for words. I can only assume she feels the sexual tension radiating between us as well.

I draw circles on the backs of her hands with my thumbs, pressing my body against hers more firmly. My mind suddenly has flashbacks to the night at The Library when she danced with me, our bodies moving against each other in a way I so desperately want them to in the intimacy of a bedroom. I remember the feel of her warm, smooth skin, and my fingers involuntarily twitch in hers at the memory of the smooth lines and planes I want to drag my lips across every single inch of.

Our eyes bore into each other, and it's like time has magically stopped, until inevitably, by some sort of cruel fate, our little bubble is burst.

"Miller!" I hear someone boom from across the atrium. Involuntarily, I peel my eyes away from Olivia's to glance over my shoulder, and see Brennen walking up to us, beaming. He has a knowing, teasing grin on his face, and the glint in his eye gives it away that he's purposefully interrupting our little moment to torture me. Asshole.

"What?" I almost snap, but I'm able to reel in the hostility of my tone.

He lifts the jacket in his hand in a grand fashion before throwing it at me. I only let go of one of Olivia's hands, catching the jacket one-handed. "Toby found it the other night after his shift at the club. Gave it to me in our nine a.m. to pass off to you," he informs me.

"Thanks." I give him an appreciative nod, and catch his gaze falling on Olivia's hand still in mine. He smirks.

Olivia's grip loosens and I can feel her starting to pull away, but I keep my grip firm, not letting go of her hand. I steal a quick glance at her to see that her cheeks now match her red nose, but it's not from the cold.

"You guys are staying in town for Thanksgiving, right?" Brennen asks. "Apparently they just announced that there's a nasty storm heading this way in about three hours or so, and whoever hasn't already skipped classes for the day is running like a bat out of hell to get to wherever they're trying to go."

Olivia's brow furrows with worry. "A storm?"

"Yeah, a winter storm. We're going to get freezing rain and all that. Roads are going to turn into an ice rink—so they predict."

Olivia frowns. "I wonder if Delilah knows?" she wonders out loud, since they carpooled together.

I give her hand a reassuring squeeze. "If you want to leave, I can always take you home," I offer.

She worries her lip. "I don't know, I don't want to skip lab. I'll just see what Delilah's going to do."

"Well, you guys have fun. If you need me, I'll be manning my shift behind the front desk at the dorm," he says, giving a little salute before heading off in that direction. He's been working at the athletic dorm's front desk since sophomore year.

Olivia's hand still in mine, I lead her down the hall to the anatomy lab. We walk in to see Delilah and Rat Boy already in their seats, and he doesn't fail to shoot me a glare, his beady little eyes zooming in on our joined hands. I can't help but smirk as I watch him practically snarl.

Olivia's steps pick up as soon as she spots Delilah, and she rushes over to her best friend. "Have you heard about the storm?"

Delilah's brows knit together over her thick-rimmed glasses. "Storm?"

"Yeah, we just heard there's a winter storm on the way," Olivia informs her, letting go of my hand to shrug off her backpack and take a seat. I take my seat next to her.

Delilah reaches for her phone, pulling up the weather app. She scans the forecast, her lips pursing into a frown. "This doesn't look good," she comments under her breath.

"What do you want to do, Dee? I know you were planning on driving back home tonight."

"Good thing is that it doesn't look like its heading south, but still. I want to avoid it as much as possible," she says, looking up at Olivia from her phone.

Olivia nods. "After the quiz we can head out, if you want. It doesn't look like half the class is showing up anyway, and I'm sure Tracy will understand." She looks around the half-empty classroom, and I'm a bit relieved when I realize Adrianna's whole table is missing.

Delilah glances out the window to observe the light precipitation already falling. "Yeah, that sounds good. I'm sorry, Liv. I hate skipping class as much as you do, but I just don't want to risk getting stuck in this."

Olivia shakes her head. "No, I don't want to risk it, either, and I know how badly you want to get home to see your family for the holiday."

"It'll be fine," Rat Boy cuts in dismissively. "It's just a little snow."

"And ice," Delilah deadpans.

Rat Boy shrugs carelessly, like he doesn't understand the severity of ice on roads. I get it, sometimes people can be real pansies about a little snow, but ice is nothing to fuck around with.

Tracy waltzes into the classroom, chipper as always. "Hey, class, I see a few of you managed not to skip lab today and head home early for the break," she jokes, setting her stuff down on her desk and jiggling the mouse to wake up the computer. "I appreciate it, and I know you are all itching to get out of here due to the break and the weather, so I promise to make this easy for you. Today, we're just going to take the quiz and breeze through next week's material. I won't keep you longer than necessary."

Olivia and Delilah share a glance across the table, the two of them having some kind of weird, silent, best friend telepathic exchange. After a moment they nod at the same time, coming to some sort of mutual agreement without saying one damn word to each other.

"What just happened?" I ask, amazed.

"What?" Delilah asks.

"That!" I gesture wildly between the two.

"Oh." Delilah smirks. "We're staying," she says simply.

I look to Olivia for confirmation. "You got all of that, just from that?" I ask, gesturing between the two of them yet again with my hand.

Olivia grins with gratification. "Yep."

I look over at Delilah, who has a matching grin.

"Chicks," I playfully mutter under my breath, causing them both to giggle.

Twenty minutes later we're all walking out of lab. As promised, Tracy just handed out the quiz and briefly went over next week's material, then bid us a good break.

Walking toward the main entrance of the science building, we all stop short when we see a line of people blocking the glass doors, looking outside intently.

"What the hell?" I mutter under my breath, walking ahead and squeezing through the small crowd to see what all the fuss is about. I look outside, not seeing much. "What's going on?" I ask some random dude to my right.

"Ice is already coating the roads. A kid from our class is trying to make it out of the parking lot, but his truck isn't going anywhere without fishtailing," he says.

I snap my gaze to the parking lot and see an old, beat-up Chevy crawl across the parking lot, the brake lights glowing every few seconds, the truck sliding around, nearly hitting other cars in the lot. This kid is fucking insane. I can appreciate determination, but this is just straight up stupidity. There's no way he or anyone else is making it out of here without hitting something or killing themselves.

"What's going on?" Olivia asks, appearing behind me. She rests her hand on my shoulder, stabilizing herself as she stands on her tiptoes to look over me.

I crane my neck to look at her, my lips dangerously close to hers as I turn my head. I try my best to ignore her breath fanning across my face and her body brushing against mine. "Guy can't make it out of the parking lot."

Her face falls, eyes immediately searching the parking lot to find the truck fishtailing yet again. She sucks in a sharp breath when the truck nearly hits another car, and she quickly glances back at Delilah.

"What's going on?" Delilah asks, immediately detecting her best friend's distress.

Olivia falters, struggling to find the words to break it to Dee gently that she's not going to be heading home for Thanksgiving to see her family anytime soon.

Delilah pushes her way past us to peek out the window herself, her shoulders immediately sagging when she sees the ice glimmering across the pavement. "No," she whines, looking back at us with utter disappointment.

"I'm sorry, Dee," Olivia says, her voice dripping with guilt.

Delilah turns back around to look outside, intently observing. "What do we do?"

Olivia glances up at me helplessly.

"There's nothing much we can do," I admit honestly. "It's below freezing, and the ground temperatures aren't going to get much warmer as we approach nightfall. It looks like everyone on campus is stuck until at least morning."

A few more kids file into the atrium, no one really knowing what to do. Only a few brave souls attempt to leave the building, slipping and sliding around as they trudge to the dorms. Two guys I recognize from the hockey team are walking more effortlessly on the icy concrete than some others who are falling on their asses.

"What's going on?" I look over my shoulder to spot Tracy all bundled up, bag tossed over her shoulder and keys in hand, looking like she's ready to leave for the day.

"Roads are already covered in ice," I inform her.

She frowns, fighting her way to the front of the doors to look outside for herself. "What the—they said it wasn't supposed to hit for another couple of hours."

"Right?" Delilah grumbles bitterly, arms tightly crossed over her chest as she looks outside with hatred.

Tracy does her best to try to compose herself. "All right, everyone, don't panic," she instructs, despite her voice rising a few octaves. "This should all blow over in a couple of hours," she says optimistically, but I can tell deep down even she knows that isn't true.

"We're never getting out of here," Rat Boy grumbles cynically, walking away and throwing himself down on one of the lounge chairs.

"No, no, that's not true," Tracy says, but her voice wavers a bit. "Everything is going to be okay. We just have to wait out the storm for a bit."

Moments later the lights flicker, and everyone looks up, a low murmur of panic ensuing.

"Fuck," I mutter under my breath, and shoot my gaze to the power lines outside, seeing them already coated with ice.

Olivia's hand wraps around my arm, and I look down to find her wide, worried eyes looking up at me.

"It's going to be okay," I try to reassure her, my arm instinctively circling her waist.

Just as the words leave my lips all the lights go out with a low, ominous droning noise.

"You have got to be kidding me," I hear Delilah grumble before everyone breaks into a panic.

TWENTY-THREE

Body Heat

"Everyone, stay calm," Tracy instructs, sounding anything but, her authoritative resolve cracking under the pressure of unforeseen circumstances. "The lights will come back on," she says optimistically.

We all stand still for a moment, looking up at the lights as if they'll magically turn back on. With no luck, everyone turns to their phones, typing out frantic texts.

"I guess I should call my parents," Delilah huffs, looking disappointed.

"I'm sorry, Dee," Olivia says sympathetically, giving her friend's arm a reassuring squeeze.

"It's okay." Delilah gives a small, halfhearted smile before walking off down the hall for a bit more privacy.

Olivia's shoulders slump. "I guess I should call my parents too. Hopefully my mom made it home already," she says, pulling her phone out of her back pocket to check if she has any missed messages. "I'll be back." She slips out of my grasp and walks down the hall, opposite to the direction Delilah went.

I take a seat on one of the couches, watching the chaos slowly ensue. There's about fifty kids loitering around the front entrance of the science building, not knowing what to do or where to go. Then there's Tracy, sprinting down the hallway to the offices.

I pull out my phone to text Chase and Brennen, seeing if other buildings and the dorms have power. By the sounds of their replies, it seems like there's a campus-wide power outage.

Olivia reappears, and plops onto the couch beside me, looking bummed.

"Guess we're not going to English today, huh?" I joke, trying to lighten the mood.

She lets out the tiniest amused huff and pulls out her phone, checking her email. "Professor Hobb just sent out an email thirty minutes ago. Class is canceled for today."

"Darn."

She elbows me in the ribs, trying her best to throw me an unamused glare. I grin, slinging my arm around her shoulders and pulling her into my side. She lets out a little shriek of surprise, giggling as she tries to squirm out of my hold.

I feel the couch shift, and Olivia and I both still. Looking down at the opposite end of the couch, I see a pair of beady little eyes staring back at us.

Olivia slips out from under my arm, sitting up straight and fixing her hair. When Delilah appears in front of us, plopping into the armchair across from the couch with a huff, Olivia sits on the edge of her seat, all her attention focused on her distressed best friend.

"Were you able to get a hold of your parents?" Olivia asks.

"Yeah," Delilah says, dejected. "They told me to stay put and just come home tomorrow whenever the roads are safe again."

Olivia purses her lips into a remorseful frown. "I'm sorry, Dee. We should have just skipped lab and gone home."

Delilah shakes her head. "It's not your fault. I decided to stay too. Maybe it's better that we did. Who knows what we would have gotten caught in if we'd left a little earlier? At least we're spending the night in a building instead of in a car on the side of the road somewhere," she says, trying to be a little optimistic.

My stomach twists uncomfortably at the thought of them driving in this weather, possibly getting stranded on the side of the road. Or worse. Much worse.

"Honestly, these chairs are probably more comfortable than my car seats. So there's that," Delilah says, trying to ease some of Olivia's obvious guilt.

"We're not spending the night here," Rat Boy grumbles irritably.

"And where exactly do you think we're going to go? Home? Because I don't think anyone brought their ice skates," Delilah fires back, equally as annoyed, if not more so.

Rat Boy huffs, crossing his arms over his chest and rolling his eyes.

I swear, if I have to spend the whole night in his proximity I'm shoving his ass in the lab supply closet with all his relatives. It'll be like he never missed a minute of Thanksgiving.

Looking determined, Tracy skids around the corner with a flashlight, even though it's still daylight and everything is visible inside the building with all the large floor-to-ceiling windows. She makes her way to the center of the crowd, then stands on top of one of the side tables to make herself more visible.

"All right, everyone!" she calls, trying to gain everyone's attention by waving her arms above her head. "It looks like we're going to be stuck here for a while, but don't worry, the science department has some water bottles, granola bars, and flashlights to get us through however long we're going to need to stay here. If there is an emergency, I and some of the staff are going to be in our offices just down the hall," she informs us, acting as if she's taken on the role of the main character in a postapocalyptic movie. "Just hang in there and we'll be out of here in no time," she chirps before hopping down from the table and heading back to the offices.

"Aye, aye, Captain," Delilah mumbles sarcastically, giving a less-than-halfhearted two-finger salute.

She turns to Olivia. "Have you talked to your parents?"

"Yeah, Mom just made it home, but it looks like Dad's going to be stuck at the store. At least the store has electricity. For now. If it goes out, though, I'm pretty sure there are some battery-powered space heaters in stock, thankfully."

"Speaking of that," Delilah says, shifting around in the chair to slide on her winter coat. "How long do you think it'll be before we freeze our asses off?"

"I don't even want to think about it," Olivia groans, pulling her coat tighter around her body.

Instinctively, I drape my arm over her shoulders and pull her into my side to provide her warmth. Delilah grins, her brows rising suggestively, and while I don't look at Rat Boy, I can practically feel the steam rolling off of him. Maybe if I piss him off even further we'll have heat for the whole damn building. Problem solved.

On a serious note, I can't help but worry about Olivia as night approaches. I know her tall, willowy frame won't retain a lot of heat, and there's only so much body heat and layers I can provide her. If we're without power for the rest of the night, we're all fucked.

"We can go to my apartment," Rat Boy suggests, looking solely at Olivia. I don't think his *we* included either me or Delilah. "It's less than a half a mile from here."

"Again," Delilah chimes in dryly, "how are you going to get there?"

"Walk," Rat Boy says, like it's the most obvious thing in the world.

Delilah snorts. "*Okay*. I'm pretty sure Liv would rather stay here than freeze to death trudging to your apartment in the ice, with the possibly of breaking a bone."

At least she said it and not me. Thank you, Delilah.

"We'd be fine," he spits, throwing her a glare.

"Oh yeah? If it's that easy, run to your place and bring us back some blankets, will ya?" Delilah counters, and the two of them bicker back and forth, Delilah clearly having the upper hand.

Olivia lets out a tired sigh, mildly surprising me by closing her eyes and laying her head on my shoulder. I stroke her hair, marveling at the silky smooth caramel-colored strands.

A couple of hours in everyone is bored out of their minds, and have resorted to using the flashlights Tracy handed out as the sky faded to black. Some kids sit on the floor, playing with them by making shadow puppets on the walls while others use theirs to explore and scope out a place to sleep tonight. Everyone is using whatever furniture is available as a makeshift bed.

Everyone has also slipped on their winter gear, the heat in the building significantly dropping. Olivia has her gloves on, and is struggling to tear open the wrapper of her granola bar. I gently take the food from her hands, using my ungloved hands to open it for her.

"Thanks." She nibbles on it, looking down at my bare hands with concern. "You didn't bring any gloves. Are you sure you don't want your jacket back?" she asks, already trying to hand me the jacket that Brennen returned to me this morning. I draped it over her about an hour ago.

"Nah, Finch. I'm all right," I assure her, securing my jacket back over her.

She frowns. "Aren't you cold?"

"I'm all right," I lie. It's fucking freezing in here, but I know she needs it more than I do.

Her frown deepens and then her eyes widen as if a light bulb just went off inside her head. "Are you sure? I can check if Professor Cooper has a blanket in her office or something. I don't think she'd mind if I borrowed it."

"You have a key to Professor Cooper's office?" Delilah asks, stunned.

Olivia looks away nervously. "Yeah."

"Why am I even surprised," Delilah mutters under her breath. "I told you, that woman's in love with you."

Now Olivia rolls her eyes. "Whatever." She sits up straighter, leaning over to reach inside her backpack on the floor and pulling out a key ring with about five keys on it, including her car keys. She stands up, adjusting all her layers of clothing. "I'll be right back."

"Uh-uh," Delilah says, popping up from her chair. "I'm coming with you."

"What? Why?" Olivia asks, brows pinched together in confusion.

"Because I want to see what her evil lair looks like."

"Dee," Olivia groans, exasperated. "No."

"Come on," Delilah pleads, mustering up her best puppy dog pout.

"Forget it." Olivia sighs, sitting back down. "I shouldn't be going into her office when she's not there anyway."

"Bull. I know that's code for you're just going to sneak off to her office later without me," Delilah argues.

"No," Olivia lies, her voice rising a few octaves higher. "I shouldn't be going in there without permission. It's rude."

Delilah walks over to her best friend, somehow managing to sneakily and swiftly pluck the set of keys from her hand like a snake. "Well, then, what's the purpose of giving you a key? And guess who's not always polite," Delilah says menacingly, smirking as she takes off down the hall.

"Delilah!" Olivia scolds, hopping up from her seat and running down the hall after her.

Instinctively, I hop up and follow them, Rat Boy hot on my heels.

I catch up just in time to see them fighting over the key at Professor Cooper's door, the light from their flashlights dancing around the walls in the scuffle, but ultimately Delilah wins, shoving the key into the lock and twisting. She lets out a triumphant laugh when the door swings open, and she slips inside Professor Cooper's office. Olivia shakes her head with exasperation, following her inside.

"Whoa," Delilah says, spinning around three hundred and sixty degrees in the middle of the office with her flashlight, observing. She takes in the white walls and light-gray accent furniture that includes a desk, couch, some chairs, and side tables. It's minimal, modern; the only decorative aspects some throw pillows and succulent plants scattered around. "It's a lot more zen than I expected."

Olivia grumbles something under her breath, shouldering past Delilah to go behind Professor Cooper's desk where she opens a drawer and pulls out a dark-gray blanket. "Here you go," she says, locking her eyes with mine and offering the blanket to me, her voice surprisingly soft despite her clear irritation.

I shake my head, stepping closer and leaning my shoulder against the door frame, blocking Rat Boy, his beady little gaze burning into my back. "No, Finch, you take it. You need it more than I do."

She frowns, shrugging off my jacket. "Then at least take your jacket back," she argues.

"Uh-uh," I argue back, pushing off the door frame to step inside the office.

Rat Boy pushes his way in behind me. "Why don't you just go back to your dorm? I'm sure you have extra layers there," he comments, jaw and voice tight.

"Oh," Olivia says in realization, her voice and eyes projecting disappointment. "I didn't even think about it. Bronx, why don't you go back to your dorm? Sleep in your own bed."

I grab my jacket from her hands, throwing it back around her shoulders. "I'm not going anywhere. The dorms are out of power, too, and the beds are hard as rocks anyway. I'm not going to risk busting my ass for that. Plus, as I told you before, I play *football*. Not hockey," I tease.

"Tonsil hockey, though," Delilah muses under her breath, a smirk playing on her lips.

Even in the dim light that's provided by flashlights, I can see Olivia's cheeks burn bright red. I even feel my own cheeks heat up a little.

"We got the blanket, can we go back out to the lounge now?" Rat Boy spits, souring the mood, like he always does.

Delilah rolls her eyes. "You know the second we stepped away from that furniture people swooped in like hawks to steal it."

Rat Boy grits his teeth. "Well, where are we supposed to sleep now? I'm not sleeping on top of a desk or on the floor, that's for sure."

"We could sleep here," Delilah says, shrugging and plopping onto Professor Cooper's couch.

Olivia's expression turns wary. "I don't know, Dee. Let me text her just to make sure it's okay," she says, slipping her phone out of her pocket.

"You *text* her?" Delilah blurts, baffled.

I see Olivia roll her eyes as she types out a text.

In less than a minute her phone pings. "Professor Cooper said we can stay here tonight."

"Of course she did," Delilah grumbles. "I swear, that lady's stuck so far up your a—"

"Delilah!" Olivia scolds her, her patience clearly wearing thin.

Delilah raises her hands in surrender.

With a tired sigh Olivia plops on the couch next to Delilah, and I quickly claim the last seat on the end next to her before Rat Boy can weasel his way in. He shoots me a glare before angrily throwing himself in the armchair across from us, pouting.

The room illuminates a little more when Delilah pulls out her phone, checking the time, yawning. "It's already past ten thirty."

Olivia involuntarily yawns as well. "Yeah, I guess we can all try to shut our eyes for a few hours. Hopefully it will be better in the morning."

She unfolds the blanket, trying to cover as much of Delilah and me as she can with it. Instinctively, I throw my arm around the back of the couch, around her shoulders, to pull her closer to me for body heat. She lays her head on my shoulder, and I reach down to grab her legs, swinging them up and over to lay across my lap so she can be more comfortable—and more importantly, to try to provide her some more of my body heat.

Her body stiffens. "Are you sure about this?" she asks, almost nervous.

"Positive," I assure her, loving the feel of her body on mine.

Eventually, she relaxes, snuggling into my side as I soothingly run my hand up and down her leg.

"I know you're pissed at me," Delilah says, "but can I get in on this cuddle session? I could really use the body heat."

Olivia sleepily mumbles an approval and Delilah curls up into a ball and plasters herself to Olivia's back, trying to soak up as much heat as she can while simultaneously using Olivia as a pillow.

"You need more meat on your bones. Even with your puffy coat on I can feel your spine jutting into my cheek," Delilah playfully gripes, adjusting herself every few seconds to try to get comfortable.

After a few minutes everyone is settled, and I'm pretty sure I hear Delilah faintly snoring. Olivia has her cheek pressed against my chest, her eyes closed, but I don't think she's actually asleep yet.

I glance at Rat Boy, whose face is slightly illuminated by the lone flashlight resting on Professor Cooper's desk, so it's not pitch black in here. I catch him glaring at me in the dark, like some sort of demon. Normally, I'm not someone who scares easily, even after watching a horror movie, but I'd be lying if I said he didn't give me the heebie-jeebies. If it wasn't for the girls, especially Olivia lying comfortably against me, I'd get up and drag him to the nearest supply closet and lock him in.

For a good remainder of the night, I stay awake just to make sure he doesn't try to kill me in my sleep. Once I'm sure he's asleep, I give myself permission to close my eyes.

>> <<

I feel Olivia shift, causing me to stir awake. I blink a few times, momentarily confused as I try to regain consciousness.

I let my eyes adjust to the bright light pouring in the small window and harshly reflecting off the white walls. When I'm pretty sure I have my sight back, I glance down to see a pair of honey-colored eyes staring back at me, the light hitting them perfectly.

"Hi," I rasp out, running the hand that's not wrapped around her back and trapped by Delilah's body through her hair, pushing some of it out of her face.

"Hi," she whispers back, fighting back a yawn.

"What time is it?" I ask, rubbing my eyes with the heel of my hand. I stretch a little and a sharp pain shoots up my spine, causing me to flinch.

She looks up at me with worry. "Are you okay?"

"Yeah, just stiff," I admit. While Professor Cooper's couch isn't bad, sitting up all night isn't the most comfortable. I've slept worse, though.

Olivia moves to get off me, but I hold her securely, not wanting to lose the feeling of her quite yet. She gets the hint and rests back against me, checking her watch.

"It's almost eight thirty," she says, her eyes drifting to the window. "I wonder if the sun melted anything yet."

Delilah lets out a groan, stirring. "Shhh."

"Dee, it's morning," Olivia says.

All Delilah does is let out a grunt.

Olivia blows out a breath, resting her head back on my shoulder. After a few moments I feel her body stiffen and she lifts her head, looking alert.

"What is it, Finch?"

"Shhh." Her brow creases in concentration. "Do you hear that?"

I strain my ears and manage to hear the low hum of the heater and electricity.

"The power's back on?" I ask.

"I think so. Dee, wake up, the power's back on," she says, elbowing her.

Delilah mumbles under her breath, then sits up, rubbing her eyes. I take the opportunity to move my numb arm, shaking it out.

"Huh?" Delilah asks groggily.

"I think the power's back on."

Delilah seems to wake up more. "Really?"

"Let's go find out," Olivia says, throwing the blanket off of us. She folds it back up neatly and puts it back in the drawer.

When the drawer snaps closed Rat Boy stirs. "What's going on?"

"Power's back on," Delilah says, standing.

Rat Boy shoots up from the chair, nearly falling over. "Seriously? Let's get out of here."

He and Delilah are the first ones out the door, but Olivia waits for me as I slowly stand up like a ninety-year-old man, my back and neck killing me.

"Let's get out of here," I say, grabbing her hand and leading her to the front of the building.

Only a few people still linger inside, most of them sleeping.

"How do the roads look?" Olivia asks Delilah as we meet her at the front doors.

"Roads seem to be fine," she says, her face bright. "We just need to take it slow for any lingering patches of ice."

Olivia lets out a relieved breath. "Good. You should be able to make it home today, then."

"That's the plan. Now let's go home!" Delilah says cheerfully, dragging Olivia outside to the parking lot.

I walk out with them to Delilah's car, still holding Olivia's hand to make sure she doesn't slip on any lingering ice. Rat Boy unfortunately follows, since his car is parked close to Delilah's.

I open the passenger-side door for Olivia.

"Thank you," she says, her tired eyes lingering on mine.

"Go home and get some rest, Finch," I tell her as she slips into the car.

"You too. I'll see you later," she whispers, a small smile gracing her lips.

"Text me when you make it home safely," I instruct before shutting her door.

I watch them safely pull out of the parking lot and onto the main road before trucking it back to my dorm room, where I flop down on my bed to try to get some decent sleep. I only fall asleep after I get Olivia's text message saying that she made it home safe, and I make sure to set an alarm to get up and get ready to go spend Thanksgiving at her house on time.

TWENTY-FOUR

Deal

I park in front of Olivia's house at 3:37 p.m., over thirty minutes late. I was so tired after hardly sleeping in Professor Cooper's office last night that I overslept. I texted Olivia to let her know and she seemed fine with it. She said she'd also slept longer than she intended, but I still can't help but feel guilty.

I jump out of the car and jog up to her porch, knocking three times. It takes a few seconds for Olivia to answer.

"Hey." She beams at me, wiping her hands on a dish towel. She's dressed in an oversized cream sweater and black leggings, fuzzy socks on her feet. She looks so cute and cozy. "Come in."

I walk into the house, shrugging off my jacket and hanging it on the coatrack. "Thanks. It smells amazing in here," I observe, the smells coming from the kitchen making my mouth water and stomach growl. "Sorry I'm late," I apologize again, cringing a little.

Olivia waves her hand dismissively. "Don't worry about it. We're still cooking anyway," she says, heading for the kitchen.

Instinctively, I follow her after greeting her dad, who is sitting in the living room watching the game, promising him I'll join shortly.

We walk into the kitchen to find her mom opening the oven,

peeking inside to check on the turkey. "I think it's finally done," she declares, turning to look at Olivia and spotting me. "Bronx, glad you could make it," she exclaims.

"Thanks for having me over, Mrs. McCausland. Let me get that for you," I insist, before she can take the turkey out herself.

"Oh, what a gentleman," she coos, handing me the oven mitts before patting me on the back, making Olivia blush with embarrassment.

After I pull the turkey out of the oven, Olivia and her mom finish preparing the rest of the food, refusing to let me help since I'm the guest. I go and watch some of the game with Stan until dinner is ready.

Stan carves the turkey, piling a hefty portion on my plate before offering me a beer from the fridge. Once we all fill our plates, I'm shocked to see them migrate into the living room to eat on the couch and watch TV. Not that I'm complaining, though. To be honest, I was a little nervous they would have us file into the dining room to eat with fancy china, say grace, and go around the table to say what we're thankful for—and I was fully prepared to answer that question by saying I was thankful to have met Olivia this year.

After dinner I help Olivia wash the dishes as her parents playfully bicker about how to stack all the leftovers in the fridge. Just as they put the last of the containers away, the doorbell rings and Olivia waltzes over to the front door to answer it.

"Cora, glad you could make it!" she exclaims, giving the woman a hug. I recognize her as the nurse Olivia had dinner with at the hospital. The one she has dinner with every Tuesday.

"Yes, I ended up getting off a little early. I hope you don't mind," she says sheepishly.

"Not at all," Mrs. McCausland insists, taking Cora's jacket and purse before also giving her a hug.

We all exchange greetings before Olivia and her mom whisk Cora off to the kitchen to make her a plate, and Stan and I head back to the living room to watch the end of the game.

Stan and I stay in the living room, giving them their girl time. I can't help but glance over at Olivia frequently, though, loving watching her talk and laugh with her mom and Cora, completely at ease with herself. There's something refreshing about observing her in her own home—not that she's a completely different person outside of school, but it's just nice to see her so comfortable.

"You really like her, huh?"

I quickly snap my attention to Stan, a punch of embarrassment hitting me at having him catch me staring at his daughter. "Yes, sir," I admit. No point in denying it.

He nods, returning his gaze to the TV before taking a sip of his beer. "I'll let you date my daughter on one condition," he states, completely shocking me.

Nevertheless, I raise a brow, intrigued.

He looks at me out of the corner of his eye. "You get me tickets to watch you boys in the playoffs."

I huff out a relieved laugh. "I can do that. I'll even throw in tickets to this Saturday's game," I add.

He tries to hide his smile by taking another sip of beer. "I always knew I liked you."

"One condition, though," I counter, making him raise a brow questioningly. "You bring her. Maybe teach her a thing or two about football."

He chuckles. "Deal."

The girls emerge from the kitchen, Mrs. McCausland clapping her hands. "Who's ready for PJs and Christmas movies!" she exclaims excitedly.

I glance at Olivia, and she cringes sheepishly. "I'm sorry, I forgot to tell you it's tradition to change into pajamas after dinner and watch

Christmas movies. I'm sure Dad can lend you something," she offers.

I stand, shaking my head. "I have my gym bag out in the truck. I should have something in there."

She smiles, relieved. "Okay, you can go grab it and change in my room," she says, already heading up the stairs as I grab the keys and go out to the truck.

I find a pair of gym shorts and an old hoodie, and carry them up to her room. I walk in to find her bathroom door shut, and assume she's changing in there.

I close her bedroom door, and am pulling off my sweater just as she emerges from the bathroom in a baggy shirt and pajama pants. Caught off guard, she freezes, her honey-brown eyes wide as she takes in my naked chest.

I refrain from chuckling, and take a few strides toward her. "Nice pajama pants, Finch."

Her eyes immediately dart down to her light-blue plaid pajama pants, the tips of her ears burning pink with a blush. "Oh, uh, thanks," she adorably stutters, pointing with her thumb over her shoulder. "You can go change in the bathroom now."

I chuckle this time, grabbing my shorts and hoodie to quickly change out of my jeans.

I come out of the bathroom to find her standing in her closet, the hoodie I gave her homecoming night in her hands as she seems to be contemplating whether to wear it or not.

"Wear it."

She jumps, spinning around to look at me. "Huh?"

"Wear it," I repeat, setting my jeans on her bed before walking over to her, grabbing the hoodie, and helping her put it on. Once her head and arms are through, I pull her ponytail out of the back and drape it over her shoulder.

"There," I say, satisfied.

She blushes, her gaze shying away from mine and fixating on the large rip at the collar of the black hoodie I'm wearing.

"Nice hoodie," she teases, trying to fight back a smile.

Surprisingly, almost as if mesmerized, her hand reaches up, her finger lightly tracing my collarbone through the rip, making goose bumps blossom across my skin.

Any hint of a smile left on her face vanishes as I take a step closer, my chest brushing against hers. I hear her soft gasp as I plant my hands on her waist, drawing her that much closer.

With no space left between us, she lifts her chin to look up at me, and I swear I can feel her heart pounding against mine.

God I want to kiss her. But not with her parents and Cora right downstairs.

"We should probably go downstairs," she whispers, as if reading my mind.

I nod in agreement, but neither one of us moves.

I lift my hand to cup her cheek, my thumb stroking the soft skin. Her eyes flutter shut, as if savoring the moment, and I do the same. The need to be impossibly closer to her has me leaning forward and pressing my forehead to hers, yearning to be trapped in this moment for as long as possible.

But when I hear the floor creak outside her door as someone walks by, I finally force myself to pull away and take a step back. Reaching for her hand, I lead her down the stairs to the living room, where her parents and Cora are already in their pajamas and picking out a movie.

Olivia and I take a seat on the couch and toss a blanket over ourselves, and she surprises me yet again when she curls her legs under her and hesitantly rests her head on my shoulder.

After a moment she tips her head back, looking up at me questioning if it's okay. Instead of replying verbally, I grab her hand under the blanket and thread our fingers together, jerking my chin in the direction of the TV. When her gaze finally lands on the screen, I take the opportunity to tilt my head, resting my cheek on the top of her head, and she snuggles into me as the movie plays.

TWENTY-FIVE

Brutal

The week back after Thanksgiving break is brutal. Everyone is walking around like zombies, probably still hungover from the holiday, but most of all, they're dreading the next three weeks.

The few short weeks leading up to finals are utter hell. Kids are running around like chickens with their heads cut off, some of them crying or jitterier than an addict from running solely on caffeine, and most look like pure death. Everyone is already so worn down from the semester, and they've all gotten a taste of what the month-long Christmas break is going to be like, so there's no turning back now. We're all just trying to push through these next three weeks to survive and keep our sanity, but the professors are ruthless.

As if cramming a semester's worth of material into one final test isn't gruesome enough, some even tack on last-minute projects and papers like it's no big deal. They act as if they're asking you to just add one extra item to your grocery list.

Aside from stress and pure mental exhaustion, finals are usually the time of year everyone starts getting sick. From Thanksgiving to Christmas, every year without fail, campus seems to be the breeding ground for the plague since everyone's immune system is depleted due to stress.

Wednesday afternoon, I stroll into the science building for lab. I walk down the hall and round the corner to find Olivia standing outside our classroom, talking to Delilah.

My steps falter a bit as I take in her appearance. Her skin is pale and her eyes are tired as she tries to focus on what Delilah's saying. She looks so worn down and fragile, like she's sick.

At this point I wouldn't doubt it, with the time of the year and with the number of times she was out in the cold for extended periods this past week. Aside from the ice storm and walking to and from class, she also sat out in the cold with her dad the Saturday after Thanksgiving to watch me play.

Walking closer, I can see the dark circles under her eyes, which are a dull brown, not their usual warm honey color. She's blinking slowly and heavily, her breathing labored as she struggles to keep her eyes open. Her face seems to grow paler, and she sways.

As if in a movie, time slows to an antagonizing speed as I watch Olivia's legs buckle beneath her. Without a second thought, I take off, running full force toward her. It feels like I'm running from yards away to reach her, when in reality, it's probably less than thirty feet.

Just as she's about to hit the floor, I dive, somehow managing to catch her and break most of her fall.

I hear Delilah scream, interrupting the movie-like trance, and everything snaps back to regular speed so fast it gives me whiplash.

With shaky hands, my heart thumping wilder than it ever has on any field during a game, I gather Olivia up in my arms. I barely hear the commotion from everyone around us, and everything happens in such a blur that I don't even realize I'm rushing her to Chase's truck, Delilah hot on my heels.

"Ohmygod, ohmygod, ohmygod," Delilah repeats. "What happened?"

Olivia makes a small groaning noise, and I look down at her in my arms. Her eyes slowly flutter halfway open as she comes to, looking disoriented.

"Olivia?" My voice sounds strange.

"What happened?" she asks.

"I was going to ask you the same thing."

I get to Chase's truck and get Delilah to grab the keys out of my backpack and open the door. I gently place Olivia in the passenger seat.

"Are you all right?" I ask, my eyes scanning her for any serious injuries. I brush some hair out of her face as she blinks, trying to regain her bearings.

"Yeah, I'm okay," she says uncertainly, her hand coming up to lightly rub her forehead. "Just tired." I notice the rasp in her voice, the strain of it. She also sounds a bit nasally, like her nose is stuffed up.

"You scared the shit out of me," Delilah says, pressing her hand to her heart. "I've never seen someone just drop like that."

"Let's get you to the hospital and get you checked out," I murmur, buckling her in.

A look of fear flashes across her face. "It's okay, guys. I'm fine. Really."

Delilah and I glance at each other, as if to say *Yeah, right.*

"Better to be safe than sorry," Delilah tries to persuade her.

"Yeah, Finch. You really scared the hell out of both of us," I admit.

She scans my face, and my expression must say it all, because she slowly nods, agreeing.

Delilah offers to stay back to let Tracy know why we aren't there and to fill us in on what we're going to miss in lab today. I take Olivia to the emergency room, and they get her back into a room fairly quickly to take her vitals and begin some standard testing.

Olivia allows me to go back into the room with her after the nurse and doctor check her out. Once they step out to go evaluate her tests and I step in, Cora rushes through the door, looking frantic.

"Olivia," she says, shocked and breathless. "Baby, what happened?" She walks over to Olivia's bed, gently grabbing her face in her hands as her wide, worried eyes scan Olivia head to toe. "I saw your name on the board and came running as fast as I could."

"I'm okay, Cora," Olivia assures her, filling her in on what happened.

Cora frowns, her eyes darting to the monitors Olivia is hooked up to, reading her vitals.

"We just had dinner last night. You seemed fine other than a stuffy nose," she mutters to herself, trying to figure out what went wrong.

Cora runs through taking Olivia's vitals again. She takes her temperature and blood pressure and pulls out her stethoscope to check her heart and breathing. In my opinion, she seems to go over the top with it, doing unnecessary and excessive nurse-y type things. But what do I know.

Once Cora is done with her own personal examination, the doctor steps back into the room with her clipboard.

"Miss McCausland." She hugs the clipboard to her chest. "Good news. As far as your tests go, everything looks fairly normal. Other than some dehydration and signs of a common cold, everything looks fine."

Olivia pinches her brows together. "Then why would I pass out?"

The doctor purses her lips in thought. "It could be because of the dehydration. Have you been getting enough sleep lately? How are your stress levels?"

Olivia shrugs. "I guess I haven't been getting much sleep with finals coming up and the stuffy nose—not being able to breathe at night. Then, finals and medical school application deadlines probably have my stress levels up, more so than normal," she admits sheepishly.

The doctor gives her a sympathetic and knowing smile. "Ah, I remember those days. Well, we're just going to give you some fluids to help you feel better. Then I want you to go home and get some rest. The combination of the cold, dehydration, stress, and exhaustion are probably what did you in. Before you leave, I'm going to write you an excuse slip for your classes tomorrow. Stay home and get some rest," she instructs.

I knew Olivia was stressed about finals, about keeping her 4.0 GPA for medical school—even though she could probably fail all of her finals and still manage to get an A in all of her classes—but I didn't know it was this bad.

Over the weekend, she had already started cracking down on her books instead of soaking up her last few days of break. I didn't think much of it. I just thought it was Olivia being Olivia, getting a few hours of studying in a day, but now I wonder just how hard she's been pushing herself. Not to mention she's been working ruthlessly on her med school applications too.

With a friendly smile, the doctor exits the room, and Cora gets working on Olivia's IV. As soon as Olivia gets the bag of fluids, the door opens and both of her parents rush in, looking panicked.

"Olivia," they say in unison, hurrying to her bedside.

"Are you okay?" her mother says worriedly, checking her over.

"I'm fine," Olivia says.

Cora steps in. "Why don't we go grab some coffee and let her rest for a minute. I'll fill you guys in."

Her parents nod, and at the same time I manage to catch their eyes.

"Bronx." Her dad smiles, eyes lighting up with recognition. He comes over to give me a pat on the shoulder. "Thanks for bring her in."

"Yes," her mother says, sounding relieved. "Thank you." The sincerity in her voice and the look in her eyes makes me feel like I'm some big hero or something.

"It was no problem," I assure them. "I just wanted to make sure she's okay."

Her dad gives me a nod of approval. "Thank you. Would you mind staying with her for a few more minutes while we run to grab some coffee? I can bring you back something," he offers.

I shake my head, stuffing my hands in the pockets of my jeans. "Nah, I'm good. Thank you, though. I'll stay with her for as long as you need."

He gives me an appreciative smile before he, his wife, and Cora leave the room and walk down the hall to the cafeteria.

I glance at Olivia, who is struggling to keep her eyes open. She looks so tired and fragile hooked up to all the monitors and with an IV in her arm. Walking over to her, I take a seat on the edge of the bed.

"You don't have to stay," she tells me. "I know you have football practice later."

"I'm not going anywhere," I assure her softly, placing my hand on top of hers, mindful of the pulse reader on her finger. "Get some rest, Finch."

As if she finally has permission to sleep, her eyes flutter closed, her long lashes resting on the tops of her cheeks. I watch as her breathing evens out and her body relaxes and becomes heavy with sleep.

A little while later her parents and Cora come back to the room. We all wait for her IV to finish and for the doctor to write her an excuse slip before she's discharged. I insist on following her parents home and carry her up the stairs to her bedroom, tucking her in for the rest of the night.

After football practice I take a quick shower and rush out of the locker room, not wanting to linger and bullshit around with the guys like usual. Instead, I hop in Chase's truck and drive to Olivia's house.

When I arrive and throw the truck in Park across the street, its past ten thirty. All the lights in the house are off, so I assume her parents are asleep.

Quietly, I get out of the truck and close the door, then walk around to the back of the house. I look up at her bedroom window and find a light on in her room.

With an annoyed huff, I look at the tree next to her house skeptically, not believing what I'm about to do.

"I thought this shit only happened in movies," I mutter to myself, struggling to climb the tree.

Finally, I manage to make it to the roof and walk over to her window. I peek inside the room, noticing the lamp bathing the room with a dim, warm glow. I find Olivia at her desk instead of in her bed, her computer screen on, illuminating her face as she stares at it intently.

Sharp and quick, I rap my knuckle on her window. She jumps at the sound, spinning around in her desk chair, her wide eyes locking with mine. Placing a hand on her chest, as if willing her heart to slow down, she scrambles up from her chair and comes over to the window, opening it.

"What are you doing here?" she whisper-shouts, the shock evident on her face.

I reach my hand through her window and place it on her waist, gently moving her out of the way. Contorting my body, I manage to get my large frame through the window and practically tumble into her bedroom.

I shut the window behind me to keep the cold from seeping in and straighten out my clothes before facing her. I try my best to throw her a stern glare and be mad at her, but it's nearly impossible when her big brown eyes are looking up at me guiltily. It also doesn't help that her hair is thrown up in a messy bun and she's in her plaid pajama pants and my hoodie, looking so soft and vulnerable.

"Finch." My voice comes out huskier than I intend it to. I swallow thickly. "Why aren't you asleep?"

She worries her bottom lip between her teeth, giving a small shrug. "I couldn't sleep."

She turns and crosses her room to sit back down in her desk chair, bringing her knees up to her chest. Hugging her arms around her legs, she rests her chin on her knees, looking up at me in a way that makes my heart melt.

I walk over to her, the computer screen catching my eye. I scan the page pulled up and realize it's one of her med school applications. Leaning in and reaching my arm around her, I grab the mouse and scroll through the application. "Is this what's been keeping you up?"

"Part of it," she admits sheepishly, unfolding her legs and turning around to face her computer.

I sigh, minimizing the screen. Sinking to my knees, I swivel her around to face me, placing my hands on her thighs. "Finch, you literally just got home from the hospital. You shouldn't be worrying about this right now."

She frowns. More like pouts. "But it's due in almost four weeks."

I tuck my lips in, trying to refrain from laughing. "Baby, exactly, you still have four weeks," I remind her gently.

I watch as her cheeks redden, and she shyly looks away. It's then I realized I slipped up and called her *baby*.

She clears her throat, not meeting my gaze. "But between studying for finals, all the extra assignments, teaching Professor Cooper's lab, tu—"

"Shh," I cut her off. I frame her face with my hands, her soft cheeks squishing together a bit, making her look utterly adorable. "Finch, you have time. You got this. You could literally fail all of your finals and maintain your 4.0."

She frowns. "That's not true, and it's not like I'm not going to try. Plus, it looks better to submit your applications early."

"Well, how much of it have you done?" I ask, curious. I'm honestly surprised she hasn't turned them in already.

"They're all almost done, I'm just trying to perfect my essays. I'm scared they're not good enough."

"Finch," I sigh, running my hands from her cheeks down to her shoulders. "You are the smartest person I know. Any medical school would be completely stupid not to accept you."

I watch a hint of a smile tug at her lips.

"How about this, once you feel better, I'll go over your essays with you and we can get these applications off your plate," I offer.

She looks at me wearily. "No, it's okay. The topics are stupid anyway. I'd be embarrassed to have anyone read them."

"Really? What are the topics?"

She shrugs. "Most of them focus on explaining your biggest life struggles and what shaped you into the person you are today. The typical clichéd and impossibly hard and evasive questions."

I nod, wishing I could relate to help her more. But since I'm gunning for the NFL, I'm not looking to enter any master's programs. My college application days are well over. "Well, if you need me, I'm here."

She gives me a small, appreciative smile. "Thanks, Bronx."

"Anytime," I say, standing. I extend my hand to her. "Now let's get you to bed."

Reluctantly, she grabs my hand and stands from her chair. I walk her to her bed and flip down the covers, taking off my shoes and crawling in first. She stands at the edge of the bed, looking at me skeptically.

"Come on, Finch. I don't bite." I chuckle, patting the space next to me in her queen-size bed.

"You're staying the night?"

"Probably not the whole night, but just long enough to make sure you actually go to bed."

"Bronx." The slight whine in her voice tells me she's about to argue with me.

"I'm not going anywhere until you get in this bed," I tell her with finality.

She huffs, jutting out her bottom lip in a disapproving pout. Regardless, she crawls into bed with me, laying her head on my chest.

"Get some rest, Finch," I say, stroking her hair, her signature vanilla scent surrounding me like a warm blanket.

She snuggles into my chest and closes her eyes. She falls asleep quickly, but I wait an hour to make sure she stays asleep, her breathing deep and even.

Watching her sleep, I realize, is the best fucking thing in the world. She looks so soft and peaceful, and the little snores from her stuffed-up nose are surprisingly adorable.

Reluctantly, when the clock strikes midnight, I slowly move out from under her and crawl out of bed, being extremely careful not to wake her. I'd stay the night with her in a heartbeat, but I'm not sure how her parents would feel about finding me in her bed the next morning. I feel like I'm in a really good place with them right now, and I don't want to fuck that up.

Before I leave I make sure she's comfortable and situated one last time. Kissing her forehead, I turn off her bedside lamp and slip on my shoes before climbing out the window and heading back to Chase's truck.

TWENTY-SIX

Nap

Friday morning, I walk down the hall of the science building after my biology class. I pass the room where Olivia teaches Professor Cooper's lab and instinctively look inside, stopping in my tracks when I spot her.

The classroom is empty as she sits on top of the front lab bench cross-legged, consumed by the binder resting on her lap as she munches on a granola bar. She must have just finished teaching her class—even though I told her she should stay home another day to rest. But a part of me knew she wouldn't listen.

Thankfully, she followed doctor's orders yesterday and stayed home. Delilah and I made sure of it with Mission: Make Sure Olivia Doesn't Dare Step Foot on Campus. We made a pact that if either of us saw her in any of her classes yesterday we'd send her ass right back home to rest.

Frowning, I walk into the classroom, and she looks up at me from her binder, giving me a half smile, half grimace. She knows my stance on her coming to classes today.

"I thought you were skipping today?" I say, coming to stand in front of her. I rest my hands on the counter on each side of her, bracketing her legs.

"I was going to, but the other TA said she couldn't fill in for me.

I couldn't just leave the class hanging this close to finals," she explains.

"So what I'm hearing are excuses," I say, a teasing lilt to my voice. "Did you talk to Professor Cooper about it?"

"No, I didn't want to bother her," she says lamely, refusing to meet my gaze because she knows it's a bad excuse, and that I'm not going to let her off that easily.

"Finch," I groan, exasperated.

I gently grab her chin, making her tilt her head up to look at me. I examine her face; her soft features are livelier than they were the other day. The bags under her eyes have noticeably reduced and she has more color to her complexion, but I can tell she's still not 100 percent. Looking at her, getting lost in her eyes, I almost forget what I'm mad at her for. Almost.

"You have to take care of yourself," I remind her. "I'm sure Professor Cooper could have scrounged up another TA to teach in your place."

"But—"

"No buts," I cut her off.

I hear a slight crinkling noise and look down to spot the granola bar in her hand. I pluck it from her grasp, finding the generic honey and oats bar only half eaten.

"What's this?" I ask, flashing her the wrapper.

"Uh, breakfast?" she says, confused.

I lean to my left and spot the trash can on the floor at the end of the lab bench, and toss the granola bar inside.

"Hey," Olivia whines, a cute little pout forming on her face.

"Come on, Finch," I say, leaning over to grab her backpack. "You need real breakfast, not that junk."

I grab the binder in her lap and pack it away inside her bag. Despite her protests I pick her up off the counter and set her on her feet before grabbing her hand and leading her to the truck.

>> <<

"Thank you, Bronx," I tease, melodramatically mimicking a high-pitched female voice before stuffing my mouth with a bite of pancakes.

Olivia purses her lips together, trying her best not to laugh. She picks up a grape from her fruit bowl and throws it at me from across the table.

I manage to catch the tiny fruit deftly, and pop it into my mouth as soon as I do.

Olivia's jaw drops in amused astonishment. "You're unbelievable," she mutters under her breath, shaking her head.

"Thank you." I smirk, causing her to roll her eyes.

Currently, we're sitting at Patricia's Pancake House, a small local favorite among the college crowd. Especially when you're hungover. Not that I would know anything about that. . . . Nope. Not at all.

Patricia's is about a five-minute drive from campus and actually has really good food. Better than anything served on campus anyway. Hence why I brought Olivia here.

"Are you sure you don't want anything else?" I ask, pointing with my fork at her measly waffle, fruit cup, and yogurt.

She giggles, shaking her head. "I'm good. I'm not a massive football player," she teases, eyeing my full plate of pancakes, bacon, sausage, ham, eggs, and toast.

I place a hand to my chest in mock offense. "Are you calling me fat? At least I don't eat like a bird, *Finch*," I joke.

She scowls at me, snatching a strip of bacon from my plate and munching on it. "Excuse me for watching my cholesterol levels."

I laugh. "Like you need to. Hey, when's your next class?"

She looks at her watch, frowning. "Eleven."

"What class is it?"

She swallows her last bite of bacon, looking anything but enthusiastic. "Art appreciation."

"You're skipping, right?" I ask.

"No, why would I?" she asks, serious.

"You can't be serious. It's an elective you can totally afford to skip. I took it three semesters ago and all the professor did was drone on and on about art pieces. I maybe showed up to class ten times total the whole semester and still passed. The final is an essay, writing about a piece you've gone over during the semester and bullshitting what it's about and what it's supposed to represent. *I* passed the class. *Me*, Finch. If I can pass it, you sure as hell can."

"You sure endorse skipping, don't you?" She smirks.

"Come take a nap with me instead."

She blinks, surprised. "What?"

"Skip and come take a nap with me," I repeat, hoping she'll say yes.

"I don't know . . ." She trails off.

"Come on, we can take an hour nap, and both make it to our one-o'clock classes. Then I'll meet back up with you for a quick lunch and we can go to English," I say, trying my best to persuade her. "Please." I give her my best puppy dog eyes, turning on the charm full throttle.

She worries her bottom lip, contemplating.

"You know the doctor filled out that excuse slip for two days, right?" I say, trying to sway her. "So if you're really feeling that guilty about skipping class, you can email the professor that you have an excuse. Not that he's going to care anyway. No offense."

She lets out a sigh, seemingly coming to a conclusion. "Fine."

"Yes!" I cheer, throwing my fists up in the air triumphantly, causing her to giggle. "Patricia, give me the check, its nap time!" I call, a huge grin on my face.

After finishing up our food and paying the check, Olivia and I hop into the truck and drive back to campus. I lead her to my room, glad to find it semi-clean, given this was unplanned.

"Let me take your bag," I say, reaching for her backpack.

She hands it over and I place it on the floor next to mine by my desk. We both toe off our shoes at the same time, and I climb into my bed first, gesturing for her to follow. She shyly climbs in, having to snuggle close to me in the small, twin-size bed.

"Is this okay?" I ask as soon as she seems to get comfortable, her head resting on my chest. I pull the covers up to her chin, making sure she's warm.

"Yeah," she says softly. "Is it okay for you?" She tilts her head up, her eyes meeting mine.

"Perfect," I admit, stroking her hair and running my hand down her back.

I catch the smile on her lips before she snuggles farther into my chest and closes her eyes.

My heart melts before surprisingly racing in my chest in realization.

Olivia is the first girl in my bed.

Granted, we're both fully clothed and only napping, but still. I've never had a girl in my personal bed before. And she's the only girl I've ever even let into my room at all.

I let everything digest for a moment, a dozen emotions swirling around in my stomach, and I come to the realization that it all feels so strangely intimate, but ultimately, it feels so right. Having her fall asleep on my chest is without a doubt one of the top-three all-time best feelings I've ever experienced. Maybe even number one, if I'm being honest.

It takes about fifteen minutes for her to fall asleep, and as soon as she does, I feel myself start to drift off.

As soon as I'm about to slip into unconsciousness, I hear a key slide into the lock and the door opens, Chase's stupid blond head stumbling in.

"Dude, you'll never believe—"

"Shhh," I cut him off sharply.

"Sorry," he says, voice dripping with sarcasm as he throws his hands up in mock surrender. When he finally looks at me, his eyes snap open wide in shock. "Wait, who the hell is that?" he asks, coming closer and weaving his head in different directions, trying to get a better look.

"Shhh," I reiterate harshly, his tone still too loud for my liking. At this rate he's going to wake her up.

"Dude, is that Olivia?" he whisper-shouts, his jaw dropped.

"Yes," I hiss. "Now get out!"

"Okay, okay," he says, hands up in surrender again as he backs away to the door. He opens the door, slowly walking out backward. "Is she naked?" he asks, an amused lilt in his voice.

I grab the half-empty water bottle on my nightstand and chuck it at him. Unfortunately, he closes the door just in time and the plastic smashes against the wood, the water sloshing around inside, causing a lot of noise.

The door opens back up, and Chase sticks his hand in, flashing a thumbs-up. "Get it! Have fun and don't forget protection!" I hear his muffled voice from behind the door, and even though he can't see me, I flip him off.

Olivia stirs and I freeze, praying she doesn't wake up.

She adjusts, snuggling closer into my side, and I finally let out a sigh of relief when her breathing evens out once more and I know she's back asleep.

I maybe get twenty minutes of solid sleep before my alarm goes off. Olivia and I both startle, and I quickly fumble for my phone, silencing it.

Olivia sits up, rubbing the sleep from her eyes. She looks around for a moment, getting her bearings before twisting around to look down at me.

I can't help but smile, taking in her sleep-puffed cheeks and her slightly ruffled hair.

"Hi," I rasp out, running my fingers through my own hair. I stretch, lacing my fingers behind my head.

I watch her eyes drift down to the small sliver of my stomach showing, my shirt hiking up a bit after my stretch. “Hi,” she squeaks.

I can’t help but grin, loving that I have at least some sort of effect on her.

“Do we have to go to class?” I whine, wishing we could stay here all day.

She blinks, clearing her head. “Don’t you think we’ve already skipped enough classes for the day?” she asks, amused.

“No.”

She laughs and climbs off my bed, making it feel oddly empty. “We have to turn in our rough drafts for Hobb’s class today, remember?” she says, straightening out her clothes and throwing her long caramel-colored hair up into a ponytail.

“More like rough, rough draft,” I admit, sitting up.

She throws me a look that says *Really?* while putting on her shoes.

I only shrug, climbing out of bed, stretching again. “All right, Miss Goody-Two-shoes, I guess we’re going to class.” I huff dramatically and slip on my shoes.

We both grab our things and head to our respective classes, meeting up for lunch after.

TWENTY-SEVEN

Finally

Monday afternoon, after our English class, Olivia and I head to the library to study. When we enter, we're shocked by the number of people inside. The library is packed, people hustling and bustling about with large stacks of books in their arms, the volume in the usually quiet building louder than normal.

I glance at the corner table where we normally study only to find it occupied. Scanning the room, I realize *all* the tables are occupied with students who have their noses buried deep in their books and notes. Some are highlighting profusely while others chug from Styrofoam coffee cups every few seconds, blinking rapidly to stay focused.

This place looks like utter hell.

"Whoa," Olivia breathes, eyes still scanning the room for a place to sit besides the floor.

"Welcome to finals," I mumble. "Aka Hell Week."

She shakes her head, baffled. "We could see if there's any space in the science building lounges. Maybe even in the business building?" she suggests.

I shake my head, knowing everyone else probably came to the same conclusion. "Everywhere on campus is sure to be packed," I say, trying to think of an alternative. We could go somewhere off campus, but I don't know how beneficial that would be. I'd probably lose focus pretty quickly. "We could go back to my room," I offer.

Her eyes widen a fraction in surprise. "We could . . ." She trails off, but I can tell she's trying to think of another alternative. "But what about Chase?"

I wave my hand dismissively. "He's going to the Delta Psi Beta party tonight, so he won't be back until way after midnight. If he even comes back at all."

She looks at me skeptically. "A frat party? On a Monday night?"

"What can I say. Some people just have their priorities straight."

She shakes her head in disbelief.

"And you're not going to said party?" she asks, a teasing smile playing on her lips.

Admittedly, in the past I probably would have gone to that party and gotten absolutely trashed. Delta Psi Beta's parties right *before* finals are legendary—not to mention a great stress reliever. In the moment, at least. The hangovers are pretty fucking brutal, though, which is why they always throw it the week before finals. We all may not be the brightest, but we're not totally stupid enough to show up to finals hungover.

"Me?" I place a hand to my chest, flashing her a feigned look of innocence. "Never. Plus, why would I go to a dumb frat party when I can spend time with my favorite girl instead? Even if it is to just study."

She rolls her eyes but I catch the blush creeping up on her cheeks. "Fine, we'll study in your room. But no fooling around," she instructs, jutting a stern finger in my direction.

Fooling around.

I hadn't thought about it until now. Well, I have—undeniably—but I actually wasn't thinking about it currently when suggesting we go back to my room to study. And now I'm definitely not thinking about it as innocently as she is.

"Whatever you say, Finch," I say, flashing her a playful grin.

She shoots me an exasperated look before leading the way to the exit. We leave the busy library and head back into the cold. On the walk over to my dorm, I try to stay close to her, huddling together for warmth. Since last week, Olivia has been much better. Her sinuses have cleared and she seems back to her old self, but I don't want to risk her getting sick again.

Halfway to the dorm I feel my phone vibrate in my pocket. Pulling it out, I glance at the screen and see a number I don't recognize. It's out of state, and I worry that it may be a football scout trying to get in contact with me.

I glance at Olivia, finding her already staring at me. "Sorry, I should probably take this," I say, giving her an apologetic look.

She waves her hand dismissively, telling me to answer it. She pulls away, putting over a foot of distance between us as we walk, politely trying to give me a fraction of privacy.

I step closer, closing the gap between us, not caring if she hears my conversation, before answering my phone. "Hello?"

"'Bout time you answered my call." An annoyed, raspy, chain smoker–like voice comes through the line, making my blood run cold.

Caught off guard, I stop in my tracks. Olivia jerks to a halt a couple of steps in front of me, sensing something is wrong. She looks at me over her shoulder, a look of concern on her face.

"What do you want?" I ask, my voice cold.

"Grandma is sick," my mother says, as if the news is some sort of new revelation.

"She's been sick for years," I spit, wondering where she's going with this. Why she's really calling me.

My grandma has been stuck in a nursing home for over ten years now due to declining health. Admittedly, my grandma and I never had a very close relationship, solely because of my mother. I would only see her once every blue moon, sometimes when there was a holiday, or when my mother was sober enough to remember to show up to a family function.

When I was a baby, my teenage mom pushed me off on my grandma most of the time. Hell, she practically forced the woman to take care of me, sneaking out of the house to go get trashed, leaving me with her. My grandma finally had enough of her and her out-of-control drug addiction, and kicked her out.

While my grandma didn't want me to be stuck with my mother, she couldn't keep me either. I guess I can't blame her for not taking me in. I wouldn't want to be stuck with a baby, either, after I thought I was done raising my own kids and my health was starting to decline.

At least she seemed to care about me, though. Just because she couldn't take care of me herself didn't mean she didn't try to find me a good home on her own. But when all of my family members and the friends she trusted declined to take me in, she had no other choice than to put me in foster care. She figured it was a lot better than being with my mother, who could put me in danger or overdose herself any second. That was the first time I went into the system.

I've kept in touch with my grandmother minimally over the years. Not so much after I became an adult. The last time I talked to her was probably over four years ago, and her dementia was pretty bad. She didn't even remember my name.

"Well, she's really sick now," my mother says almost blandly. "They say this will be her last Christmas, and she really wants to see you."

Bullshit.

The last time we spoke she hardly remembered who I was. There's no way in hell she personally requested that I come see her. This is just a gateway for my mother to get me to Florida to see if she can snag any cash from me.

"I'm busy," I say through a clenched jaw, my patience wearing thin.

"Too busy to come see your dying grandmother?" she asks, trying to manipulate me, making my blood boil.

"I'll see," I say sharply, and hang up the phone, not wanting to deal with her anymore. I know this is all just a game to her. She couldn't really care less if my grandmother is dying, especially since my grandmother left her out of her will, and my mother sure as hell doesn't call me for anything important. She only calls if she needs something.

Not even ten seconds after hanging up, the same number calls back and I instantly hit Decline. I turn off my phone and shove it into my pocket, not wanting to deal with it.

Blood boiling, I look up and see Olivia's concerned face. I instantly snap back to reality. I'd forgotten where I was and what we were doing, spiraling in my anger.

She approaches me slowly, cautiously. "Hey, you okay?"

I look deep into her warm brown eyes, seeking comfort. Letting out a long exhale through my nose, I loosen my shoulders, my muscles taut from stress. "Yeah, I'm good," I say, my voice rough.

She frowns, seeing through my lie, but her eyes are patient.

Those damn eyes, they get me every time.

Usually I'm a very reserved person. I'm not a big talker, especially when it comes to personal things, but when it comes to Olivia, all I can seem to do is talk. It's almost scary how much I've told her in comparison to anyone else. But those eyes: big, warm, innocent, patient, inviting; they make me feel safe. Like I actually want to open up.

I let out another exhale, my hand coming up to cup the back of my neck. "That was my mom."

Her eyes widen in surprise. "What did she say?"

I shake my head. "Nothing important."

I can tell that's not the answer she's looking for just by the look on her face, but her eyes are still patient, breaking me.

I swipe a hand down my face, rubbing my jaw. "My grandma's sick."

Her eyes fill with worry and sympathy. "Bronx—"

I cut her off, saving her from a pity speech by waving my hand dismissively. "She's been sick for years. It's nothing new," I inform her, my anger suddenly prickling again. "My mom says she wants me to come visit her for Christmas, but it's just a ploy to get me to come to Florida. My grandma has dementia, and the last time I spoke to her she barely knew who I was, so I know my mom is just trying to get me down there to see if I'll give her cash or something. Like she always does," I scoff bitterly.

She frowns, nodding in understanding. "But do you want to go see your grandmother for the holiday?"

"No," I answer honestly.

I see the disappointment in her eyes, and I realize how harsh that must have sounded.

"We were never close," I explain gently, grabbing her hand, hoping she doesn't think of me as some kind of monster. "I only saw or spoke to her once every couple of years."

"Oh." I see the sadness behind her eyes. "When was the last time you saw your grandma?"

"Not since middle school," I admit, inwardly cringing at how awful it must sound. "But I've talked to her on the phone a handful of times since."

"Is she in Florida?"

"Yeah."

A silence falls over us and I can tell she's in her head about the subject, and the longer we stand here I feel myself start to brood. She doesn't deserve that. She doesn't deserve my shitty mood after another family issue. Again.

"Hey, let's forget about this, yeah?" I ask, desperate to change the topic and the mood. "Let's just go back to my room and study."

She nods, but I can tell she's still distant, thinking.

Hand still in mine, I lead her across campus to the dorm. When we walk through the doors, Brennen instantly looks up from his phone behind the front desk, his feet kicked up as he leans back in the desk chair.

"Miller!" he greets me, his eyes landing on Olivia's hand in mine before lifting to her face. "McCausland!" He beams. "What are you two up to?" he asks, sitting up straight in his chair.

"Just going to go study, man," I say, hoping he doesn't keep us long.

"Study? In your room?" he asks, raising a curious brow because he knows I don't bring girls to my room.

"Yep, it is getting close to finals," I say, straining to keep it casual, wishing he didn't have to sound like that to tip Olivia off.

A slow, seemingly knowing grin spreads across his face. "Ah. Well, you two kids have fun," he drawls suggestively.

I mentally face palm, dragging Olivia past Brennen and down the hall to my room.

Reluctantly letting go of Olivia's hand, I grab my keys from my pocket and unlock the door. I hold it open and let her step in first.

She steps through the door and heads straight for my desk. Shrugging off her backpack and her coat, she sets her bag on the floor and hangs her coat on the back of the desk chair. She pulls out all of her study materials, laying them neatly on the desktop before taking a seat in my desk chair.

A heavy, uncomfortable feeling rests on my shoulders but I ignore it, shaking the feeling off with my backpack and coat. Again, she doesn't deserve my shitty mood. She already had to put up with me the last time, and she's taking time out of her busy week to study with me.

I toss my backpack and coat at the foot of my bed, and hop onto the firm mattress, which lets out a loud whine under my weight. Shimmying up to the headboard, I lean my back against it, lacing my fingers behind my head.

Olivia looks at me skeptically, and I can't help but grin. "Come sit up here, Finch," I instruct, patting the space in front of me.

"Do you really think that's the best place to study?"

"Yes."

She gives me a doubtful look.

I lean over and snatch her binder full of notes, holding it hostage to bait her.

"Hey!"

She stands, trying to grab her binder back, but I hold it tightly.

"Bronx!" She tries to sound stern, but she laughs. "Give it back!"

"Uh-uh." I grin.

She places her knee on my mattress to gain leverage, trying to reach above my head, but she can't. Lunging forward, trying to snatch the binder back, she manages to grab the corner of it but loses her balance and falls forward on top of me, her face inches from mine.

We both freeze, eyes locking.

She slowly pulls away, sitting back on her knees.

"Looks like it worked," I say, breaking the silence. "Guess we're studying here." I grin victoriously.

She blinks slowly, clearing her head before glaring at me. She snatches her binder back, huffing playfully before sitting back and crossing her legs, sitting in front of me. "And what did I say about funny business?" she mutters under her breath sarcastically.

Opening her binder and setting it in her lap, she flips through her notes, deciding where to start.

Feeling playful, I grab her crisscrossed calves and pull her closer until our knees knock together.

She lets out a little shriek, gasping. "Bronx," she says, a hint of warning in her tone.

"There. Better." I smile.

She gives me a look before glancing back down at her notes. "Okay, so I was thinking . . ." She trails off, tabbing off pages. "We can go over these sections today for lab. I can list off a few bones and you can tell me where they're generally located."

She looks up at me through her lashes for confirmation.

"Sure. Sounds good." I lace my hands back together behind my head, getting comfortable.

We study for about ten minutes, her listing off bones and me pointing them out on my own body. Until I get bored.

Suddenly, a brilliant but semi-dangerous idea comes to my head.

"Acromion," Olivia says.

Feeling bold, I lean forward, pressing my lips to the end of her shoulder.

She softly gasps, eyes wide. "Bronx, what are you doing?" she asks, a slight waver in her voice.

I shrug, confident. "I was right, wasn't I?" I ask innocently.

"Yes," she sputters adorably, clearly flustered.

I watch her throat work on a swallow as she fidgets, nervously tucking a strand of hair behind her ear. "Patella," she says, refusing to look up from her notes.

I grin, leaning forward to place a kiss to her bent-up jean-clad knee.

"Lunate," she squeaks.

Gently grabbing her hand, I pull it toward me to place a delicate kiss to the top of her wrist.

"Humerus." Her voice turns softer, breathier.

I kiss her upper arm.

"Clavicle."

I kiss her sweater-covered collarbone.

"Sternocleidomastoid."

I pause, a grin forming on my face. Leaning forward, I let my lips brush against the side of her neck. "That's not even a bone, Finch," I rasp against her skin, pressing an open-mouthed kiss there anyway.

She takes in a sharp breath, her hand landing on my knee.

"Jaw."

I skim my lips upward, lightly nipping at her jawbone, seeing where she's going with this.

"Auricular lobe."

Moving my lips higher, I lightly flick my tongue over the skin just under her ear before kissing her earlobe.

She shudders, her voice coming out shaky. "Buccal."

Slowly, torturously, I skim my lips to her soft cheek, placing a soft kiss there. "Where next, Finch?"

She pulls back an inch, those brown eyes locking on mine, hazed over. Her eyes drift down to my lips for a brief moment, then she looks at me with uncertainty and fascination.

"Say it, Finch," I urge her softly, desperately.

I lean in until the tips of our noses are touching, our lips inches apart. I lean in farther, lingering until our lips almost brush against each other, teasing.

"Say it," I whisper, wanting her to be the one to willingly seal the gap between us.

She takes in a jagged breath, and instead of using her words, she tilts her head to the side and leans in to press her unbelievably soft lips to mine.

That's it. I'm done for. Every inch of me feels like I'm on fire.

I take her face in my hands, deepening the kiss, being mindful to be gentle with her. But, damn, is it hard not to fall all in. To kiss the absolute sense out of her. Devour her. But instead I take it slow, savoring the feeling of her lips on mine. Because I'll be damned if I scare her off too quickly.

This isn't like any other kiss I've had before, and Olivia is definitely not like any other girl I've kissed before.

Before I get too carried away, I slow the pace, pecking her lips before pulling away, smiling.

Opening my eyes, I watch her beautiful ones flutter open, her lips twitching up as her cheeks turn an adorable shade of pink.

"Finally," I sigh, resting my forehead against hers.

TWENTY-EIGHT

Trust Me

I walk into the science building feeling like I'm floating on air, smiling cheek to cheek. Everyone who walks past me must sense my good mood—during the week before finals, of all times—and gives me long, sideways glances.

When I enter the lecture hall, my eyes automatically land on Olivia's face. Her attention is focused on Delilah, but it only takes her a few moments to sense my gaze, her eyes finding mine.

She smiles shyly, blushing adorably.

The grin on my face widens.

Taking the stairs two at a time, I jog up to our row and stand beside her. She tilts her head back to look up at me, the long, smooth lines of her neck on full display. Her eyes lock on mine, a hint of questioning and longing set deep within them.

Gladly, without hesitation, I lean down and plant my lips on hers in a short but meaningful kiss. When I pull away, she's blushing madly, the smile on her face matching mine.

"Hi," I whisper, pecking her lips once more before shrugging off my backpack and taking my seat. "What are you blushing for?" I tease, resting my hand on her thigh.

Her blush deepens and she shyly looks away, shrugging. "Nothing."

Grinning, I lean in, pressing my forehead to hers. "Is it because I get to kiss you now? Whenever I want," I whisper lowly.

"Maybe," she whispers, a playful edge to her tone. "That and the fact that everyone is staring."

I furrow my brow, pulling back to glance around the classroom to find people gawking at us. Especially Delilah.

Delilah's face over Olivia's shoulder is almost comical. Her eyes are wide behind her thick-rimmed glasses, jaw practically on the floor. I try my best not to laugh.

"Wha—you and you . . ." she sputters, trying to digest it all, her eyes shifting between me and Olivia rapidly. "You didn't tell me!" she bursts out, her angry, accusing eyes homing in on Olivia.

Olivia cringes. "We just got here, and you were talking about debate club!" she tries to defend herself.

"Debate club, sh-mate club! This is way more important!" Delilah insists, sitting forward, thoroughly interested. "Tell. Me. Everything."

Olivia looks back at me with uncertainty. I nod, giving her full permission to give her best friend the details. She starts off slow, Delilah hanging on her every word, but then they both turn into giddy schoolgirls, smiling and talking excitedly, animatedly, all the while trying to keep their voices down, making me chuckle.

Not long after, Rat Boy walks in with that seemingly permanent scowl on his face, his dark hair doing nothing for his pale skin, which is only getting whiter with winter. He walks up to our row, quirking a brow at the excited shrieking before taking his seat next to Delilah. "What are you two going on about?"

"Olivia's got a boyfriend," Delilah says in a singsong voice.

I watch as a dozen different emotions scroll across his ratlike face. He starts with shock and eventually lands on rage. "Who?" he asks sharply, miserably failing to leash his emotions. I think he already knows the answer to his question, his beady little eyes snapping to me and my hand resting on Olivia's thigh.

While Olivia and I never fully established our relationship status as boyfriend and girlfriend, I have to admit it has a nice ring to it. I've never had a girlfriend before, never wanted one, and I'm surprised when no alarms go off in my head and my stomach doesn't twist uncomfortably at the thought. In fact, I feel pretty damn good—excited—about it. And I'm definitely getting satisfaction out of Rat Boy knowing our unconfirmed but basically confirmed status. At least he finally has some color to his face. Red, but whatever.

"Seriously, Olivia. You and this guy?" he spits, prickling my anger.

Olivia jerks her head back in surprise at his hostility, a hint of shock and annoyance pulling on her features. "What about it?"

He huffs out a humorless laugh. "You do know you can count the number of girls he's slept with on this campus on your fingers at least five times over, right?"

I watch Olivia's face fall, and I remove my hand from her thigh, balling both of my hands into tight fists.

"Why don't you shut the fuck up, you jealous little prick," I say through gritted teeth.

"I'm just looking out for her," he insists.

"No, you're not." Olivia speaks up, turning her gaze to him. "You're suffocating me, Quinton," she confesses. "I feel like I have to constantly walk on eggshells around you because I know you still have feelings for me that I told you I don't reciprocate. I thought you could get past it, that you could accept it, and we could actually be friends, but clearly that isn't the case."

"What are you saying?" he demands, alarmed.

"I'm saying, it's probably best we don't try to be friends anymore," she says, her tone almost sad, but her intent clear.

His face twists in shock and anger, his complexion turning an unflattering shade of red. He balls his hands into fists and abruptly stands. Delilah shifts closer to Olivia to get out of his way as he snatches up his backpack, flinging it over his shoulder before storming out of the classroom, causing a scene.

A low, hushed murmur falls over the lecture hall, all eyes on our row.

I watch Olivia uncomfortably sink into her chair, folding into herself, clearly mortified by all the attention.

I glance at Delilah, who has her gaze on Olivia, frowning in pity. Her eyes shift up to meet mine and she gives me a helpless look, not knowing what to do.

"Hey," I say softly, scooting closer to Olivia and taking her hand in mine, rubbing circles into her palm with my thumb. "You okay?"

She nods, refusing to lift her gaze.

Delilah rubs her hand up and down Olivia's arm to comfort her. "I'm proud of you, Liv. Deep down, you know it's for the best. You can't feel bad for telling him how it is."

"I know," Olivia sighs.

"Finch." I lean in closer, tucking some of the hair curtaining her face behind her ear. "Look at me." Lightly grabbing her chin, I turn her face toward me.

When she gazes at me, it feels like a sucker punch straight to the gut. She looks conflicted, and it has me worried that it's not just about her guilt over her fight with Rat Boy, but about what she thinks of me after what he said.

I wish I could say the words that came out of his mouth about me were completely untrue, but I have had more than my fair share of random hookups throughout the years. I used to brag about them not too long ago, but I feel ashamed now.

I know she's probably overanalyzing his words about my crude past, but I pray she doesn't think she's just another girl I'm trying to get with.

She's so far from that. All the other girls, I wanted them in the moment. But Olivia, I want her for the long haul.

"I'm sorry." The words fall thick from my lips, loaded.

I'm sorry this happened. I'm sorry he lashed out at you. I'm sorry for my past. I'm sorry I didn't find you sooner. I'm sorry for coming into your life, probably making it more complicated than it already was. I'm sorry for wanting you even though I don't deserve you. I'm sorry for falling for you even though I know I'm not good enough for you. I'm sorry for all of it. Everything.

As she looks at the expression on my face, staring into my eyes, I watch her face drop with an emotion I can't quite decipher.

Surprising me, she leans forward and places a soft, lingering kiss on my cheek.

"It's okay," she whispers, her small voice packed with meaning.

I bring her hand up to my lips, pressing them to the back of it. "Are you sure?"

She nods, a small but genuine smile gracing her lips.

I let out a sigh of relief, the weight lifting off my shoulders just as our professor walks in and stands at the front of the room, gaining everyone's attention.

"Good afternoon, class. As I'm sure you all know, finals are next week. For this class you will have a final for both lecture and lab. The final for lecture will be held next Tuesday at regular class time and your lab final will be based on your lab section, so please refer to the university website for the scheduled times.

"Now, I know it's a lot to have a final for both lab and lecture," the professor continues, "so I'm willing to compromise. For the lab portion, since it's a lot of memorization, I want you to work with your partner and take the final as a pair. You two will have to count on each other, so make sure to study wisely. Your best bet is to split the memorization up fifty-fifty."

The room bursts into a mix of emotions at the news. Some are thrilled while others are annoyed or uneasy at the thought. Me, I'm pretty stoked.

I glance at Olivia to find her expression blank, making me somewhat uneasy.

For me, this is great, getting to work with the smartest girl in the class. I guess you could call it an unfair advantage for me and a disadvantage for her, since I'm admittedly not the brightest student. But that doesn't mean I'm going to make her carry all the weight. I'm willing to split the work evenly.

"Hey." I gently nudge her side with my elbow. "We got this," I assure her. "I got this."

She gives me a small, tight-lipped smile, turning her attention to our professor as lecture begins.

After lecture, Olivia, Delilah, and I pack up our things and head out of the lecture hall. Walking through the building, I hesitantly grab Olivia's hand, lacing our fingers together.

She glances down at our hands, a smile playing on her lips.

I've never been one to engage in PDA. The few times I have, it was in the spirit of meaningless fun or to tease, like making out in a dark corner of a crowded frat party and getting handsy. But now it's to actually show affection. To proudly claim my feelings for one girl in particular.

Holding Olivia's hand feels different from the other times before. It feels secure, confident, easy. I've never held a girl's hand, unless you count the times Adrianna would possessively grab my hand, dragging me along, trying to declare some sort of relationship. But now all I want to do is hold Olivia's hand or touch her in some way. I used to make fun of guys who would practically hang off of their girlfriends or act like if they weren't touching them, they'd die. Now I'm starting to understand.

As we walk outside and down the sidewalk, I dread the upcoming fork where we'll have to go our separate ways to our next class.

Olivia stops her conversation with Delilah as we make it to the fork and stops at the same time I do, turning to face me.

"I'll see you later," I say, leaning in to place a quick kiss to her lips. "Study in my room tonight?"

"Your room?" I hear an all-too-familiar voice ask, appalled.

I turn my head to find a pair of piercing green eyes gawking at us, envy blazing behind them.

"Your room?" she repeats, as if it's some kind of joke.

I clench my jaw, mentally counting to three, willing patience. "Mind your own business, Adrianna."

She barks out a humorless laugh. "Seriously? Is this some sort of sick game you're trying to play? After all we've been through, you're acting like this is suddenly something special?" She eyes Olivia and me up and down skeptically.

"Watch it," I warn her softly.

A malicious smirk plays on her lips, and her eyes lock with Olivia's. "Careful, sweetheart. He only wants one thing. Trust me."

With that, Adrianna turns and walks away, her long raven hair swishing back and forth behind her.

"Hell hath no fury like a woman scorned," Delilah mutters under her breath, possibly almost as annoyed as I am.

I exhale long and hard, my breath visible, mingling with the cold air. I gently grab Olivia's face in my hands, pleading with my eyes. "Finch, don't listen to her, okay? I just, I—"

She turns her head, placing a delicate kiss to the inside of my wrist. "I get it. She's your Quinton."

I smile sadly, remembering the day in the cafeteria when I told her that. It was the first time we had lunch together. I was copying her notes and asked if Rat Boy was her boyfriend after he acted so possessive over her. Then she asked me about Adrianna, and I explained to her that Adrianna was like my Rat Boy.

"I'll see you later," she promises, walking away to her next class with Delilah.

I watch them go, Delilah throwing me a sympathetic look over her shoulder that says she'll talk to Olivia, mildly putting me at ease.

I swear, every time something good happens something always has to come along and fuck it up for me.

TWENTY-NINE

Only You

I walk into my dorm room and see a sight for sore eyes. Olivia is sitting on my bed, propped up against the headboard. She's dressed in one of my old football hoodies, absentmindedly twirling one of the drawstrings around her finger, with a pair of simple black leggings and blue socks adorning her feet. She has one of her knees bent up, propping up her binder to study from, all her other study materials sprawled out around her.

I grin, leaning against the door frame for a moment to watch her flip through her notes.

Sensing my gaze, she peers up at me, catching me staring at her. "What?" she asks, self-consciously.

My grin deepens as I push off the door frame, making sure to close the door behind me, and saunter to the end of my bed, tossing the two water bottles I just picked up from the small café down the hall to the side. I lay my hands flat on the mattress, leaning on my arms.

"Nothing," I muse, raking my eyes up her body, all the way from her sock-covered toes to the messy bun of caramel-colored locks piled on top of her head.

She flashes me a dubious look.

"Okay . . ." I drawl, lazily skimming one of my hands up the bed toward her.

Quickly, I grab hold of her ankle, pulling her down the bed toward me. She shrieks at the sudden movement, tossing the binder she's holding to the side before crashing into me. I grab her legs, wrapping them around my torso once she's perched on the edge of the bed. Giggling, she places her hands on my chest, stabilizing herself.

I grin down at her. "Maybe I'm thinking about how good you look in my bed," I admit in a low, raspy whisper.

All the laughter drains from her eyes as she draws in a sharp breath, her eyes clouding over at my confession.

But as fast as she fell into the trance, she snaps out of it, giving me a smirk that doesn't quite reach her eyes. "I'm sure I'm not the first girl you've said that to," she says, her voice light, joking, but I sense the insecurity behind it.

I frown, my shoulders slumping. Since I met back up with her after our classes, I can tell she's not fully recovered from all that happened today with Rat Boy and Adrianna. I can tell their words are still swirling around in that pretty little head of hers, no matter how hard she's trying to hide it.

"Finch," I sigh, not knowing where to start. I slide my hands up her calves, which are still wound around my waist, to her thighs, rubbing soothing circles into the soft fabric of her leggings as I try to find the right words.

I hate that she knows my past. I hate that I even have a past. And that after all these years, when I thought it wouldn't matter, it matters. Not just to her, but to me too.

"You're the first girl in my bed," I admit.

She flashes me another dubious look, her hands on my chest falling until the tips of her fingers are barely resting on my stomach. Her legs also begin to go slack, but I run my hands down them, locking her ankles back into place around my waist.

"I'm serious. You're actually the only girl I've ever let into my room," I confess softly, suddenly nervous.

A small frown mars her brow, telling me she doesn't quite understand.

I sigh, leaning forward and hiding my face in the crook of her neck, embarrassed. "I've never brought a girl back here," I mumble against her skin. "I've never done anything with a girl in here because . . . I don't know." I huff, pulling my face from her neck, but I'm still too ashamed to look her in the eyes. "It's too personal," I admit.

After a moment of silence, I finally gain some courage to glance at her face.

I bring my hands up to gently rest on each side of her neck, my thumbs stroking the edge of her jaw as I look into her eyes. "My number-one rule has always been to never let a girl into my room, so they don't get any ideas or stay. Hell, I never even let a girl walk into my room before, just because. I broke that rule for you, though, Finch," I whisper. "Only you."

A look I can't quite decipher washes over her face.

I lick my dry lips before continuing. "I know the things said about me today aren't necessarily untrue." I cringe. "But just know that you're nothing like the other girls. Me breaking my rules for you, just know that means something," I promise. "That you mean something to me."

Her eyes grow soft, and a look of adoration mixed with appreciation graces her face. "Okay," she says softly, nodding in understanding.

I lean forward and press my forehead to hers. "I promise you, you're the only one who's mattered."

A small smile tugs at her lips and she places her hands on my forearms, her thumbs stroking back and forth. "Is that why Adrianna was so shocked?" she asks, a hint of laughter in her voice.

Reluctantly, a laugh bubbles up the back of my throat. "Yeah. She's tried on multiple occasions to get in, but . . ." I trail off, not really wanting to discuss Adrianna, or any other random hookups I've had, any further.

"Ah." She nods once, understanding.

I can tell the thought of other girls is still a sore subject for her, naturally. If she had old flames coming up to her or a notable reputation of hooking up with randoms, there's no doubt I'd be jealous as hell.

"So, are we good now?" I ask, hopeful.

She smiles genuinely. "Yeah, we're good."

"Thank god," I groan in relief, closing my eyes briefly. "Does that mean I get to kiss you now?" I smirk, leaning in and hovering my lips dangerously close to hers.

I don't miss the smirk playing on her lips as she loops her arms around my neck. "What happened to kissing me whenever you want?" she teases, quoting me from earlier today.

"You're right," I say, my lips just brushing against hers. "I can kiss you"—I lean forward all the way, nipping her bottom lip—"whenever I want."

Urgently, I crash my lips against hers, sliding my hand into her hair, threading my fingers through it. A small, approving hum comes from the back of her throat when I lightly skim my tongue across her bottom lip, spurring me on. I stand up a bit taller, causing her to tilt her head back, her jaw naturally slacking.

With one of my hands still on her neck, I use my thumb to angle her head just right and slip my tongue past her lips, inside her mouth, to brush against her own. The second my tongue touches hers, I'm a goner.

A low moan erupts from the back of my throat and Olivia pulls me closer, her hands grabbing at the back of my shirt as her legs tighten around my torso. I untangle my fingers from her hair, running my hand down her spine to that dip at the small of her back that drives me wild. Boldly, I sneak my hand under the hem of her shirt, splaying it across her warm, smooth skin, sending my brain into a fritz.

Leaning forward, I press our bodies impossibly closer, causing her to lie back as I lean over her. I kiss her over and over again, getting caught up in how good her body and lips feel against mine.

I know we should stop, or at least slow down, but I also know I'd be an idiot to stop. Unable to convince myself to, I keep kissing her, continuing to brush my lips against hers slowly, passionately, desperately.

We only manage to break apart when we hear the door rattle and fling open, Chase obnoxiously and unknowingly barging in, bringing our moment to an abrupt halt.

Olivia gasps against my mouth in surprise, pushing me away and sitting up to frantically adjust her clothes while simultaneously trying to fix her hair. Her pupils are dilated and her cheeks are flushed, while her lips are wet and rosy. She looks absolutely stunning as we both try to catch our breath, and it takes everything in me not to shove Chase out of the room right this second.

"Whoa," Chase breathes, caught off guard himself. He stands frozen in the doorway, looking at us with wide eyes.

"Ever heard of knocking, asshole?" I practically growl, staring at him over my shoulder.

Chase blinks at me, confused. "Dude, it's my room too! You never have girls over so how was I supposed to know?" he tries to defend himself.

Olivia leans forward and hides her reddening face in my chest, flustered and embarrassed by being caught making out in the middle of my room by my airhead roommate.

I wrap an arm around her, leaning down to press a kiss to the top of her head and to whisper in her ear. "See?" I say, a teasing lilt in my tone as I try to lighten the mood. "I told you you're the only girl who's ever been in my room."

She pulls back a little to look up at my face, her eyes brightening.

"Hi, Liv," Chase drawls, a knowing grin on his face as he walks past us to throw his backpack on his desk and toe his shoes off.

"Hey," she says shyly, unable to look at him.

Chase chuckles, jumping on his bed and folding his hands behind his head. "So, what were you two up to?" he asks, feigning innocence despite the mischief sparkling in his eyes.

"Studying," I bite out, giving him a warning glare that tells him to back off.

Chase hums in acknowledgment, his grin deepening. "Studying what?"

"Anatomy," I say through gritted teeth, knowing he's purposefully trying to piss me off and tease Olivia.

Chase lets out a laugh. "Well, I could definitely see that."

Olivia lets out a small groan, hiding her face behind her hands.

Annoyed, I snatch up one of the water bottles I tossed to the side earlier and chuck it at Chase. The plastic bottle flies across the room, hitting him square in the knee.

"Ow!" Chase yelps, his body nearly folding in half as he abruptly sits up. He frantically rubs a hand over his knee, trying to ease some of the pain.

"That's your patella, asshole," I mutter, referring to the knee bone I just hit.

Olivia lets out the smallest laugh, leaning forward and pressing her face to my chest.

After Chase stops whining about his knee, Olivia and I get back to studying, Chase watching over us like an authoritative parent to make sure we actually study. We study for almost two hours before she has to go home, and I walk her out to her car.

She leans back against her car door, looking at me expectantly.

Grinning, I lean down and press a chaste kiss to her lips. "I'll see you tomorrow, Finch. Good night," I whisper against her lips, leaving her with one final peck.

"Good night." She smiles, her voice just above a whisper.

She opens her car door, and before she can slip inside, I grab her wrist, remembering something that's been weighing heavily on my mind since earlier today, unable to let it go.

"Hey, about what Delilah said earlier today," I start, suddenly becoming nervous. "The whole boyfriend thing . . . is that—do you . . ." I cup my hand around the back of my neck, struggling to find the right words to say. "Is that something you're interested in?"

Her lips twitch up at the corners, her eyes laughing at my humility. "Is that something *you're* interested in?" she counters.

"Yeah," I admit through a *whoosh*ed breath, relieved she doesn't seem repulsed by the idea. I take a step forward, resting my forearm on the top of her open car door, caging her in between it and the car. "So, it's official?" I ask, hopeful.

"I don't know, you haven't asked me properly yet," she teases.

I take another step forward so that our bodies are almost touching. Bringing my hand up, I rest it on her cheek, looking down into her warm brown eyes. "Olivia McCausland, will you officially be my girlfriend?"

She smiles up at me, eyes bright. "Yes."

I lean down, pressing my lips to hers once more as we both smile into the kiss. It's slow, soft, playful, and it takes everything inside of me to finally pull away and let her leave.

When I walk back into my dorm room, Chase peers at me from his bed with an amused look.

"What?" I spit, trying to pretend to be annoyed to hide the huge-ass smile that threatens to break out across my face. I peel off my shirt and rummage through my drawers for some new clothes to change into after my shower.

"So you and Olivia, huh?" he asks with mirth. "It's serious?"

I bite the inside of my cheek, doing my best to act neutral. "Yeah, I guess," I say with a causal shrug. I try to downplay it, only because if Chase knew how serious I was about her I'd never hear the end of it. All I'd hear all day are comments about being pussy-whipped or going soft.

His grin tells me that he can see right through me, but he surprisingly refrains from telling me verbally. "She's a good one, man. Don't fuck it up."

God, I hope not.

I give him an appreciative nod and grab my towel and shower caddy, finally letting my smile break free as soon as I step into the solitude of the empty hall.

THIRTY

Punished

After nearly a semester of anatomy lab, the lingering stench of formaldehyde doesn't bother me as much anymore. It's become familiar as I step into the small classroom and walk over to my table, where my girlfriend has her back to me.

Delilah looks up and sees me, a knowing smirk on her face. Olivia probably filled her in earlier this morning about our new official relationship status.

Slowly, quietly, I sneak up behind Olivia, leaning over her shoulder to smack an unexpected kiss on her cheek. She jumps, mildly startled.

Twisting at the waist, she looks back to see my grinning face, a grin breaking out across her own.

"Hi, girlfriend," I murmur, leaning down to plant a proper kiss on her mouth.

"Hi," she responds, a cute little blush spreading across her cheeks. I don't know if I'll ever get over how adorably shy she gets when I show her affection.

I shrug off my backpack and jacket before taking my seat, reaching over and grabbing the leg of Olivia's chair. Dragging her closer to me,

I drape my arm over the back of her chair and place another kiss to the side of her head, causing her to giggle and shake her head, amused at my likely overkill of affection. But I can't help it. It's like everything inside of me itches to be near her, to touch her.

"All right, you two lovebirds are so cute I want to throw up in my mouth," Delilah sarcastically jokes.

Olivia's cheeks burn red in embarrassment as she shrinks in her chair, and I can't stop beaming. I glance at Delilah, and she gives me a secret smile, letting me know she's happy for her best friend—and amused by her agony.

For the first time I glance across our table to find Rat Boy not there, giving me a sense of relief. After he stormed out of class yesterday like a child, I figured he wouldn't show up to lab today, especially since it's just a review session for the final. He probably thinks he's too good, too smart, to even show up and go over any of the material.

Tracy walks into the classroom, winded, carrying stacks of papers. She sets them on her desk and walks over to the computer, booting it up while smoothing out her hair, which has fallen out of her haphazard bun. I guess the week leading up to finals is taking its toll on her as a grad student *and* as a TA.

Watching Tracy, I accidentally catch a pair of envious green eyes.

Adrianna scowls at me—or at Olivia, rather—her arms tightly folded over her chest. I can tell she's analyzing every little thing, scrutinizing. Wondering where she went wrong in her attempt to get us to end up together. Wondering what makes Olivia so special or what game I'm trying to play.

"All right, everyone," Tracy cuts in, getting everyone's attention. Adrianna's eyes reluctantly peel away from my direction. "As you know, the final for this lab section is next week on Wednesday at eight a.m.," Tracy announces, causing a couple of students to groan at the reminder. "I know it's way earlier than our normal time," she cuts in, "but just think, at least you're getting it over with first thing," she finishes, trying to be optimistic.

"For today," she continues, grabbing her stack of papers and passing them out, "I've made some review sheets for you to study and a mock final for you to try out. Turn it in by the end of the class period and I'll give you a few bonus points.

"Now I know your professor has come up with the *brilliant* idea of having you take the finals in pairs," she says cynically, letting us all know she's not too keen on the idea. "So work with your partner on the mock final and figure out how you want to execute the real thing by either divvying up the sections or each studying it all and coming together. Whatever you want. Rats are in the back corner if you want to grab one to study and let me know if you have any questions."

Wordlessly, Olivia and Delilah stand up and get in line to grab a rat, leaving me at the table alone.

While waiting for them, I pull out my phone to scroll through some of my socials to distract myself from Adrianna's returning gaze, until I hear a small collision and a loud, surprised gasp.

I immediately look up to find Olivia frozen, her eyes wide and jaw slack. Taking a closer look, I see something spilled all over her light-pink sweater. A girl from Adrianna's table is standing in front of her, holding one of the trays that the cadaver rats are usually in, and I look down to see a rat at Olivia's feet.

"Oops," the girl—one of Adrianna's minions—says insincerely, giving her best grimace.

The legs of my chair screech loudly against the tile as I get up and immediately go over there.

"Seriously?" Delilah spits at the girl, her eyes narrowing and growing hard behind her glasses. "Don't you watch where you're going?"

I come up behind Olivia and wrap my arm around her to tuck her protectively into my side, getting a large whiff of formaldehyde. Looking down at her, I realize it's formaldehyde spilled down her sweater from the rat Adrianna's minion must have dropped on her.

"What's going on here?" Tracy jumps up from her chair and walks over, her eyes flicking between the four of us.

"It was an accident," Adrianna's minion insists, her overly sweet tone telling me she's lying.

I glance over at Adrianna, catching a smirk on her lips. This was no accident.

"She ran right into Olivia and spilled the tray all over her," Delilah informs Tracy, annoyed, gesturing at Olivia's soiled sweater.

Olivia grabs the front of her sweater, trying her best to pull the wet fabric away from her skin, grimacing.

"Olivia, you need to go change right away," Tracy instructs her, her voice surprisingly calm. "Do you have any extra clothes?"

A flash of worry passes in Olivia's eyes. "No."

She immediately looks at Delilah, who gives her an apologetic look, letting her know that she doesn't have any extra clothes with her either. Instantly, I whip off my hoodie and offer it to her.

"Olivia, go change in the restroom and be sure to wash your skin off thoroughly," Tracy says. "It should be fine, but if your skin starts to get red or irritated let me know immediately."

"Come on, Finch," I say, gently grabbing her arm and leading her out of the lab.

She carefully steps over the dead rat at her feet and follows me down the hall to the nearest restroom, still clutching the front of her sweater, preventing it from touching any more of her skin.

"Are you okay?" I ask, holding the ladies' restroom door open for her.

"Yeah," she mumbles. "Thankfully my sweater is pretty thick, so not much seeped through." She breezes past me, and I go to follow her inside. "What are you doing?" she asks, looking back at me, eyes wide.

"Um, coming to help you?"

She looks at me as if I have two heads. "Bronx, this is the *ladies'* room," she whisper-shouts, like it's the biggest crime of the century if I step foot inside to help her.

I try my best not to roll my eyes. "Finch, I'm just coming in to help you, people will understand. No one's even in there anyway," I point out. "Hello!" I call into the restroom, my voice echoing off the tiled walls of the small space.

Silence.

"See," I say, my point proven. "I'll even make sure to lock the main door so no one comes in."

"No, it's okay. I'll just clean up and change and you can stand outside the door to make sure no one tries to come in."

I open my mouth to argue but end up shutting it, realizing she may not be comfortable with me being around when she has to change. I think about offering to turn around when she swaps clothes to still try to help her, but decide against it, not wanting to push her or waste any more time.

"Okay," I grumble.

She gives me an appreciative smile, standing on her tiptoes to place a kiss on my cheek before slipping into the restroom. The lock to the main door clicks into place once the door is fully shut, and I lean on the wall right next to the door, my arms crossed over my chest.

In the silence of the hallway I'm able to hear the faint sound of the faucet running behind the door, water splashing as Olivia washes off the formaldehyde that touched her skin.

Standing here, I mull over what just happened, knowing this without a doubt was some sort of petty revenge instigated by Adrianna, which makes my blood boil.

It's one thing to mess with me, but there's no way I'm going to allow her to make Olivia's life a living hell at my expense. I did Adrianna wrong, not Olivia. Adrianna has another think coming if she thinks she can get away with this.

I make a mental note to talk to her later to set things straight.

Down the hall I hear a door open and close, and I peek around the corner to see Delilah walking down the hallway, her dark curls bouncing with each step.

"How is she?" she asks, walking closer.

I give a helpless shrug. "She could be better."

Delilah frowns, rounding me and the corner to push open the restroom door, only to find it locked. She knocks on it twice, her voice cutting through the wood. "Liv, it's me. Do you need any help in there?"

"No, I'm okay." Olivia's voice drifts from behind the door over the sound of the running water.

Delilah huffs in defeat and I frown, wishing she would at least let Delilah in to help her.

Delilah slumps on the other side of the door, waiting with me.

"What happened in there?" I ask, my tone hushed so Olivia doesn't hear.

"Malibu Barbie with highlights brighter than the sun totally dumped that rat on her on purpose," Delilah insists, crossing her arms tightly over her chest with a slight sneer on her face.

I scrub my hands over my face, cursing under my breath. "Fucking Adrianna."

Delilah lets out a humorless laugh, shaking her head in disgust. "Of course. The classic pretty, popular, mean girl revenge."

I sigh, unable to argue that. Not that I'm looking for excuses for Adrianna at all.

"I'm going to talk to her," I say, determined. "This is bullshit."

"Damn straight it is."

I glance over at Delilah, appreciative of how protective she over her best friend. Not to mention, she's headstrong and upfront. I'm surprised at how fond I've become of her and how we've somehow formed a bond over the semester.

The sound of running water stopping and paper towels being pulled from the dispenser make both Delilah and me perk up. A few moments later the lock on the restroom door clicks and the door opens a couple of inches, Olivia sticking her arm out.

"Hoodie, please," she asks.

I hand her my hoodie through the crack in the door. A minute later the door finally opens and Olivia walks out wearing my hoodie, the fabric hanging loosely on her thin frame. Her old clothes are carefully cradled in her hands, so that she doesn't touch any more formaldehyde, and her hair is thrown up in a high, messy ponytail.

I take a step toward her and run my hand up and down her arm. "You okay?" I ask, ducking my head to meet her eyes. My heart tightens uncomfortably in my chest when I see the dejection behind her eyes, but she tries to hide it with a soft smile.

"Yeah, I'm okay."

"Do you want to go home?" I ask, knowing she probably wants to take a real shower.

She shakes her head. "No, I'm okay," she insists. "I washed my skin at the sink for at least ten minutes so I should be fine."

"You sure?" Even Delilah presses her.

"Yes," she says, flashing us a smile that doesn't quite meet her eyes.

Delilah and I both glance at each other, coming to some sort of silent, mutual agreement to let it go for now.

I hook my arm around Olivia's shoulders and the three of us go back to the lab and take our seats.

Sitting down, I can't help but let my eyes drift over to Adrianna's table for a second, catching her and her three minions staring at us with scowls. Her green eyes sizzle with envy and her jaw ticks when she notices Olivia wearing my hoodie.

I turn back around and grab the mock final, writing *Bronx* and *Finch* at the top. That puts a genuine smile on Olivia's face.

We both glance over the skeletal figure printed out on the paper, filling in the answers where indicated, starting top, down. When we get to the scapula, I lean over and press a kiss to her shoulder blade, making her cheeks immediately burn red.

"Bronx," she scolds in a hushed tone.

I grin at her cheekily, leaning over again to press a kiss to the edge of her shoulder. "Acromion," I mumble against the fabric of the hoodie.

Her teeth sink into her bottom lip, eyes worriedly sweeping across the room to make sure no one is paying attention.

"I thought you liked studying like this," I whisper teasingly into her ear.

Playfully, she pushes me away, but I swoop right back in, hooking my arm around her waist and resting my chin on her shoulder. I whisper the answers to her, causing her to giggle whenever my breath tickles her ear.

We finish the mock final and study for a bit before heading out with Delilah. As we walk outside, a flash of raven hair walking the opposite direction catches my eye.

"Hey, baby," I cut into Olivia and Delilah's conversation. "I forgot, I have Brennen's water bottle he left at the gym this morning in my backpack. I'm going to go run to the café and give it to him," I lie.

"Okay." Olivia nods, pausing with Delilah on the sidewalk.

I lean down and press a quick kiss to her lips. "I'll catch you in English," I say, kissing the back of her hand and letting go of it before jogging in the direction I last saw Adrianna go.

Gaining sight of Adrianna again, I watch her slip into the old math building, and I follow, catching her at the bottom of the stairs.

"What the fuck?" I spit, not having the patience to exchange any sort of pleasantries, cutting right to the chase. "I hope you're happy with your little stunt back there."

She spins around, the slight smirk on her face telling me she was expecting this sort of reaction from me. "Oh, hi, Bronx," she says, her voice sugary sweet as she bats her eyelashes at me.

"Cut the shit, Adrianna."

"What are you talking about?" she asks, feigning innocence.

"Leave. Olivia. Alone," I instruct curtly.

Her eyes narrow, mask slipping. "Or what?"

My hands involuntarily ball into fists at my sides. "Or you'll regret it. Come on, Adrianna, she didn't do shit to you," I point out, roughly raking a hand through my dark hair and taking a deep, calming breath.

"I'm the one who fucked up, not her," I state, placing a hand on my chest. "I was the one who kept blurring the lines of our relationship when I should have just cut it off cold turkey. I'm sorry," I admit earnestly. "Don't fault her for my dumb mistakes."

Her eyes widen in shock at my confession before they narrow, glittering with mischief, a small smirk tugging at her lips. "So you're saying you're the one who should be punished?"

I grit my teeth. "Listen. I can handle whatever shit and twisted games you try to throw at me but leave her out of it."

She takes a step toward me, and I take one back, retreating. Her grin is sharp as she eyes me up and down, assessing. "Noted."

With that, she flicks her hair over her shoulder before turning around and heading up the stairs, leaving me with an uncomfortable feeling in the pit of my stomach.

THIRTY-ONE

Alarm

"We should really . . . get back . . . to studying," Olivia breathes between kisses, weakly trying to pull away.

"Mmm, five more minutes," I protest, running my hand up her spine to plunge my fingers in her soft, silky hair, deepening the kiss.

She giggles against my lips before a small moan escapes when my tongue slips past her lips and massages hers. With her knees planted on each side of my legs, straddling my lap, I tighten my hold on her hip, pulling her even closer. The small movement causes her to tantalizingly brush her hips against mine and I nearly combust at the contact.

Olivia gasps, breaking free of the kiss, pulling away and tilting her chin back, unintentionally giving me full access to her neck. I lean in and press my lips to the column of her throat, leaving a variety of delicate and open-mouthed kisses.

"You do know our lab final is in less than twelve hours, right?" she asks, her throat vibrating against my lips as she speaks.

"Mh-mm," I hum, still planting kisses along her neck.

"We should really be studying," she says, despite tilting her head to the side, giving me more access.

"I am," I insist. "Trachea. Hyoid bone. Mandible," I list, getting closer and closer to her lips.

Before I can reach her mouth, she grabs my chin, preventing me from going any farther. She gives me a stern look but all I can focus on is her mussed hair and kiss-swollen lips.

"We need to study," she states more sternly.

I groan dramatically. "I'm tired of studying. We've been studying nonstop all week," I point out.

It's true. All week—all month, really—we've been studying for finals. But thankfully that all ends tomorrow for me. Luckily, the majority of my finals were Monday and Tuesday, and my last one is lab tomorrow.

"Can't we have just a little bit of fun?" I plead. "At the very least I deserve some sort of reward for all the studying I've done."

She gives me a pointed look, raising a brow. "A reward?"

"Yeah."

"And what kind of reward, exactly?"

My grin is sharp as I grip her hips. "I was thinking something along the lines of you . . . right here, in my bed." Swiftly, carefully, I roll us over so she's under me, mindful of the limited space provided by the twin mattress. "Like this."

Her big eyes stare up at me, and her dark hair is splayed across my pillow. The image is so perfect I burn it into my memory to remember for a long, long time.

In awe, I lean down and seal my lips to hers, kissing down her neck, sucking on that tender sliver of flesh at the crook of her neck where her shoulder meets it.

"How did you do on the final today?" she asks, breathless.

"Wow, I love it when you talk dirty to me," I mumble sarcastically against her skin.

She giggles, playfully shoving my shoulder. "But really, how did it go?" she asks, suddenly serious, concern in her eyes.

I huff, moment over. Of course she would be thinking about that right now.

Lying down on top of her, I make sure to put most of my weight on my forearms on either side of her so I don't absolutely crush her. "It was fine." I shrug.

She looks at me skeptically.

"Seriously, Finch." I chuckle. "I think it went well. I have a pretty great tutor, you know."

That causes a smile to tug at her lips. "So does that mean I get a reward?" she asks, a glint in her eye.

I grin, hovering my lips just millimeters above hers. "What do you want?" I ask huskily.

Her teeth sink into her bottom lip as she looks at me, her eyes shifting between my eyes and my lips. "Remember when you said for the next bet I could set the wager?" she asks, nervously fingering the collar of my shirt.

"Uh-huh."

"Well, what if I said I want to go to Florida?"

I blink, surprised. "Florida?"

She nods. "Over winter break. I've never been to the beach before, and maybe we could go see your grandma."

My body stiffens.

A flash of worry crosses her face as she senses my unease. "We don't have to see her or interact with your mom whatsoever," she insists hastily.

I will my body to relax. "I don't know, Finch," I admit, still uneasy.

Her bottom lip juts out in an adorable pout. "Please? You said to come up with something crazy, something I've never done before. I want to go to the beach. With you. Seeing your grandma was just a suggestion."

I let out a sigh, contemplating. I haven't been to Florida in forever. That place doesn't hold any good memories for me, and the thought of taking her there unnerves me a little.

I have a feeling, in her head, the trip will be some sort of nostalgic bonding experience. That it will make me see where I grew up with fresh eyes and reconsider.

Looking at the hope in her eyes, I realize maybe going back won't be so bad if it's with her.

And I made her a promise, after all, that she could set the wager. I won't back out on that.

"Fine. If you get an A on the final and I get a B, we'll go to Florida," I bargain reluctantly.

A wide grin breaks across her face. "Really?" she asks excitedly, her voice rising a few octaves.

I chuckle. "Really. So you better hope you didn't flunk," I tease.

She rolls her eyes, looping her arms around my neck and drawing me closer. Gladly, I reconnect our lips and kiss her eagerly.

As we kiss, her hands slide around my shoulders, stroking down my chest to my abdomen. Electricity shoots through my veins when her hands hesitantly slip under my shirt, her cool fingers touching my bare skin, running along the planes of my stomach.

I growl at the contact, kissing her harder and grabbing her left leg, hooking it around my waist. Unable to restrain myself, I lean my weight into my pelvis, pressing it against hers. Slowly, tantalizingly, I gently rock my hips against hers.

Olivia gasps at the feeling of my arousal pressed against her, and I take advantage, slipping my tongue between her parted lips to brush against hers, loving the sweet little noises coming from the back of her throat. Her legs tighten around my hips, and she surprises me by gliding her hands around to my back, her fingers pressing into my skin, pulling me closer.

Just as I grab the collar of my shirt, ready to yank it off, an ear-piercing shriek goes off, nearly giving us both a heart attack.

We both pull away, panting heavily from the kiss and sudden surprise.

"What the hell?" I mumble, unhooking Olivia's leg from my waist and jumping off the bed, the shriek of the fire alarm persistent and deafening.

I crack open the door and stick my head out, watching the warning lights flash in the hallway with the alarm and people unenthusiastically file out of their rooms, heading outside.

I groan in agony, looking back over my shoulder to see Olivia already slipping on her shoes.

"Fucking fire drill," I mutter, grabbing the nearest hoodie and slipping it on with my shoes.

Once Olivia has her coat on, I grab her hand and lead her outside to the front parking lot where everyone else is standing, freezing their asses off.

I stand behind Olivia and pull her back against my chest, wrapping my arms around her to huddle together for warmth. Plus, her body acts as the perfect shield to hide my raging hard-on from all the surrounding spectators.

Everyone stares at the building, annoyed that there's a fire drill this late at night during finals week. Especially when it's this cold out. It's kind of cruel, really.

A few minutes later, the sound of an engine can be heard along with sirens, and a fire truck rolls up, the fire crew hopping out.

I furrow my brow. Normally, firefighters don't show up if it's just a drill. They only show up if it's a real emergency, and I don't see any flames or anyone seriously injured.

Then again, it's probably just some drunk idiot who set their microwave on fire by cooking ramen without adding water. Sadly, that's a pretty common occurrence. But who's getting that drunk during finals week?

The lights on the truck bounce off the building and cast shadows across faces as we all stand around impatiently in the parking lot, waiting to go back inside.

Out of curiosity, I fish around for my phone in my pockets, wanting to text Brennen to see what the hell is going on. He's working the front desk tonight so he probably has some sort of insight, but to my dismay, I can't find my phone. I guess I forgot it in my room.

Waiting, I catch a flash of hot pink out of the corner of my eye, and turn my head to see Adrianna standing at the other end of the parking lot, talking with one of the guys from the hockey team who lives on the floor above me. She catches my gaze and gives me a slow, wicked smirk, one that sends an uneasy chill up my spine.

Ripping my eyes away, I look back at the building to catch the fire crew walking out, the chief giving the all clear.

Like a heard of wild animals, everyone charges forward in an disorderly fashion, desperately wanting to get out of the cold. I stand firmly planted, wrapping my arms tighter around Olivia to wait it out, not wanting to get shoved around in the crowd.

Subconsciously, I keep my eyes peeled for a bright-pink coat, but it seems as if Adrianna is long gone.

When I feel it's safe enough, I lead Olivia back inside and stop at the front desk to see Brennen standing around with some officials and university staff. I catch his gaze, and he excuses himself, coming over to the edge of the desk to talk.

"What's going on?" I ask, eyeing everyone behind the desk.

Brennen shakes his head in annoyance. "Someone pulled the fire alarm."

I feel my eyebrows shoot up a fraction.

"Why would someone do that?" Olivia asks, her brows furrowed in concern.

Brennen shrugs casually. "Probably just some asshole trying to be funny. It's not going to be so funny though when they catch him and his ass ends up in some deep shit."

"Do they know who did it?" I ask.

"Nah, not yet. They're reviewing the surveillance footage now, but all they can see is some kid in a black hoodie with the hood pulled up," Brennen says, thumbing behind him.

Olivia shakes her head in disapproval, and someone behind the desk calls Brennen back over.

Saying our goodbyes, Olivia and I head back to my room.

"Now, where were we?" I say, smirking, closing the door behind me and locking it.

Thankfully, I don't have to worry about Chase barging in this time. His lucky ass finished with finals this afternoon and he headed straight home after.

Olivia gives me an amused but warning look. "Uh-uh. We have to study."

Slowly, I stalk toward her.

"Bronx," she says firmly, pointing a stern finger at me.

Abruptly, I charge her, grabbing her by the hips and pushing her onto the bed, falling on top her and straddling her hips.

"Bronx!" she squeals, giggling uncontrollably. "No!"

"Please," I whine, leaning down and peppering kisses along her neck.

She places her hands on my chest, pushing me away. "Study," she demands sternly.

I let out a huff and roll off her. "Fine. But it's not like you even need me to study anyway. You could literally ace that entire final by yourself in your sleep," I tease.

She rolls her eyes. "No, because I need my *partner* to help me since this is a *partners* final," she emphasizes, giving me a pointed look. "I'm counting on you, mister."

"*Oof*, call me *mister* again," I tease.

She grabs my pillow and smacks me in the face with it.

"All right. All right!" I grab the pillow out of her hands. "Damn. I promise you can count on me. Although, I may just need you to double-check some of my answers for me," I admit sheepishly.

For the final, we decided to split it evenly. She will memorize the top half of the skeleton while I memorize the bottom half. But I know as well as she does, she's going to memorize the whole thing to ensure we get an A. I know I should be offended that she doesn't trust me to memorize my half, but I guess I can't blame her with my less than model track record of skipping class and not getting the best grades.

Olivia gives me a softer look and grabs her study sheets. We study for about thirty minutes until she has to go home, wanting to get some quality sleep for our earlier-than-sin final.

"I'll see you tomorrow," she says as she slips on her coat, ready for me to walk her out to her car. "Remember, our final starts at eight a.m."

"Already got my alarm clock set," I assure her, gesturing to the digital clock on my nightstand. "Got my phone set too."

She gives me an appreciative look, some of the anxiety dissipating from her eyes. I can tell she's nervous about completing the final in pairs. I know if it was up to her, she'd prefer to do this solo, not having to rely on anyone. Again, I can't blame her. I know I'm a liability.

Admittedly, the old me probably would have just expected my partner to carry my ass, pass or fail. I wouldn't have cared or tried. But for her, I really want to.

"I promise, I won't let you down," I whisper, rubbing my hands up and down her arms.

After a short kiss, I walk her out to her car and watch her drive off.

Once her taillights are out of sight, I walk back to my room and get ready for bed. Crawling into bed, I double-check my alarms one last time before letting my head hit the pillow, Olivia's sweet vanilla scent clings to the pillowcase, helping me drift off to sleep.

THRITY-TWO

Down the Drain

The sunlight pouring in the window pierces my eyelids and I roll over with a groan, trying to block it out.

After a few minutes of not finding myself drifting back off to sleep, I peel my eyes open and blearily stare at the clock on my nightstand, wondering what time it is. I blink a few times, trying to make out the numbers, only to realize there's no numbers on the clock.

Alarmed, I shoot up and grab my phone to see the alarm going off with no sound. I stop it and a looming dread creeps up my spine and swarms my chest when I realize what time it is.

Fuck.

Not wanting it to be true, praying I'm stuck in some crazy nightmare, I repeatedly smack the digital clock on my nightstand, willing it to work and show an alternate time. It was working last night but appears completely dead this morning.

My eyes flash back to my phone, reading 8:42 a.m. Forty-two minutes after the lab final has started.

Nauseated, heart thumping madly in my chest, I jump out of bed and throw on my shoes. Without a second thought I race out the door without my coat or anything, only wearing my pajamas, which consist of some old sweats and a ratty T-shirt, and sprint to the science building.

Out of breath, my lungs on fire, gulping in the cold air, I force myself to push forward and race across campus as if my life depends on it. Halfway, I stumble over my feet and nearly fall flat on my face, the rough texture of concrete scraping my palms as I catch myself.

I hop right back up, pushing my legs to go faster, and eventually, after what feels like miles, I burst through the science building doors. Skidding around the corner to the anatomy lab, I stop in my tracks, spotting a group of three huddled outside the door.

Delilah and Rat Boy's backs are to me initially, each of their hands on Olivia's dejected shoulders in a comforting manor. Olivia's face is on full display, the hurt written across her face eminent, destroying me.

My less-than-subtle entrance catches their attention, my breathing rapid, chest inflating and deflating quickly as I stand frozen. Helpless.

Rat Boy looks over his shoulder at me, a hard, knowing glint in his beady little eyes, like he expected this to happen. Even Delilah's eyes are hard, cold, as they land on my face.

Olivia's eyes glance up at me and her face crumples. I nearly stumble back at the look in her eyes. The disappointment—the betrayal—in them.

Hesitantly, on wobbly legs, I take a cautious step forward.

"Finch," I say softly, a plea in my voice.

She shakes her head, tears misting her eyes.

Words clog in my throat as I take more steps toward her, my feet feeling like cinderblocks.

"Finch, I'm sorry," I whisper remorsefully, my throat unbearably tight.

She only looks at me, hurt and confusion in her brown eyes.

"Finch," I plead desperately, reaching for her. "I didn't intend for this to happen, I swear."

Reluctantly, Delilah moves out of the way, but all one hundred and twenty pounds of Rat Boy stands firmly rooted in front of her.

"Clearly she doesn't want to talk to you," he spits.

"Clearly, you need to stay the fuck out of this," I spit back venomously, shoving him out of the way.

"Finch," I say, much more gently, softer, reaching for her face.

She flinches away, like she can't bear for me to touch her, absolutely breaking my heart. "Don't," she says, her voice firm but weak.

"Finch, I swear—"

"You're lucky Tracy is nice enough to not make her take the final alone," Rat Boy cuts in, not knowing when to shut the fuck up. "Not that she needed your or anyone's help anyway."

"I told you to stay out of this," I bite out curtly over my shoulder at him.

"But at least she got to work with us. People she can *count on*," he persists, clearly provoking me. "And don't for a second think you're getting credit for *our* work."

I spin around, baring my teeth. "Shut the fuck up!"

He squares his scrawny shoulders. "You were just using her to pass the class, weren't you? You're only showing up now to make sure she took the final for you, right?" he accuses. "I always knew you were good at using girls. I just thought you only used them for sex."

White-hot rage flashes though me, and without a second thought I swing, and my fist collides with his jaw. He stumbles back, tripping over his feet. Landing flat on his ass, he yelps in surprise and pain.

"Throw my past in my face one more time," I challenge him, looming over him. "I fucking dare you."

I snatch him up by the collar of his shirt as he tries to scramble away and slam him back against the nearest wall. "She's nothing like the others," I spit dangerously, my knuckles turning white as they wrap tighter around the collar of his shirt as he squirms to get away.

The fear in his eyes gives me a sickening satisfaction, and I imagine the nice dark bruise that's going to bloom across his pale skin.

Out of pure hate and spite, I draw my arm back and punch him in the face again. And again. Something I've dreamed of doing multiple times since I met him.

"Bronx, stop!" I manage to hear Olivia over the blood roaring in my ears.

A delicate hand wraps around my bicep, and I freeze. Looking over my shoulder, I see Olivia's face filled with fear and horror. Immediately, she lets go of my arm, as if I scorched her, and takes a few steps back. She stumbles into Delilah, who catches her, wrapping a secure arm around her shoulders.

"Finch." I let go of Rat Boy and he crashes to the floor. I take a step toward her slowly, carefully, not to scare her any further.

She closes her eyes, willing the tears away, and suddenly I notice a small crowd has formed around us. Students trickling out of nearby classrooms stop and watch the show. All of a sudden, it seems like time has stopped and I'm standing outside of my own body, watching a fiery train wreck unfold.

I scan the faces of the crowd, feeling like a caged animal on full display for their pleasure. All of them anxiously waiting to see what happens next.

My eyes catch on a pair of wicked green eyes, Adrianna's mouth turning up in a satisfied smirk, making my blood run cold. Just as I'm about to confront her, a large, strong hand grips my shoulder, pulling me back to real time.

"Dude, what the fuck is going on?" Brennen asks, his eyes hard, questioning.

My eyes flash between Olivia, Delilah, and Rat Boy, who is still crumpled on the floor, a small amount of blood trickling from his nose.

"Let's go, Liv," Delilah whispers gently to her friend, pulling her toward the exit.

"Finch, wait!" I call, ready to run after her, but Brennen's hand grips my shoulder tighter.

Brennen flashes me a warning look, telling me with his eyes to let them go, but I'll be damned if I let her walk away. I shove Brennen and shoulder my way through the crowd, pushing through the doors of the science building to run after my girl.

"Finch! Olivia!" I call, running behind them, begging her to stop.

Delilah looks over her shoulder at me, flashing me a warning glare.

I stop in my tracks, my chest heaving.

No, no, no, no.

My chest seizes, and I feel like I'm losing everything. Losing her. Like my life is spiraling out of control. And the fact that Olivia won't even talk to me—will hardly look at me—I can't handle it. The look on her face; she has all the power to single-handedly destroy me.

"I love you!" The words desperately tumble out of my mouth without warning, and I instantly wait for the regret to creep in—the dire need to shove the words back into my mouth—but it doesn't.

Olivia freezes, Delilah jerking to a stop next to her.

"You know I wouldn't do that to you, Finch," I call. "You know it," I plead.

"I don't know what happened," I confess. "I swear, I had both of my alarms set! Adrianna—" I harshly scrub my hands over my face, not knowing how to explain. I know she had something to do with this, I just don't know what. "I'm sorry."

Olivia remains frozen, but she doesn't dare turn around to look at me.

"Please, Finch. You have to believe me," I say, my voice barely above a whisper.

Delilah rubs her back soothingly, whispering into her ear. After a few moments, Olivia squares her shoulders, standing up taller, and the two of them begin to walk away.

"No," I breathe, my heart shattering into a million pieces.

My eyes sting and my chest grows incredibly tight. I want to chase after her, catch her in my arms and promise everything is going to be okay, but my feet are rooted to the ground.

I watch Delilah settle Olivia into the passenger seat of her car then close the door and round the hood. She flashes me a look before she gets behind the wheel, and the two of them drive off.

A frustrated scream rips from the back of my throat. I slam my fist into the brick wall of the building repeatedly, loving the scrape of the rough texture on my skin. I only stop when Brennen finds me and locks his arms around me, pulling me away.

"Man, stop!" he yells, his grip tightening around me until I settle down.

When he loosens up enough, I push him away, storming off to the dorm. I burst into my room and grab my shower caddy, marching off to the showers. Going into a stall, I rip off my clothes and turn the water to the hottest setting, steam already looming.

I step under the hot spray, letting the scalding-hot water practically burn my skin, hoping the memories will burn with it. I let the water spray onto my cuts, savoring the sting, wanting to feel something other than the sickening acid in my stomach and the wrenching pain in my chest.

I watch the smallest amount of blood tint the water, the red liquid swirling down the drain with everything else in my life.

Scan the QR code to discover what Olivia is feeling right now.

THIRTY-THREE

Fight

I stay in the shower long after the water turns cold. Until not only my brain but my body is numb too.

When I finally find the energy, I turn off the water and dry off, slip on some new clothes, and pad back down the hall to my room. Once inside, I lean back against the door and slide down the wood, sitting on the floor and bringing my knees up to my chest.

I examine my busted-up knuckles, the cuts starting to scab over after the brutal clashing against Rat Boy's face, the brick wall, and another round of punches thrown at the tiled wall of the shower.

My eyes drift up my arms to the scars on my forearms, the burns still haunting me.

Anger bubbles up inside me again and I slam my fists down on the floor.

I hate the power these stupid scars still hold over me, no matter how much I pretend they don't. I hate the man who put them there. I hate my mother for being such a shitty parent. I hate my entire childhood. I hate being such a fuckup. I hate everything and everyone. Myself included.

Not since I was a child have I felt so confused, so lost, so broken.

All my life, people have come and gone. I got so used to it, so used to only depending on myself. No one ever cared for me—except for maybe Lexi, but I lost her too—and I learned to live with that. Learned to cope. Learned to not need anyone. To want anyone. To be alone.

But, god, do I need Olivia.

I've never cared about anyone or anything before. And I certainly never had anyone care for me, not like she has. Sure girls have been interested in me, thrown themselves at me, but they only cared about one thing. Sex. Or they saw—fantasized about—me as some project. Something they could fix to have potential and be a version of something only they could love. Something that could love them back.

With Olivia, I wasn't a challenge or a problem to be repaired. I never felt like she was trying to fix me, even though I'm beyond broken. She cared for me despite my flaws and always looked at me as if she understood. With her, I want to be better, even though I know I'll never measure up to be someone she deserves.

But I love her.

I've never loved anyone before, and it scares the absolute shit out of me. No one has ever wormed their way into my heart like she has. And she didn't even try.

From the moment I set eyes on her I knew she was special. I was hooked the second those honey-colored eyes met mine and she gave me a smile. Then I found out how smart, sweet, funny, caring—how perfect—she is.

I feel like Olivia McCausland was made for me. That she walked into my life to steal my heart, only to break it. But maybe I deserve it.

Because I don't deserve her.

Olivia and I are total opposites. She's the sweet girl next door with the perfect life and family, while I'm the angry, messed-up son of a bitch with mommy issues who couldn't keep it in his pants. But somehow we're like magnets, two polar opposites attracted to each other by force, like it or not.

I sit on the floor for hours, staring up at the popcorn ceiling until the sun starts to set, lost in my own dark, self-loathing, and pitiful thoughts.

Finally, I manage to get up to get some proper blood flow back to my body, my limbs stiff and my ass sore from sitting on the floor for so long. I scrub a hand over my face, moving down to my chest, rubbing there too. Trying to ease the pain. But the thought of losing her crashes into my mind again, making me restless.

I pace around my room, every second ticking by, making me jittery, making me long for her even more. Picking up my phone, I feel a pang of hurt in my chest when I look at the screen to find no new messages and her face as my wallpaper, smiling back at me.

Fuck this.

Determination sparks inside me, and I realize my pity party is over. If I want her, I have to fight for her.

Slipping on my jacket and shoes, I snatch the keys to my bike lying on my desk and head out to the parking lot. Putting on my helmet, I swing my leg over the motorcycle and rev the engine, then race onto the street.

The cold wind slaps my face and bites into my bare hands, but I ignore it, too fixated on where I'm going and what I'm about to do to care.

I pull into her subdivision, my engine rumbling loudly on the quiet suburban streets. My heart pounds as I approach her house and park my bike in front of the mailbox. I take off my helmet and get off the bike, staring at her front door. I glance to the left, into the living room windows to see the lights on behind the curtains; it's only a little past seven.

With a shaky breath, I walk up her driveway to the front door. To my surprise, running purely on adrenaline, I knock without hesitation, not pausing to fully collect or mentally prepare myself.

I shift my weight anxiously from foot to foot, waiting for her to answer the door. Shoving my cold hands into the pockets of my jeans, I stand off to the side so she can't peek through any of the windows to see me and dodge me.

After a few very long moments, I hear the knob rattle and the front door opens. I sidestep in front of the door to find Mr. McCausland staring back at me. His face shows his surprise to find me on his doorstep unannounced, but nonetheless, he smiles, his eyes sparkling with fondness. "Hey, Bronx. What brings you here?"

He steps back from the door frame, his body language welcoming and clearly relaxed, which I'm thankful for. I guess Olivia hasn't filled her parents in on recent events, because I have a feeling if she had, there wouldn't be any pleasantries.

Mr. McCausland isn't the type of man to threaten my life with a shotgun if I dare to hurt his daughter, but he wouldn't be pleasant either. Rightfully so, there would be some sort of resentment or hostility.

I clear my throat. "Hi, sir. Is Olivia home?"

His lips turn down into a remorseful frown. "Sorry, son. You just missed her."

My shoulders deflate. "Do you know where she went?" I ask, hoping I don't sound too desperate.

"She's going over to Cora's for dinner tonight."

I blink, racking my brain for what day it is. "But it's Wednesday."

Olivia's weekly dinners with Cora are always on Tuesdays.

He gives me a small smile. "They switched up nights so you guys could study last night for your final."

My heart squeezes at the realization that she did skip dinner with Cora last night—something she never misses—so we could study together for our lab final. But she did for me.

Fuck.

Sensing my guilt, Mr. McCausland continues. "It's okay," he assures me. "It's actually an anniversary for Cora today. So it worked out that they did dinner tonight instead."

I nod, some of my guilt subsiding. "Her and Olivia are pretty close, huh?"

He smiles fondly. "Yeah. Cora's a good family friend. Olivia and her daughter were very close."

I can sense a shift in his mood, the way his face turns solemn, smile timid.

"Oh. I didn't know Cora had a daughter."

Olivia never mentioned it. I just thought Cora was someone she met while shadowing at the hospital and that's as far as their connection ran.

He nods, hesitant. "Yeah, that's actually why Olivia is with her tonight. It's, uh—it's the anniversary of her daughter's death."

My face blanches, and my stomach knots.

He swipes his hand over his mouth uncomfortably, smoothing out his mustache afterward. "It's been a number of years since she passed, and Olivia's been helping Cora cope. It's just Cora by herself since her daughter is gone, so Olivia spends time with her frequently to make sure she doesn't get too lonely. I think she sees Olivia as a second daughter," he informs me, voice thick with emotion. There's a deep sadness in his eyes, but I also see the sparkle of adoration, how proud he is of his daughter for being that outlet for Cora.

Oh, Finch. Once again, proving why she's too good for me. Too good for anyone.

"Wow," I whisper, really not knowing what to say now.

Mr. McCausland nods and we stand in silence for a moment, him reminiscing and me absorbing this new information.

He shakes his head, seemingly clearing his thoughts before squaring his shoulders, his usual charismatic demeanor returning. "Yeah. I'm sorry you missed her, but I'll let her know you stopped by."

I shake my head. "Don't worry about it, sir. I'll just catch her tomorrow."

"You sure? I mean, you're more than welcome to come in if you want and wait for her. I'm not sure how long she'll be, she'll probably be out late, but there's a game on that I'm going to watch if you want to stay," he offers politely.

I give him an appreciative smile, respectfully declining his offer. I'm sure after the day she's had, the last thing Olivia will want to do when she gets home is to see me and hash things out. She's already had such an emotionally taxing day that I don't want to send her over the edge, ruining any sliver of a chance I may still have left with her. And I definitely don't want to seem like the domineering boyfriend who can't let her breathe, especially to her parents.

"No, thanks, Mr. McCausland. I'll catch her tomorrow," I repeat, backing away from the door. "Have a nice night."

"All right, Bronx. You too."

He watches me from the doorway as I walk down the driveway and hop on my bike.

I drive back to campus, my chest tight and mind racing a million miles an hour. While I may not have gotten what I wanted to get accomplished tonight, I know there's always tomorrow. Even if the wait kills me.

My fight isn't over yet. I'm going to fight for her with everything I have in me tomorrow morning, first thing.

THIRTY-FOUR

Know

I wake up the next morning, feeling worse than I have from any hangover I've ever had. I got a total of maybe two hours of sleep, too anxious and distressed to rest, going over and over in my head what I'm going to say to Olivia.

I check the time on my phone to see it's just past seven o'clock. I know Olivia has a final at eight for the lab she teaches for Professor Cooper so I jump out of bed and get dressed, wanting to catch her before it starts.

I wander down the halls of the science building until I reach her lab room. Peeking inside, I spot a few early bird, eager freshmen already sitting inside, going over their notes one last time. I glance at the front of the classroom to find one of them talking with Olivia.

She looks wrecked. The dark circles under her eyes tell me she's probably gotten just as much sleep as I have, and the dullness in her usually bright eyes tells me just how emotionally drained she must be after all the events that have taken place in the past twenty-four hours.

Seemingly sensing my gaze, she looks up and her eyes lock on mine. I nearly gasp at how dull and empty her expression is. At how differently she's looking at me. That usual sparkle of fondness, happiness, isn't there. It's like she's looking at me as if I'm just a ghost from her memory.

I don't miss the quick flicker of surprise, as well as the lingering pain set deep beneath the usually warm brown irises. For a moment I think I see a flash of longing in them, but that may just be wishful thinking.

She stares at me with a mix of emotions, until her attention is taken back by the freshman in front of her, asking a million questions.

With fifteen minutes remaining until the exam starts, a few more students filter in. Olivia glances up at me frequently, and eventually she excuses herself, standing up and walking across the lab to the door.

My heart reaches out for her, but my feet stay glued to the floor, unsure of whether or not to meet her halfway or have her come to me.

"Finch."

She looks at me, subtly shaking her head. She places her hand on the door, making my heart sink.

"Finch, please, let's talk," I beg.

She continues to shake her head. "Not here," she says, voice hardly above a whisper, a plea rolling off her lips.

I open my mouth and close it, as her wounded eyes beg me to leave. I know I shouldn't be doing this here, in front of her students, but I can't stand not talking to her, not seeing her. I've been going crazy not being near her, knowing nothing has been resolved between us.

"Olivia, I—" The words get caught in my throat. Everything I planned on saying to her, everything I rehearsed over and over again last night, escapes me.

Another one of her students arrives, passing between us and into the classroom. Olivia gives me one last long look before closing the door behind her, leaving it cracked open a quarter of the way for the students still making their way in. My heart breaks at the knowledge that she's physically and emotionally trying to keep me out.

It takes everything inside of me not to push through that door and hash it out with her right here, right now, but I know how distressed that would make her and how bad that would look. Not only for me, but for her if the students complained to Professor Cooper.

Completely dejected, I take a seat on the bench across the hall, watching the remainder of her class file in, the door cracking open a little wider with each body that passes through. At eight o'clock on the dot, Olivia closes the door all the way and doesn't spare me a single glance.

I hear her giving instructions for the final, her voice not as bubbly or lively as it normally is.

With a sigh, I sink back against the wall, waiting impatiently until the last student leaves the room.

I hop up from the bench and walk inside the lab to find Olivia quickly collecting papers, no doubt trying to dodge me.

"Finch, we have to talk." I walk up to where she's standing at the front lab bench.

I watch her bite the inside of her cheek, avoiding looking at me.

"Finch," I plead, unable to resist the urge to reach out for her, but she shrinks away. "Just let me explain."

"Explain what?" she asks. Her voice has a cold edge that I've never heard from her before. It's then she finally looks up at me, her eyes just as cold.

I realize in the past twenty-four hours her sadness has rolled over into anger. Rightfully so.

"I'm sorry," I begin, desperately needing her to listen to me. "I'm so, so sorry. I don't know what happened. I had both of my alarms set, I swear. They were set before you even left!" I explain, still scrambling to try to figure out what happened. "I know Adrianna had something to do with this."

I watch Olivia's face crumple, the absolute hurt resurfacing. "Why?" she asks, so softly I barely even hear her, her voice wavering as she fights back tears. "Is it because she slept in your bed that night?"

The accusation is so out of left field it feels like a hundred-mile-an-hour fastball just hit me right upside the head. "What?" I ask in a rushed, disbelieving breath.

She shakes her head again, collecting all the final exams in her arms, hugging them to her chest. She rounds the bench, trying to leave, but I stop her, moving in front of her.

"Where on earth did you get that idea?" I ask.

The tiniest scoff passes her lips. "Oh, I don't know, Bronx," she says, some of the coldness returning. "Maybe it's because she came parading into lab that morning bragging about it, and about how you wouldn't wake up no matter how hard she tried to wake you."

My jaw goes slack in shock. This is why her demeanor is so cold. Not only does she think I ditched her to take the final by herself, but she also thinks I cheated on her.

"You know I would never do that to you," I claim definitively, my voice thick with emotion.

"Do I?" she asks, tears welling in her eyes. "Tell me, Bronx, were you just using me this whole time?" Her eyes are locked on mine, begging me to tell the truth. I can see the desperation, the insecurity, the hurt behind them.

I know what Rat Boy, and others on this campus, have been whispering in her ear all this time: That I'm a scumbag who could never commit to one woman. That I'm just using her to pass the class. That she's naive enough to let me do it and believe I actually care about her.

"Of course not! Finch"—I take a step toward her and she retreats, breaking my heart—"do you really think I'd ask for you to tutor me and actually show up to every single study session if I was going to use you to just take the final for me?"

I see a flicker of something—hope?—in her eyes, and I cling to it desperately.

"I used tutoring as a gateway to spend more time with you because

I liked you, and I wanted to do better *because* of you," I admit. "The bets—why would I try so hard to get good grades if I was just going to use you in the end? If I didn't care?" I swallow past the lump in my throat. "Why would I let you be the only girl I've allowed in my room? The only one I've ever shared my past with? Why would I literally beat myself up over disappointing you?" I hold up my hands, flashing her my busted-up knuckles.

She gasps and her eyes flood with worry, her body tense like she wants to reach out and touch me, showing me that beneath her anger there's still some sort of affection for me. But she refrains from doing so.

"I'm in love with you, Olivia," I admit, feeling the most vulnerable and transparent I have ever been. "And I know I don't deserve you. I know that, but I'll be damned if I don't at least try."

The tears in her eyes spill over as she looks at me, utterly conflicted. "I wish I could believe you," she says eventually, her voice a broken whisper.

"What?" I breathe, going into utter panic mode. I feel like I'm hanging off the edge of a cliff by a rope and the rope is frayed down to a single strand. I grab her arms, begging for her to believe me. "No. I love you, Finch, and I would never purposefully do something to hurt you."

"Then why would you sleep with her?" she cries.

"I didn't," I assure her. "I swear to god I didn't. I would never do that to you. Never," I vow.

"She was wearing your hoodie!" she yells hysterically, raising her voice, something I've never heard her do.

Dumbfounded, I stumble a step backward. "It was probably an old hoodie she stole years ago," I try to reason, knowing that could be the only explanation.

Tears stream down her face, the look in her eyes shattering. She shakes her head. "It was the hoodie you wore at Thanksgiving. The black one. The one with the large rip at the left collarbone."

My face pales, my heart stopping while my mind runs a million miles a minute. How the hell could Adrianna have gotten that hoodie?

"I don't . . . I swear, this is just a big misunderstanding."

Olivia squeezes her eyes shut, as if she's in pain. "Just stop," she whispers, her voice a broken plea. "Stop lying. Stop trying to play games with me. You already basically admitted it yesterday."

"What?" I blurt, baffled.

She opens her eyes, looking right at me. "Yesterday, outside the building when you came running after me. You said her name." Her voice wobbles. "You were talking about your alarm and then you said her name. Then you paused and said you were sorry, like you were guilty."

"No, no, no." I shake my head, stepping toward her. "I was sorry for not showing up on time. For letting you down. And when I said her name, it was because I know she has something to do with my alarms not going off." I rack my brain, trying to think of a logical explanation. "She must have snuck into my room during the fire drill to mess with them and steal my hoodie."

"Then how was she outside so fast with the rest of us?" she asks. Apparently she'd noticed Adrianna outside the night of the fire drill too.

"I don't know," I choke out helplessly.

I can see it in her eyes, somewhere deep, deep down she wants to believe me, but there's too much evidence stacked against me. The negative voices of everyone else are too loud, influencing her judgment about me.

She tips her head back, trying to keep her tears at bay.

I grab her arms again, begging her to look at me. "Finch, I swear I would never do that to you. I would never be that cruel. You have to know that."

She looks at me with such vulnerability, such confusion that it completely breaks my heart, shattering it into a million pieces.

The door to the lab creaks open and Professor Cooper sticks her head in. "Olivia?" she asks, concern in her tone as she looks at the both of us—at her prized TA crying in the middle of the lab. She steps inside, looking at me skeptically. "Is everything all right?"

Olivia sniffles, quickly swiping at her tears with the sleeve of her sweater. "Yeah, Professor Cooper. Everything's fine," she says, her voice rough as she hugs the papers in her arms tightly to her chest.

Professor Cooper doesn't take her narrowed eyes off of me. "Has everyone finished taking the exam?"

"Yes," Olivia replies, shrugging out of my hold and skirting around me.

Professor Cooper holds the door open for her, shooting me one last disapproving and warning glance before slipping out of the room with Olivia.

As soon as the door closes with a soft *click*, I lose it. Beyond frustrated, feeling utterly hopeless, I kick the nearest stool, sending it toppling with a loud bang.

I feel my phone vibrate in my pocket and I grab it, glancing at the incoming call from Brennen. I hit the Ignore button and shove my phone back into my pocket, not in the mood or mental state to talk to anyone right now.

Heart pounding, I race back to my room and immediately rifle through my hamper. I tear each piece of clothing out one by one, not finding my black hoodie, which should be in there.

"Fuck," I spit, kicking the plastic hamper.

My phone keeps buzzing in my pocket, pissing me off further. I grab it and throw it at the wall out of blind anger.

Taking a seat on the edge of my bed, I try to even out my breathing and calm my nerves, but I make the mistake of glancing at my alarm clock, which is still dead, taunting me and absolutely sending me over the edge.

I pick up the dead clock and throw it as hard as I can at the back of the door with a scream.

Restless, breathing heavy, I snatch my keys and pick up my phone from the floor, ignoring the large crack in the screen. I hop on my bike and race five minutes down the road to an all-too-familiar apartment complex.

My tires squeal when I slam on the brakes, fishtailing a bit as I haphazardly pull into the nearest parking spot. I jump off my bike and march up to Adrianna's door, pounding my fist against the wood.

Nothing.

I pound again persistently until the door flies open, revealing an annoyed and tired-looking Adrianna.

Once her eyes land on me, some of the annoyance disappears, replaced by amusement.

"Hey, Bronx," she says with smugness in her voice, leaning against the door frame in her pajamas. "Long time no chitchat."

"How the fuck did you get my hoodie?" I practically growl.

"Whatever do you mean?" she ask, feigning innocence.

I clench my jaw, not in the fucking mood to play games with her. "You pulled the fire alarm and snuck into my room, didn't you?" I accuse her.

"No," she says simply, eerily calm and nonchalant.

"Do you think I'm fucking stupid, Adrianna?" I seethe. "I know it was you who pulled the fire alarm and messed with my alarms."

"Do you really think *I'm* that stupid, Bronx?" she says, her voice condescending. "Pulling a fire alarm can get you expelled if you're caught. But I guess some people aren't smart enough to know that. I'm honestly kind of surprised you haven't figured it out yet."

Something in her tone makes me very uneasy.

"What the fuck is that supposed to mean?"

She lets out the tiniest noise of indifference. "Have a good break, Bronx. See you next semester."

She pushes herself off the door and shuts it in my face, leaving me dumbfounded and fuming.

Not even ten seconds later, my phone vibrates with another incoming call from Brennen.

"What?" I snap, finally picking up his call.

"They know who pulled the fire alarm."

THIRTY-FIVE

On My Way

"What?"

"Yeah, they were able to trace more surveillance footage around campus and track down who it was," Brennen informs me.

"Was it Adrianna?" I ask, eager to find out if she's bluffing or not.

"Not quite," he says, voice hesitant. "I was talking to her at the front desk when the alarm went off. She came waltzing in with that guy from the hockey team who lives on the second floor and started talking to me as if we were long-lost friends. I thought it was odd, but I figured it was just some game she was trying to play to make him jealous or something. We talked for about five minutes until the alarm went off and everyone had to evacuate."

"So wait, if it wasn't her then who . . ." I trail off, racking my brain. Because my second guess would have been that she got the hockey player to pull it, but it seems as though he was with her the whole time she was talking to Brennen.

"You know that scrawny kid Olivia and Delilah hang out with?"

My blood runs cold, every muscle in my body tensing.

"They found out this morning that he pulled it," he continues when I don't say anything. "It took a while, but they finally pulled enough footage from the other security cameras around campus to catch him in one of the parking lots twenty minutes prior, talking to Adrianna with his hood down.

"It looks like they were working together, except he did most of the dirty work. They actually ran into the guy from the hockey team, and he was their way into the dorm. He used his key to get them inside, and then Adrianna dragged him over to the front desk, pulling both of us into a conversation so that nerdy kid could sneak behind the desk while I was distracted and go into the back room to steal the master key."

"Fucking rat bastard," I mutter, raking a hand harshly through my dark hair.

"From there he snuck back out and pulled the fire alarm. When almost everyone was out, cameras caught him using the key to get into your room for about three minutes, then carrying something out in his arms. Have you noticed anything missing?"

"My fucking hoodie," I seethe. "The fucking asshole messed with my alarms, making me late for my final the next morning, and he gave that hoodie to Adrianna to make it look like I slept with her."

All this time, all this fucking time, the little rat was right under my nose, and I didn't even see it.

"Shit," Brennen curses under his breath. "Well, campus security should be contacting you soon to see if you want to give a statement and possibly press charges."

"The fuck I do," I reply. There's no way I'm letting him get away with this. I know he's going to get into a lot of trouble with the school anyway, but he deserves everything coming to him and then some for not only fucking up my life, but messing with Olivia too.

"Hey, man, thanks for letting me know," I say, feeling slightly guilty for dodging all his calls and snapping at him when I finally answered.

"No problem. I'll keep you updated. Do—"

I hang up and run back to my bike, not wasting any time. I kick-start the engine and speed down the road, adrenaline coursing through my veins. I pull into Olivia's driveway and run to her front door, knocking three times.

Mr. McCausland opens the door again, a smile on his face. "Pleasure to see you here again, Bronx. Let me guess, you're here to see me," he teases with a knowing grin.

I try my best to be polite and give him a laugh, hoping it doesn't sound too forced or strangled. "Actually, sir, I'm here to see your daughter."

His smile turns apologetic. "I'm sorry, Bronx, she's not home right now. My best guess is that she's either at Delilah's or still at school."

I refrain myself from muttering out a curse, and scratch at the light dusting of stubble on my jaw from not shaving for a couple of days. "All right, thank you, Mr. McCausland." I slowly inch toward my bike, wanting to leave, and he gives me another knowing smile.

"I'll let her know you stopped by again," he says, bidding me goodbye, sensing I don't have time for small talk.

"Thank you, sir," I call over my shoulder, jogging to my bike and speeding off again.

I decide to swing by Delilah's first to hopefully save me some time. It's in the opposite direction of campus, past Olivia's house, so I head that way, praying I know which apartment complex it is. I've never been to Delilah's apartment, but from what I've gathered, it's just a few minutes down the road from Olivia's home.

I pull into the parking lot of the first apartment complex I see, knowing it's one of the more popular apartment complexes among college students. If I remember correctly, Delilah said she lived here. Now if only I knew which apartment she lived in.

With nothing to lose, I walk into the office building at the front, where an older woman greets me unenthusiastically.

"May I help you?"

I throw her my most charming smile, leaning against her desk on my elbow. "Hi, ma'am. Do you by chance know what apartment number Delilah Harper is in?"

She looks at me skeptically, a scowl forming on her thin lips. "I'm not sure I can give you that information."

"Please," I beg, giving her my best puppy dog pout. "I'm actually her cousin from across state here to see her. We haven't seen each other in forever and I'd love to surprise her," I lie.

She looks at me long and hard, but eventually she huffs and starts typing on her computer. I suppress a triumphant grin, buzzing with impatience and nervousness.

"She's apartment B11," she tells me, as if it was a big chore.

"Thank you."

I exit the office and run up the stairs two at a time to the second floor, muttering Delilah's apartment number over and over again to myself until I find her door. I knock as calmly as I can, despite my heart slamming against my rib cage.

Delilah opens the door, looking at me with a distrusting scowl. "May I help you?" Her voice is cold, colder than the lady downstairs when she uttered the same words.

"Is she here?" I ask breathlessly, looking over her shoulder to see if I can spot Olivia perched somewhere in her living room or kitchen.

Delilah stands her ground, blocking the doorway, refusing to let me inside. She crosses her arms over her chest. "She's not here."

"Come on, Dee," I beg.

She squares her shoulders, uncompromising. "She's not here," she insists. "You can even check the parking lot for her car."

I look over my shoulder to scan the cars in the parking lot, not finding hers. I let out a low curse, turning around to see Delilah's door closing in my face.

"Wait!" I plead, placing my palm on the wood to stop it from closing. "Do you know where she is?"

"I don't think she wants to talk to you. And quite frankly, I don't want to either."

I grit my teeth, losing my patience. "Come on, Delilah. I would never do that to her! Adrianna and Rat Boy, they set me up."

She looks at me skeptically, interest piqued. "What do you mean?" she asks slowly.

"Adrianna and Quinton," I clarify. "They staged the whole thing! Brennen just called me, and they have surveillance footage of Quinton pulling the fire alarm and sneaking into my room. He messed with my alarms and stole my hoodie to give it to Adrianna."

Delilah's eyes widen, her demeanor completely flipping. "To make it look like you slept with her," Delilah says under her breath, more so to herself. I see the gears turning in her head, watch as she puts all the pieces together. "Oh my god!" She gasps, covering her mouth with her hand. "Olivia!"

She spins around and sprints down the hall, presumably to her bedroom. I step inside, not thinking she cares anymore if I come inside or not, no longer the enemy. A short time later, Delilah reemerges, her phone pressed to her ear as she anxiously chews at her bottom lip, pacing back and forth across her small kitchen.

"Come on," she mutters impatiently under her breath. "Liv?" She perks up, voice rushed and relieved.

Without thinking, I walk over to Delilah and take the phone from her, pressing it up to my own ear. "Olivia?"

"Bronx," she says, her voice surprisingly breathless, desperate.

"Finch." I close my eyes, soaking in the sound of her voice, relief washing over me. "Baby, I—"

"I know," she cuts me off, tears in her voice. "I know. I just found out. Brennen told me."

All the tightness in my chest evaporates and I feel like I can finally breathe easy again. "He did?" I ask, surprised.

"Yeah, he called me about thirty minutes ago. I've been trying to call you since then," she informs me.

I furrow my brow, fishing my phone out of my back pocket to find it dead. After not charging it all night and all of Brennen's previous calls and texts, I shouldn't be surprised.

I curse under my breath. "I'm so sorry, my phone must have died. I've been everywhere looking for you."

A choked laugh comes from the back of her throat through her tears. "I guess that's why I'm talking to you on Delilah's phone?" she asks with slight amusement.

"Yeah." I unexpectedly laugh with her. "Your dad said you would either be here or at school. I stopped here first."

"My dad?" she asks, the surprise evident in her voice.

I swallow thickly, nervous again. "Yeah, I stopped by your house again to see if you were home."

There's a pause before she replies, "I'm actually outside your dorm room. I thought you left for the break." She whispers the last part.

I feel my heart squeeze in my chest, knowing we've been chasing after each other all along and that she thought I'd leave without resolving things.

"No, baby. No," I assure her, wishing I was there right this second to hold her. "Stay right where you are, I'm on my way," I promise.

THIRTY-SIX

Everything

My heart nearly beats out of my chest when I spot Olivia, right where she said she'd be. She's still in the same clothes from this morning, a pair of jeans with a dark-blue sweater, her ponytail swishing behind her as she paces in front of my door, nervously biting at the nail of her index finger.

Spinning around, she stops in her tracks as her eyes meet mine. Her shoulders drop, hands falling to her sides. She looks nervous, uncertain, but also relieved.

I take a step toward her, the feet between us feeling like miles. "Finch," I breathe.

Tears mist her eyes as her bottom lip quivers. "Bronx," she whispers, my name caught in her throat. "I'm sorry."

I shake my head. "Don't be sorry."

I don't need apologies. All I need is her.

From the look on her face, I know how sorry she is. How confused and hurt she was, thinking I purposefully ditched her and cheated on her. With all the evidence stacked against me, and my reputation, I know it was hard for her to believe me, but I always knew beneath the surface she clung to hope that I wasn't that guy anymore. That I loved her.

But I don't want to think about that any longer. Right now, all I want to do is hold her.

I extend my hand to her. "Come here."

More than willing, she walks toward me, and I meet her halfway in three long strides, gathering her in my arms. I hold her tightly, her arms looping around my waist, holding me just as tight. Her soft vanilla scent engulfs me, soothing me, and I feel like I can breathe again.

Her body melts against mine, and I press my lips to the top of her head, savoring the feeling of her touch. When I lean back to look at her, those warm brown eyes are already looking up at me, full of longing.

Dipping my head, I press my lips to hers, kissing her softly, slowly. I take my time with her, loving the way her lips and body feel against mine. She must feel the same way, her hands sliding up my torso to my chest, one landing on my cheek while the other reaches the collar of my shirt, fingers curling inside, fisting the fabric and pulling me that much closer.

I let my tongue skim across her bottom lip and dip inside her mouth to sweep across her own, tasting her. She sighs in contentment but pulls away from the kiss, catching her breath.

I furrow my brow, afraid I moved too fast, scaring her off, but the thumb of her hand still resting on my cheek glides back and forth, soothing.

"Let's go inside," she whispers, and I'm suddenly aware that we're in the middle of the hallway. Not that I care—almost everyone has left for the break already—and even if there were people still lingering around, I wouldn't give a damn if they saw.

I take a deep breath, getting my head back on straight. The second I left Delilah's to the time I reached the parking lot and walked inside the dorm has all been a blur, seeing Olivia the only thought crossing my mind.

Reluctantly, I let go of her to grab my keys and unlock the door, holding it open for her. She walks in and crosses the room, standing in front of my desk as the door softly shuts behind us. We stand facing each other, nervous energy suddenly humming between us, neither one of us knowing who should speak first.

Clearing my throat, I shrug off my jacket and lay it over the top of my dresser, leaning back against the door. I long to touch her, but I give her space, give her the option to come to me. I don't want to fuck this up.

She fidgets, nervously picking at the skin at the edge of her fingernail. "I'm sorry," she says softly, sincerely, her voice cutting through the silence.

I push off the door, standing up straight. "You don't have to apologize."

She shakes her head, eyes looking up to capture mine. "No, I do," she insists, and tears prick her eyes again. "I'm sorry I didn't believe you," she whispers painfully.

Unable to not touch her, I cross the room and wrap her back up in my arms, her cheek resting against my chest.

"When she came into class wearing your hoodie, saying those things, I—" The words get caught in her throat. "Then in class and the night before the final, you were saying I wouldn't even need you, and I thought—"

I kiss the top of her head reassuringly before pulling back, taking her face in my hands so I can look her in the eyes. "I get it," I admit painfully. As much as I hate it, I understand. I have a shitty past. Mix that with Adrianna's master plan, and I probably wouldn't have believed me either.

I should have known the levels that Adrianna would stoop to to get back at me. I know how twisted and manipulative she can be, and I was a fool to believe that she would only hurt me. But of course, Olivia was collateral damage in her and Rat Boy's grand scheme.

"I know I don't have the best track record, that I have a lot going against me, but just know from here on out I would never do something like that to you," I vow, swallowing thickly. "I meant what I said, Finch. I'm in love with you, and I don't plan on losing you anytime soon."

Her eyes soften, looking at me with longing and need.

Slowly, I dip my head to gently press my lips to hers in a long, sweet kiss, pulling back and resting my forehead against hers.

"I love you too," she whispers, causing my heart to jump.

I pull back, searching her eyes for any hesitancy, fraud. All I can find is truth. She's not saying this just to say it back. She means it.

I lean back down and crash my lips to hers, kissing her passionately, communicating just how much hearing those words means to me. To not only love someone but have someone love me back feels good. Exhilarating, even. It feels like a sense of security I've never had before. Something I know I can only have with her.

After some time, we both pull away to catch our breath.

"So what happens now?" she asks, looking up at me with those big brown eyes.

I don't know if she means in general or between us, but I reply, covering all the bases.

"Well, Brennen said the school should be contacting me soon to get a statement and see if I want to press charges," I say carefully, gauging her reaction, but I don't detect any sort of objection. "I know they're going after him, but I'm not sure about Adrianna." I don't know how much evidence there is to make her an accomplice.

She nods, absorbing everything.

"And as far as us, I'm still yours, if you want me."

She looks at me with so much affection it hurts. "Of course I do," she says, placing her hand on my cheek and standing on her tiptoes to seal her lips to mine. "I want all of you . . . the good, the bad, everything," she breathes between kisses.

And just like that, I fall all in. One hundred and ten percent, without a doubt, this girl owns me.

I thread my fingers through her hair, deepening the kiss, and I take a step forward, causing her to take a step back. The backs of her thighs press against my desk, and she sits on top of the wood surface, spreading her knees to allow me to stand between them.

I remind myself to take it slow, to be gentle. I didn't plan on this escalating to anything more than a kiss, but when her fingers run down my torso and sneak under my shirt, touching my bare skin, those thoughts fly out the window real quick.

I don't dare remove my shirt, not wanting to accidentally misread her actions and move too fast. But when she inches the fabric up, tugging at it, I think I'm reading her cues pretty well.

My lips only briefly break contact with hers as I reach behind me and grab the collar of my shirt, tugging it up and off. The second my shirt hits the floor her cool, delicate fingers brush across my naked skin, setting it on fire.

I groan into her mouth, grabbing her thighs and pulling her closer to the edge of the desk so our bodies are pressed against each other. My fingers itch to reach for the fabric of her sweater but I don't, wanting and needing her to be the one to willingly escalate things fully.

"Bronx." She breathes my name against my lips, the tiniest whine in her tone.

"Yeah?"

Damn. Why does my voice sound so rough?

Instead of using her words, she places her hands over mine, skimming them up her thighs. When my fingertips graze the hem of her sweater, I pull back.

"You sure?" I ask, breathless, my heart hammering in my chest.

She looks up at me with hazy eyes, then her gaze drifts over to my bed. "Yes."

Hands practically shaking, I grab the hem of her sweater and tug it up. She raises her arms, allowing me to slip the fabric up and over her head, revealing a simple white T-shirt underneath.

She pulls me in for a searing kiss, her fingers raking through my hair. I grab the backs of her thighs, lifting her and carrying her the few steps to my bed, gently laying her down.

I crawl on top of her, one hand pressed into the mattress near her head while the other rests on her hip, slowly creeping up and under the thin fabric of her T-shirt, my fingers grazing her soft, warm skin.

"Wait." She pulls away from the kiss, breathless, her hand shooting down to capture my wrist.

I freeze automatically, pulling away. Looking down at her, her eyes land anywhere but mine.

"We don't have to do this, Finch," I assure her, afraid everything is happening too fast.

"I know. But I want to. I just—can we . . ." She takes in a deep breath, her eyes finally meeting mine. "Can I keep my shirt on?" she asks shyly, her cheeks flaring red.

"Baby, you have nothing to worry about," I promise softly, brushing some hair out of her face. "You're perfect."

She looks at me, eyes hesitant, and it breaks my heart that she would be so insecure about her body. But I won't push her. I'll gladly accept whatever she's willing to give me and fully cherish her with zero questions asked.

I know this isn't the most ideal place for our first time being intimate; the harsh florescent lights in the dorm rooms are far from romantic. If anything, I pictured candles casting a soft glow and flowers everywhere, along with a plush king-size bed, not a shitty twin-size mattress that's almost as stiff as cardboard. But I know what hooking up in this room symbolizes, since I've refused to bring anyone back here before. How it would change everything and show her just how much she means to me. How she's nothing like the other girls. Not even close.

I swallow thickly. "Yeah, baby. You can keep it on if you want to, and just know we don't have to do anything you don't want to," I reiterate, needing her to know that I expect nothing from her. That she doesn't have to feel obligated to do this just because we made up and emotions are running high.

A flash of relief passes in her eyes before they turn soft, adoring. "I want to," she affirms, her voice absolutely sure.

It takes everything in me not to take her right this second.

"Finch—" I strain, fighting against my most basic instincts to start-tearing her clothes off.

She leans up and gently presses her lips to mine, letting me know she's sure, and I'm a goner.

Slowly, I skim my hand up her spine under her shirt until I reach the clasp of her bra.

"Can we take this off?" I ask, hesitant, not wanting to completely push her boundaries.

She nods, and with one flick of my fingers the back comes undone, and she works her arms through the straps and the holes of her shirt, managing to pull her bra out, dropping it to the floor. I can't help but stare down at her perfect, petite breasts, her nipples pebbling through the shirt. Unable to resist, I dip my head low and take one into my mouth, sucking softly through the fabric.

She takes in a sharp breath, arching her back. Her hand flies to the back of my head, fingers carding through my hair. Sweet little moans pour from the back of her throat, and I automatically decide it's my favorite sound ever.

Switching breasts, I give the other one the same treatment, and my hands find their way to her jeans and my fingers work on popping open the button and pulling down the zipper.

I kiss down her clothed torso, leaving an open-mouthed kiss when my lips finally graze skin, only a small sliver of it showing between the hem of her shirt and jeans.

I hook my fingers under the waistband of her jeans and panties, looking up at her through my lashes for permission. Panting, she pushes up onto her elbows and nods, observing my every move.

Carefully, I ease the fabric down her long legs, revealing her sex. I swallow thickly before looking up and meeting her gaze, her eyes hooded and cheeks flushed.

Keeping eye contact, I spread her legs open and press my lips to the inside of her thigh, purposefully grazing the stubble of my jaw against the tender skin as I work my way up. She whimpers, her head lolling back as her legs fall open more.

Just before my lips reach her center, I quickly swap over to the other leg, placing another string of kisses up the inside her other thigh. But this time, right before I'm about to bury my face between her legs, she grabs my face and pulls me up to her mouth, kissing my lips.

Her whole body is tense, and I can tell she's nervous. Something like that is probably more intimate to her than actual sex, and I get it, I'm not going to push her to do anything she's uncomfortable with.

"We don't have to do anything you're not ready for," I assure her.

I watch her throat work on a swallow, her eyes suddenly shying away from mine. "I'm sorry, I've just never done that. I've actually never done anything before."

"Wait." My stomach swirls with a mix of emotions. "You've never?"

She shakes her head, still refusing to meet my gaze.

I close my eyes, clenching my jaw to reel in any shred of restraint I have left.

Cool fingertips run along my cheek and land on my chin, tipping my head up. I open my eyes to meet hers, and she slowly leans up and presses her lips to mine. It's so soft, gentle. Intimate. The fact that she's willing to give me more—give me something she's never given anyone else—somehow makes me love her even more.

I place my hand on her cheek and marvel at her beautiful features, loving every inch of her. She turns her head and presses a delicate kiss to my wrist, nearly destroying me.

Gingerly, I ease her hair out of its ponytail, watching it splay across my pillow like a halo. I slide her hair tie around my wrist and lean down to kiss her once more.

"Let me make you feel good," I murmur against her lips, wanting to warm her up and have her first time be as pleasurable as possible.

Reaching down, I let my fingers skim the inside of her thigh before moving up to the apex of her hips and between her legs. She gasps into my mouth as soon as my fingers find her soft, warm, wet skin, rubbing circles.

A string of sighs and moans falls from her lips as my hand explores between her thighs, and eventually her trembling legs squeeze my hips as her head falls back into the pillow.

"That's it, baby. Let go," I urge her.

Her back arches off the bed and her fingers dig into my back, pulling me closer. With just a few more strokes of my fingers she shatters beneath me, and I swallow her cries as she comes apart.

I let her catch her breath, stroking her hair as she comes down from her high. She slowly blinks her eyes open, her pupils contracting back to a normal size.

I kiss her slowly, sweetly, groaning when her fingertips trail down my body to the waistband of my jeans. With shaky fingers, she pops open the button and pulls down the zipper, tugging at the fabric.

I capture her hands, threading our fingers together and placing them above her head. I kiss her lips a few more times before crawling off the bed and kicking off my jeans, then walk over to my dresser and pull out a condom.

Crawling back on top of her, between her legs, I stare deep into her eyes, searching. I can tell she's nervous.

"Finch, you're sure about this?" I ask, afraid to ask again, but I feel like I have to.

I've imagined this moment for so long, spent so many nights thinking about her, but I won't pressure her into anything she isn't ready for. I'll wait if she isn't ready, no matter how badly I want her.

She hesitates, her eyes flickering with realization of what we're about to do. She stares at me long and hard, vulnerability written all over her face. And then I detect it. Insecurity.

I can practically see the mental barrier, the warning signs going off in her head, telling her this isn't my first time. That this is nothing new to me, nothing special. But, god, is she wrong. No one has or will ever compare to her.

"I love you," I whisper. "I've loved no one but you. Will love no one but you," I confess.

And just like that, her eyes clear and any lingering negative thoughts fade away. She knows I'm not going to use her and leave right after I take from her what no other man has. She knows I'll stay for as long as she'll have me.

She grabs my face and brings me down for a kiss. "I love you. I'm sure."

I press my hips into hers, grinding against her, showing her just what kind of effect she has on me, while kissing her senseless.

She trails her fingers down my body once more, hooking her fingers into the waistband of my boxers, pushing them down. I kick them off and grab the condom, pulling my lips away from hers to tear the foil packet open with my teeth, then roll it on.

Tenderly, I caress her face, staring into her eyes as I line myself up at her entrance.

"No one but you," I murmur before sealing my lips to hers and pushing into her.

Gently, I feed into her inch by inch, groaning at how good she feels, how tight, warm, and wet.

She whimpers against my lips, pulling away from the kiss to push her head back into the pillow, her eyes squeezing shut in discomfort.

"I'm sorry, baby. I'm so sorry," I apologize. "Do you want me to stop?"

She shakes her head, letting out a slow, shaky breath. "No, just—" She gasps when she tries to shift her body. "Just give me a second."

I plant kisses on her face and neck, trying my best to distract her from the pain. "It'll ease soon," I promise.

Slowly, I skim my fingers down between our bodies to reach between her legs, pressing on her bundle of nerves again, making her moan.

After a while, she experimentally shifts her hips and I freeze, gauging her reaction. The knot between her brows is gone and her eyes are hooded as she looks up at me with need. Cautiously, I roll my hips and her eyes blissfully flutter closed, a small moan coming from the back of her throat.

I thrust into her slowly, in and out, pushing a little deeper each time until she has all of me. I take my time with her, not wanting to fuck her meaninglessly or race to an end, like all the others. I want to make love with her. Kiss, caress, and worship her whole body until we're both trembling and breathless.

It's like a dance, the way my hips roll against hers and the way her tongue brushes against mine. I've been with plenty of women, but none of them will ever compare to her. To the girl who stole my heart without even trying. Who took my breath away at first glance, whose smile could light up a whole room, whose heart could love mine completely. She's smart, beautiful, and kind. She single-handedly has all the power to break me, to drive me to my knees if she wants.

No one will ever compare to her.

I feel her walls tighten around me, my name mixed with pleas of release falling from her lips, telling me she's close. I drive into her slowly, languorously, hitting that spot that makes her thrash beneath me every time.

She sobs, her back arching off the bed as her arms and legs wrap around me. I pick up the pace, thrusting into her harder, faster, and she shatters beneath me, her body shaking with the force of the orgasm that tears through her.

Her walls squeeze and flutter around me, sending me over the edge. I release, her name the only thing rolling off my tongue.

I collapse on top of her, breathing heavily, sweat coating my skin. My lips find her neck, placing kisses as we both come down from our high, trying to catch our breath. She wraps her arms around me, her hands running up and down my back before her fingers settle at the hair on the back of my neck, playing with the short strands.

"Stay," I plead, the word falling from my lips, even though I have no right to ask. I don't deserve it, especially after so many girls have asked the same of me and I've refused, walking out and leaving right after with zero remorse.

"I'm not going anywhere," she promises, kissing the top of my head.

When we both catch our breath, I crawl off of her and discard the condom in the trash can. On my way back to the bed, I grab a towel to clean both of us up before crawling back into bed and wrapping my arms around her.

Her head rests on my chest right over my thumping heart, her fingers absentmindedly tracing a lazy pattern along my skin. I watch her fingers graze my chest, swirling around the two scarred cigarette burns placed there long ago.

I grab her wrist, bringing her hand to my mouth where I kiss her palm and the pad of each of her fingers.

Leaning over, she places two delicate kisses on the tiny scarred-over tissues, her big eyes looking up at me through her lashes after, making me a whole new level of fucked.

My throat clogs with emotion when I see her look up at me with so much love in her eyes it hurts. Never have I had someone look at me like that before, make me feel worth something. Unashamed of the scars placed on my body. Understood.

I grab her face and bring her up for a slow, lazy kiss, unable to stop kissing her.

"I love you," she breathes, melting my heart.

"I love you too."

God do I love this girl.

THIRTY-SEVEN

Jackpot

I wake up to warm lips pressing kisses along my back, a few damp strands of silky hair gliding across my skin. I sigh in contentment, snuggling my face deeper into my pillow.

I focus on her lips as they place several kisses across my back, shoulder blade to shoulder blade, kissing every letter of my tattoo. *U-N-K-N-O-W-N.*

My chest tightens with an emotion I can't quite decipher, the meaning behind my tattoo starting to crumble since she walked into my life.

I roll onto my side, blindly reaching for her. My arm lazily hooks around her waist, and I realize she's standing at the edge of my bed.

"Hi," I rasp, pulling her closer and burying my face in her stomach, smelling a familiar soap and shampoo. *My* soap and shampoo.

Damn it. *Damn it.* She smells like *me*, and for some reason that ignites something primal and possessive deep inside of me. She must have stolen my shower caddy and snuck off to the shower earlier this morning while I was asleep.

She giggles softly, carding her fingers through my hair. "Hi," she whispers, leaning down to place a kiss on my cheek.

I hum in contentment, feeling a sense of peace and satisfaction I haven't felt since, well, ever.

"What are you doing up?" I ask, my eyes still blissfully closed, heavy with sleep.

Her fingernails continue to gently graze over my scalp, sending a shiver down my spine.

"I still have the final for my other section of Professor Cooper's lab," she reminds me. I completely forgot about it.

I groan in protest, tightening my arm around her waist. "No."

She giggles sweetly. "No? Come on, I have to go," she urges me gently, managing to slip from my hold. "And I need this," she mutters under her breath, her fingers grazing my wrist and hand as she slips her hair tie from my wrist.

Before it can slide up and over my fingers, I capture the small band in my fist, holding it hostage. Blearily, I blink open my eyes to stare up at her beautiful face, her cheeks rosy and hair damp from her shower. Her long caramel-colored locks cascade over one shoulder, the ends dripping onto one of my sweaters, which adorns her torso.

"Not until you kiss me first," I state, tilting my lips up in offering.

A small, amused smile tugs at her lips before she leans down and presses them to mine. I kiss her lazily, lovingly, letting go of the band to cup her cheek in my hand. Savoring the kiss, not wanting it to end anytime soon, I slide my hand back to tangle my fingers in her wet hair, gently fisting the dark strands, deepening the kiss.

She giggles and hums against my lips in protest, eventually breaking free. "Bronx," she whines adorably through a string of giggles, an infectious smile on her face. "I'm going to be late."

I attempt to wrap my arm back around her waist to prevent her from leaving but she steps back quickly, escaping my hold.

My arm hangs limply off the mattress, and I let out a dramatic huff, causing her to laugh. I peek up at her through my lashes, and watch her tie her hair up in a ponytail.

"I should be done around eleven today. Would you maybe want to meet me around that time and do an early lunch?" she asks, suddenly a little shy, making me smile.

"Of course, baby. I'll meet you outside of Professor Cooper's office," I promise.

She smiles, a light blush spreading across her cheeks. "Okay, I'll see you later. I love you."

My grin widens. "I love you too," I state, watching her slip out the door.

I roll over onto my stomach, hooking my arms underneath the pillow and smiling into it, satisfaction thrumming through my veins. I let out a long, contented sigh, replaying last night's events in my head, wishing I could hold her just a little longer.

Last night was perfect, unlike anything I've ever experienced before. Sure, I've had sex countless times, but last night—with her—I craved something more. It meant something more.

Ultimately, I think what we both craved wasn't sex, but intimacy. To be wanted, touched, looked at, adored—to have our actions speak louder than words can. We wanted to be vulnerable, to fall all in and have a sense of security, safety. Trust.

My eyes flutter closed, and I drift off to sleep for another hour or so, a smile on my lips, thinking about her.

>> <<

I walk into the science building, grinning cheek to cheek, nothing able to sour my good mood. I take a left down the hallway lined with professors' offices, and take a seat on the bench closest to Professor Cooper's office.

Five minutes later, I hear a door creak open and Olivia's melodic, cheerful voice floats down the hall as she bids Professor Cooper goodbye and wishes her a good break. She slips into the hall, her mouth spreading into a grin as soon as she spots me, a slight skip entering her step.

I stand and extend my hand to her, reeling her in as soon as her hand lands in mine. Our chests press together, and she stands on her tiptoes, winding her arms around my neck before molding her mouth to mine.

I smile into the kiss, gripping her hips and pulling her that much closer. "Hi."

She leans back, her face absolutely glowing and eyes shining with happiness. "Hi. Ready to go grab lunch?"

"Mh-mm."

I peck her lips a few more times before pulling away, grabbing her hand, threading our fingers together, and leading her down the hall. Her opposite hand curls around my tricep, her head resting against my bicep as we walk out of the science building and into the chilly December air.

"How did the final go?" I ask as we walk across campus.

"Good. Everyone passed and left me a good review for Professor Cooper."

"That's great," I state, kissing the top of her head.

"Yeah, I'm just glad everyone passed." She sighs in relief, knowing it will reflect well on her and prove her teaching capabilities.

I hum in acknowledgment, happy for her. "Of course they would with you as their TA."

She gives me a grateful smile and plants a delicate kiss on my arm, making my heart melt.

"How are you feeling?" I ask softly, changing the subject, my thumb rubbing circles into the back of her hand.

She looks up at me with confusion, a small knot forming between her brows.

"After last night," I clarify.

"Oh." Her eyes light with realization. "Uh, good," she says, suddenly becoming shy.

I can't help the smile that tugs at my lips, finding her adorable.

She clears her throat, desperate to change topics. "How was your morning?"

I refrain from making a crude joke about missing and only thinking about her while she was gone.

"Good. Really good, actually," I admit, breathing out an airy chuckle, an uncontrollable, goofy smile making its way onto my lips. After I got up and got ready, good news upon good news just fell into my lap this morning. "A lot happened while you were gone."

She arches a dark brow, a curious smile teasing her lips. "Oh?"

"Mh-mm. I'll tell you over lunch."

She continues walking toward the school's cafeteria, her body jerking and stumbling backward—her hand still in mine—when I unexpectedly turn right and heading toward the parking lot.

She lets out a little noise of surprise. "Where are you going?"

"To get some real food," I state.

>> <<

After the waitress leaves our table to go fill our orders, Olivia scoots forward in her seat, crossing her arms over the tabletop. "Well, what's your good news?" she asks, bouncing with excitement and interest.

The smell of grease hangs in the air and the soft sizzle of the oil in the fryers behind the counter increases in volume when the kitchen staff drop another load of fries in. For lunch I brought Olivia to a popular burger joint off campus to celebrate the end of finals week and reward ourselves for not only making it through finals, but for also making it through all the other unexpected bullshit thrown at us.

I comfortably recline back in the booth, debating where to start, still feeling the ecstasy of the high I'm currently on—have been on since last night—slide through my veins. I swear, it feels like I've hit the jackpot and luck is finally on my side.

I list all my good news the way I received it this morning, in chronological order. Normally, I'm never one to enjoy phone calls—hell, half the time I don't even answer them—but today they just kept rolling in, one after the other, with *good* news. I didn't even have a single spam caller.

"School called me this morning," I start off, watching her expression sober. "Quinton is being expelled," I say flatly, trying not to show any emotion in order to gauge her honest reaction.

Her expression is almost stoic, neutral as she absorbs the information, but I can tell she's conflicted. At the end of the day, she, Delilah, and Rat Boy were a pretty tight-knit friend group for the past four years. But that doesn't excuse his behavior. He purposefully hurt her for revenge.

I go on to explain that the school brought him in this morning for questioning and he squealed like the little rat he is. He confessed that Adrianna approached him and originally came up with the plan to pull the fire alarm and sneak into my room to mess with my alarm clocks, making me miss the lab final. He said she paid him to help her.

Apparently, when he snuck into my room he swapped out the batteries of my alarm clock with nearly empty ones—explaining why my clock was working the night before and wound up dead the next morning. He also managed to hack into my phone, which I'd forgotten on my desk when Olivia and I walked out, going into my settings to put my alarm on silent.

While Quinton is for sure being expelled for getting caught, they are still working on a case of action for Adrianna since there's not much solid evidence against her, only his word. But I don't doubt she'll get what's coming to her eventually. I can't imagine Rat Boy not putting up a fight to drag her down with him.

"Then I got *another* call after that from the local police department," I continue carefully. "They asked if I want to press charges."

Her eyes briefly flicker with worry and suspense.

"I told them I'd think about it," I say.

Admittedly, I want to press charges, but they're not quite certain on what I can go after him with yet because he broke into my room, which is technically campus property, and only stole a thirty-dollar hoodie from me. It's a bit complicated and I'm not sure if it's really worth the time and hassle. Plus, I want to get Olivia's input before I do anything.

She still looks conflicted.

"Hey." I reach over the table to grab her hand in mine. "You okay?"

She stares at our joined hands for a moment, unblinking. "Yeah. No. I don't know," she admits, shoulders sagging. "I honestly don't know how to feel."

I rub my thumb back and forth over the back of her hand. "I get that."

She opens and closes her mouth, trying to form her thoughts into words. "I just can't believe it," she says eventually. "I thought he was my friend. I guess I just feel a little shocked and confused right now."

I nod sympathetically. "If you don't want me to press charges, I won't," I promise her. I don't want to cause her any more distress for my own vengeance.

"No," she says with certainty. "He broke into your room and purposely did those things. He knew what he was doing was wrong," she says, sighing sadly. "He intentionally tried to hurt you . . . and me. He should have to face the consequences."

I nod.

"Well, we don't have to make any decisions right now," I tell her. "We can think it over for a few days." Plus, it'll be a little fun making the rat sweat, but I won't tell Olivia that.

She gives me a grateful look before pulling her hand from mine, then leans back to give the approaching waitress room to set down our plates.

"On a lighter note," I say, perking up and picking a fry off my plate and popping it into my mouth. "Coach called me this morning."

She looks at me, puzzled. "He did?"

I grin, taking a big bite of my burger, chewing and swallowing before I continue. "Yeah. He called to let me know a scout from the West Coast called him the other day to discuss me."

Her eyes go wide, and her voice rises a few octaves. "Really?"

I wipe my hands on a napkin. "Yep, said they're really interested in me, and he gave them a great review and verbal résumé about me to really drive home their decision. He said I have a high chance of getting drafted next year."

"Bronx, that's amazing!" she states, eyes warm and proud.

"Thanks, baby. According to Coach, they're coming to watch me play during the playoffs after the break and plan on sitting down to talk with me."

Her eyes sparkle with happiness. "That's great news!"

"And that's not all of it," I confess, excitement buzzing through my chest. When I said the good news kept coming this morning, I meant it. "I got another call from testing services."

Her head jerks back in surprise, confusion written all over her pretty face. "Testing services?" she asks, slight alarm in her voice.

"Yeah, since I missed the lab final due to reasons that were out of my hands, they're giving me a chance to take it instead of receiving a zero." Not that taking the lab final was weighing heavy on my mind. Honestly, I was more worried about getting Olivia back to even think about not actually taking the final. "I have an appointment at the testing center at two."

She looks at me baffled before guilt washes over her face. "Oh my gosh, Bronx, I didn't even think about you missing the final," she says worriedly, knowing a zero would really tank my final grade.

"I didn't either." I chuckle and wave my hand dismissively. "Zero or not, I'd still pass the class. Barely, but I'd pass."

She looks at me disbelievingly. "Huh?"

I grin. "Final grades for the class were posted this morning on the online portal. My barely passing, overall grade obviously isn't set in stone anymore with my now-tentative zero for the lab final, but for the lecture final I got a B plus."

Shock and excitement light her eyes again. "No way!"

"What can I say?" I shrug casually, taking a sip of my soda, smirking around the straw. "I got a kickass tutor."

With an excited little squeak, she stands and slides into my side of the booth, and wraps her arms around my neck. "I'm so proud of you!"

I wrap my arm around her waist, hugging her back. "I couldn't have done it without you," I whisper sincerely into her hair.

Leaning back, I capture her lips with mine, kissing her briefly. I grab her plate and drink from the other side of the table and slide them over in front of her, not wanting her to leave my side of the booth.

She settles in next to me, my arm draped around her shoulders as I watch her pick up her phone and log into her student portal to check out her final grade. No surprise, she finished the class with an A+.

"Great job," I say, kissing the top of her head.

"So, wait." She pauses, looking over at me expectantly. "Since we both got the grades we agreed to for the bet, does that mean we're going to Florida?"

Shit.

I completely forgot about that.

As much as I don't want to go to Florida, a bet is a bet. And the look on her face, the hope and excitement in her eyes—I'd be a complete dick if I told her no and went back on my word.

I sigh, forcing myself to smile despite the unsettling feeling in my stomach. "I guess so. Pack your bags, Finch, it looks like we're going to Florida."

And just like that, the smile on her face makes it worth it.

Maybe going back won't be so bad with her. It'll be nice to have a little getaway and see her experience the beach for the first time, something I know she's excited about. I think I can manage to set aside my bad memories and make new, better ones with her.

"But first I have to pass the lab final. Think we can squeeze in a quick study session before two?" I ask, my grin sharp as I waggle my eyebrows suggestively. "A little anatomy refresher with you would really do me some good."

Her cheeks burn red at my innuendo, and she swats me in my chest with the back of her hand.

I just laugh, leaning over to kiss the side of her head. "I'll take that as a maybe," I tease.

THIRTY-EIGHT

Red Light

I shift in the driver's seat, trying my best to get comfortable, my ass numb and body stiff from the five-hour drive. I blink a few times and reach for the coffee in the cup holder, gulping down the remaining cold contents. Olivia offered to drive for a while, but I refused, letting her rest since we woke up at the crack of dawn to leave.

Glancing to my right, I catch a glimpse of her curled up adorably in the passenger seat, her long hair slicked back into a ponytail, revealing the side of her face that isn't pressed to the window. Her elbow is planted on the door, her fist under her chin as her dark lashes rest against her cheeks. She tried her best to stay awake for my sake, but the blur of the scenery passing by won, lulling her to sleep.

We left her house early this morning, the day after Christmas, to head to Florida and get there just before noon, to enjoy as much sun as possible. We ended up taking her car because no way were we making the drive on my motorcycle, especially at this time of year.

Christmas just so happened to fall on the Wednesday right after finals, and I spent the holiday with her and her family instead of locked up in my dorm like previous years. Just like Thanksgiving, spending the holiday with her family was amazing. It was literally perfect, like something straight out of one of those cheesy family Christmas movies.

I glance down at the dash and notice the needle of the gas gauge flirting with the large *E*, telling me we need to stop for gas. *And to stretch*, I think as I shift in my seat for the umpteenth time, feeling a twinge of pain in my lower back.

I drive until I find a decent enough gas station, then pull in and fill the tank. Locking the car doors with Olivia still asleep inside, I jog inside the small gas station to grab us some drinks and snacks, and on my way to the cash register I pass the cheap liquor section and grab a bottle of the nicest wine they have, which is less than ten dollars, if that says anything. Thankfully, I don't think Olivia drinks often, if ever, so hopefully she won't notice the low-end bottle. I just want to make tonight and this little vacation special.

Since last week, aka the best night of my life, I haven't been able to stop thinking about Olivia and how perfect that night was. But despite it being perfect, it was far from romantic. I can't help but think about how she deserves more, and I want to give her more. The best. She deserves flowers, candles, wine, and a decently sized bed, and I'll be damned if I don't give her at least that much. I want—need—to show her how much she means to me and how much that night meant to me too. I'm determined to make our second time beyond perfect.

I walk up to the register and the man behind the counter looks zoned out, a far-off look in his eyes. He's tall, rail thin, disheveled, and the scabs on his arms are a telltale sign that he's a total drug addict.

I set my things down on the counter with a *thud* to grab his attention. His blank eyes slowly find mine and wordlessly, mechanically, he starts scanning my items.

"ID," he asks after scanning the wine, and I'm honestly surprised he bothered to ask.

I grab my wallet from my back pocket and pull out my driver's license, handing it over. He glances at it, not even really looking. Just before he goes to hand it back, something catches his eye and he snaps the little plastic card back a few inches in front of his face, examining it intently. Something actually seems to start churning in his empty brain, making me uneasy.

"Any day, pal," I snap, wondering why he's staring at my ID like that.

He blinks and reluctantly hands me back my card. I slide it into my wallet and pull out my credit card, shoving it in the card reader before he can rattle off the total. As soon as the transaction is approved I gather up my things, not bothering to stay a second longer to ask this weirdo for a bag.

I jut my hip into the handrail of the door, pushing it open and getting the hell out of there, that guy giving me beyond creepy vibes. As quietly as I can, I open the back door of Olivia's car and dump everything into the back seat before jumping back behind the wheel.

As soon as I turn the key and the engine rumbles to life I hear Olivia take in a deep breath through her nose, and look over to see her stir. Tiredly, her eyes flutter open, and she sits up straight, getting her bearings. Her eyes flicker over to me, and I can't help but chuckle at how adorably sleepy she looks with the small red mark on her cheek from it being pressed against the window.

"What?" she asks through a yawn, stretching a bit, her stiff bones cracking.

"Nothing. You're just really cute."

She blushes slightly, rolling her eyes.

I grab her chin and pull her lips to mine, kissing her longingly. I only cut the kiss short because I still feel perturbed by the creepy gas station guy, needing to get as far away from here as possible.

"How much longer?" Olivia asks as soon as we pull onto the main road.

"We're about thirty minutes out from the hotel," I inform her, reaching over to grab her hand and bringing it to my lips.

"When we get there do you want to unpack and rest before grabbing some lunch? Then maybe we can head to the beach?" she asks, and I can hear the excitement in her voice. She's been dying to go to the beach, talking about it nonstop for the last couple of days.

I can't help but smile against the back of her hand. "Whatever you want."

>> <<

Her caramel-colored hair flies in the wind and the skirt of her navy dress whips against her thighs in the slight breeze, flaring out when she twirls around in a circle. Pure happiness is written across her face as her bare feet pad around in the wet sand, the waves lapping at her feet whenever the tide rolls back in. She looks so effortlessly beautiful, her head carelessly thrown back as a wide, blissful smile consumes her face.

The sun is setting around us, the blue sky streaked with various pinks and oranges. Behind her, the ocean and the sunset create the perfect backdrop. I don't know if I'll ever see or experience anything as beautiful in comparison again.

She straightens, smiling at me over her shoulder while holding out her hand, beckoning me closer. So much life lights up her eyes that looking into them I feel like I've hardly lived.

More than willing, I walk up behind her, wrapping my arms around her waist and resting my chin on her shoulder. I kiss the shell of her ear, and she leans back into my chest, a content sigh leaving her lips.

"Is it everything you dreamed it would be?" I tease, knowing how excited she had been.

"Definitely," she says, a lazy smile gracing her lips.

I plant a series of kisses along her neck as she watches the ocean and the sky changing colors beyond it.

"Did you come to this beach often?" she asks, and I know she's lightly probing me for answers about my childhood.

"Once or twice," I admit vaguely, my lips still attached to her neck. "I rarely ever came to the beach."

It's true, I've only been to the beach a handful of times. Most of those were when I was in high school, sneaking out to attend parties late at night that were typically busted by the cops. None of my foster parents were fans of that. But I imagine in Olivia's head the experiences I've had here are filled with family fun and sunshine.

She hums in acknowledgment. "Maybe one day you could show me around all the places you used to go to. Your house, school, wherever," she says, and I can hear the hesitancy and nervousness in her voice, knowing I won't be too keen on the idea.

I sigh into her shoulder and gently spin her around to face me, brushing her hair out of her face. "I wish I could, but I can't even count the number of different houses and schools I was shipped off to when I was a kid. I never stayed in one place for long, and all the houses I stayed in with my mother were either abandoned or shitty apartments owned by her lousy boyfriends. I don't want you to see that," I admit shamefully.

I watch her eyes fill with sadness. She takes my face in her hands, standing on her tiptoes to place a tender, understanding kiss on my lips. "Okay," she whispers, resting her cheek against my chest, her arms wound tightly around my waist.

I stroke her hair, resting my chin on top of her head. Heavy silence falls between us; the only sounds are the waves crashing on the shore.

"Do you want to see your grandmother at all?" she asks, breaking the silence.

I close my eyes, holding my breath. "Would you be mad if I didn't want to see her?"

She hesitates for a moment. "No." I can tell she's lying, that me not wanting to see my grandmother is bothering her—which is bothering me because I don't want to disappoint her.

"I just don't want you to regret it one day when it's too late," she admits softly into my chest, and my arms instinctively tighten around her.

Oh my sweet girl.

Would I regret it one day? Probably not.

But then my mind oddly drifts off to ten years from now, when I have a house of my own and a family, a couple of kids running around. Two little girls with big honey-colored eyes and caramel-colored hair swim into my vision, and my stomach tightens as I think of the day they ask about their grandmother, and possibly their great-grandmother, along with other aspects of my life. While I may never allow them to meet their low-life grandmother, and I have no clue who their grandfather is, maybe I could at least give them a positive outlook about their great-grandmother.

I take a deep breath before exhaling slowly. "All right."

Olivia stiffens in my arms, leaning back to observe my face. "All right?"

"Yeah, I'll go see her."

She looks at me skeptically, a small frown marring her brow. "I don't want to force you to do anything you don't want to."

I shake my head. "No, you're right. This is probably the last time I'll ever get to see her. I might as well. She probably hasn't had visitors in years."

Her features smooth over and her eyes grow soft. She leans in and presses her lips to my neck.

"How about we go see her after dinner tonight?" I offer, honestly wanting to get the interaction over with. Plus, if we go tonight it'll limit the number of hours we'll be able to stay.

"Sure, if that's what you want to do," she says, looking up at me with her big brown eyes, making me melt.

"Yeah, I want to."

After dinner we go to my grandmother's nursing home, which smells heavily of antiseptic and death, making me very uneasy. A nurse leads us to a large dining hall where residents are lingering. She walks us up to a round table where a lone, frail elderly woman is sitting, and I almost don't recognize her.

"Mrs. Miller," the nurse says, raising her voice a little and placing a gentle hand on my grandmother's shoulder to gain her attention. "Someone is here to see you."

My grandmother stops poking at the pudding cup in front of her with a plastic spoon and glances up at me, her eyes brightening. "Bryan!" she says cheerfully. Close enough, I guess. Due to her dementia, I'm surprised she even recognizes me.

The nurse smiles politely, excusing herself, and heads back to the front desk.

"Hi, Grandma," I say, awkwardly stepping forward to lean down and give her a one-armed hug. My stomach tightens in realization that this is one of the few times I've gotten to hug her. And it's most likely my last.

"Oh my goodness, you've gotten so big!" She gawks at me. "How old are you now, twelve?" she asks in all seriousness.

I clear my throat. "Uh, no. I'm actually twenty-two."

Her thin lips purse into a confused, disbelieving frown.

"This is my girlfriend, Olivia," I say, switching the subject and stretching my hand out to Olivia. She places her hand in mine and steps forward into my grandmother's line of vision.

"Hi, it's nice to meet you," Olivia says sweetly, despite shyly tucking herself into my side.

My grandmother's eyes widen with surprise and joy. "My, aren't you just the prettiest thing," she says, fawning over her.

Olivia blushes madly, and thanks her.

Olivia and I take a seat next to my grandmother at the table, Olivia taking the reins on conversation, keeping the topics light and generic. I can tell how excited my grandmother is to have visitors, even if she hardly knows who we are.

We sit and talk for a while, and thank god my grandma doesn't seem to notice or even mind the tension radiating off me in waves. It feels so weird to be here, talking to a practical stranger I feel obligated to have a strong relationship with. I do my best to be polite and engage in conversation as much as I can.

I subtly look at the clock and realize it's just past seven and visiting hours are over at eight, meaning I thankfully have less than an hour longer to endure. It's honestly not even that bad, just really awkward. And sitting here, staring at this fragile lady who's almost skin and bones in front of me, is stirring up conflicting emotions.

"Well, look who's back," a familiar rough, sadistic voice says from behind me, making my blood run cold.

I turn around to look at my mother's face, and she looks so much worse than the last time I saw her. She looks like she's in her fifties, even though she hasn't turned forty yet. Her eyes are sunken in, hair wiry and graying prematurely. Her yellow, rotting teeth look like a dentist's worst nightmare as she smirks at me like she just caught her prey, and the man standing next to her doesn't look any better.

"Weren't even going to tell me you were in town?" she chastises me.

I grit my teeth, every muscle tensing as I slip into defense mode. I stand up from my chair, subconsciously stepping in front of Olivia, shielding her. "How did you know I was here?"

She shrugs a shoulder. "I have my sources."

Sources?

What the hell does that mean? The only way she could have known I was in town is if someone told her. And then it clicks. The guy at the gas station. Not a doubt crosses my mind that they run in the same circles, and he put two and two together.

She waltzes up to the table, bypassing me to sit at the other side of it, the man, who I only assume is another one of her boyfriends, following her. Even my demented grandmother stares at them with skepticism and distrust.

I remain standing, itching to get out of here, and just as I'm about drag Olivia away, my mother speaks up.

"So, what, you're just here to make sure you collect the money without even consulting me?" my mother continues, leaning back in her chair.

"What the hell are you talking about?" I spit, in no mind to play games.

"Don't play dumb with me," she snarls, leaning forward with her elbows on the table. "You heard she put you in her will instead of me and you're only coming down here to make sure it stays that way."

I shake my head, feeling like I just got hit by a freight train. "What?"

She growls impatiently. "That money belongs to me," she insists.

I blink, growing frustrated. "I have no clue what you're talking about," I reply honestly, not knowing where she's getting all these ideas about money. Did my grandma seriously put me in her will? Why?

She slams her hands on the table, gaining the attention of nearby residents. "The hell you do!" she accuses. "I talked to an attorney, and the demented old broad is leaving *everything* to you! And she's so far gone now that she won't switch it over to my name because she barely knows who I am anymore!"

A humorless, bitter chuckle escapes from the back of my throat. Of course. It all makes sense now. All the phone calls, why she wanted me to come down here to see my grandmother so bad. She wants me to have everything switched over to her name.

I pinch the bridge of my nose, trying my best to leash my temper.

"Of course. I should have known. You only ever call me when you need money."

"I deserve that money! I'm her daughter!" she states hysterically.

"Yeah, and a shitty one at that!" I roar back, any reserve I have left cracking. All the emotions I had festering inside of me are coming to the surface. "You don't deserve anything!"

"And you do?" she counters, and for some reason her words hit me straight in the chest.

"I never said I deserve shit," I growl. "But I'll be damned if I give you any money so you can go blow it all on drugs. Like you always do. Always have. That's probably why you're not getting anything in the first place. You were a shitty daughter who only cared about getting your next high. You stole money from her all the time to get drugs and wound up getting pregnant at fifteen because you were so reckless. Then you were a shitty mother, never caring about your own son and shoving me off onto her for as long as you could until she had to kick you out."

Her jaw ticks in anger and annoyance. "I was a good mother. You always had a roof over your head, didn't you?"

I bark out a laugh. This lady is fucking delusional. "Yeah, because seventy percent of the time it was provided by other people!"

Zero remorse crosses her face, sending me over the edge. Suddenly I feel angry, hurt, *vulnerable*. Like I'm a little kid all over again, just wanting my mommy to care about me.

"Let's get out of here," I say, grabbing a stunned Olivia by the arm and leading her to the exit.

"We're not finished here!" my mother calls, and I hear her get up. She grabs my arm, and I spin around to face her, towering over her.

"Yes. We are," I say with finality. "Never in a million years will I give you a penny."

Her eyes look up at me with pure hatred. "Fuck you."

"Right back atcha."

I back away slowly, sending her one last warning glare before placing my hand on Olivia's lower back and steering her out to the parking lot. I open the car door for her, and she gets in, speechless. I get behind the wheel and start the engine, peeling out of the lot more aggressively than I intended to.

The silence inside the car is almost deafening as I drive back to the hotel, my teeth clenched and hands white-knuckled around the wheel. Olivia stays silent, sensing that I'm an emotional ticking time bomb right now.

Driving down the road, a few streets up from the beach, I spot a small shop that has motorcycle rentals. Without thinking twice, I quickly veer into the parking lot, haphazardly parking in a parking space. I unbuckle my seat belt and open the car door, stepping out.

"Bronx." I hear the panic in Olivia's voice. She gets out of the car and briskly rounds the hood to meet me, placing her hand on my chest, eyes full of worry.

I cover her hand with mine, voice strained. "Baby, I just need to clear my head for a bit," I explain.

Back home, whenever I'm stressed or angry, I just hop on my bike and take off. I ride until I'm able to think straight. I'm afraid if I don't find some sort of outlet, some sort of escape, I'm going to explode in front of her.

"I just, I don't want you to see me like this," I confess, feeling too restless, too vulnerable. "I feel like I'm about to explode and I don't want you to be collateral damage."

She nods in understanding, despite the tears misting her eyes. She knows I would never physically hurt her, but she also remembers that the last time I exploded in front of her wasn't so pretty. I can see it in her eyes that she desperately wants me to stay, wants to help me. I know I could—probably should—lean on her and confide in her, but I'm so used to handling everything on my own. It's the only way I know how.

But I'm working on it. I've already shared with her so much—more than I ever have with anyone else—but I just need a moment to myself to get my emotions in check. To figure them out before I can express them to anyone else.

I lean down and press my lips to her forehead, letting them linger there for a beat before pulling away. "Take the car back to the hotel. I'll be back in a few hours," I promise.

I go to brush past her but she grabs my arm, making me turn around. Without warning, she stands on her tiptoes, crashing her lips to mine in a desperate kiss.

"I love you," she breathes, looking deep into my eyes.

Damn it. This girl is going to be the death of me.

"I love you." Cupping the back of her head, I pull her in for one more kiss. "I'll see you soon."

I watch her reluctantly get into the car and drive away safely before walking into the rental shop. The man behind the counter spares me a glance from his computer, monotonously asking how he can help me, and I'm honestly relieved he's far from a perky, in-your-face salesman.

"I'm here to rent one of your motorcycles," I say, already shoving my credit card at him.

He rings me up and hands me back my card, along with a pair of keys. "The bike in the very left corner of the lot," he informs me, and I'm out the door, grabbing a helmet along the way.

I fasten the helmet before swinging my leg over the bike and roaring the engine to life. I rev the engine a few times, already feeling a sense of control and power that I so desperately long for in this moment. In no time I'm taking off down the back roads, trying not to overly exceed any traffic regulations.

The wind whips my face and drones in my ears, helping to drown out my thoughts. I drive with no destination, my mind on anything but direction.

I curse under my breath when I approach a red light, willing it to turn green so I don't have to fully hit the brakes. To my surprise, given all the glorious luck I've had today, the light switches to green and I accelerate, ready to breeze through.

Halfway through the intersection, I hear a car horn blare to my right just as I see a pair of headlights in my peripheral vision speeding toward me from the left. In a split second, icy fear and dread slide through my veins before pain courses throughout my entire body.

THIRTY-NINE

Whole

The light from the TV casts shadows along the hotel room walls as I mindlessly flip through the channels, hardly paying attention to what's on the screen. I'm sitting on the bed, propped up against the headboard with a wrap around my chest and a cast on my leg.

After two days in the hospital, they released me. I don't remember much from the accident, but the driver who hit me ran the red light at the last second and smashed right into me as I was going through the intersection. I was in and out of it for a while, only recalling bits and pieces of the ambulance ride, and by the time I was fully conscious they already had me bandaged up and Olivia was at my bedside, scared out of her mind. The doctors claim I'm lucky to have come out of it with only a couple of broken ribs, a broken leg, a shit ton of bruises, and some road rash.

The bathroom door clicks open and Olivia quietly pads into the room, her vanilla body wash wafting in the air. She's in an oversized sleep shirt and shorts, her hair damp from her shower as she walks over to her suitcase, neatly placing her clothes from today inside.

She glances over at me, finding me awake. Her eyes drift over to the clock hanging on the wall, and I can see her doing the math in her head to calculate how many hours it's been since the last time I took my pain meds.

Since we got back from the hospital a few hours ago she's been taking her role as my nurse very seriously. It's like every ten minutes she's asking me if I'm okay or if I need something, and while I know she's being helpful, I can't help but find it extremely frustrating that I can't do anything myself. It's aggravating to feel so useless.

Olivia walks over to the desk where she has all my pills neatly lined up next to the papers the hospital provided. She pops a few of the pill bottles open and shakes out the correct dosages, recapping the bottles after. Grabbing a water bottle, she walks over to my side of the bed and places it along with the pills on the nightstand.

"Take these," she urges softly, giving me a small smile before wandering back into the bathroom to brush her teeth and finish getting ready for bed.

I grab the water bottle and uncap it, taking a few swigs before grabbing the pills off the nightstand, one accidentally slipping from my fingers and falling to the floor.

With an aggravated huff, and without thinking, I go to lean over the side of bed to pick it up. Pain rips through my side, and I suck in a sharp breath through my teeth, letting out a curse. "Fuck!"

I hear the faucet turn off in the bathroom and Olivia rushes out, eyes wide, alert. "What's wrong?"

"Everything!" I snap, all my pent-up emotions bubbling to the surface and boiling over. "Everything is wrong!" I reiterate.

Olivia stares at me, stunned.

After a beat she approaches me slowly, worry and concern flooding her eyes. "Hey," she coos calmly. "It's okay."

"It's not okay!" I shout. "My fucking leg is broken!" I gesture to my leg, which is covered in plaster from my foot to midthigh. "How the hell am I going to play football now? You can't fully come back from something like this, and no scout is going to want to talk to me when they find out about it!" I explain, furious.

"You don't know that," she says softly, optimistically, making my blood boil further.

In a way—deep down—I wish she'd yell at me, be just as furious. Somehow, I think it would make things easier.

To me, anger is better than pity. I'd rather have someone screaming at me, reminding me of what a fuckup I am, than give me pity. Pity makes me feel weak, vulnerable, and I hate people seeing me that way. At least with anger they think I'm strong enough to take it, or that I'm not completely torn down yet.

"Yes, I do! My whole future is down the drain. What the hell am I supposed to do now?" I fight back.

She carefully sits on the edge of the bed, gently placing her hand on my knee. "You're still getting your degree. You have options."

I let out a low growl, scrubbing my hands harshly over my face in frustration. The NFL has been my dream for years; I can't swallow the fact that it's all over just yet, and she obviously doesn't understand that. She has her whole future ahead of her, all perfectly mapped out and tied up with a fucking decorative bow.

"Hey." Her thin, cool fingers wrap around my wrists, pulling my hands from my face. "Don't shut me out. Talk to me," she begs.

"I don't need or want to fucking talk, Olivia," I snap, pulling my hands from her grasp. "Talking isn't going to fix anything," I insist.

Hurt flashes across her face. "You're mad at the world right now. I get it. But—"

I bark out a laugh, cutting her off. "How could you possibly get it?" I argue. "Olivia, you have the perfect fucking life! You have amazing parents and you're so fucking smart that you're going to become a cardiac surgeon. You literally have a white picket fence! So don't tell me you *get it.*"

Her lips press into a thin line, pain written all over her face at my harsh words. I instantly regret them.

Fucking hell.

I know I'm being a dick, and the tactless words tumbled out of my mouth before I could stop them.

I feared this would happen. That I'd lash out at her and make her my emotional punching bag. Anger always seems to be my default setting. I use it to mask my weakness and not show what I'm really feeling. It makes me feel strong, powerful. In control when I actually feel anything but.

"Fuck, baby." I grab her wrist as she stands from the bed, ready to walk away. "I'm sorry."

Reluctantly, she sits back down, refusing to meet my gaze.

"I'm sorry," I repeat sincerely. I exhale a harsh breath. "It's just that after all that's happened between the other day and today, I feel like everything is crashing down around me. I feel like everything I've worked so hard for is gone in the blink of an eye. And being here of all places . . .

"As a kid, I always promised myself I'd be something. I wanted to prove everyone wrong. Myself wrong. With football, I thought for once that I was going to be something. Make something of myself. All of my childhood, I felt so unhappy, unstable. I just wanted a life I could finally be proud of."

Her honey-colored eyes finally meet mine, full of sadness. "I understand," she says softly, and I bite my tongue about how she'll never understand.

Sensing my restraint, she stands from the bed once more, and I'm certain she's about to walk away. I wouldn't blame her. She should have walked away from me a long time ago, because she deserves better. Not a miserable son of a bitch who can't do anything right.

Instead of walking away, she places both of her knees on the bed, carefully swinging one of her legs over me, straddling my lap. Instinctively, I place my hands on her hips and urge her to sit down, but she hardly puts any weight on me, scared she'll hurt me.

She takes my face in her hands, her thumbs lightly stroking my cheeks. "I know you don't think I understand," she says, staring deep into my eyes. "But I do. I understand what it feels like to be scared, alone, *broken.*"

I furrow my brows, wondering when she could have ever felt that way; her life seems perfect.

She nervously chews at her bottom lip, looking contemplative, unsure.

Eventually, she comes to a conclusion. As she sits back, her hands fall from my face to reach for the hem of her shirt. Taking a deep breath, she hesitantly lifts the fabric up and over her head, the oversized T-shirt landing beside us on the mattress.

My heart stops.

Not only are her bare breasts on full display a few inches away from my face, but so is the large scar between them.

Down the center of her chest, running from her collarbones to just below her breasts, is a long, pale pink scar that looks to be a number of years old.

Leaning forward, I press my lips to the center of the scar, dragging my lips down to the end of the line before kissing the path up to the top. I look up at her through my lashes, my eyes asking a million questions.

She grabs my face, planting a soft kiss on my lips.

My hands on her hips travel up her waist, to her ribs, and round her shoulders before gently resting on her neck. "Baby," I breathe, throat tight as a tornado of thoughts swirl around in my head.

She looks at me, eyes vulnerable. "When I was born," she starts off shakily, her eyes drifting down to the pad of her finger that's tracing my collarbone to distract herself. "I had a heart complication. The first few weeks of my life, I had multiple surgeries on my heart to get it working properly. I was fine for a while, my problems were manageable, but when I turned ten my heart became unrepairable."

Tears pool in her eyes and she tips her head back to keep them at bay. She grabs her shirt, next to us on the bed, and uses the sleeve to wipe her eyes before draping the fabric over her bare chest, hugging it to her.

"At ten years old I had to have a heart transplant," she continues. "I was put on the waiting list, and just when I thought I was never going to get a heart in time, one showed up at the last minute that was a match. The heart they brought in was Cora's daughter's. Her daughter was walking home from school that day and got struck by a car."

Tears pour down her cheeks and my chest grows uncomfortably tight.

"They brought her to the hospital and pronounced her brain dead. Cora was absolutely devastated, as any parent would be, but as a nurse she knew she had to act fast and make the toughest decision of her life. She knew her daughter wasn't going to come back, so she decided to donate her organs to other dying kids who could be saved, and give them a fighting chance. She didn't want any kid to go through what her daughter went through, or any parent to go through what she went through."

Her tone changes halfway through her last sentence, sounding hard, cynical.

"When I woke up from surgery"—she swallows thickly—"the only person by my bedside was Cora. My parents, they were gone."

I jerk my head back, utterly confused. "What?"

She wipes away more tears falling from her eyes. "Stan and Monica, they're not my real parents. They're my adoptive parents," she confesses, throwing me for a loop. "My real parents split during the transplant. They claimed it was too much and that they would never be able to afford all my hospital bills."

Anger bubbles inside my chest. "They can't do that," I argue, not knowing how any parent could just up and leave a kid who just came off of the operating table.

A small, bitter laugh escapes the back of her throat. "They did. After I recovered from surgery I was placed in foster care, but no one wanted a kid with my medical history. Cora wanted to adopt me herself, but she knew she didn't have the funds or the time with her job to take care of me like someone else could. But she always stuck by my side, her daughter a piece of me, and finally I found Stan and Monica. As transplant recipients themselves, they understood and accepted me with open arms."

A genuine but sad smile makes its way onto her lips. "They adopted me when I was thirteen, and I moved to Georgia with them. Cora came along with me," she explains. "She feels like her daughter is a large piece of me that she can't let go of quite yet."

Oh this girl. My sweet, strong, beautiful girl. I don't know how I didn't figure it out sooner. Never in a million years would I have guessed she'd grown up the way she did. That our stories could ever compare.

I grab her face in my hands, bringing her lips to mine in a desperate kiss. I kiss her fervently, conveying just how much I adore her.

"You are so, so strong," I praise her, placing stray kisses along her neck and shoulders. "I don't know how you did it," I confess. Not once has she ever given the slightest hint about her shocking past. Despite all the misfortune, she came out on top, seemingly unaffected.

Now it's her turn to grab my face, looking me in the eyes. "I didn't become a prisoner to my past," she says, voice packed with meaning, her message directed to me. "An unfortunate past isn't a life sentence."

I feel as though she just punched me in the gut, knocking some sense into me. I never looked at it that way. I was always so focused on being such a miserable, angry kid because my mother was such a shitty parent that I never cared to give anyone else a chance. I was so consumed by my past that I forgot to enjoy the present half of the time.

So completely in awe and mesmerized by her, I reclaim her lips with mine, kissing her with everything I have. I trail my hands all over her body, not missing a single beautiful inch.

If I could, I would flip her over right now and worship every inch of her body, not leaving a single part of her untouched. I want her to feel beautiful, desired, loved. *Whole.* Because she is so far from broken.

I won't make love to her right now, though. I'm not sure if I'd even be able to properly with all my injuries, but that doesn't mean I can't hold her close and profess my unyielding love for her.

Tenderly, I grab the shirt draped over her chest and remove it, throwing it to the side and exposing her to me once again. I admire her for a moment before leaning back in and pressing my lips to her damaged skin, my hands running up and down her back, sending a shiver down her spine.

She threads her hands through my hair, letting out a small sigh of appreciation.

"So damn beautiful," I murmur against her skin, kissing every available inch. "I love you," I breathe against her lips.

She smiles into the kiss. "I love you too."

FORTY

Finches

My crutches click loudly against the tiled hospital floors as I struggle to hop along the corridor. Everything still hurts, and all my bruises are starting to turn a nasty yellowish color, while the road rash is scabbing over nicely.

After my accident Olivia and I stayed in Florida a few more days to rest, cooped up in the hotel room, before attempting the uncomfortable five-hour drive back home. I profusely apologized for ruining our vacation, but she insisted I hadn't.

Since the incident at the nursing home, my mother's calls have been persistent, but I've blocked her number and dodged any unknown caller IDs to avoid her at all costs. I have nothing to say to her anyway. For a minute I was scared she was going to find out about my accident or find out which hotel I was staying at and hunt me down, but I haven't seen her since the nursing home, thankfully. And I plan to keep it that way, as harsh as it may be.

Back at home now, Olivia helps me through the hallways of the hospital after completing the follow-up appointment with my doctor. He said everything is going to take time, but it should heal properly. As far as my football career goes, as I suspected, he doesn't expect me to bounce back and be the athlete I once was, basically crushing any dreams I have of making it to the NFL.

A heavy rock of disappointment and uncertainty sits in the pit of my stomach as I scramble to figure out what the hell I'm going to do now. I know I'm going to graduate in a few months with my degree in exercise science, but I've honestly never given much thought about actually using it. I always pictured myself going straight to the NFL, not even needing my degree, but now I have to digest that's not a possibility anymore.

Olivia walks beside me like someone who would walk with a toddler, tense and observant, ready to catch me in case I fall over. I don't know how she expects to catch me though, given I'm twice her size.

Halfway down the hall, a voice calls Olivia's name, and we both look over our shoulders, finding Cora coming up behind us.

Cora smiles. "I thought that was you," she says, walking up to us and hugging Olivia.

"Hi, Cora," Olivia greets her, hugging her back.

Cora glances down at her watch, her brow furrowing. "You're early."

Olivia lets out a small laugh. "Oh, no. I was going to run home first before I came back up for dinner," she says, and I suddenly realize it's Tuesday. "I'm here now for his appointment," she clarifies, placing a gentle hand on my shoulder.

Cora frowns with worry, observing my injuries. "Oh my. What happened?"

"It's a long story," I admit.

"I'll fill you in later," Olivia assures her. "Let me just run him back home and I'll be back up in about a half an hour or so."

"That's okay, baby. I can just wait around here somewhere while you guys catch up," I insist, not wanting her to drive me all the way to the dorm just to come back here.

She frowns. "No, I don't want you to be uncomfortable."

I smile, leaning over to press a kiss to the top of her head. "I'll be fine," I promise. "You guys go enjoy your dinner."

She still doesn't seem sold on the idea. "Why don't you come have dinner with us?" she offers. "Is that all right, Cora?"

Cora looks hesitant for a moment, and before I can insist on not wanting to intrude, Olivia speaks up, noticing the look on Cora's face as well.

"It's okay. He knows," she tells Cora with a reassuring look.

Cora's eyes widen a fraction in surprise before she turns almost sheepish. She clears her throat, looking at me as if I hold all of her secrets. But deep down I also see the gratitude behind her eyes, like a weight has finally been lifted off of her shoulders by having someone else know about her tragedy and accept her decision. I feel as though she has trust in me now, knowing her truth.

"Yeah," Cora says definitively. "Let's all have dinner together."

The three of us head to the cafeteria, grabbing some food and sitting down. Olivia and Cora mainly engage in conversation. I accept being the third wheel and only cut into their conversation when prompted, letting them have their time together.

Conversation starts to slow once we're all finished eating and an uncomfortable charge hangs in the air. Cora eyes me warily, almost unsure about something.

Olivia leans over and places a comforting hand on her arm. "It's okay," she reassures Cora before turning to me. "She's just going to listen to my heart," she explains solemnly.

I swallow thickly, nodding. I remember the first time I saw Olivia at the hospital with Cora and she was listening to her heart then, telling me this is a weekly ritual.

With a shaky breath Cora grabs the stethoscope draped around her neck and Olivia scoots closer to her. Cora puts the earpieces in her ears and positions the chest piece over Olivia's heart, listening.

Cora closes her eyes, a pained expression crossing her face as she listens to her daughter's—now Olivia's—heartbeat. I can tell this is hard for her, that she's reliving that day all over again in her head, the wound of her daughter's death still not fully closed.

Cora listens to Olivia's heartbeat for several minutes before pulling away with misty eyes. She places her stethoscope back around her neck, folding her hands in her lap and staring down at them.

"We were finally getting our lives together," she confesses sadly, her voice a raspy whisper. "I got a great job in a different state, and we were able to move away from the awful apartment we were in."

She sniffs, wiping at a lone tear that rolls down her cheek.

"We moved all the way from Florida to Louisiana, thinking we were going to have a fresh start," she continues, clearly vulnerable talking about her daughter. "It was just me and her. I started a great job, and she was in a good school, and not even a month in, she was walking home when a driver swerved off the road and struck her."

Tears streak down her face, and I glance over at Olivia to see silent tears running down her own cheeks too.

"Lexi was such a good kid," Cora declares through her tears.

Lexi.

That name makes my stomach lurch, my mind drifting to Lexi from my childhood and then to what Cora said, my heart dropping.

Lexi. Shitty apartment. Florida. Nurse. My mind homes in on those facts. *There's no way*, I think. There's no way there could be any connection. This has to be one of those freak coincidences, right?

My hands begin to shake, and I can't bite back the question haunting my mind. "Cora, what was Lexi's last name?"

She looks at me skeptically, wondering why I would ask such a question. "Sampson," she says slowly. "Why?"

My chest tightens and I suddenly feel like I'm going to throw up.

"Lexi . . . you guys lived on the third floor of the Watson apartment complex," I state, voice shaking. "I lived below you. Lexi and I were friends. She used to see me sitting out on the steps all the time when my mom and her boyfriend were fighting. She helped save my life. *You* helped save my life," I inform her, remembering her and Lexi rushing me to the hospital after Lexi found me the night Benny pushed me down the stairs.

Cora's teary eyes widen in realization and disbelief. "You . . . you're that little boy," she realizes.

Tears prick my eyes, and I feel like I'm lost in an alternate universe.

My mind races a million miles a minute, trying to digest everything.

Lexi's dead, I realize, my heart cracking. I haven't seen her since I was placed in foster care, but I always hoped to find her again one day to thank her for saving my life.

My eyes drift over to Olivia, who's got a hand covering her mouth, absorbing the new revelation.

Not only did Lexi save my life, but she saved Olivia's too.

Just when I thought I knew Olivia's story, I realize I didn't know everything after all.

From the moment I set eyes on Olivia, I knew there was something special about her. Something that beckoned me closer, to take a second look. She hid her original secret from me so well that I completely missed it. Then once she told me, I thought I had her all figured out, but it turns out there's so much more to her story than we both thought.

My heart is racing with so many emotions it feels like it's going to burst.

My eyes drift from Olivia's face down to her chest, staring at her in awe. Just when I thought I couldn't love her and her sweet heart more, she surprises me yet again. As a kid, Lexi was one of the few people to actually care about me, show me kindness, and knowing she's connected to Olivia feels oddly fitting.

Emotionally raw, we all stare at each other in disbelief and silent understanding of our unbelievable connection.

"Thank you," I whisper, my words directed to Cora.

Not only did she give up her daughter to save others' lives, but she also took care of Olivia. She stuck by her side all these years. She sat by her hospital bedside when no one else did, only after sitting with me at mine a couple of years prior. Cora is an angel in disguise, and I can't thank her enough.

A whole new flood of appreciation for this woman rushes through me, and I'm forever indebted to her for all she's done. Without her—without Lexi—the love of my life wouldn't be sitting here with me right now. I probably wouldn't even be sitting here right now.

In the end, it's amazing how small the world really is, how things can turn out.

>> <<

The first day of the spring semester I'm woken up by Chase loudly stumbling into our room, dropping his bags on the floor before rifling through his desk, throwing things around and rushing back out the door to his first class.

Unable to fall back asleep, I decide to get up before my alarm goes off, allotting myself extra time to get ready, given my broken leg. Only five more weeks to go with this damn hunk of plaster and then I'm free.

I carefully sit up in bed and gingerly swing my legs over the edge. Grabbing my crutches propped up against the nightstand, I lift myself up from the bed and glance around the room. It looks like a fucking tornado ripped through.

Chase's duffel bags are haphazardly thrown next to his bed and half of his desk drawers are open, their contents strewn all over the floor.

I sigh in aggravation, maneuvering around all his shit to put some clothes on and get ready.

After getting dressed, brushing my hair and teeth, and applying some deodorant and cologne, I hobble back over to my desk where I already have all of my stuff packed and ready for class, thanks to my lovely girlfriend. On the short trip over, the bottom of my crutch lands on top of a folder and it nearly slips out from under me.

"Fucking Chase," I growl, bending over to pick up the folder. To my luck, all the papers spill out all over the floor.

Pissed, I throw the folder on his bed and angrily grab my desk chair, dragging it over to at least sit down to pick up the papers so I don't fall flat on my face trying to balance. Gathering up the papers, I realize they're notes from our biology class last semester, the class code scribbled in the top corner of every page.

I observe the handwriting, determining it's not Chase's. The handwriting is big, bubbly, *legible*. Yep, definitely not Chase's. He hardly ever took notes in class anyway. He must have taken them off the girl in our class that he has a massive crush on to study for the final.

Reaching for another paper, I see a bunch of bird names highlighted as subtitles, several bullet points listed under each species. My eyes automatically find the finch and I can't help but smile reading the notes written down.

Finch:

- *Darwin's theory of evolution*
- *Differ in beaks, body size, and behavior*
- *Quiet*
- *Social in their own groups*
- *Need other finches for stability and to thrive*
- *Live in large groups out in the wild and rarely migrate*

I remember giving Olivia the nickname Finch at the beginning of last semester just because I thought she was sweet and quiet and never left her hometown. But there's way more to her than that.

Sitting back, I now realize most of the people around us are just finches living among other finches. Olivia and I found each other because we're one and the same. Stan and Monica found Olivia because they were all similar. Lexi, Cora, we're all the same. Connected. While we all may differ physically and emotionally, we're all parallel.

Just like finches, we thrive together. We lean on each other and understand one another.

When Olivia found me, I was a lonely, miserable individual. And despite being polar opposites, we somehow naturally attracted each other. My life completely flipped when she walked into it, and now I realize it's because we were just two finches who found each other, finding our niche. Our flock. Everything falling into place.

I gather up the rest of Chase's papers and throw them on his desk, my heart surprisingly happy.

A soft knock comes from the other side of my door, and I instantly know it's Olivia. After a beat she slowly opens the door and sticks her head in. "Ready?" she asks.

I can't help but smile. "Yeah, I'm ready, Finch."

I shrug on my backpack and grab my crutches, hopping out the door.

She walks me to my first class, making sure I get there all right with my leg.

"I'll see you later in the Anatomy II lab," she says, kissing me goodbye at the door of my first class.

I grin. "I'll see you then. Hopefully we both get good partners," I tease.

Olivia and I already planned it out last semester that we'd pick the same lab section this year just so we could be partners again.

She smiles, playing along. "I hope so."

Epilogue

I zip up my gym bag and sling it over my shoulder, rounding the wooden desk and locking the door to the office behind me on my way out. The sound of metal clanking against metal echoes off the walls as players pack up for the day and head home.

"Great session today, Bronx," Coach says, coming up behind me and clapping a strong hand on my shoulder, looking proud. There's only a few weeks left until the playoffs and everyone is working their asses off to win the championship.

"Thanks, Coach."

Since freshman year, Coach has been the closest thing I've had to a father figure. I was his star pupil all four years of my college career, and when we found out I would never fully bounce back from my injuries and make it to the NFL like we both dreamed, he took me under his wing, offering me a trainer position right after I graduated. As an NCAA Division I team ranking in the top three for years, the pay is decent, but Coach is trying his best to work me up to assistant coach, where the starting pay will be almost six figures.

For now, to pay the bills while Olivia is in medical school, I work for the college as well as part-time at a high-end gym downtown as a personal trainer. Both of our schedules are pretty hectic at the moment, me with preparing the team for the championships while Olivia's rounding out her fourth year of med school, but we always manage to fall asleep together every night and wake up to kiss the other goodbye in the morning.

Thinking about her, I add a little more pep to my step as I head out to my truck in the parking lot, jumping in and driving home. Arriving at our apartment complex, I frown, not seeing her car in the parking lot, meaning she got stuck at clinicals late. Again.

I park in my designated spot and step inside the main floor lobby, veering to the mailboxes. I slip the brass key into the lock, and find a few pieces of mail.

Junk. Advertisement. Junk. Junk. Bingo.

A smile spreads across my face. I know exactly what's in this envelope from the DMV.

Elated, I tuck the mail under my arm and slip into the elevator to ride up to the fourth floor. I unlock the front door of our apartment and hang my keys on the hook, setting the mail on the counter on my way to the bedroom. I put away my gym bag and strip for a quick shower, throwing on a T-shirt and some sweats after.

Padding to the kitchen, I open up the refrigerator to pull out some butter and cheese, grabbing the loaf of Texas toast on the counter on my way to the stove. I pull out a pot and a pan and throw them on the stove, ready to make Olivia's favorite meal—grilled cheese and tomato soup.

When I talked to her briefly on the phone earlier today, I could tell she was having a rough day. She's currently in her pediatrics rotation and I can tell it's taking a toll on her physically and emotionally. She's been spending so much overtime at the hospital lately, getting home late at least three nights out of the week, that she deserves a night of spoiling.

As soon as I'm done dumping the tomato soup into the pot and adding extra spices to it to give it more flavor, I hear the front door open. I look over my shoulder to see Olivia walk in and set her keys and purse by the door.

"Hi, baby," I greet her, flipping one of the grilled cheeses over in the pan before turning the heat down to give her my attention.

Her tired eyes look over at me, a fond smile gracing her lips. "Hi," she says, her voice soft and a bit raspy. She walks over to the kitchen in her navy scrubs, and I turn away from the stove to kiss her. As she glances at the stovetop, an adorable pout forms on her face. "Bronx, you didn't have to do this."

"Yes I did," I insist, brushing some of the tendrils of hair falling out of her bun and framing her face behind her ear. "We've hardly seen each other all week."

Her eyes grow soft. "Have I ever told you how much I love you?" she says, appreciation clear in her voice.

"Once or twice," I tease, kissing her lips one more time before turning back to the stove, making sure nothing is burning.

She wraps her arms around my middle from behind, resting her cheek against my back.

"How was your day?" I ask gently, already sensing it wasn't great.

She lets out a disheartening sigh, her arms tightening around my torso. "I don't want to talk about it," she says, voice muffled by my T-shirt.

I frown, placing my hand on top of both of hers resting on my stomach. "Why don't you go change and get comfortable. Dinner will be ready in a few minutes."

She lets out a hum of acknowledgment, kissing my back before unwinding her arms from around my waist and heading to the bedroom.

By the time I'm finished plating the food and carrying it to the table, Olivia emerges from the bedroom in her pajamas. She gives me another look of appreciation and adoration before we both sit down and dig in.

Olivia picks up the sandwich, taking a bite, the cheese pulling from the center. She lets out a hum of appreciation, her eyes practically rolling to the back of her head as she savors the gooey, cheesy goodness. "Remind me again, have I told you how much I love you?" she says after she finishes chewing.

I chuckle, taking a large bite of my own sandwich, the perfectly toasted bread providing the slightest crunch. I chew and swallow before replying, "I love you, too, baby."

"How was work?" she asks, adjusting in her chair to sit with her legs crisscrossed.

"Good," I say genuinely, the generic reply not leaving a bitter taste in my mouth anymore.

I'll admit, I was absolutely crushed when my NFL dreams went down the drain. All I ever pictured for myself was making it to the NFL and retiring after a long, successful career. It's what I thought I wanted—needed—to feel validation, but I realize I was all wrong. Looking at the girl sitting across from me, I'm not sure that's what I needed after all.

Picturing it now, I don't know how sustainable an NFL career would have been for our relationship. I have no doubt in my mind that she would have been supportive, and we'd have made the part-time long distance work, but now getting to fall asleep next to her every night is something I can't imagine giving up. Being miles away and not being able to hold her when she has a bad day, being away from her for certain holidays, I don't think I could do it. I never factored in finding the love of my life when calculating my original, seemingly inflexible, plans.

I think back to everything that's happened since the accident. I haven't seen my mother since Florida. But that doesn't mean she's stopped trying to contact me—especially after my grandmother died. She passed about six months after I saw her, and it turns out she did leave everything to me. Not that she had much, but my mother wants every penny she can get to feed her addiction.

And keeping on the topic of annoyances of my life, Rat Boy and Adrianna finally got what was coming to them. After their little stunt, they both ended up getting expelled. As suspected, Rat Boy squealed and provided text messages as evidence to drag Adrianna down with him.

At the complete opposite end of the annoyance spectrum, Delilah graduated with me and Olivia, the three of us throwing our caps up in the air side by side. But while Olivia and I stayed in Georgia, Delilah got accepted into a great medical school out on the West Coast. The two girls talk at least once a week over FaceTime. It used to be more, but as they are both ending their fourth year it's almost impossible to even squeeze in one FaceTime with how busy they are.

"The team is doing great this year. You're still able to make it to the championship game if we make it, right?" I ask. I know her schedule is hectic and changing day by day, but she promised she'd be there.

She smiles. "I wouldn't miss it for the world."

I give her an appreciative smile. "Thanks, baby. I know you're superbusy with clinical rotations, so it means a lot. How were your kids today?" I ask, knowing she's grown attached to some of the kids at the hospital, having her favorites.

Her smile depletes. "Carter isn't doing so well," she admits sadly.

Carter is a cute little blond-headed boy who's managed to capture her heart. The five-year-old has been having some trouble with one of his heart valves and doctors are trying their best to get him better. I know Olivia feels a connection there, and it's crushing her to see the kid get sicker and sicker.

Olivia continues to talk about Carter and his declining health, as well as other things that happened at the hospital today. Now I understand why she wasn't having the greatest of days. I do my best to try to comfort her.

"Anyway." She sighs, exhausted, seemingly mentally shaking off the bad day and putting on a smile for me. "How was your day?"

"Good," I admit enthusiastically. "Really good, actually." I hope my good news also puts her in a good mood.

She gives me a strange but amused look at my sudden giddy behavior.

Excited, I hop up from the table and grab the piece of mail addressed to me on the counter and bring it over to the table. "I got something in the mail today," I state, sliding the envelope across the table to her.

She picks it up, her eyes immediately landing on the words *Department of Motor Vehicles*. "What's this?" she asks, frowning. Then her eyes scan who the envelope is addressed to. "Bronx!" she scolds me, her eyes wide. "You can't just give the DMV my nickname!"

I bite back a laugh, knowing her brain must be going haywire right now reading *Bronx Finch*, thinking I did something to mess everything up and the DMV really screwed up big-time by letting it slide. But that's not the case at all.

A couple of months ago I started the process of legally changing my last name, wanting it to finally have some meaning. So what better than Finch?

I laugh, unable to suppress it any longer. "No. It's *my* name."

She looks at me, more confused than before, and I can't help but smile.

"I changed my last name," I explain.

"You what?" she breathes in disbelief, looking at me as if I'm playing some kind of weird prank on her.

My grin deepens. "Open it," I instruct, nodding to the envelope.

Slowly, almost cautiously, she peels open the envelope and plucks out my new driver's license, gawking at it.

A dozen emotions scroll across her face, and I lean over the table, taking the plastic card from her and setting it off to the side. I lace our fingers together before speaking. "Don't be mad," I say, suddenly feeling nervous.

I remember when I came home with a tattoo of a finch. I had the little bird permanently perched on top of the last *N* in the UNKNOWN tattoo splayed across my back, making the word less significant by proclaiming my love for the girl who changed my life and helped erase the meaning of that tattoo. But I'd be lying if I said that Olivia didn't have a mild freak-out over it, claiming tattoos are an automatic curse for disaster in relationships. It's grown on her though, thank god, and after the freak-out stage she found it sweet.

"Why would you change your name?" she asks, her head adorably tilting to the side in confusion.

I shrug, playing with her fingers. "I want a last name that means something. I've wanted to change it for a while now, but I never knew what to change it to," I admit softly, glancing up to catch her staring at me with understanding. "I know finches are sort of our thing, and they symbolize joy and better days ahead, and that's what I want," I explain. "A fresh start." Without the weight of my last name—which is connected to the person I used to be—dragging me down.

She gives me a thoughtful smile, her eyes glossy as she stands up from her chair and rounds the table to take a seat on my lap, wrapping her arms around my neck. I gladly accept her, holding her tight and kissing her lips.

"I love it," she whispers against my mouth, approving my new, legal last name.

"Good," I whisper back.

We finish dinner and begin to clean up.

"Let me get it," I insist, taking her plate from her hands with a kiss. "Go relax. Maybe run a bath and I'll meet you in a bit."

She gives me another soft, appreciative smile before retreating to the bedroom. I clean up everything as fast as I can to meet her in our attached bathroom, finding her standing in the middle of it in her robe, staring down at her phone, probably checking emails.

I sneak up behind her, wrapping my arms around her waist. "None of that," I lightly scold, kissing the side of her head and taking her phone from her hands, setting it on the counter.

She spins around in my arms, a guilty, sheepish smile adorning her face, telling me she was, in fact, reading hospital emails.

The tub is full of water, and a generous number of bubbles float on the surface while a few scented candles litter the counter. I reach between our bodies to toy with the silk tie of her robe.

"I think this is the part where we strip," I whisper.

A small blush rushes to her cheeks. After all these years, I find it adorable that I still have this kind of effect on her. Shyly, she reaches for the hem of my shirt, her fingers slipping up and under the fabric, touching my naked skin. My eyes flutter shut as I let out a groan, loving the feeling of her hands on me.

Impatient, I reach behind me to grab the collar, pulling my shirt up and off. I tug at the tie of her robe and it comes undone, the fabric now limply hanging on her body. Gently, I push the silk off her shoulders, peppering the newly exposed skin with kisses. She sighs in contentment and reaches for the waistband of my sweats.

When all our clothes are discarded on the floor, I grab her face, kissing her softly before dipping my head farther and kissing just between her collarbones, pressing my lips to the tip of the light-pink scar running down the center of her chest.

I hold out my hand and help her step into the tub first, watching her sink into the warm water. Once she's settled, I slip into the tub behind her, pulling her back against my chest. She relaxes, her body melting against mine. Her eyes flutter closed as she tilts her head back onto my shoulder, letting out a contented sigh.

My lips find her neck as my hands massage her sides. She giggles and I think I've accidentally hit one of her ticklish spots.

She laughs quietly again, and I pull back to see a large smile on her face. “I can’t believe you changed your last name to Finch,” she says, more to herself, giggling happily.

I smile into her shoulder, my eyes drifting to look through the door frame of the bathroom and into our bedroom. My eyes land on the bottom left drawer of the dresser and my stomach flutters. There, at the very bottom of the drawer, deep inside the pocket of a random pair of pants, is a ring. After Olivia is done with med school and things slow down a little, I plan on proposing.

I’d be lying if I said I didn’t have her in mind when picking out the last name. Not only is it her nickname but I think it represents us well; just two finches who found each other and became one, sticking close to the other finches around us. Our family. I did some light research and found out that finches symbolize diversity, happiness, vulnerability, and family, among other things, and I think it’s perfect.

“Believe it, baby.” I grin.

“Bronx Finch.” She pauses, mulling over the name, testing it out. “I like it,” she declares, smiling.

“I’m glad you approve,” I tease. Because it’s going to become her last name soon too.

Scan the QR code to discover what Olivia is feeling right now.

Acknowledgments

I know I wrote a book full of words, but I seem to be at a loss for them now to properly express my excitement and gratitude.

First and foremost, thank you to Wattpad and the readers for making this possible. I can't thank you enough for your support, love, and encouragement. It has been an absolute pleasure growing as a writer with you and working with such an amazing team to make this happen. I would especially like to shout out my editor, Fiona, for making me look good by helping me shape this story and these characters into something worthy of being on an actual bookshelf. I sincerely appreciate all of your time, hard work, and expertise.

To the very few friends and family I shared this exciting news with from the beginning, thank you for all of your excitement, kind words, and support. You'll never know how much I appreciate you.

Lastly, thank you to that scared, lonely, depressed girl who decided to give herself purpose again through writing.

Growing up, I was always the A+ model student who thought she had her whole life planned out at ten years old. I thrived in academics and measured my self-worth based on my grades. It was just how I was wired. I graduated high school with honors and a 4.0 GPA, and I thought I was going to excel in college as well. But once I got to college, things were not as easy as I expected. The course material was harder, I struggled with being away from home for the first time, and experienced some big life changes. My As started becoming Bs, and things just weren't turning out the way I'd planned.

Then after graduation, I got rejected by the master's program I'd dreamed about for over a decade, and I felt like a complete failure. I was so lost, humiliated, and confused, and I started writing as a distraction, an escape as I struggled to figure out what to do with my life next. I used it as a coping mechanism to give myself purpose again, sharing my work online to receive validation from others—which in return gave me some self-validation. But never did I anticipate writing to lead me here today.

Eventually I found a new career path, and I realized that what I thought I always wanted may not have been what I needed—and it certainly wasn't my only option. I didn't fail because I didn't achieve my goal, I actually won because I broke free of the box I'd put myself in.

I guess what I'm trying to say is, never give up on yourself. When one door closes, another will open. You just have to have faith, patience, and give yourself grace.

Also, shout out to everyone involved in making transplants happen, from the donors, to the doctors, to everyone else working tirelessly behind the scenes, especially my lab crew! Funny enough, I wrote this story long before working in transplants, and now I have a whole new appreciation for organ donation. If you feel inclined, please consider becoming an organ donor and giving the gift of life to those in need.

About the Author

Nicole Alfrine is a new adult contemporary romance author from St. Louis, Missouri. She loves a good "opposites attract" and "he falls first and harder" trope. When she isn't writing and being a complete recluse, you can catch her doing hot girl stuff (which occasionally includes crying) in a lab, making use of her bachelor of science. You can also find her playing bingo, ghost hunting, or doing something else completely random with her friends.

Want more from Nicole Alfrine?

Brain Games

Coming soon from W by Wattpad Books!

Don't miss this sneak peek!

ONE

Strike a Match

I curse my hands for trembling as I run them over the skirt of my maroon dress, smoothing it out. I'm going to be a neurosurgeon for crying out loud. I can't have my hands shake this much with silly little nerves.

But today is a big day. A life-changing day, I remind myself.

I huff out an impatient, anxious sigh, assessing and nit-picking my reflection in the mirror, noting the changes my body has gone through these last four years.

My face is more defined, despite the fourteen pounds I've gained since undergrad. My natural golden skin has only gotten a half shade darker, despite living in California. I guess that's my fault; I spent too much time inside studying instead of soaking up the beautiful sunshine.

Lastly, I note how much older I look. It's most likely due to stress, and I don't look like my eighty-year-old grandmother yet. I just look more mature and wise. At least that's what I tell myself.

But there's something off . . .

I stare long and hard at my reflection before scanning the bathroom counter, finding nothing that sparks my intuition.

When I open up the medicine cabinet, the first thing I spot is my contact lenses case, and then it dawns on me.

I take the small case out and set it on the counter before walking into my bedroom to grab my signature thick-rimmed glasses off the nightstand. I take them back to the bathroom and wash my hands before removing my contact lenses and putting on my glasses instead.

There.

Now I feel more like me.

Ever since second grade I've had to wear glasses—since my eyesight is pure and utter crap. I've worn glasses all my life because contacts sort of freaked me out, but I had to suck it up once I reached medical school.

Once I hit rotations in the operating room, I decided to ditch my glasses for contacts because my glasses would slip off my nose, or they'd frequently fog up when I wore a mask. Though I despise contacts, they have made working in the OR easier.

Plus, wearing contacts sort of makes me feel like Superman. By day, I'm in the OR helping save lives, while at night, and on my rare days off, I'm like mere mortal Clark Kent in my beloved thick-rimmed glasses.

Running my fingers through my dark shoulder-length curls one last time, I can't help but smile at my reflection in the mirror—at the brilliant and resilient woman staring back at me. I've worked my ass off my whole academic career to get to this moment, and I'll be damned if it doesn't go how I always dreamt it would.

A soft rap on the bathroom door tears me away from my thoughts, and I turn to see my momma standing in the doorway. She's also dressed up for the occasion, wearing a forest green dress that complements her warm, golden skin tone. She gives me a soft, meaningful smile, knowing I'm freaking out in my head.

"Ready?"

I let out a shaky breath and flash her a wary smile. "As ready as I'll ever be."

She extends her hand to me, and I instinctively place mine in hers, savoring her touch.

Since moving away for undergrad and medical school, I haven't been able to see my family much. Especially when I moved all the way to the West Coast for med school.

At least in undergrad I was only a five-hour drive away from home—four and a half if I sped—so I could go back home every once in a while. But med school has only allowed me to go back home and visit on major holidays. So to say I've missed my momma would be a huge understatement. I'm super grateful she and my daddy were both able to fly out to be with me on my special day. Not that they'd miss it for the world.

She pulls me close, grabbing hold of my other hand and squeezing it. "Delilah Kareena Harper, I am so proud of you," she states, her voice soft but strong and proud, pricking tears in my eyes. "You've become the woman you've always dreamed of, and no matter what happens today, no matter where you end up, you're going to be the best neurosurgeon the world has to offer."

I try my best to swallow the lump in my throat, but my voice still comes out strained. "Thanks, Momma."

She gives me a tight smile and I can tell she's holding back tears of her own. "I want to give you something," she whispers, letting go of my hands. She reaches for the dainty gold ring on her right hand, sliding it off.

My throat grows uncomfortably tight. "Momma, n—"

"Shhh," she hushes me, already knowing I'm going to object. "I want you to have it," she insists, grabbing my right hand and sliding the small ruby on my ring finger.

I admire the ring my daddy gave my momma years ago when they first started dating. He bought it for her on their third date, at the market where they'd first met in India.

My momma is originally from India, while my dad is from the States. He was studying abroad and claims it was love at first sight when he found her—even though she rejected him multiple times before he eventually wore her down and scored a date.

It's a long-running joke that my momma rejected my daddy so many times because she thought he was just some horny American college boy trying to find a fling to keep him occupied for the semester. Little did she know he was head over heels for her and that he'd worm his way into her heart with his "undeniable charm and wit" (his words), and she'd end up marrying the weirdo and move with him to a whole new country to start a family.

While the ring is simple, it's beyond beautiful and makes me think of my parents' perfectly imperfect and humorous love story.

My momma used to catch me sneaking into her jewelry box all the time as a kid to admire the ring, and I'd make her tell me their love story every time. She'd always promised to give me the ring when I was older, I just didn't think today would be the day.

"Momma," I say, and she gives me a warning look, daring me to protest. "Thank you."

She kisses my cheek before grabbing my hand to lead me into my tiny apartment living room where my daddy is sitting on the couch, pretending not to be wringing his hands in anticipation.

Once we have everything, we run downstairs to the parking garage and jump in my car.

>> <<

I lead my parents through one of the many academic buildings I've come to know like the back of my hand over the past four years. We walk down the long stretch of hallway before finding the correct auditorium, a sign outside the door welcoming us to McCord University's Match Day Ceremony. Butterflies instantly swarm my stomach, everything becoming that much more real.

I peek inside the auditorium and find people still setting up. Reaching into my small cross-body purse, I pull out my phone to check the time. Forty-five minutes early. In true Delilah Harper fashion.

One of my many personality traits is being early. To class, to appointments, to functions, and especially to match day. While it may have only been a ten-minute drive over from my apartment, you never know when the world is going to throw you a ten-car pileup or a doomsday-apocalyptic situation of some sort. Therefore, it's always good to have a totally sensible and reasonable forty-five-minute cushion. You know, because doomsday-apocalyptic situations typically include flesh-eating zombies that are certain to cause a traffic delay.

"Looks like we're the first ones here," my dad comments, a teasing lilt in his voice. He knows and loves to mock my arrive-unnecessarily-early policy.

"Not quite," a deep voice rumbles from behind us, smooth and rich. There's also a teasing, amused lilt to the voice.

Of course. I don't even have to turn around to know who that voice belongs to.

Bradly Gallow, aka the biggest pain in my ass.

Since day one of medical school, Brad and I have had some sort of silent agreement to be sworn mortal enemies—the pair of us fighting to be top of our class. Throughout these past four years, we've been neck and neck, putting in the most hours while managing to kick and kiss all the appropriate asses. We're both gunning for the same highly competitive residency, and I'll be damned if he gets picked over me.

"Oh, hello," my daddy says, surprised that someone could be even earlier than his daughter. He sheepishly runs a hand through his salt-and-pepper hair, now embarrassed that his teasing me is invalid.

Reluctantly, I turn around and I'm immediately embraced by the cool, clean, delicious scent of Brad's cologne. I have to tilt my head back to look up at him, and I silently curse myself for not wearing heels today.

But I feared that I would end up falling and busting my ass if I tried walking up and down the auditorium steps in anything other than flats. Hell, I'm so jittery I may even trip in flats.

"Delilah." My name rolls off of Brad's tongue as soon as my brown eyes meet his.

I cross my arms tightly over my chest, hating that I always have to look up at him because he's so freaking tall. Heels would have only helped so much. "Bradly."

A triumphant grin graces his full lips as he realizes he's already got me agitated. "I'd like you to meet my parents: Dr. Kalani Gallow and Dr. Anthony Gallow," he says, gesturing to his left where two other people are standing behind him.

Of course both of his parents are doctors, I think, somehow managing not to roll my eyes.

Politely, I turn to the middle-aged man and woman and flash them a smile. They look nice enough, and it's no surprise they're both gorgeous and well-polished. "Nice to meet you."

Brad is almost a spitting image of his mother, with the same naturally tan skin and dark wavy hair. They have similar facial structures and the exact same rich, brown eyes and long, dark lashes. Both of his parents are a few inches shorter than him, so I'm wondering where on Earth he got the height. His father has fair skin, gracefully graying blond hair, and brown eyes. He stands about an inch taller than his wife, who's in sensible one-inch heels. The more I look, Brad and his father have the same bone structure, but Brad is definitely his mother's child.

"Are you going to introduce me to your parents?" Brad asks with a hint of condescension. If I could smack him across his stupidly pretty and chiseled face, I would.

Before I can even start introductions, my dad jumps right in.

"James Harper," he introduces himself a little too enthusiastically, extending his hand to sworn public enemy numero uno.

Brad steps forward, purposely brushing his arm against mine as he reaches to shake my father's hand. "Bradly Gallow, sir."

When Brad pulls back, he brushes my arm again, and I glance down to catch his tan, taut, and just the right amount of veiny forearm because he has the sleeves of his crisp white dress shirt rolled up to his elbows.

Damn him.

I grind my teeth to maintain my composure and try my best to ignore the feel of his radiating body heat. If our parents weren't here right now, I'd take a large, purposeful step back. Maybe even push him away.

Brad turns to my mother, giving her that brilliant, easy-going smile of his. "And I'm guessing you're Mrs. Harper?" he says, extending his hand to her next.

She smiles, and I can see it clear as day on her face that she's falling for his charm. I want to scream at her, *Keep it together, woman!*

I know he seems cute, Momma, but don't fall for it.

Bradly is the definition of tall, tan, and handsome. But he's also the definition of a complete and utter jackass.

I'll never forget the first day we met at orientation for med school. I was the first to arrive and he was the second. He was so confident and smug, introducing himself as if he were the CEO of a billion-dollar company. Although, I have a feeling a CEO would have been much humbler. Then, he had the audacity to eye me up and down, like a piece of meat, and tell me we should have an anatomy refresher before classes started, preferably later that night in his bedroom. And when that line absolutely did not work on me, he used it on the next girl who came along. That was automatically red flag number one.

Red flag number two was that he wore a full-blown navy suit to orientation and shoes—ironically the same shoes he's wearing today—that probably cost more than my rent. And they're ugly shoes! They remind me of loafers my eighty-year-old grandpa would wear, but somehow, Bradly still manages to make them look fashionable. Like he's a damn *GQ* model or something.

Red flag number three was that his name is Brad. I mean, come on. Brad is basically the male equivalent of a Karen.

But unfortunately, despite his devastatingly good looks and stereotypical air-headed frat boy name, he's actually unbelievably intelligent. I found that out on the first day of class when he blurted out the correct answer to the first question our professor asked, beating me to it. He could tell I was shocked, even impressed, and I sensed that gave him an enormous sense of satisfaction, because I think he was still ticked I refused to sleep with him. Since that moment, he decided to make my life a living hell by trying to compete with me in everything. But then again, I'm very competitive by nature so maybe I egged him on. Either way, it's been all out war ever since.

"Priya." My mother places her hand in his, shaking it.

"Nice to meet you, Priya. I have to admit, I almost mistook you for Delilah's sister." He smiles his most charming smile, the one that crinkles the corners of his eyes.

Vomit. I want to vomit. The projectile kind. Everywhere.

I also want to knock every one of his perfectly straight, pearly white teeth out—but one thing at a time.

My mother giggles. *Giggles!* Like, full-on schoolgirl giggles.

Traitor!

"Well, looks like we're all a bit early. How about we grab some coffee?" my dad suggests, not even fazed by Brad's comment to his wife. "I saw a small coffee cart and some tables when we walked in."

Is my family all just a bunch of traitors?

"That sounds wonderful," Kalani says, looping her arm through her husband's.

Our parents begin walking to the coffee cart, instantly chatting like they're all long-lost friends. My feet stay rooted to the floor as I blink at the backs of their heads, trying to wrap my head around what just happened.

Beside me, Brad clears his throat, and I snap my eyes in his direction. He gives me an almost knowing smirk and stretches out his arm, gesturing for me to follow them.

With a huff, I reluctantly do so, Brad right behind me.

TWO

Game, Set, Match

We all crowd around a small round table that should really only hold four people, max. Why we didn't just push two tables together, I don't know, but I really wish we had because I'm currently molded to my mother's side and trying my best not to brush against Brad, who's sitting to my left.

Of course the seating order has me sitting next to him, and of course he's practically manspreading, daring me to brush my knee against his by purposefully keeping his within an inch of mine. Hence why I'm plastered to my mother's side.

At the other side of the table, our dads are chatting up a storm like they're two old best friends catching up.

Again, traitor.

Not that my mother is any better. At the rate she and Kalani are going, I wouldn't be surprised if they make plans to go shopping and get mani-pedis together soon.

What is my life?

Brad leans over, lips inches from my ear. "Looks like they're hitting it off, huh?"

I only *harrumph* in response, and he has the audacity to smile at my displeasure. Jackass.

"Yeah, I can tell Dee's nervous." I hear my dad's voice across the table, and I turn my attention to him. He has an amused but proud look on his face as he stares at me. "If this were a normal day, she'd be on her third cup of coffee by now. She maybe drank a fourth of a cup this morning while she was getting ready, and I don't think I've even seen her take two sips of this one," he calls me out, gesturing to my coffee cup.

Subconsciously, I fidget with the cardboard sleeve around my cup as all eyes turn to me, making me nervous. I force myself to take a sip, the warm liquid immediately sinking to my stomach and churning uncomfortably.

Kalani gives me a comforting smile. "Where are you hoping to match today, Delilah?" she asks, making polite small talk.

"Warner Central Hospital in New York," I spew out immediately, like I have so many times before. It's a reflex at this point.

"Oh!" Her eyes light up with genuine interest and excitement. "That's a great hospital. Arguably the best in the country. What are you wanting to specialize in?"

"Neurosurgery," my parents and I all say in unison.

Kalani's smile grows. "That's what Bradly wants to go into as well!" She shoots a proud look at her son.

My parents fawn over the revelation, and soon enough, all four parents start swapping childhood stories about me and Brad.

I tune them out, my attention homing in on two classmates who just arrived with their families. More classmates trickle in, making me itch in anticipation to get into the auditorium and grab a perfect seat for the most important day of my life.

I don't realize all my muscles are tight and my leg is bouncing up and down obnoxiously until a hand lands on my thigh, squeezing it reassuringly. I look over at my mother to catch her giving me a knowing look.

"Well," my mother announces, setting her coffee on the table and lifting her hand from my thigh to glance at her watch. "Looks like there's about twenty minutes until showtime."

"Oh, yes," Anthony says, checking his own watch. "We should probably go grab some seats." He takes two more large gulps of his coffee before standing.

We all follow suit, standing up and recycling our cups in a nearby bin before walking back to the auditorium. I try my best to walk at a normal speed, but the nerves and anticipation have me leading our tiny pack by a margin of several feet.

Brad catches up to me easily with his naturally long strides, his hands shoved in the pockets of his dress pants, looking as cool as a cucumber. "I missed the glasses," he states casually.

I do my best not to trip over my own two feet. Glancing at him, I narrow my eyes in distrust. "What kind of game are you trying to play?" I accuse.

He shrugs. "No game, just a compliment. Haven't seen the glasses in a while since you started wearing contacts. They're cute."

I glare at him skeptically and he just chuckles, smirking as he slows his stride, letting me walk through the auditorium doors first. The room is already about a third of the way full with our fellow classmates and their families.

Without any consensus, I immediately head for the fifth row, claiming the aisle seat. I'm surprised when Brad follows, walking down the row and leaving four seats in between us for our parents.

Soon enough, our parents take their seats as more and more classmates show up. At 8:30 a.m. sharp, the auditorium is packed, and the head of the department takes the microphone at the front of the room to begin her speech about how hard we all have worked and how proud we should be of ourselves—as if I don't know how hard I've busted my ass for this.

For the next thirty minutes, all the medical school bigwigs give similar speeches, trying to make us feel all mushy and gushy inside and pull on the heartstrings of the parents, buying themselves time until the clock strikes 9:00 a.m.—12:00 p.m. EST— when we're officially allowed to start opening envelopes.

While everyone is talking, my eyes stay glued on Cindy, one of the department secretaries, who has all of the envelopes in her hands. The envelopes that seal our fates. While Cindy is one of the sweetest people on the planet, right now I want to tackle her to the ground and find my envelope. She's a petite sixty-two-year-old lady standing at a whopping five-foot-two. I think I can take her.

Finally, at 9:00 a.m. on the dot, the first envelope is distributed.

One by one, classmates are called up to the front to announce their fate, some walking away with shaky hands and tears of joy, while others are not nearly as ecstatic. I anxiously await my turn as names are being called in no particular order.

"Bradly Gallow."d

Brad stands up and his parents, along with my parents and a number of classmates, cheer him on as he makes his way down the row to the front of the room. As he passes behind me, his fingers skim the back of my chair before he walks down the stairs, and I get another waft of his cologne.

He walks to Cindy, grabbing his envelope and walking to the microphone. He gives the audience a spectacular smile before introducing himself.

For the first time today, I take a moment to really observe him. He's wearing a crisp white dress shirt, charcoal gray dress pants, and those stupidly ugly and overpriced dress shoes. Yet, he looks like a hotshot-millionaire-bad-boy ready to grace the cover of *Forbes*. His tan skin is extra glowy today, making him look radiant, while his dark, wavy hair is mussed to perfection.

Looking at his large, strong hands, I notice how steady they are.

He opens the envelope skillfully with a swipe of his finger under the flap, not tearing it or crinkling it whatsoever, and takes out the paper inside, his brown eyes scanning. A grin breaks out across his face, and I automatically know what he's about to say, my heart sinking to the pit of my stomach.

"Neurological surgery. Warner Central Hospital, New York."

He looks directly into my eyes as he says it, and I deflate faster than a balloon being stomped on. The crowd goes wild, but all I can hear is the ringing in my ears.

That's it. Just like that, my dreams are shattered. All that time I wasted busting my ass to beat him is useless now.

Bradly won.

A residency at Warner Central is exceptionally competitive, but a residency in their neurosurgery program is practically a one in a million chance. There's no way two people from the same school are going to earn a spot in the same residency.

Completely numb, I watch as Brad walks off the stage, doing a victory lap back to his seat. I don't look at him. I can't.

The few sips of coffee I had this morning begin to churn around in my empty stomach all over again, and my skin feels uncomfortably clammy. I try to even my breathing and ignore the urge to throw up until they call my name.

"Delilah Harper."

Like a newborn baby deer, I stand and my whole body is trembling with nerves. I somehow manage to make it down the steps without falling and grab my envelope from Cindy. She gives me a proud smile before my icy cold hand brushes hers and her smile falters to one of concern as she stares at me. I can only imagine the look of panic on my face.

Standing in front of the microphone, I stare down at the envelope in my trembling hands. Inside this envelope is the fate of my entire future. I almost want to laugh, possibly even cry, at how silly this all seems. How one piece of paper is going to change my whole life and determine my future. How one piece of paper is going to stare me in the face and remind me that Bradly Gallow won, and I'll have to settle for second best.

It would be one thing if he matched at any other hospital, but the fact that he matched at one of the best hospitals in the country—my dream hospital since I was seven years old and knew how to work a computer to research how to become a neurosurgeon—and in one of the most competitive specialties is like a knife straight to the heart.

At least you matched, I remind myself. *Some people don't*. I've heard horror stories about some people not being placed in a residency program on Match Monday, leaving them to scramble to try to scrape up one of the bottom-of-the-barrel positions leftover.

And now on Match Friday, I finally get to know where I've been placed.

This is it. This is what these past four years—my entire life, really—have come down to. All of the studying, work, tests, strategic planning, research, interviews, networking, money, sleepless nights, tears, stress, and worry come down to this. A few words typed out on a single damn piece of paper.

I may not be going to Warner Central, but hopefully I at least got one of my top-five picks.

I scan the crowd and lock eyes with my momma, who gives me a reassuring smile and nod. Subconsciously, I twist the ring she gave me around my finger, praying that no matter what this silly little piece of paper says, everything will work out.

Without thinking, my eyes drift over a few seats to find a pair of rich brown eyes staring back at me intently, face almost void of any emotion. Almost. There's something there, swirling just beneath the depths of his stoic demeanor, but I can't quite put my finger on it.

I tear my eyes away from Brad's and take a deep breath before speaking into the microphone. "Hello, I'm Delilah Harper," I announce to the crowd, my voice embarrassingly shaky. I'm surprised when I get a hefty amount of applause and cheers.

Staring at the envelope in my hand one more time, I tear it open with anxious fingers and scan the page, my heart jumping to my throat as tears sting my eyes.